ALL WOMAN
AND SPRINGTIME

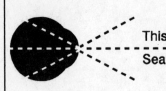

This Large Print Book carries the
Seal of Approval of N.A.V.H.

ALL WOMAN AND SPRINGTIME

BRANDON W. JONES

THORNDIKE PRESS
A part of Gale, Cengage Learning

GALE
CENGAGE Learning·

Detroit • New York • San Francisco • New Haven, Conn • Waterville, Maine • London

GALE
CENGAGE Learning®

LIBRARY OF CONGRESS CATALOGING-IN-PUBLICATION DATA

Jones, Brandon W., 1972–
  All woman and springtime/ by Brandon W. Jones.
    pages ; cm. — (Thorndike Press large print core)
  ISBN-13: 978-1-4104-5192-7 (hardcover)
  ISBN-10: 1-4104-5192-5 (hardcover)
  1. Female friendship—Fiction. 2. Human trafficking—Fiction. 3. Korea (North)—Fiction. 4. Large type books. I. Title.
  PS3610.O618A79 2012b
  813'.63—dc23   2012025879

Published in 2012 by arrangement with Algonquin Books of Chapel Hill, a division of Workman Publishing, Inc.

Printed in the United States of America
1 2 3 4 5 6 7 16 15 14 13 12

For my mom, Kathy Jones.
May she rest in peace.

AUTHOR'S NOTE

Parts of this novel reveal the physical and psychological traumas associated with human trafficking and sexual slavery. Because of the graphic and mature nature of these themes, the contents of this book may not be suitable for young readers.

A NOTE ON VERNACULAR

Throughout this novel, I have used the regional word *Hanguk* to refer to South Korea and South Koreans, and the word *Chosun* for North Korea and North Koreans. I apologize in advance to those who are familiar with Korean language, history, and politics, for whom this may be an oversimplification — I wanted to acknowledge this split in Korean identity, but without complicating the story with lengthy explanations, since usage of such terminology is a complex issue.

PART I

Part 7

1

Gyong-ho fed another pant leg into a powerful, old cast iron machine, counting the stitches as she ran a perfect inseam. She watched intently as the needle danced across the rough fabric, plunging in and out of the cloth with methodic violence — she was amazed the fabric did not bleed. It was a paradox of sewing, that such brutality could bind two things together. A distant cloud shifted, liberating a pocket of sunlight that had been building up behind it, flooding the dirty windows high on the factory wall and illuminating her work station in smeared and spotted light. Now the needle glinted as it stabbed. Gyong-ho felt grateful for the light because of its illusion of warmth — she could still see her breath, and her dry fingers ached. The factory was a cold concrete cavern, full of fabric scraps and echoes, a container for damp and chilly air.

She glanced up only momentarily. The Great Leader, Kim Il-sung, and his son the Dear Leader, Kim Jong-il, looked down on her from behind their golden frames. They perched on the wall, smiling, like they did on every wall, looking down on her, watching and weighing her every move. Reflexively she prostrated from within, bowed her head and worked harder. She was not good enough. The portraits filled her with awe and fear. *It is by the grace of the Dear Leader that I live so well,* she recited to herself mechanically.

Gyong-ho was in a nest of sound. The air around her hummed and stuttered with the staccato of one hundred sewing machines starting and stopping at random. Electricity buzzed from lights and machines, and seemingly from the factory women themselves, who were plugged into the walls by unseen tethers. Scissors snipped and clipped at threads in punctuating chops, sharp steel sliding on sharp steel. Holding the sounds together, corralling them, was the shuffling step of the foreman pacing his vengeful circuit of the factory floor, dragging his mangled foot as he walked — thump, slide . . . step; thump, slide . . . step. The sounds were a kind of music to Gyong-ho, helping her focus, occupying a busy part of

14

her mind that was always looking to distill order from chaos.

The pained and lumbering gait of the foreman drew nearer, and Gyong-ho tensed. His powerful body odor preceded him, pinning her to her chair. He was both sour and flammable. He stopped in front of her, and she could hear his raspy breathing, could smell the smoke on his breath. Without looking up at him, she could see his scarred and slanted face, lined with disapproval. He grunted and then labored onward, shuffling away. Gyong-ho exhaled. She knew that his obvious pain was an example of his impeccable citizenship: He walked all day in spite of it for the glory of the Republic.

Foreman Hwang would tolerate no disruption to production, and even restroom emergencies were met with heavy scorn and public humiliation. There was a sign on the wall that read, Eat No Soup. It was a campaign designed to increase production by curbing restroom visits. Unfortunately for Gyong-ho, thin soup had been the only food available that morning at the orphanage. She had tried not to eat too much of it, but she had been hungry; so she danced around her straining bladder, working her hips back and forth in coordination with her sewing.

She worked in rhythm, fast and precise, feeding legs and waists and cuffs into her hungry machine as fast as it could chew them. She worked to outpace a memory that was pursuing her, reaching for her, breathing on her. She was afraid that if she slowed down for even a moment, it might catch up with her, grasping the back of her neck with a black-gloved claw. It was a demon chasing her down a long corridor, his hard shoes echoing, his stride longer than hers, leather hands grazing the little hairs on the back of her neck as they snatched for her, always catching up with her. She kept up a mental race in an effort to evade the memory, her mind in overdrive to distraction.

She chanced a brief look to her right. Her best friend, Il-sun, was finishing a cuff. The seam staggered drunkenly, and one of the trouser legs appeared a little longer than the other. It was a wonder how she could get away with it; but then, she was the pretty one. Sunlight, whenever it shone, seemed to cling to her. Most days it condensed right on her, running in bright rivulets down her body, drawing eyes down the length of her. She was even beautiful with dark circles under her eyes from lack of sleep, and her lethargic motions were fluid — seemingly an open invitation to caress. Her heart-shaped face was set off by pouting red lips and eyes that gazed mischievously from the corners of their sockets. Her skin was flawlessly smooth and her pin-straight hair hung in a black curtain just below her shoulders. In just the last year her body had taken on a new shape that made her hips and shoulders move in hypnotic opposition as she walked. People turned to watch her whenever she glided by, their gaze causing her to radiate even more, to be even more beautiful. Men in particular were affected by her presence, losing their ability to speak, looking both fearful and hungry. Gyong-ho did not like the change.

She worried that Il-sun would again not meet the day's quota. This would make the fifth day in a row. How long could she go on like this, so indifferent to authority? It was as if she did not understand the consequences of being so . . . individualistic.

They had been working at the factory for less than a year. At seventeen years old, they had been excited to join the ranks of working adults — the novelty of going to the factory every day was a welcome break from the tedium of school. They had felt a sense of maturity as they left the orphanage each morning in their factory uniforms — bright red caps, pressed white shirts, and navy blue trousers — the younger girls gazing at them with awe and respect. Their heads had been filled with images of going to the factory with a feeling of pride and purpose, as if every day was going to be more exciting and fulfilling than the last; after all, this was called the Worker's Paradise. In a short time, however, all the basics of sewing were mastered, and the job itself did not require much more than that — cut, match, sew, snip, cut, match, sew, snip. Every day, day in and day out, it was the same pair of trousers over and over again. The work transformed quickly from excitement to drudgery, especially under the thumb of the fearsome and cranky foreman.

Finally, a whistle blew and the foreman announced, as if it were against his better judgment, that lunch was being served in the cafeteria. Gyong-ho and Il-sun stood up and, in rigid military fashion, filed out the factory door. Gyong-ho wondered if there really would be lunch, or just the sawdust gruel that was served most days.

The women splintered into small groups as they exited the workroom, and the air filled with chatter. It seemed an odd contrast between the martial atmosphere of the workroom and the casual muddle of the lunch room, as if they were ants that morphed into women and then back into ants again. Occasional laughter could be heard, and a Party anthem played in the background on tinny speakers. Gyong-ho made a break for the latrine. When she returned, she and Il-sun queued up in the cafeteria, waiting for the day's ration, which turned out to be a small scoop of rice and a slice of boiled cabbage. On the wall behind the service counter was a poster with a drawing of stout *Chosun* citizens handing food across a barbed wire fence to the emaciated and rag-clad *Hanguk*. American soldiers with long noses and fierce, round eyes were holding the *Hanguk* down with their boots, the hands of the *Hanguk* out-stretched in desperation. The poster said, simply, Remember Our Comrades to the South. Gyong-ho and Il-sun received their bowls and sat down at a corner table.

"How long do you think we will have to stockpile food for the *Hanguk?*" Il-sun asked, looking despondently at her meager ration.

"Until the Americans stop starving them, I suppose," Gyong-ho answered. It was widely known that the imperialist Americans were harsh overlords to the oppressed *Hanguk* people, who craved reunification of

19

the Korean peninsula under the Dear Leader. That is why the Dear Leader was stockpiling food for them, asking his own people to sacrifice much of their daily ration to aid the unfortunate people of the South.

"Yeah, but what I wouldn't give for a bite of pork," another woman at the table chimed in, not quite under her breath. The whole table fell into a tense, uncomfortable silence. The cold of the concrete room drilled bone deep. Nobody dared inhale. Such a statement was as good as slapping the Dear Leader — it could leave the stain of treason on anyone who heard it.

"But it is worth it for the benefit of our dear comrades to the south," she added quickly, forcing a smile at the rice balanced on her chopsticks. "It is by the glory of the Dear Leader that we eat so well."

Conversation resumed. It was a broom sweeping dust under the corner of a rug. Such talk was dangerous.

Twenty minutes later a whistle blew, signaling the end of the midday break. It ended all too soon for the weary Gyong-ho and Il-sun, who were ants once again, marching back into the workroom. They stood next to their sewing stations, feet apart, hands behind their backs. Not all factory foremen demanded such military strictness of their workers, but Foreman Hwang was decidedly old-guard. The shift began with a song in praise of the country's founder, then the foreman spoke.

"Comrades, I do not need to tell you that there is no higher purpose than serving our Dear Leader." His voice was low and gravelly, like stones rolling around in a tin can. "It is an honor that he has bestowed upon you, allowing you to serve him in the People's garment factory. But sometimes I think you do not fully appreciate this gift. Every day I see complacency and laziness." His eyes landed on Il-sun, and Gyong-ho tensed. "These must be stamped out!" He punctuated the statement by slamming his fist into the palm of his hand, sending a shock wave down Gyong-ho's spine. She nearly gasped out loud. "We must be prepared for the day when the imperialist dogs, the American bastards and their flunky allies, attack us. Even though we no longer hear their bombs or feel their bayonets in our hearts, we are still at war. They are afraid of the Dear Leader and the mighty *Chosun* army. They are afraid like cornered animals; and like cornered animals they must eventually strike at us, even as hopeless as they know it will be to do so. So we must be prepared for that day. Each of you must ask, 'What can I do for the Dear Leader?' " He let the question hang in the air for a moment to collect drama. "You must do exactly what is asked of you, without question, without complaint." He paced thoughtfully for a moment.

"We are falling short of our quotas. Each of you must work harder, sew faster, and make no mistakes. Errors have become quite a problem on this floor. Every time you have to restitch an inseam . . ." He paused, looking to the dirty ceiling for words that seemed to be eluding him. "For every stitch you have to redo, a good *Chosun* man or woman pays for it with blood." He laid heavy emphasis on the word "blood," probing the room with heartless, accusing eyes.

The room was captivated in breathless, guilty silence. Gyong-ho felt as if she were solely to blame for the imperialist scourge and wondered how she could possibly work any harder to rout it out. She stole a glance toward Il-sun, whose eyes were closed with her head pitching forward. It could have been humble introspection in response to the foreman's speech, but Gyong-ho saw it for what it was: sleep. She was amazed, offended, and, in spite of herself, impressed by the way her friend could so casually flaunt her disrespect for authority. That she could fall asleep standing up was impressive in its own right. Il-sun was always on the edge of trouble, just skating by without suffering any real consequence for her insubordination. Gyong-ho felt deeply fearful for her safety. For Il-sun, the dangers lurking around every corner and under every rock were impotent, imaginary shadows; for Gyong-ho they were real. Il-sun did not understand what she was risking by being impetuous, rebellious, and unique. *If only she knew what I have been through.*

With that thought, Gyong-ho bumped into an unspoken boundary of her consciousness, treading accidentally into an area where she dared not go. A memory flared in brilliant colors, growing on the dry tinder of her fear, and the factory began to fade around her. Suddenly she was hearing again the footsteps she had been evading. They were catching up with her swiftly from behind: hard soles echoing down a long, bare corridor, muffled voices, rough laughter, the light of a naked bulb, cold, wet feet, an electric shock.

In desperation, to fight off the sensation, she began counting things. Anything.

She counted needles in a pincushion —

forty-eight.

She counted bare lightbulbs — *sixteen.*

She counted buttons on the foreman's shirt — *seven.*

She multiplied lightbulbs by buttons, and then divided them by needles — *two point three, recurring.*

Two point three, recurring, multiplied by itself is five point four, recurring.

Five point four, recurring, multiplied by two point three, recurring, is twelve point seven zero three seven zero three, recurring . . .

With each number her mind gained ground, her demon receded, inky black thoughts fell further and further behind. She was once again ahead of the echoing footsteps, could hear them falling back.

The square root of twelve point seven zero three seven zero three, recurring, is three point five six four two —

"Comrade Song!" the foreman barked loudly, shocking her back into the room. He was standing toe to toe with her, bathing her in a cloud of sour kimchee breath. Kimchee was a luxury of his rank that the times did not afford for the likes of Gyong-ho. "Comrade Song Gyong-ho! Is there something you would like to say?" It was more of a threat than a question.

She looked around to see that the other

seamstresses were already sitting at their machines, looking fearfully at her. She had been lost in counting and had missed the command to sit. She felt very much like an errant nail in a wooden deck that had worked its way upward, standing out, begging to be struck with a hammer until its head is again flush with the wood. In any moment of uncertainty, she had learned, there is only one safe course of action. As if by reflex she brought her hands together in front of her chest, hoisted a gleaming tear into her eye, and, with a catch in her voice, said, "I am so very grateful, comrade foreman, sir. It is by the grace of the Dear Leader that I am here. I am not worthy to be here. I am lower than mud. Lower than pond silt. Even so, our Dear Leader has had the grace to allow me to work in his garment factory. I am just so grateful." She bowed her head, but remained standing.

"Very good, Comrade Song," rasped the foreman. "I hope that the others here will learn from you." He turned to address the room, seeming to relish the pain shooting up his damaged leg. "You see? Comrade Song knows that she was given a rare second chance. She knows that she is unworthy. This makes her grateful. You may

25

sit, Comrade Song. Everyone, get to work!"
Relieved, Gyong-ho sat and began sewing.

2

When Il-sun first walked through the front door of the Home for Orphan Girls, she sneered at the portrait of the Dear Leader. His frozen smile only confirmed for her that his omnipotence was a lie — he was only made of paper. Either the orphanage mistress did not see the offense or she chose to ignore it. Il-sun had certainly made no attempt to hide it. She was thirteen years old and had just watched her mother crumble, piece by piece, before her eyes, and she was in no mood to be placatory.

Il-sun had grown up in relative luxury, with extra food rations, almost new clothes, and in a nice apartment in the middle of the city. These were her birthright, handed to her through her father's good *songbun.* She did not belong in the orphanage; not with lowly girls who had no home — that was not her. Her mother had been doting and kind, her greatest ambition being to raise her children well. Her social position afforded her the ability to do just that. Less fortunate women had to trudge off to the factories and farms each day, leaving their children to raise themselves. Il-sun dearly loved her mother.

Il-sun's father had been in the army, and his military uniform hung in the small family closet throughout her childhood. It was the only thing she knew of him. He had been an old man when he married her mother, and then died shortly after Il-sun was born. Some days, when she was in a particular mood, she would glide her fingers on the fabric of the uniform, and smell it for any trace of the man who had worn it. Sometimes she thought she could detect a masculine scent around the collar, but other times it was only mildew.

Her father had been loyal to Kim Il-sung, had fought for him in the war, and had been decorated with medals. These were kept in a special box on a high shelf, and Il-sun would sometimes ask to hold them. They were a comforting weight in the palm of her small hand, and they were a tangible reminder of her own privilege and duty. For his dedication, her father had been awarded the apartment in the center of the city and enjoyed an elevated social standing. His first wife had died of something; of what, Il-sun did not know or really care. The children from that marriage had already grown and had families of their own. She never even knew their names. As soon as Il-sun's mother reached marrying age, her father took her for his second wife. Even though he was already an old man, his excellent *songbun* made him a desirable husband, at least from the parents' point of view. Il-sun hoped no one would make her marry an old man, when her time came.

It was generally known that times were hard, and yet a person could disappear just for saying so out loud. That had happened to Il-sun's older brother; or at least she believed so. She could never be sure. He had been an angry young man who tended to say whatever dangerous thought was on his mind. Their mother tried punishing him, reasoning with him, and then finally pleading with him to change his thoughts; or, at the very least, to keep his heretical ideas to himself. He never listened. One day he simply did not come home. During Il-sun's more upbeat moments, she liked to think that he had made a run for the northern border into China. Late at night, when their mother was asleep, he had whispered tales of people who braved crossing the frozen

Tumen River, risking their lives for the opulence and endless feasts awaiting them on the other side. Il-sun had idolized her brother, even if she thought his ideas were a little crazy. He was the only person she ever heard speak that way. It was known that *Chosun* was the wealthiest, most prosperous nation — the envy of all the world. Why would anyone want to leave it? In her more realistic moments she knew that her brother had been picked up by the police and taken away forever, as so many other people had, and nobody ever talked about it. Why else had the authorities not come asking for him when he did not show up for his Party Youth meeting? She missed him terribly.

Her brother's disappearance had been too much for her mother to bear. It first broke her spirit, and then it broke her body down. It was not the grief of losing him that did it; it was having to pretend that he had never existed. It was having to get up the same way each day, doing the exact same routine, trying to convince herself that she had never had a son, had never suckled him, had never watched him grow handsome and strong. Neighbors and friends likewise pretended, as if by unspoken consensus, that there had never been a son, a brother, a friend. They never asked about him, never offered consolation, or even a knowing nod. To acknowledge him would be to acknowledge some guilt by association. Such smudges were hard to polish off a person's badge of loyalty.

Il-sun watched it all with the clear eyes of childhood.

Shortly afterward, her mother became ill. It came on gradually. At first she became clumsy, dropping things and tripping over nothing. Over months it became increasingly difficult for her to stand up and walk across the floor, which she eventually had to do using a cane. Then her body trembled uncontrollably and she could no longer operate chopsticks, or even a spoon. Il-sun had to feed her, and help her bathe and use the toilet. A doctor came and went, shaking his head and avoiding Il-sun's eyes. A year and a half after the symptoms appeared, her mother could no longer move from her sleeping mat. She could not speak, but only roll her eyes and make helpless grunts. Her mother ached, and Il-sun tried with all the force of her imagination to bring the affliction into her own body instead. Her mother suffered all the same.

The hardest part was knowing that her mother was still aware inside her broken and useless body, looking through the scuffed and milky windows of her eyes, aware that it was the futile end of her life. The *Chosun* were not allowed an afterlife — it was against the law — and nor was there any solace given to the survivors. Life was service to the Republic, and nothing more. Life was service to the Dear Leader, and everything outside that was forbidden. The very words for those things were rubbed out of the language until all that was left of them were impressions under the eraser marks where the first pencil had originally scratched them into being. Only the brave or the stupid dared to exhume them. Truth was an agreement, in *Chosun,* not an absolute. For the first time Il-sun fully understood her brother's anger.

One by one, her mother's organs shut down. Her skin became a sickly, pale green and her breath came in short gasps. Her body jerked in uncontrollable fits, with less force each time. She was a tire deflating. In one moment she took her last breath, and then gave up the thin tether of control over her lungs. Il-sun watched, powerless, as her mother slowly suffocated.

The jerking stopped. Il-sun had thought they had been fighting a disease — an unseen, unknowable enemy — but then realized they had actually been fighting against death itself. Unavoidable, inescapable death.

It was then she realized that, no matter what, death would always triumph; and that death's victory, after the struggle of life, is liberation. Il-sun had not allowed herself to cry since her mother had fallen ill: She had needed to stay strong. Sitting in front of her mother's empty shell, as understanding came to her in waves, she wept — not from grief, but from relief. The sweet release of death. An insupportable weight had been lifted from her, and, in spite of herself, she was glad that it was over. And she hated herself for being glad: It felt like betrayal. With nowhere else to cast her blame, she blamed . . .

No. There would be no talking about who she blamed.

The Home for Orphan Girls was no comfortable place to grow up, espe after having lived in a private apar with her family in a nice part of Still, it was better funded and less than its counterparts outside th even if she did not recognize it she was lucky to be there. specifically for orphans from loyal to the Party.

Il-sun did not adjust orphanage. She develor

being vindictive, sly, and cunning in her abuses. Many girls tried to befriend her, but she shunned them all. She had been accustomed to better food, cleaner conditions, a doting mother, and more privacy. Now she was just one of many girls in the care of a lone, overworked state employee. She had been told all her life that, with her excellent *songbun,* she would be able to find a good husband high in the Party ranks, that she would always enjoy greater comforts and privilege than most. All that was gone now. Now she was a castoff, a throwaway, a burden to the Republic — an undesirable.

Her pique found its sharpest focus on one girl in particular, who had arrived at the orphanage under mysterious circumstances a few months after her. To Il-sun, Gyong-ho looked more like a half-starved rodent than a thirteen-year-old girl. She was a skeletal wisp with long arms and a lopsided posture. Her spine was twisted and her left arm hung lower than her right, as if she were perpetually carrying a heavy sack of rice over her shoulder. Her wavy hair was matted and ry, and she made no effort to straighten Her skin was pale and cold, made all the so by the contrast with her black hair. wretchedness was exacerbated by her Gyong-ho was a boy's name, a souve-

nir from a bygone era when parents, wishing for a boy, gave their girls masculine names. Gyong-ho refused to speak, instead only shaking or nodding her head. She had a wide, blank look in her eyes that seemed a permanent part of her features.

Gyong-ho arrived at the orphanage in the middle of the night in a big black automobile. It was an unusually opulent arrival for an orphan, especially considering her soiled state. The first thing Il-sun noticed about her was her smell, which filled the entranceway of the orphanage and assaulted Il-sun at the top of the stairs from where she was spying. She smelled filthy, but not in the way of a person who has worked hard between regular baths. She smelled as if she had crawled out of a sewer in which she had wallowed for months or years. Grime streaked her face and stained her hands. The orphanage mistress scolded Il-sun for being out of bed, and then whisked the girl off to the bath. Il-sun had never seen a face before that was completely blank, that showed absolutely nothing; but that was the only way to describe Gyong-ho's face on the night of her arrival. She was empty, devoid of feeling — devoid of self — and that scared Il-sun.

For the first few weeks Il-sun ignored

Gyong-ho because she looked and behaved oddly, stuck as she was in a state of near catatonia. But after a while something about her began to eat away at Il-sun's patience. She hated her for her weakness. She hated her for being collapsed. She feared Gyong-ho for showing her how low the human spirit can be degraded and still not die. Gyong-ho was pathetic, broken, useless, and yet still alive. It meant that Il-sun herself could be broken further — things could get worse. Gyong-ho's wretchedness stimulated such anger that Il-sun felt compelled to strike out at her. She tripped her, and shoved her when the mistress was not looking, and threw pebbles at the back of her head. She called her names and tried to rally the other girls into the cause of ostracizing her. Gyong-ho became the focus of a deep, stirring rage about the weakness of humankind and the apparent lack of any accountable or benevolent overseer.

One day, a few months after Gyong-ho's arrival, the girls were given a rare treat of pork with their vegetables and rice. The portion was small, as usual, but the sliver of meat put a smile on Il-sun's normally scowling face. Some of the other girls had never even tasted meat before. Il-sun ate hungrily until her bowl was empty, and then scraped it with her finger to make sure none of the valuable juices would go to waste. When she was finished, she looked up to see Gyong-ho staring blankly at her bowl of untouched food. It was an affront. Life was precious and hard, and the meat was such a rare opportunity to gather strength that Gyong-ho's inability to respond to it provoked Il-sun's fury. She walked over to her, stripped the bowl of food from her hands, and said, "If you're not going to eat it, stupid cow, I will." She then shoveled the food into her mouth, greedily scraping it out of the bowl with her fingers, making exaggerated sounds of pleasure. When the food was finished and the bowl licked clean, she forced it back into Gyong-ho's hands and stood over her, waiting for a response. What she most craved was for Gyong-ho to protest, to yell at her or fight back. She wanted her to stand up and hit her, or scream obscenities — that would have meant she was alive. But none of that came. Instead, Gyong-ho kept her head down, a silent stream of tears running down each cheek and falling into her empty bowl.

"I hate you!" shouted Il-sun. "I hate you, I hate you, I hate you!" With each time she yelled it, something capped and frozen moved and dissolved inside of her. With each time she screamed, she realized more deeply that it was not Gyong-ho she hated; it was herself. She had failed her mother, had failed her brother, had even failed the father she had never known. "I hate you!" she said to herself, more softly. "I hate you!" She fell to her knees, saying, "I hate you." A torrent of grief rushed up from a dormant pool and erupted from her eyes. The relief she had felt after her mother's death had been a thin crust over a well of sadness that she had not allowed herself to feel. But she was feeling it now in full. She missed her mother more than words could say. It ached from every organ and every limb, and it all came out through her eyes and the shaking of her shoulders as she sobbed.

She felt a hand on her head. In her collapse she had laid her cheek, without realizing it, on Gyong-ho's lap. Gyong-ho had placed her small, hollow hand caringly on Il-sun's head; and when Il-sun looked up, for the first time Gyong-ho's face was not a void. It never really had been, not completely. It was then that Il-sun could see the flicker of Gyong-ho underneath the empty-looking husk. The pilot light had not gone out. She was a girl with a beating heart who had fully capitulated to some unseen suffer-ing, but whose essence still throbbed beneath the surface. She saw how alone Gyong-ho was, how she had laid herself down to a demon whose torture of her never ceased; and yet she kept soldiering on, albeit damaged, every day. What must she have gone through to be reduced as she was? She was still fighting back, in the small way that she could, just by being alive. She was a person to be admired for her strength, not despised for her weakness.

In that moment an understanding was born between them that was the foundation of a friendship — two halves finding unexpected completion. Gyong-ho's broken state gave Il-sun a constructive focus. She nursed Gyong-ho's enfeebled spirit with the irrepressible quest for girlish fun and mischief. Slowly, Gyong-ho's catatonia melted away as Il-sun, day after day, brushed her hair and chatted idly with her. Having someone to care for kept Il-sun from seeking the kind of trouble that would have led her to her brother's fate, and being cared for gave Gyong-ho a sense of safety that allowed her to come, at least a little bit, out of her shell.

"My name is Gi-Gi-Gi-Gi-Gyong-ho," she said to Il-sun, stuttering her name as they formally met each other. She often had difficulty saying her own name.

"Why don't you just tell people your name is Gi? It would be simpler," Il-sun joked. From that point on she called her Gi.

Once cleaned up, Gi was not exactly pretty, but she had a quirky personality that Il-sun enjoyed. She looked at the world in a completely different way from anyone Il-sun had ever met, reducing it in her mind to its fundamental pieces and the forces that acted on them. Where Il-sun was almost entirely focused on the people in her life and how they related with each other, Gyong-ho seemed to care only about the physical construction of the world around her. She cared little for social grace, or perhaps she had simply never been trained; and so, in the rare moments when she would speak to anyone other than Il-sun, she often came across as brusque and insensitive. She did have a subtle sense of humor that would emerge at unexpected moments, making Il-sun laugh. Il-sun was a bridge to the outside world for Gi, showing her that many of the dangers she feared were imagined: Gyong-ho startled easily at loud noises and sudden movements, as if at any moment she was expecting a great calamity to come upon her. She was shy and reticent where Il-sun was forward and often spoke out of turn.

Gi never spoke about her past, and any-time Il-sun pressed her for information she became evasive and sometimes hostile. It was as if she was fighting a lengthy and gruesome battle not to remember it; and when she came too close within her own mind, she would race away on another topic until she seemed to have forgotten what it was she was avoiding. If she got too close to her memory, her eyes would roll back in her head and her face would become a blank stone for minutes, sometimes for hours. Then, quite suddenly, she would return, maybe cheerful, maybe sullen, but as if nothing at all had happened.

One of the odd things that made Gyong-ho so puzzling and special was her obsession with numbers. It was eerie how she could do large and complicated compu-tations instantly in her head. It was as if she could simply see the numbers floating in front of her eyes, as if they drifted weight-lessly, borne on the dust churned upward by the turning of her mind. Il-sun was lost when it came to numbers, so it seemed particularly miraculous to her whenever Gi showed off her talent. It was the only time she didn't look quite so afraid. It seemed to Il-sun that Gi clung to numbers in the same way Il-sun clung to her anger — it was the only thing of which she could be absolutely certain. At times, when they were bored, Il-sun would try as hard as she could to make a calculation too complex or the numbers too large, lofting a string of numbers at Gi, all the while checking answers on a calculator she had stolen from their school. Gyong-ho never made a mistake. This was nothing more than amusement for both girls. It never occurred to them, being orphans and therefore having bad *songbun,* that Gi's talent could be used for anything practical. They would never qualify for anything more than manual factory labor.

Il-sun could not muster much enthusiasm for her factory job. Had her mother lived and her life stayed on course, Il-sun would have been given a first-rate education and lived in their fine family apartment until she left to make a life, and a family, with her undoubtedly well-connected husband. She had never gotten over the sense that she was meant for a better life, married to a man who would shield her from the common drudgery that afflicted most of *Cho-sun.* That dream was dashed, but she was still determined to climb, any way she could, out of the mire of mediocrity that her life had become. She still believed that

her way out was through a man. Perhaps
she had already found him.

3

The orphanage mistress sat in front of a scratched, old mirror, raking through her hair with a comb that was missing most of its teeth. She spent many hours, whenever she had hours, combing, looking at herself and trying to will her perfectly straight hair curly. She would have been happy if it had turned even slightly wavy, but her hair never complied. She reached back and tied it into a tight bun on the back of her head. This was her one indulgence, gazing into the mirror and fantasizing about a different self.

She applied powder from the bottom of an empty tin using a brush that held more dust than color. Again, it was the fantasy that fueled the ritual. Her face was an acreage of plainness, of nothing special, of a measure of time. It was a dull clock ticking off years, showing a late hour of youth, on the cusp of middle age. Her face might as well have been a pane of glass — eyes rolled right on past it, slid straight off it without stopping or even slowing down, seeing right through her.

She bit at her lips for color, then smoothed over them with the bottom of a taper candle, just for the sensation. On a different face they might have been nice lips, she thought, just right for kissing. She batted her eyes at herself, then sighed. Her birth certificate claimed that she was one hundred percent *Chosun,* but her eyes betrayed a hint of Japanese. This did not have any consequence for her, such as limited mobility within the Party — people were used to looking the other way for such ancestral transgressions — but it was like a small badge of shame.

She slid one foot, then the other into old, white, knee-length stockings that had dark impressions of her footprints stained into the feet. A clean toe peeked out between threads, its unadorned nail filed to a precise length, reflecting the light from her bedroom window. The stockings were ragged along the top and deftly stitched in places. On first glance, just seeing the ankles, they could have been new. *Maybe someone will notice my ankles,* she thought. Her unshapely underwear was a drab, laundered gray, and she quickly covered over it with a neatly pressed skirt and starched blouse. She took great care in her appearance, but for whom? The orphans? They certainly did not care. Her superiors? They never concerned themselves with the orphanage. Looking into her partial reflection, it seemed that there was nothing there but a uniform of efficiency, her face a mere window on her shoulders.

But I have nice ankles, she thought. *Maybe there will be a delivery today.*

Her bedroom opened into the large, plain kitchen, and as she left her room she was pleased to see that the girls were already making breakfast. She spoke her approval, causing several of the girls to beam. She had learned that having the girls take responsibility for themselves not only eased her work load but helped them gain needed confidence. She performed her morning rounds delivering praise, or a mild rebuke when necessary. Few of her girls had behavior problems.

She passed Gyong-ho and Il-sun as they were heading out the door on their way to the factory. They would soon be leaving the orphanage to live on their own, when their paperwork cleared, maybe in a couple of months. She felt both proud and heartbroken when girls flew the nest, but these two in particular had a special place in her heart and she would be sad to see them go. Il-sun was a success story of sorts. She had been the bad apple to spoil the bunch when she first arrived, and the mistress had feared her crossing a dangerous line. It was so easy to do. But now she stayed, mostly, within a safe margin of behavior, largely because of her friendship with Gyong-ho. She was ripening into womanhood in the way some girls do, like a bomb exploding, and the mistress hoped she would get plucked into marriage soon, before the world of men could leave its stain on her. A young woman with Il-sun's thirst for trouble was safer when married, in *Chosun.*

The orphanage ran without hiccups, which was a testament to the mistress's competence. When she had taken it over six years earlier, it was in complete disarray. The girls were filthy and the grounds unkempt. Violence was commonplace, and several of the older girls were openly prostituting themselves, perhaps even to the profit of her predecessor. The food shortage had been worse in those days: Many of the girls were sick, and all were malnourished. She could not have been successful if she had allowed herself to get attached. There was no time for coddling or mothering. She was

47

the only caretaker for twenty-five girls, and she understood that routine and structure were more important than pampering, given the limited resources at her disposal. Besides, if these girls were going to survive, they needed to be tough.

The Home for Orphan Girls had been a factory during more prosperous times, but was hastily transformed into an orphanage during the outset of the food shortage in the 1990s. It was a blocky, two-story concrete building with large rooms and few homey embellishments. In the foyer were the obligatory framed portraits of the Great and Dear Leaders. The upper floor was a large, open room where the girls kept their sleeping mats and their few personal possessions. The building was wired for electric light, but most of the time the electricity did not work and they had to use oil lamps and candles. Even those, they used sparingly. Similarly, the building had at one time been plumbed, but the water system had long been shut down. Water had to be hauled daily from a spigot two blocks away, which worked only intermittently. As part of her shared responsibilities, each girl was required to carry two buckets of water every day to a large storage tank on the second floor of the building. As an example to the girls, the mistress did not exclude herself from the duty.

Once the girls had all left for school or work, there was an endless pile of paperwork to attend to. The mistress had to run the orphanage completely on her own, and her superiors preferred to remain ignorant of its operations, lest they should ever have to fill in for her. They viewed it as a problem better left ignored, and complained loudly if they were ever asked to do anything more than sign the necessary requisition forms and ration requests. *Chosun,* they said, was founded on the *juche* ideal, the idea of self-sufficiency, and she should lead by example. She wanted to remind her superiors that *juche* was meant to be self-sufficiency for all of *Chosun,* a nation built on the foundation that all citizens work *together* for the common good, but she thought better of it. Besides, her autonomy had unforeseen benefits.

Midway through her pile of morning paperwork there was a loud knock on the kitchen door. The mistress's heart missed a beat and her cheeks flushed red. She wondered at how biology took precedence over rationality: A knock at the front door would never excite her blood in such a way. Perspiring now, she checked her hair in the mirror, made her way to the kitchen door, hopeful in spite of herself, and opened it.

4

Gyong-ho was eight years old. She had always looked forward to the private meetings with Comrade Uncle Kim. He came to school every few months with his kind eyes and his bottomless bag of sweets. He told funny stories and liked to ask questions.

"Good morning, Gyong-ho!" he said brightly.

"Good morning, Comrade Uncle Kim!" she responded.

"Would you like a sweetie?"

"Yes, please."

"I hear you are almost old enough to join the Children's Party. You must be very excited."

"Oh, I am."

"That will make the Dear Leader very happy."

"Will you come to the ceremony, Comrade Uncle Kim?"

"I certainly will! Will your parents be there?"

"I think so."

"You're not sure? Wouldn't your parents

want to see such an important event?"

"They are so busy. They go to meetings all the time."

"But don't you think they would make an exception this time?"

"I hope so."

"Me too." Comrade Uncle Kim paused thoughtfully for a minute. "Gyong-ho is a boy's name, isn't it? Why did your parents give you a boy's name?"

"My parents wanted to have a son, but they got me instead."

"I see. I thought people stopped doing that a long time ago. Do you think your parents love you?"

Gyong-ho sat quietly. She had never wondered about that before, and suddenly she was worried. Her parents seemed to love her, but the way Comrade Uncle Kim asked the question put a shadow of doubt over her heart. "I think so," she said timidly.

"Tell me, Gyong-ho, do you have a portrait of the Great Leader hanging in your apartment?"

"Yes, we do! I love it very much." She was relieved to have something else to think about.

"I'm sure you do. You are a very good little girl. Tell me, where is the portrait now? Is it tucked away on a shelf somewhere?"

"No. It is on the wall."

"I see. Well, is it on a wall with other pictures, or is it on its own wall?"

"It is on the wall next to the picture of the Dear Leader. They are the only pictures we have hanging in our apartment."

"Well, that's very good, indeed. So who takes care of the portraits of the Great Leader and the Dear Leader? Do your parents take care of them?"

"No."

"No? Are the portraits all dusty, then? Is the glass spotted?"

"Oh no, definitely not! My grandmother cares very much for the portraits. She maintains them perfectly."

"Your grandmother must be a very good citizen."

"Yes, she is!"

"Do your parents ever bow to the portrait of the Great Leader?"

"Sometimes."

"Only sometimes? Not every time they walk in the door?"

"Well, most of the times when they come in the door. Sometimes they are so tired that they just fall on their sleeping mats and go to sleep."

"Oh, I see." Comrade Uncle Kim scribbled something on his notepad.

5

At the end of the day, a whistle blew and the seamstresses began to tidy their workstations. At each station there was a pile of trousers to be inspected and tallied, the resulting numbers to be graphed and recorded in a file. Each day's number was added into the mysterious equation that determined the quality of a worker's citizenship. The consequences for being deemed unworthy were dire — people disappeared and no questions were asked. Occasionally falling short of a quota was not the worst possible offense — they were often set unrealistically high; but consistently falling short of them could be seen as unpatriotic. That is why the whistle at the end of the day brought on a wave of tension for the seamstresses.

"Hey, Gi!" Il-sun whispered urgently.

Gi raised her eyebrows in Il-sun's direction.

"Gi, I'm five short!" There was rising panic in her voice. Being short by five pairs of trousers would not go unnoticed. "How did you do?"

Gi knew that the question was really a plea for help. She felt tempted to ignore her and let her suffer the consequences of her own irresponsibility. She also knew that she could never be so heartless.

"I'm three over."

"Could you . . . ?"

"Here," said Gyong-ho, scowling as she handed four pairs of trousers to her while the foreman was looking the other way. "Now we're both only short by one."

"Thank you, Gi. I owe you one."

"Actually, you owe me thirty-two."

"Why do you have to be so damned precise?"

The foreman shuffled painfully over and tallied Gi's and Il-sun's trousers. Exactly five of the lines on his disapproving face were angry-looking scars. One scar began above his left eye and continued below it, though leaving his eyeball intact — a fortunate near miss. Did he feel lucky to still have his eye, or just embittered to have the scar? Gi guessed that it was probably the latter.

"You are both under the quota by one." His raspy voice sounded painful, and Gi

55

unconsciously touched her own throat in sympathy. "I am very disappointed in you, especially, Comrade Song." Gi flinched at her name. "I would think that you of everyone would want to make a good impression. Do better tomorrow."

"Yes, comrade foreman. I will do better tomorrow, sir."

The foreman walked on to the next station, but his powerful body odor weighed the air down like a damp blanket around them. With heads down and breath held, the girls made their way to the workroom door.

After work, the seamstresses attended "voluntary" continuing education classes. The meetings were not considered strictly mandatory, but it was well known that not going would invite inquiry, which would lead to trouble. Classes were held in the cafeteria and, as with most events, began with a patriotic song. Il-sun and Gi took seats near the back of the room. At the front stood a smartly dressed woman in her early thirties, in a white blouse and ankle-length beige skirt with matching dress shoes and nude stockings. She was considered a loyal expert seamstress and she taught at the White Butterfly garment factory once every week. She always spoke through a forced smile, and Il-sun admitted to Gi that she would have been happy to slap it off with a large, dead fish.

The evening's lecture began with a parable about the Dear Leader's honorable mother, Kim Jong-suk. Kim Jong-suk was an inspirational revolutionary woman whose self-sacrifice and purity of spirit any good *Chosun* woman should do her best to emulate. As a guerrilla fighter, Kim Jong-suk supported her husband, the Great Leader Kim Il-sung, tirelessly, even in the frigid mountain winters of their remote revolutionary camp. She raised their son, the Dear Leader Kim Jong-il, while they were cold and hungry, with the *juche* ideal as her guiding light. *Juche* was the cornerstone on which the great *Chosun* nation was founded. It was a philosophy of self-sufficiency and cultural superiority — the ideal socialism.

During the anti-imperialist war that divided the Korean peninsula in half, depriving their southern neighbors of the utopia that was developing in the north, the honorable guerrillas, fighting under the flawless leadership of Kim Il-sung, captured an imperialist Yankee soldier. At the last moment, as he was about to be executed, the great mother of the country stopped the firing squad because she could see in the

57

Yankee's eyes that he could yet be educated in the ways of *juche*. She took the prisoner in and, with a minimum of language between them, was able to convey the absolute superiority of the *juche* ideal over any other way of life. The soldier begged forgiveness for his imperialist ways, which Kim Il-sung saw fit to grant. The soldier was later allowed to serve in the war against the Americans, who had been his own people, in which he fought savagely and passionately. The soldier was killed in battle, and his last words were, "Long live *juche!* Long live the Great Leader Kim Il-sung!"

They had heard the story before. The girls were bored.

"The way she always smiles like that drives me crazy," Il-sun whispered into Gi's ear.

"I have a theory about that," replied Gyong-ho.

"Oh?"

"Yeah. I think that she pulls her pantyhose on so high that they force the corners of her mouth to rise."

Il-sun chortled loudly at the image this created, and heads turned toward the commotion. She loved Gi's unusual sense of humor. The presenter continued with her oratory unfazed, as if nothing had happened.

Embarrassed by her outburst and surprised that the teacher kept talking in spite of it, Il-sun was struck with an uncontrollable urge to giggle. For some reason, though she did not know why, it was all unbearably funny: the lecturing seamstress, her story, the factory, all the women in their silly uniforms. The strain of trying to hold in a giant wave of laughter was causing her belly to hurt, which made her want to laugh all the more. Unable to control herself, she snickered through her nose, louder with every effort she made to quiet it.

The presenter suddenly stopped speaking, and the whole room turned toward the two girls.

"Is something funny?" asked the presenter, still holding her frozen smile.

Gi was horrified. It was bad enough to disrespect the presenter's authority, but to disrespect the important and honorable history of the Dear Leader could have serious consequences. The blood drained from her face and she shifted away from Il-sun in an effort to escape the fallout of guilt by association.

"I'm sorry . . . It's just . . . I can't explain . . . ," Il-sun said, trying to pull herself together; but looking again at the presenter's smile and remembering Gi's comment, the wave broke through and she began laughing in earnest.

A nervous tension filled the room. No one knew how the presenter would respond to such an insolent outburst. There was no punishment that was beyond her reach. It could be as light as a mild rebuke; or, if she were wanting to make an example, could be as heavy as —

It was better not to think about that.

To Gi's relief — she was becoming increasingly afraid of the outcome — the forced smile on the presenter's face softened and her eyes relaxed. She even began to chuckle.

"Young lady, your laughter is contagious," she said. "I don't see enough of that."

Obediently, as if on cue, the other seamstresses started laughing. It came timidly and forced, but then picked up speed, like a boulder rolling down the side of a mountain. Faces turned red and tears glistened on cheeks. It seemed strange to Gi that everyone laughed, and yet nobody knew why. Perhaps it was only relief.

After a while the laughter began to die down, but some of the women forced their laughter to continue in spite of the natural lull, as if to show off their dedication. As they did this, more and more women forced their laughter, in a chain reaction, so that what was a room filled with hearty laughter at nothing in particular was now a room of forced and compulsory laughter upheld for self-preservation. Everyone was looking around the room, wanting to be neither the first nor the last one to stop. No one wanted to take that chance.

In an attempt to end the cycle, an elderly seamstress stood up and walked to the framed photograph of the Dear Leader on the wall. She kneeled and called out to the picture in gratitude. Then another woman did the same. Then another. Only after prostrating oneself to the Dear Leader was it truly safe to stop laughing. Now that it had started, it would not stop until every person in the room had gone to the photo of the Dear Leader. Not even the presenter could interrupt a person's display of devotion without fear of punishment. Once it had started, anyone not seen doing it would be considered suspicious. People had disappeared for as much.

"This is going to be a long night," Il-sun said to Gi.

6

The orphanage mistress opened the box slowly — restraint was a quality she prized in herself. It was just an ordinary box, like so many others she had seen. She could guess at its contents: several kilos of rice, some kind of dry beans, perhaps a few onions, canned vegetables if she was lucky, maybe some aging root vegetables, and possibly a little bit of soap. Whatever it was would be enough to keep them all from starving. It was the extra thing in the box, the more personal inclusion, whether or not it was even there, that caused her chest to pound. She scolded herself: The food is more important. For the girls.

She removed bags of rice and beans from the box and set them on the counter. She was pleased to find several large carrots, only slightly wilted, and two whole cabbages with more green leaves than brown. There were about a dozen tin cans, all with the labels torn off, presumably to hide their foreign origin. If anyone bothered inspecting the cans closely, they could see that they were not manufactured in *Chosun;* but nobody would be checking them. There was no way to know what was inside the cans until she opened them, but that hardly mattered. There was a small stack of forged ration coupons, neatly banded together. She would have to check them against her legitimate ones to see if she could risk using them, but on first glance they looked passable. For a moment her breath faltered. The box was empty. She brought her hand to her cheek in an unconscious gesture to make sure her face was still there, and not a plate of glass. It was only a small comfort when her fingertips met warm flesh.

Then she saw it. It would have been easy to miss the flat package, wrapped in plain brown paper the same color as the box. She reached in and gingerly lifted it out, relishing all its properties of weight, texture, and color. She brought it to her nose and mouth and inhaled. It smelled vaguely like onions and cardboard, but in her mind it was both sweeter and earthier — a little bit like tree bark, leather, fresh sweat, and ground spices. It was the same aroma still clinging to the air around her from the brief visitor who had come and gone only moments before, delivering the box. Bringing her a gift. She let the package drag at her bottom lip as she lowered it from her face.

The package was thin and rectangular, and the paper was folded with a careless sort of care — the corners and edges sticking out randomly, but the surfaces smoothed over and flattened. She clung to these details as if they were a map to a secret terrain, clues to the heart of the hands that wrapped it.

The mistress savored the action of peeling the paper back, drawing it out for as long as she could. If it were possible, she would take a whole week to open the package. She had to fight an urge to rip at the paper, but she knew that the anticipation of opening it was as much the gift as whatever was inside. Finally the paper was open and slid onto the floor. Her hand went again to her face — her flesh and blood face. She was not invisible.

Finding enough food for the girls was the first obstacle the mistress had to overcome when she took the job at the orphanage six years earlier. Officially, the food shortage was nothing more than a mild inconvenience. In truth, people were dying every day on the streets. According to the state, the *Chosun* people were well cared for in the hands of the Dear Leader, and the distributed ration cards were more than sufficient to feed everyone. Yet even the most obedient *Chosun* could not pretend away the truth, though most of them tried in earnest. If she had relied solely on the rations allotted to the orphanage, many more of the children would have died.

The mistress supplicated her superiors for aid, and when they proved deaf she tried going above them. No one would listen. No one could afford to listen — the food did not exist to be distributed. In desperation, the mistress took the older children and went to the streets to beg.

There was little charity to be found there. People who wanted to help simply could not — it was every person for herself. Three of the younger children became critically ill, and still there was no help. When they died, there was no time or energy for ceremony. A cart came and took them away. There was no shortage of bodies. There was also no shortage of carts, or well-fed carters. This was both a relief, for the sanitation, and an outrage. Once again, the façade of the functioning of the state was more important than the well-being of the people. But that was a dangerous idea. She found it hard to swallow.

The mistress had reached a breaking point. It was a nightmare, and the only thing keeping her from suicide was the thought that so many children needed her. With her, there was little hope; without her, there was no hope at all. She had reached a level of despair and sadness that she had never thought possible. Just when she thought she might lose her mind to the tragedy she was witnessing, a small ray of hope opened up to her.

A man approached her on the street. He was clean and his salt-and-pepper hair was neatly trimmed.

"I think I might be able to help you," he said. His voice was smooth and reassuring.

There had already been so much rejection and anguish that the mistress was shocked in disbelief, unable to speak.

"I can help you," he continued. "But you must meet me later at my apartment."

If the times had been any less desperate, the mistress would have sent the man down the street fleeing a screeching torrent of obscenities. She could not, however, afford to turn down any offer, even dubious or illicit. Either she survived in shame, or she and the children perished in hunger.

"Do you understand what I'm offering you?" the man asked.

The mistress nodded, still not able to find words.

Scared but resolved, the mistress sought out his apartment building on the outskirts of town later that same afternoon. It was a particularly shabby building, with many boarded windows and cracked walls. The stairwell smelled strongly of urine, and she had to stifle her second thoughts — children were starving. She made her way to a door on the fourth floor and, as she had been told, knocked exactly seven times, slowly. The man from the street answered and invited her inside with a subdued hand gesture. He was more handsome than she remembered, having morphed in her imagination, during the intervening hours, into an ogre of sorts. His clothes were a little frayed, but clean, and he had a warm, friendly face. The apartment was mostly bare, except for the portraits of the Great and Dear Leaders, a sleeping mat on the floor, and a small bookshelf with the works of Kim Il-sung. The mistress had an uneasy feeling, but she had already committed herself this far.

At the time, she was in her midtwenties and she had still not lain with anyone. There had certainly been advances from men, but their lurid nature had left her feeling cheap. She wanted her first time to be something special and meaningful. She wanted to be caressed and loved, taken gently by a man who looked *at* her and not through her. She was not holding out for the man of her dreams; she did not care if he was bald, or toothless, or worn out. She just wanted someone who could see her. This was not the scenario she had waited for, but at this point she would have done anything to feed the girls in her care.

"I am sorry to have to be so discreet," said the man in a near whisper.

The mistress only nodded in response.

"I believe I can help you, but first let me introduce myself. I am Father Lee, but in public please call me Lee Won." He had a habit of lifting the right side of his lip as he talked, as if he were smelling something foul through only one of his nostrils. This tic was at odds with his otherwise calm demeanor.

The mistress nodded.

"Have you heard of the teachings of Jesus Christ?"

Reflexively she looked over her shoulder at the closed door behind her. This was dangerous talk: To be implicated as a Christian could have dire consequences. She hoped she had not been recognized going into his apartment — there were eyes everywhere. She turned back to him and nodded.

"If you are willing to accept Jesus Christ as your savior and allow me to baptize you in his name, then I will bring food to your orphanage."

That explained the secrecy. The proposal sounded both easier and more risky than what she had thought she was going to have to do.

"What kind of assistance can I expect, if I do as you say?"

"There are Christian organizations outside the country that work very hard to bring food across the border for their *Chosun* brothers and sisters. The less you know about it, the better it is for everyone. But suffice it to say that every week, more or less, I get a shipment of food and supplies from them. I can make sure that some of that shipment makes it to your orphanage."

"And what do I have to do, to assure this charity?" She thought she knew the answer, and had steeled herself to go through with it. Surely there had to be a steeper price. She only hoped that it was a onetime fee.

"All I ask of you is to accept Jesus Christ

as your savior. Pray to him."

She would have accepted anyone or anything, animate or inanimate, as her savior for a regular shipment of food for the orphanage. And it seemed that his proposition ended there.

"Fine," she said, relieved.

"So now I will baptize you in the name of Christ. Please kneel." Father Lee then performed an incantation and dribbled water over her head. "Now you are officially in the fold of Jesus. Let us pray." The whole ritual seemed like nonsense to the mistress, but she was not in any position to deride a man who claimed he could help her.

As she was leaving the apartment, Father Lee handed the mistress a book, one of Kim Il-sung's more popular works. She was confused by the gift until she opened the cover. Instead of the words attributed to the Great Leader, she found, in bold characters, the words *The Holy Bible.* Looking closely, she could see where the binding had been cut and the prohibited book glued in place of the original text. The book was hot lead in her hands — it burned her fingers and exhausted her arms. She knew that if she were caught with it she would be taken away, tortured, and possibly killed. To hold the book was at once frightening and thrilling. She now possessed a deadly secret, which felt both powerful and liberating. Suddenly there was a sense of meaning for her; not because of what was in the book, but for the simple fact that it was forbidden. There was now a place within her where the rigid tendrils of society could not reach. She was no longer just the plain girl with a window for a face — she was a woman with a secret.

7

When the girls finally left the factory and began their walk back to the orphanage, it was already dark. The street was lit by the moon, which was low in the sky over the city, and climbing. The street lights were not working, and there were no vehicles on the road at night to offer even temporary light. The cold, early spring air bit into the bare skin of their faces and hands, and their breath came out in cottonlike puffs. They walked in silence because Il-sun, who was normally animated, was too tired to talk.

During the rare moments when Il-sun was quiet, Gi's mind had to work double-time to keep itself distracted. On the way home she turned her thoughts to the puffs of steam coming from her mouth as she exhaled. The girls had completed high school, but were not expected to go to university because of their low *songbun*. They had been taught rudimentary mathematics, as well as reading and writing. Being able to read the works of the Great Leader was considered extremely important, and even the lowliest of citizens was expected to have at least some proficiency in reading. Science was a topic that was generally glossed over in favor of the honorable history of the great *Chosun* nation and its leaders. In spite of this, Gi had developed a curiosity about the physical world and the way it works and tried to piece together the mysteries it held. Il-sun took it for granted that when it was cold, her breath would rise from her mouth as a visible vapor. But Gi was aware that there is a subtle order to the workings of nature, and she wanted to figure it out.

She had noticed that when a kettle is full of boiling water, a similar vapor escapes the mouth of the kettle. She had also noticed that breathing on a mirror or window causes a moist fog to appear on the glass. *Maybe there is water trapped in the breath itself,* she thought. *When the water inside, warmed by the body, meets with the colder air outside the body, it somehow makes the water visible in the air. Maybe that is why the closer the temperature of the outside air is to the temperature of the body, the less visible the vapor is. But why does it become more visible? When water is very cold, it freezes. When water is very hot, it turns into vapor and rises away. But what happens when vapor gets cold? Maybe it turns back into water. So I wonder, is the breath that I see really just tiny particles of —*

"Thanks for covering for me with the mistress last night," Il-sun burst out suddenly.

"What?" Gi's body shook.

"Sorry, I didn't mean to startle you. Thank you for helping me last night."

"Oh." Gi had tried to forget it. She was feeling bitter.

"I know you don't like doing that sort of thing. You know, lying."

"It's okay," Gi replied, though she did not mean it. She knew that Il-sun wanted her to ask about her illicit adventure of the night before, the reason for her being so tired and unable to meet her quota at the factory. Gi felt like punishing her, and she let silence linger in the space of her expected response.

"Aren't you going to ask?" said Il-sun after too many beats of silence.

"What?"

"Don't play dumb. You know what."

"No, I don't."

"About last night!"

"I don't want to know."

"Oh, come on. Just ask," begged Il-sun.

"Why don't you tell me what you want to tell me and stop playing this game?"

"Because it's more fun this way."

"For you."

"You're just jealous."

"Just tell me and be done with it!" Gi had raised her voice. She almost never did that.

"You're no fun," Il-sun said, pouting.

"Maybe that's true." Gi was genuinely hurt. She could no longer hide her feelings from herself: She *was* jealous, but not for the reasons Il-sun believed.

The girls walked along in uncomfortable silence for a little while. Finally the storm passed between them and Gi gave in.

"Okay, I give up. What happened last night?"

"That's more like it!" Il-sun grabbed Gi's arm. "It was wonderful!"

"What was wonderful?"

"Everything!"

"Everything?" Gi felt embarrassed by her lack of sophistication. She knew that "everything" actually meant something specific, that it implied something that older people would make knowing eye contact about but never speak of directly. But she did not want to seem uninformed, so she said, "Oh, *everything.*"

"He met me on the street last night, and

he took me on his scooter to a park over-looking the water."

"On his scooter! Il-sun! You know that you can get into a lot of trouble for driving vehicles at night!"

"Relax, Gi. He knows a lot of people. He would never get in trouble. Besides, we drove with the light off so we wouldn't be seen."

"Are you insane? You could have been killed!"

"Really, Gi."

"I'm just saying."

"Can I tell you the story, or are you going to keep throwing a fit?"

"Okay, tell your story. I'm just glad you didn't get killed. Or worse. Somebody could have seen you."

"The moon was out and it was really bright outside, almost like daylight. He took me to a grassy area where we could see the outline of the city across the water. It was cold, but he had a blanket. He held me really close to him. Gi, he is so handsome!"

"You could see that at night?"

Il-sun either ignored her or wasn't listen-ing.

"He smelled really good too. He was wear-ing some kind of scent. I've never smelled anything like it before. It was so manly, I just wanted to bite him."

Gi was unsure why anyone would ever want to bite a man, but she had stopped trying to figure out Il-sun's little quirks.

"He brought a bottle of whiskey and he gave me a glass."

"He had whiskey? Where did he get it?" Gi had heard of whiskey but had never seen it or known anyone who had actually tried it. She imagined it must be delicious, by the way people talked about it.

"He has a lot of connections. Really, Gi, I think he knows everybody."

"How did it taste? Did you like it?" Gi did not think that she would have had the courage to try it.

"It was awful. It burns your mouth and throat. At first I thought he was playing a trick on me, making me drink gasoline or something. He told me it was an acquired taste. Anyway, it made me feel giggly."

There was an expectant pause, and Gyong-ho realized that again she was supposed to prod for more information. This time she decided to play the game.

"So then what happened?"

"It was so wonderful, Gi! He had his arms around me, and I was feeling really good from the whiskey, and the water was lit up by the moon, and he smelled so tasty —

and then he kissed my lips. I thought I was
going to die! It was just like *John and Daisy.*"

No, not John and Daisy *again,* Gi thought
to herself. She wished they had never found
that book.

"As soon as he kissed me, I melted. I
couldn't stop kissing him back. I felt so hot."

Feeling "hot" was a *John and Daisy* term
Il-sun had started using that didn't mean
what it was supposed to mean. Gi again felt
embarrassed by her own ignorance.

"I think he was getting hot too. Did you
know that they get big down there, when
they get hot?"

Gi had absolutely no idea what she meant
and was relieved that it was a rhetorical
question. Il-sun continued.

"So we were kissing, and then he reached
under my shirt and grabbed my breast.
Under my bra!"

Il-sun paused for maximum shock value.

"You let him touch you there?" Gi could
not imagine letting anyone touch her there,
especially a man.

"At first he squeezed too hard and it hurt,
but then I told him to be more gentle. It
feels really nice, Gi! He sort of pinched my
nipples with his fingers. I thought I was going to go over the edge!"

Gi flushed with sudden embarrassment.

She would never be able to speak so freely about such personal things. "Going over the edge" was another *John and Daisy* term, and Gi had the feeling that even Il-sun did not fully understand it.

"It sounds awful to me."

"That's just because you've never tried it. Trust me, you'll love it!"

Gi was pretty sure that she wouldn't enjoy any of what was described, but she did have a curious sensation in her body hearing Il-sun talk about it. She felt like she wanted more of something. Maybe more of Il-sun's story. Or maybe she was just hungry. There was something about the story that left her with a vague craving. It was different from other gossip.

"Then what happened?"

"That was it."

"That was it?"

"Then I started to feel dizzy. He said it was from the whiskey. It was time to go home anyway, so he brought me back to the dormitory."

Gi felt like there was something unfinished about Il-sun's account, as if it weren't supposed to conclude with getting dizzy and going home. The tale required something more punctuating and dramatic to feel truly complete. At the end of movies and popular

fiction, the hero and heroine always exchanged pats on the back and then sang
patriotic songs to celebrate their triumph.
Getting dizzy and coming home was definitely not a satisfying ending.

They reached the orphanage in silence, Il-
sun's second wind spent. They signed in
with the mistress and went directly to bed.

8

It was the middle of the night. There was a loud knock at the door, and Gyong-ho started awake. It had happened before. Normally it was just the *inminbanjang* asking if there were any unregistered guests staying at the apartment. There never were any. But this time it was different. This time there were three severe men in uniform, two of whom were carrying guns. They asked if this was the Song residence. Father bowed courteously. They said that they were there for an inspection, and for everyone in the apartment to line up against the wall outside the door. One of the men carrying a gun stood in front of Mother, Father, Grandmother, and Gyong-ho while the other two went inside. There was a lot of shuffling, sounds of ripping fabric, furniture being overturned. Eventually a man, the one without a gun, stepped outside and glared at them. Father was perspiring heavily. Mother was pale.

"A concerned citizen has reported that your loyalty to the state is in question. Upon inspection, we have found that you have failed to properly maintain the portraits of the Great Leader, Kim Il-sung, and his honorable son, the Dear Leader Kim Jong-il. You have failed to care properly for the icons representing the *juche* ideal. There is dust on the tops of the frames, and the portraits are not level. Your neglect indicates your lack of fealty and suggests that you are in danger of becoming involved in seditious activity. You are all hereby under arrest for failing to pay proper respect to the authority of the state."

Mother gasped and Grandmother lowered her head.

"You are to be immediately removed from your home and taken to prison to await trial."

"I have neglected my duties as homemaker," Mother pleaded. "Please don't make my family suffer for my unworthiness. Take me but leave my family!"

"No! I'm to blame, as the head of this household," Father tried to bargain.

"It is not only the portraits. There are other charges against you, which you will learn about at your trial. We reserve the right to detain three generations for transgressions such as this. I see three generations here. You all must go."

"No!" Father shouted. "We work very hard for the glory of our Dear Leader. We attend meetings with our work units daily. My mother takes care of our home. Look at her eyes. She can barely see! She gets confused sometimes. Please give us a chance."

"You are still found wanting. You can give the circumstances of your case at your trial. They may see fit to be lenient with you, but that is not my decision."

"No, please!" Father begged. One of the soldiers hit him hard across the face with the butt of his rifle. Blood rushed from his nose and he whimpered. Mother cried. They were led to a truck outside and never saw their home again.

9

Within a week after the mistress first met with him, Father Lee came to the back door of the orphanage with a large box of food. That was nearly six years ago. It contained mostly rice and beans, as well as forged ration coupons and some soap. It was not a lot of food, considering the many girls she was responsible for feeding, but, along with her state rations, it would keep them from starving. The mistress offered him tea, so as not to seem ungrateful or rude, but she hoped he would decline. Receiving illicit goods was grounds for imprisonment, and she did not want to be caught accepting them or fraternizing with a Christian. To her frustration, he accepted.

Every layer of *Chosun* society was organized and stratified. The *inminbanjang* was a neighborhood watcher, of sorts, who was responsible for keeping tabs on the coming and going of her neighbors. She was expected to report anyone in her district who engaged in suspicious activity or failed to participate in social events. The orphanage was considered its own independent district, and by default the mistress was made *inminbanjang*. Technically, the *inminbanjang* was supposed to attend extra meetings and training, but that would have meant the mistress's superiors having to stand in for her at the orphanage. For her they waived the requirement.

Being the *inminbanjang* meant that the mistress was beyond scrutiny from below; and because her superiors preferred to ignore her, she was practically invisible from above. It seemed that there was a tiny hole in *juche* itself in which she fit perfectly, obscured from the eyes of the Republic that otherwise could see everywhere. Still, the presence of Father Lee, who was intent on lingering, made the mistress nervous.

"I cannot thank you enough for giving this food to us," she said, impatience pushing at the restraint in her throat.

"Thank our savior, not me," he replied unctuously. "Have you been praying to him?"

"Every day," she lied.

"Good. Have you had a chance to read from the Bible?"

"I have, a little." This time she was telling the truth. Reading it was tempting, because of how dangerous it was. When she read it she felt like she was examining a relic from an alien world. She had not been given much room to contemplate life or history outside of *Chosun*. Now here, laid out before her, was a whole new history, none of which remotely involved *Chosun*. The Great Leader was not even a minor character in the stories of the Bible.

"Very good! It pleases me to spread the word of God." He held his smile a little too long. The mistress had a feeling that he wanted something. "I would like to meet some of the girls here," he blurted after an uncomfortable silence. "I would like to tell them of the wonders of Jesus Christ."

The mistress blanched. "I don't think that's a very good idea," she said. It was one thing for her to keep the illegal activity secret, but to expect children to remain quiet about it was asking too much.

"But don't you want God's precious little ones to know the truth? I would hate to have to discontinue food deliveries. There are so many deserving Christians who could use the help."

The mistress suddenly boiled inside. He was trying to manipulate her through her desperation only to gain more converts to his dangerous ideology. Did he think that this was a game? These were children, and this could kill them! She wanted to lift him by the lapels of his threadbare shirt and toss him into the mud on the street. But she *was* desperate, and he had proved that he had the means to help. She forced a veneer of self-control and tried a diplomatic approach.

"I don't think it's a good idea. You know as well as I do just how dangerous your . . . *our* . . . practices are. I cannot in good conscience endanger the lives of the girls in my care. I doubt that Jesus would want that." She monitored his face for his reaction, but it was hard to read. "Here's what I propose: I'll read the Bible on my own and pass the teachings of Christ on to the girls, but I'll say that they are conventional wisdom, or even the wisdom of Kim Il-sung, without mentioning their true origin. That way, the girls get the teachings without being put into harm's way. If the Dear Leader ever decides to soften his position on Christianity, then we can talk to them more openly about it. That seems fair, considering the charity. You can still send the food, knowing that the teachings of Christ are being taught to them."

Father Lee looked doubtful. He seemed about to refuse, so she cut him off.

"If you won't send the food, then I will publicly renounce Jesus Christ." She said it threateningly, her eyes wide and her nostrils flared.

Father Lee looked at the mistress in an appraising way. He understood her veiled meaning. *She may be plain, but she's certainly not short of wit,* he thought. He realized that he was in a perilous situation: The mistress could, out of spite, turn him over to the authorities, who would waste no time making a public example out of him. He imagined his trial and his martyrdom. And then the pain. He would surely be subjected to horrible, horrible pain. His facial tic began to work double-time. A dark cloud passed through his eyes.

"Very well, you will receive your food." With that he turned on his heel and marched out the door.

Food deliveries continued with surprising regularity over the next six years. In a country where most of the infrastructure had shut down, the black market moved with punctual regularity. Father Lee often made the deliveries himself, but sometimes they were brought by other members of his organization. The mistress never asked too many details, but received the goods with much gratitude.

It took several weeks, but Father Lee eventually recovered from the humiliation of the first contentious delivery. He even humbled himself and became a welcome visitor at the orphanage. He would engage the mistress in conversations about what she had read in the Bible. She enjoyed the stimulation, even if she did not share his zeal for the subject. She could not blame him for wanting so desperately to share his belief with others. Everyone needed to believe in something in such a dark time. Also, being denied faith by the government only made people hold their faith more dear. For his sake, she pretended to go along, and out of self-preservation he never challenged her.

The Bible, however, she cherished. It turned her into an unlikely criminal: a renegade with the power to poison the minds of the youth with imperialist dogma. Just the awareness that she could do it gave her a sense of power over the establishment, which claimed absolute authority. When she was not reading it, she would hide it behind a loose wall board in her bedroom. Knowing the danger that it could be found by the roving hands of a naughty orphan, or by the police during one of their random midnight inspections, was a brisk stimulant that lifted her above despair.

10

The moon crackled and hissed as it slid across the sky. It was the sound of the moon, as much as its brightness, that kept Gi from being able to close her eyes and go to sleep. She kept replaying in her mind the details of Il-sun's illicit adventure.

What was it about Il-sun that made her so compelling to people? She was certainly pretty — there was no doubt about that — but it seemed like there had to be more to it. It wasn't just the lush outline of her lips or the shininess of her hair, or even the fullness of her breasts. It was the way she was always reaching forward with her lips, tossing her hair casually into the light. It was the way she looked at people from the corners of her eyes while cocking her head modestly, the way she walked as if the very act was causing her pleasure. It was not the parts that made up Il-sun that captured their attention, but the way the parts worked together — the rhythm of her actions, the fluidity of her gestures, the alluring promise in her eyes coupled with the scorn of her shoulder as she turned away — that drew people to her. It seemed that the secret to Il-sun was her embodied contradictions, how she simultaneously teased and rejected; and this manipulation seemed to come naturally to her, as if from some innate womanly knowledge that Gi did not possess.

Gi imagined the scene of the night before: the man putting his arms around Il-sun. She must have felt soft to his firm touch. The newness of her body, so different from his own, must have sparked a curiosity in him. Perhaps he was trying to solve for himself the mystery of her contradictions. Maybe, as the moonlight reflected off her lips, they looked like ripe berries, and he wondered if they might taste red and sugared. Her smell was naturally sweet, and maybe this compelled him; so he put his lips to hers and kissed her, hoping to taste berries.

Gi looked over at the sleeping form of Il-sun. It was not uncommon on cold nights for them to keep warm together in the same bed. She slid from her own sleeping mat and got under the covers next to her. Gi pressed the front of her body into the back of Il-sun's, allowing her warmth to penetrate below the skin. She inhaled her familiar smell and was suddenly jealous that the man would also know this intimate detail. Il-sun had been her only friend for nearly four years, and she did not like the idea of anyone coming between them. Gi put her arm around her and brought her face to the very back of her neck, where long, wispy hairs made two trails up to the base of her skull. Her skin was soft and redolent of sweet rice.

Il-sun shifted in her sleep, turning until she was almost flat on her back. Gi lifted a leg over her, to take in more of her warmth, and the soft sensitivity between her legs made contact with Il-sun's hip. An unexpected flood of tingling spread throughout her body, warm and electric. It was wonderful. As soon as she felt it, she was parched for that sensation, as if she had become aware of a thirst that had always been there and she had just now found the well. She ground herself more firmly onto Il-sun's hip, heightening the sensation. Satisfying the urge to press down, however, only increased her desire to press more. Gi did not understand what was happening to her, or why she was doing it, but the compulsion was overwhelming. She was afraid of waking Il-sun, but she also did not want to stop — this was intimacy unlike any she had ever experienced. If she pressed hard enough for long enough, would she merge completely into Il-sun?

She had a feeling that Il-sun would not approve of what she was doing. It seemed to cross a line that had the power to redefine their friendship, but Gi had no explanation of what that line might be. The prospect of rejection was frightening. Even so, she continued doing it, charging toward an unknown goal.

She once again imagined the man's hands exploring Il-sun's body, and found herself doing the same. Her hand slid up Il-sun's belly over her nightshirt until she found the rise of her breast. She had never felt another woman's breast before. Her own were underdeveloped, and Il-sun's were a pleasant contrast. She gently cupped the breast, feeling its weighty softness. She could feel Il-sun's heartbeat, slow and steady, so unlike her own. She could feel her friend's nipple between her thumb and index finger, and she squeezed softly. Il-sun took in a sharp breath as her nipple stiffened in response to the touch.

"Gi, what are you doing?" Sleep was thick in Il-sun's voice.

Gi froze in place, as if by not moving she could deny being there at all.

"Gi?"

"I'm sorry. I was just trying to warm up." There was silence for a whole minute and neither girl moved.

"I don't think we should sleep in the same bed anymore," said Il-sun, finally.

"I'm sorry," Gi responded, removing her hand from her friend's body. Il-sun pretended not to notice.

"I mean, we aren't little girls anymore. We'll be moving out of here soon. We're practically women now."

"I'm sorry," Gyong-ho repeated, unpeeling herself from Il-sun and slinking back to her own mat. She caved in on herself, embarrassed. Before her eyes could fill with tears her head was full of numbers. By the time daylight broke through the dirty windowpanes, the numbers in her head were very large, indeed.

11

The mistress sat, gazing at the back door. She knew there would not be a delivery for several more days, but still she watched the door longingly. Impatiently. How was it that she had come to be this distracted? She had for so long dedicated her life to others, and now she needed a pursuit that was all her own. She had witnessed so much sorrow and despair, and now she knew that those were in infinite supply — what little comfort she could provide, these days, seemed so meaningless.

It started when Father Lee began having trouble with his suppliers. His shipments had been so regular over the past several years that the mistress had nearly forgotten that the goods arrived at great peril to the bearers. Father Lee explained that the secret route across the border had been compromised, and several of his flock were lost to the labor camps, along with the officials who

had been bribed to look the other way. He assured the mistress that he and his contacts would find another supplier soon — he had already been put in contact with a prominent dealer on the black market; she shouldn't lose hope. That was three months ago.

The following month was very lean at the orphanage. The state ration distribution system was working better than it did a few years earlier, but it was still not enough. The mistress and the girls had so far been spared having to hike out of the city in search of tree bark and edible mushrooms, or taking the grave risk of stealing corn from the state-run farms, as many people had to do. Now, perhaps, their luck had run out.

But then the young man arrived, and now the mistress could think of little else. She replayed the meeting over and over in her memory, to fill the space between his visits.

There was a knock at the back door. A knock could mean so many things, and the mistress tensed. It was the middle of the day and all the girls were either in school or working; she was alone in the kitchen. She opened the door to see a man in his mid-twenties leaning against a post and smoking a foreign cigarette with a filtered end. He

smoked it as if he were the one smoldering, not the cigarette. His posture showed a studied tough-guy attitude: button-down shirt carelessly untucked, shirtsleeves rolled up, a faded blue newsboy cap cocked at a no-nonsense angle, the brim partly concealing his eyes. His stance, leaning as he was, was a dare to anyone who might have the nerve to ask him to move. He was average in height, but solidly built, with firm muscles, a strong, square jaw, and long limbs that tapered elegantly to agile hands and feet. His gaze bored into her with animal intensity, and she flushed. With an unconscious flutter of her hands, she checked the buttons of her blouse to make sure she had not accidentally answered the door bare-breasted. He blew smoke from the corner of his mouth with practiced nonchalance. There was a large box at his feet.

The mistress was speechless for a moment as she took in the young man in front of her. He was not the typical sort that Father Lee employed to make deliveries. In fact, he was not a typical sort at all. His manner of dress was precariously individualistic, a badge of danger in a society where people try very hard not to be noticed. Perhaps because there were few men in her limited

social orbit, and even fewer attractive ones, she found herself looking at him with hungry eyes. His youth, his fullness and firmness, and his cocksure attitude cracked her defensive barriers. She had not felt attracted to a man in many years, which is perhaps why she fell for him so suddenly. He was an outward expression of who she was inside, a renegade standing against the current of their severely homogenized culture. And, perhaps, she had never felt this kind of attraction before. It was so instant, and so . . . physical — made all the more taut by the fact that she was older than he. Seeing him reminded her of every one of her long, chaste years.

Recovering herself, the mistress swallowed, bowed her head in the polite way and said, *"Anyang haseyo."*

The young man took a final drag from his cigarette, exhaled smoke in a long, steady stream from the corner of his mouth, then flicked the butt carelessly into the yard. Most people would have scavenged the remaining tobacco from the butt to roll into another cigarette, but clearly he did not feel the need to conserve. He held his eyes on the mistress for a long moment before speaking.

"Where do you want this?" he asked, kicking the box at his feet with his toe. His voice was smooth and steady. His phrasing was abrupt, but he spoke each word with slow deliberation. It sounded like he was trying to make his voice deeper than it actually was. Even so, the texture of his voice caused a tingling sensation to bubble up her spine.

"Inside. On the counter," she said, finding herself short of breath.

The mistress wondered how a young man could come to possess foreign cigarettes, which by all accounts were difficult to find and prohibitively expensive. They were normally a privilege bandied about by Party officials. Then she realized that, as a dealer of contraband, he probably had access to all manner of exotic things. That would also explain the full quality to his skin — he obviously ate well enough to support his muscular frame.

He set the box down with a heavy thud onto a countertop, then, turning around to face the mistress, leaned casually against a wall. The kitchen had no decoration, only stained walls that may have been white at one time. It was a large, square room surrounded by cupboards and countertops, and there was a wooden chopping block in the center. It was by no means modern, but it was sufficient for the simple meals prepared by the girls. He stood there silently, watching the mistress with his arms folded across his chest.

"Can I offer you something? Some tea?" she asked, blushing.

He looked thoughtful for a moment, as if weighing whether or not having a cup of tea would damage his image.

"That would be nice, thank you," he replied.

His politeness caught her off guard — it was at odds with his otherwise tough demeanor. She put a kettle of water on the stove.

"Would you like to have a seat?" she asked, offering him a stool.

He sat down. In contrast to the studied confidence he had been exuding while standing, sitting on the stool made him seem nervous and uncertain. It was as if his assuredness hinged on being able to lean impudently against walls. He sat stiffly upright, hands on his knees, the tips of his loafers pointing in slightly toward each other. In his discomfort he gazed around the room as if to admire ornate molding rather than the plain and dingy kitchen walls. He could have been in the lobby of a doctor's office awaiting an exam. The mistress remained standing near the stove, examining him.

After several moments of awkward silence, she spoke. "Have you been with Lee Won's organization for a long time?" She immediately felt silly for asking. He was obviously Father Lee's new black market contact.

"Me?" he laughed. "I'm not part of any organization. His friends in the South pay me to deliver goods. That's as far as it goes."

The water on the stove came to a boil and she poured it into a teapot with a scattering of tea leaves. Weak tea was all anyone had to offer, but she was still embarrassed by having to serve it that way — he seemed accustomed to abundance. Would he think less of her for serving weak tea? The mistress wanted to ask him what it was like living in constant danger, being an outlaw and trafficking goods; but she hesitated, unsure if it would be proper. She had a dangerous secret of her own, owning and reading the Bible, which she felt gave them a peculiar kind of intimacy. She wanted to share that with him.

She poured tea into chipped ceramic teacups and handed one to the young man, who nodded in thanks. She remained standing, studying the surface of the tea in her cup. They sipped their tea in a thick atmosphere of thoughts, none of which could quite condense into spoken words.

The young man finished his tea, then swirled the last drop that was clinging to the bottom of his cup as if he hoped to find something to say in it. Finding nothing, he put the cup down, the drop still in it, and stood up. The mistress, who was still staring into her nearly untouched tea, put her cup down as well.

"Thank you for the delivery. I'm very sorry, I have nothing to pay you."

"I've been paid already," he said.

When he stood, he donned once again his tough persona. He walked to the door, opened it, then closed it behind him without looking back.

The young man now made deliveries every week. As brief and infrequent as his visits were, the mistress looked forward to them. She developed an elaborate fantasy of who he was and how he lived, based on nothing more than his rebellious swagger, his nervous silences and terse answers to her few questions. Their conversations had mostly been limited to short greetings and a courteous thank-you. Sometimes he would stay for a cup of tea, but always he would sit nervously, silence prevailing between them.

She looked for clues about him, like the way he drank his tea with purpose, neither delicately sipping nor oafishly gulping. He obviously cared about his appearance, always arriving clean, his clothes spotless and in careful disarray on his frame. He kept his hair trimmed, from what she could see under the newsboy cap he always wore. That he wore the hat at all was curious: It was an unusual style and obviously foreign, yet he wore it in the open without fear and, even more puzzling, with impunity. In her imagination, she saw him as an eloquent conversationalist, once relaxed, expressing insightful ideas in direct, concise truisms. He seemed the brooding, thinking type. She imagined that his illicit line of work stemmed from a rebellious iconoclasm that ran so deeply in his marrow that he could not keep himself from it; he was an idealist fighting a dangerous establishment, ulti- mately for humanitarian aims. That must be why he so steadfastly delivered his illegal supplies to the orphanage. But she had no way of knowing for sure. Maybe he was just a criminal; but even that she found attrac- tive.

She liked watching his muscles work underneath his shirt as he hefted the heavy food boxes. She enjoyed watching him walk out the door, his trim backside flexing and relaxing in his confident stride. Most of all, she loved inhaling his earthy aroma as he stirred the air when he walked past her. She counted the hours until she saw him again.

12

Il-sun pretended nothing had happened, and so Gyong-ho did too. It was easier that way. Gi did not understand her feelings and could not even begin to explain them. They woke up, performed their morning rituals, dressed, and walked to work as normal, but the gulf between them seemed impassable. They each tried lobbing words into it, like "good morning," and "it's cold today," but the phrases echoed unnaturally in their ears. They gave up and walked in silence. This time it was Gi who was dragging her feet from lack of sleep.

Gi felt as though they were being pried out of girlhood: herself unwillingly, Il-sun enthusiastically. They were on a threshold and all their priorities were changing at once. It was too fast. Il-sun seemed to be running toward it with open arms, impatient for the knowledge and the sophistication of the womanhood fitting her new body. Gi shrank from it. She had just gotten comfortable here.

Things had begun changing when they found the book *John and Daisy.* They had come home early because the electricity at the factory had gone out. When they walked into the kitchen to check in with the mistress, she was standing and staring wistfully at the back door with her hand on her cheek. She seemed in a pleasant daze. She turned and smiled at the girls, then excused herself to her bedroom.

"What's with her?" asked Il-sun.

"I don't know, but she looks happy."

"Hey, what's in here?" Il-sun asked, noticing a box on the counter. She lifted one of the lid flaps.

"It's not ours. We should leave it alone," replied Gi.

"I'm just curious," Il-sun said, peeking inside. "There's food in here!"

"Today must have been a special ration day or something," Gi said, peeking into the box.

"Maybe we should put it away for the mistress," said Il-sun.

They began sorting through the contents of the box: a few ragged-looking onions, a bulb of garlic, several potatoes, a bag of rice, and a bag of red beans. As they removed the items, a rectangular bundle wrapped in a stained cloth and tied with a string tumbled onto the counter. Gi picked it up. It was not a food item and she was conflicted about what to do with it. Should she unwrap it, or leave it on the counter for the mistress? She was inclining toward the latter when Il-sun noticed it in her hands.

"What's that?"

"I don't know. Maybe it's for the mistress. I think we should leave it."

Il-sun snatched it from her. She turned it over, prodded and bent it. "It feels like a book to me."

"It's not for us. We should leave it like we found it."

"We can look and then wrap it right back up." Her eyes had taken on a mischievous glint.

"Il-sun, no! We could get in trouble."

"For what? Unpacking the food box? The mistress always tells us we need to take the initiative when it comes to helping out. Don't you want to see what it is?"

"But it isn't ours!"

"If we get caught, here's what we'll say: We were unpacking the food box, we picked it up by mistake, and the wrapping came undone. See? It's not even tied very well." With that she pulled at the string and the cloth fell open. "Oops," she said with exaggerated indifference.

In her hands was a book unlike she had ever seen before, a paperback with a graphic cover. The cover illustration showed two Caucasian people, a man and a woman, in a mad embrace. The woman had blond hair and was wearing a gauzy dress that appeared to be falling off, slipping over her overly large breasts. Her head was back, her very red lips seductively parted. The man in the illustration had dark brown shoulder-length hair and a face of rough stubble. He was shirtless, with rippling muscles and a narrow waist. He was gazing intently at the woman's parted lips, his arms wrapped around her tightly. The cover had both Korean characters and small foreign print. The title, spelled phonetically in Korean, was *John and Daisy,* and in smaller characters it said, "Translated from English by Andrew Kim." This was definitely not a regular-issue book.

The girls stared at it openmouthed, transfixed by the blatantly erotic cover. They had never imagined that such a thing could exist. Where could it have come from? What story could the book have to tell? It was certainly not a safe thing to possess. They looked at each other, each with a different thought about what to do next.

"We should tie it back up and leave it like we found it," Gyong-ho said, trying to sound definitive.

"I want to read it."

"We can't do that! What will the mistress say when she looks for it and can't find it?"

"She may not even know it's here. How do we know it is even hers? Besides, I don't think anyone in her right mind would publicly claim this, do you?"

"No, which is the same reason that we would be better off leaving it alone too."

"You don't have to read it if you don't want to. I'm just curious. What harm could it do?"

"You don't have any idea —"

Gyong-ho was interrupted by the sound of the mistress's door opening. Il-sun quickly hid the book in the waistband of her trousers, pulling her blouse over it to cover the bulge.

The mistress emerged still smiling. She looked from one to the other of them, and then at the empty box. Her face fell slightly.

"Is that all? Was there anything else in the box?"

There was a tense silence and Gyong-ho felt the blood drain from her face. She counted flies on the kitchen window.

"No, miss. Should there have been something?" Il-sun said a little too brightly.

The mistress deflated. "No. No, nothing." With that, she turned and left the room.

Over the next few weeks Il-sun consumed the book. She studied it with more interest and concentration than she had given to any of her studies in school. Gi refused to read it, but that did not stop Il-sun from reading passages to her or from talking about it nonstop. Gi felt certain that there were no details of the book of which she was unaware because of Il-sun's long discourses and verbalized ruminations on the subject. She had gotten quite tired of hearing about it. Besides, she really did not understand much of it.

Not long after that Il-sun met the man on the scooter, and Gi could not help but think that Il-sun had been emboldened by reading the book. Gi had only ever seen the man from a distance, and that was fine with her. There was something shark-eyed in the way he seemed to linger around the factory, and her natural inclination was to avoid him.

"Let's go talk to him, Gi!" Il-sun had said. They were on their way home from the factory. It was only midafternoon, but the factory was shut down because an expected shipment of cloth had not arrived. The man was sitting on his scooter across the street.

"Are you crazy?"

"Aren't you curious?"

"He gives me the creeps."

"He looks interesting. Maybe he'll give us a ride on his scooter!"

"No way."

"Come on, Gi. Let's have some fun."

"I'm going home."

"I'm going to talk to him. You'll be jealous after he has driven me all over the city on his scooter and all you've done is play dice with a twelve-year-old."

"You'll be jealous when I'm playing dice and you're dead."

"Don't be so dramatic."

"The mistress will kill you, if the guy on the scooter doesn't."

"You'll cover for me, won't you?"

"Il-sun!"

"Gi!"

Gi paused, then sighed. "Okay. Don't do anything stupid."

"You know me."

"Yes, I do."

13

Grandmother was the first to go. She died peacefully in her sleep during their first week at the prison camp. The guards had been merciful — mindful of Grandmother's old age and confusion, they did not overwork her. She was sitting on a stool in the garden pulling weeds the day before she died and, to Gi, looked content. That was the benefit of Grandmother's confusion: From moment to moment, she could forget who and where she was. Gyong-ho and her parents did not have that luxury.

The family arrived at the prison camp just after dawn and was immediately split up. They were told it was to facilitate reeducation; a rottenness had infected the family, and in order to keep it from spreading among them they needed to be isolated from one another.

The camp was large, like a small city, with miles of dirt roads lined with rows of barracks made of plywood and tin, plus several buildings for labor and reeducation purposes. There was a constant flurry of activity. Guards with rifles patrolled the perimeters and the streets like gangs of angry youth, looking for, and often creating, trouble. The men, women, and children were all housed in separate areas and were not free to roam between them. Gyong-ho was allowed to see her mother for thirty minutes every few days, which was how she learned of her grandmother's death, but was never permitted to see her father.

The camp was nestled in a deep valley and was surrounded by electric fences topped with razor wire. Guard posts with bored and trigger-happy sharpshooters were spaced every hundred meters, and the inmates were warned of land mines in the surrounding fields. The prisoners were a gaunt and dirty lot, their clothes stained, torn, and foul. They reminded Gyong-ho of farm beasts, wallowing in filth and excrement. The inmates had faraway looks in their eyes, weighed down by grim and sagging mouths. For weeks Gyong-ho walked on tiptoe and made a great effort to keep from making contact with the filth that was all around. Little by little, as her own clothes became stained and smelly and layers of grime coated her body, she began to recognize herself as part of her surroundings, a member of the sallow, sorry community around her.

Gi was assigned to one of the windowless barracks where more than a dozen girls slept on hard, bare planks. She was given a thin blanket, a small tin bowl, and a set of rough wooden chopsticks. These were her only possessions. The blankets had to be particularly well guarded because some of the older girls were inclined to steal them in order to better insulate themselves against the frigid *Chosun* nights.

Gyong-ho cried inconsolably the first night she spent in the crowded and dirty room. She was frightened and missed her family. The guard assigned to her dormitory, a severe woman in a crisp uniform, irritated by the noise, jerked her by the arm into the street outside and told her that if she did not stop breaking the Dear Leader's peace immediately, her mother would be brought out and shot dead in front of her. Her vivid, eight-year-old's imagination could visualize it clearly; and with every ounce of strength that she possessed, she swallowed her grief and tears. With no outlet, however, the wailing echoed inside her, filling her up, reverberating until her every moment was saturated with it. It was a constant background hum.

14

The mistress stood, holding the gift gently with her fingertips as if it might crumble into dust. The young man had seen her, and understood her, even without words. They were kindred outlaws, treasonous in their thoughts and desires.

The brown paper had fallen to reveal a clear cellophane package stapled closed at the top, together with a thin cardboard label. The label was printed with what she recognized as Chinese characters, though she could not read them, and below that was a foreign script — perhaps English or French, or even German. She carefully removed the label by prizing up the staples, and then set it on her dresser. She would hide it later in the pages of her Bible, along with the few other foreign wrappings and newsprint scraps that had been stowed away in previous food boxes. She cherished these illegal snippets.

Gingerly, she withdrew a new pair of sheer, white nylon stockings from the cellophane. They had been wrapped around a piece of cardboard to preserve their shape in the package. They were smooth and pristine, never before worn. She slipped a hand into one of them, pulling the stitched toe over her fingertips, careful not to snag any threads on her fingernails. The fabric was cool on her skin. It had been several years since she had had new stockings.

She brought her hand up to her face so that she could feel the virgin cloth on her cheeks and across her lips. The mistress ached to be a woman — she so often felt like a machine. There was something suggestive about the gift, more intimate than the hand mirror he had brought the week before, or the hair clip several weeks before that. It was as if, when she wore the stockings, he too would be sheathing her feet, her calves, her knees. What would it feel like inside the stockings, his hands sliding over her legs?

The gifts were a recent development in the boxes delivered by the young man. The first one she had found in the rice when she was unpacking the box. It was small, and wrapped in a ragged, old piece of newspaper. She pulled back the wrapping to discover a fancy hair clip tucked inside, made of polished wood with an ornate leaf pattern carved into it. It was held together with a strong spring and looked new. She fished in the box for a note, or some indication that the young man had intended it for her; that it had not accidentally fallen into the box on its way to some other, less featureless girl. There was no note, so she looked more closely at the wrapping. It was randomly and raggedly torn, with no apparent hidden message in its clipped content. Looking more closely, she realized that it was from no ordinary *Chosun* newspaper. In fact, it was not *Chosun* at all. It was clearly *Hanguk,* being torn from the middle of an article about an art installation in Seoul. It was pedestrian, commonplace, exotic, and, best of all, illegal. Potentially lethal. She smoothed the wrinkles out of the paper and hid it within the pages of her Bible.

The next time the young man came, she made a point of wearing the hair clip and showing a lot of profile in hopes that he would see it on her and mention it, or at least confirm in some way that it was truly meant for her. He said nothing, and so, in frustration, neither did she. That same day, however, there was another small package in the box. This time it was a music box that played an unfamiliar tune when its lid was lifted. The mistress realized that this was more than a coincidence, that these presents were clearly left for her.

Almost every week since then there had been something, some small token, left for her. In her entire life she had never felt so real.

15

It was late at night and Foreman Hwang was sitting in his office, poring over papers at a scratched old desk, a dim electric bulb above casting a small circle of light around him. The factory was otherwise dark and empty. Three loud bangs rang out from the large metal loading-dock doors. The foreman looked up at a clock on the wall. Ten-thirty. The boy was always punctual.

He rose painfully from his chair and limped the length of the factory to the loading dock. He lifted the rusty bar off the doors and opened one of them a crack. The faint light coming across the factory through his office door was barely enough to illuminate the face of the man standing outside. He was young and full faced, and wearing a strange foreign cap. *If this boy was not so bloody useful,* the foreman thought, *I would love to hit him across the face with a board. That would wipe off his insubordinate grin.*

"Do you have something for me?" The foreman's voice sounded like dry leaves crumbling together, which made the young man feel like swallowing.

"I do, if you are still able to do something for me," came the reply.

"Have I ever let you down, you disrespectful little shit?"

"Not yet."

"I have half a mind to turn you in just to watch you be shot."

"But before they shoot me, I will have told them all about you, you dirty pervert."

The foreman looked as if he had been slapped.

"Relax, old man. I may be many things, but a rat isn't one of them."

"You're a lowlife and a criminal."

"But I also have what you want." The young man produced a brown paper bag and handed it to him. The foreman took it quickly and held it behind the door. He unfolded the top of the bag and looked inside: two large bottles and a bundle of magazines. He felt a wave of gratitude for the young man.

"Don't let me down, Colonel. I'm going to need your help soon."

"Everything is already prepared."

16

Il-sun waited for Gyong-ho's breathing to become deep and regular. It always took so long for her to get to sleep, and tonight it seemed that she would never settle down. Gi tossed back and forth on her sleeping mat. Several times she inhaled sharply as if she were about to speak, but then said nothing. Il-sun had the sense that she was chewing on some kind of an explanation or apology but could not find the right words to begin; and she hoped that Gi would not find them. She did not want to talk about it. It was painful to be so near her internal struggle and yet not be able to offer help. The problem was that Gi wanted something that Il-sun could not provide: more closeness, when Il-sun was needing more space. Lately Gyong-ho seemed so . . . childish, clinging with ever greater tenacity to the games and play of girlhood, just as Il-sun was trying to shed them to be more womanly. She was embarrassed now to be seen with Gyong-ho, who was so awkward and insular.

Il-sun rolled over, turning her back to her friend, and feigned sleep. She was just able to shake herself awake before slipping from consciousness. The pull of dreams had almost drawn her under — she was so tired lately. Gyong-ho's breathing was now heavy and rhythmic, so Il-sun shed her blanket and sat up on her mat. She had laid out her clothes next to her sleeping mat in such a way that she could dress without fumbling in the dark. There was not even a hint of moonlight, and the room was in absolute darkness. She wished that she had better clothes; her nicest outfit was her factory uniform, which she donned with a grimace. If only her mother had not died.

She began tiptoeing toward the stairs. Just as she was starting to believe she had made a clean getaway, she stumbled loudly on a pile of books one of the girls kept near her mat.

"Il-sun?" Gi cut the darkness with a loud whisper.

"I'm just going to the latrine, Gi. Go back to sleep."

"Where are you going?"

"I told you, to the latrine. I'll be right back."

"You're going to meet him again, aren't you?"

"Shhhhhhh! I just told you, I'm only going to the toilet. Now go to sleep!"

"Il-sun —"

"Shhhh! I'll see you in the morning." With that she turned and made her way to the stairs. She descended them in twos, making an effort to miss the squeakier steps. She felt a moment of pride for having had the guile to plot the quietest route the day before. There was a certain thrill in doing what was forbidden. She had left her sneakers in the corner of the foyer at the bottom of the stairs so that she could easily find them, and sat on the floor to put them on. When she stood back up, she found herself facing the portrait of the Dear Leader. She could only barely make out the edges of the frame, but his image was already burned so deeply into her mind that her eyes did not need light to see it. Without thinking, by some latent reflex emboldened by the near perfect darkness, she formed a ball of saliva in her mouth and spit upward at the photograph. She felt a moment of tickled delight, knowing that she had just defiled the most sacred of images and that no one had seen her commit the crime. She stared into the blackness at the point where she knew the eyes to be and spit again. And again. She stood there for a moment, reeling in the power of what she had done.

Then, quite suddenly, the impact of her actions hit her full force. She felt her chest tighten and the air squeeze out of her lungs. She could not draw a breath, no matter how hard she tried. Even though she did not much believe in the Dear Leader, he still exerted power over her life. Suffocating, she reached upward to the photograph, barely able to reach it with her sleeve, and wiped the glass. She could feel the cool dampness of the saliva as it soaked through her shirt in spots — her aim had been true. She sucked at the air in tiny gasps as she polished the glass. *I'm not good enough,* she thought. It was a meaningless, superstitious incantation, but it had the power to loosen the death grip on her lungs. She hoped from the depth of her soul that the glass would not be smeared. There would be an investigation for sure if it were.

Il-sun took two steps back, her breath slowly returning to normal, and thought about the man she was going now to see. He was not the perfect man, but the only one who could, now, elevate her station in life. If her mother had not died, Il-sun would, no doubt, be courted by a handsome young Party official — a man working his way up the ranks, destined for success, and competing for her affection. He would arrive at the apartment, nervous, smelling of precious aftershave in a flawlessly pressed uniform. He would make a show of politeness and generosity to Mother, who would size him up and giggle girlishly — courting the daughter is also about courting the mother. Mother would bring out the best kimchee for him, and serve steaming pork while subtly mining him for information about his family history. A girl married the history as much as she did the man.

That life, that *songbun,* was over for her now. As an orphan she needed a strategy. She did not want to spend the rest of her days slowly becoming arthritic at the garment factory. Her new man did not have good *songbun* or Party clout, but had built a life for himself all the same. With him she could, at least, rise above her station. What did it matter if some would call it unrespectable?

Il-sun turned to the door, unlocked it, and stole into the night.

fate itself. She lay down on her sleeping mat. Using the hand mirror that the young man had given her, she watched as she allowed her fingers to trace the outline of her panties. The light touch caused a shiver to roll through her. She imagined that her fingers were the fingers of the young man exploring her body for the first time, and her eyes were his eyes watching her. Fingertips followed bones and tendons and sensitized lines where light flesh meets dark flesh. With her fingers she indulged in the power of her building desire, purposefully avoiding her most sensitive places even though they throbbed in anguish to be touched. She breathed her sweet and musky smell and imagined how the young man's scent would mix with her own. She was no stranger to her own pleasure, having touched herself many times before, but never had she so thoroughly drawn it out as if she were the lover touching her.

Her breath was ragged and heavy, and her heart beat strongly. Blood flushed the surface of her skin. She brought herself to the very brink of release and hovered there. She basked in the raw power of the moment, savoring the interplay of control and the uncontrollable. How would the young man be in moments such as this? Would he rush to the finish, or draw back from the edge? Could he stay, unmoving, super-charged, with her?

Her breath wound down slowly, and the thin film of perspiration covering her body evaporated as her skin cooled down. Her heartbeat returned to normal, but she did not. Something had changed inside her. She brought her hand to her face, and delighted in the texture of her own skin. She was made of flesh and blood.

18

The days at the camp began before sunrise and ended long after sunset. It was a constant blur of reeducation classes, labor and longing for food, water and nurturing. Gyong-ho was taught that her parents had strayed from the path of good and deserved to be punished for their transgressions. By association, she herself had been stained by impure imperialist ways and needed to work doubly hard to prove herself worthy of living in the Worker's Paradise. The Dear Leader loved her, in spite of her shamefulness; and, as his child, it was her duty to honor him by confessing the misdeeds of her relatives and friends.

From day to day the tasks of her labor changed. Commonly she was given the job of finding firewood, or working on the prison's farm. There was also a small factory at the camp that produced items for export to China, though Gyong-ho never knew what they were. When she worked there, her job had been to stamp out small, meaningless steel pieces using a hydraulic press. She was grateful that she was too young to work in the mine. The adults, when she saw them, were broken and blackened with soot. She thought of her father and ached for him. Could the earth digest an innocent man and turn him into stone? She was expected to prove herself by working tirelessly and mutely, with only the vague promise that one day a higher power might deem her worthy of reentering *Chosun* society.

Verbal self-flagellation was an integral part of her training. Gi was required to stand in front of her class each day and tell everyone the ways she had failed to match up to the *Chosun* ideal and what she would do the next day to be better. She was encouraged to devise punishments for herself. Failing that, the group would decide on the best punishment for her. Sometimes it was to clean latrines or to skip meals. Lighter punishments involved cleaning dormitories or writing repetitious lines about fealty to the Dear Leader. Beatings, isolation, and torture were part of the standard repertoire of punishments used by the prison guards.

Less common were rewards for model behavior. This usually involved the honor of reading the words of Kim Il-sung aloud during reeducation, or sometimes an extra ration of food. These rewards most often followed a confession implicating a family member or friend in antirevolutionary activity and were doled out with much fanfare.

In the fervor to become worthy *Chosun* citizens, the children often looked for ways to rat each other out. It was common for a child, taken up in the excitement of her devotion to the Dear Leader, to express some imagined or exaggerated transgression on the part of another child. The hope of reward, especially that of extra food, ensured that this happened with regularity. Some children learned that they could trick the more gullible of their peers into making transgressions that they could later report. Gi fell into that trap several times in her first few weeks in the gulag.

There was no one she could trust, and nobody to look after her.

19

The foreman stood in front of the busy seamstresses, scowling. The joints of his damaged leg were aching with particular vengeance. *There must be a storm coming,* he thought. He was a man who made use of his pain. Many other men would have become lesser people, useless and whining. Instead, he used it to propel himself forward, to make himself stronger. The Great Leader would have approved. *The problem with people today,* he thought, *is that they are out of touch with the war. The Great Leader would never have let that happen.*

He was not sure which was more painful, standing in one place or walking, so he alternated between the two. They each hurt differently, he decided. He paced the room, randomly inspecting the work of the seamstresses. "Your seams aren't straight enough, Comrade Kim!" he barked at a cowering young woman. "Comrade Ho! You're wasting fabric," he scolded another. *Yes, these women have not seen enough war,* he agreed with himself.

Foreman Hwang was a bitter man. He had been born with excellent *songbun,* but now look at him! Relegated to the impotent task of managing a bunch of snotty girls who knew nothing of real sacrifice and loyalty. His father had been a decorated veteran of the war against the imperialists: He had killed Americans and lost an arm. He had met the Great Leader, who pinned a medal on his lapel and called him a true son of the Republic. His father had earned his privilege — a high standing in the Party, a spacious apartment in the center of town, a television set. *That is the way to respect loyalty. That should have been my birthright, coming from such pure stock. The new guard doesn't understand what makes a man a man. Today it all goes to sycophants and liars. Twenty years ago I would have been elevated for my sacrifice, but now they just push me aside.*

The foreman's hard eyes scanned the room and landed on Gyong-ho. *Now, there is a girl with real Party potential,* he thought. *There is a girl who has seen the wrong end of the Party and knows what it can do. She fears it properly, like a loaded gun, which gives her the right amount of respect. Look at her, thin and pale. She looks almost like a boy. Look how she works: tirelessly, head down, efficient. She is completely focused. Every day she exceeds the quota, and yet she always gives her extras to her friend, the pretty one. I could have her flogged for doing that. If I were given a chance I could mold that loyalty to fit the Party instead. Then she would turn in her lazy friend rather than protect her. Anyway, that pretty cunt has it coming to her, I've seen to that.*

He turned too quickly and searing pain shot up his leg. He thought of Kim Il-sung and pushed the pain out of his consciousness. He thought of running a bayonet through the chest of a long-nosed imperialist. He thought of a world where respect was given to those who really deserved it — a world that made perfect, orderly sense.

20

Gyong-ho and Il-sun went out the factory double doors and into the first truly warm day of spring. Mercifully the workers' education class had been cancelled for that evening and they were able to go out and enjoy the last rays of sunshine. The air throbbed with life as birds sang, insects cut circuitous routes to buds and blossoms, and brilliant light glinted off every surface. The smell of trees was pervasive, and there seemed a general feeling of thrill to be alive.

"There he is!" Il-sun pointed to a young man on a pale green scooter parked at the curb next to the factory. The young man looked up and smiled from underneath his blue newsboy cap. His eyes were shielded by large, dark sunglasses with wire rims. "I wonder how he knew we would be finished early?" she asked.

Gyong-ho thought he looked conspicuously well-to-do, sitting on a scooter and smoking a filtered cigarette. There was something disconcerting about his careless appearance. It was not the way he looked, specifically, but the fact that he got away with it that was cause for concern. To Gyong-ho he looked dangerous, and therefore was somebody to be avoided. But to Il-sun, the danger was the most attractive part.

Il-sun started running to the young man, then stopped herself in midstride. She composed herself and instead walked with almost painful slowness, exaggerating the fluid communion between her hips and shoulders. A moment before, she had been just a girl chatting; and then, suddenly, she was all woman and springtime, the embodiment of feminine beauty. In spite of her shapeless factory uniform, the sunlight hinted at the form of her body underneath. Her coy indirectness and impudent slowness were part of a calculated torture. The young man was playing a similar game, sitting on his scooter as if time itself belonged to him, smoking his cigarette and pretending not to notice Il-sun approaching.

Gyong-ho was rooted to one spot, suddenly a witness rather than a participant. She was an unnecessary accessory to the odd ritual, and felt awkwardly exposed in her pointlessness.

Il-sun finally reached the young man and they exchanged greetings. Gi could not hear what they were saying, but she could see that Il-sun was tossing her hair often, laughing easily with her breasts held on offer. She was reminded of the cover of *John and Daisy:* She could imagine Il-sun — her head back, lips parted, her uniform blouse unbuttoned and falling off her shoulders — wrapped in the muscular arms of the young man. Jealousy stabbed at her. She wanted to be the one holding Il-sun, supporting her as she arched her back, offering the berries of her lips and the delicate mounds of her breasts.

The young man was a cockroach, Gi decided. His suspicious sunglasses were altogether too buggy, especially with his funny hat squashing his face. He looked like the kind of man who would eat bites of other people's food, leaving his droppings in their cupboards and drawers.

Il-sun and the young man finished their conversation. She turned toward Gi and was suddenly a girl again, running playfully toward her friend, smiling. It was amazing how quickly she could vacillate from girl to woman and back again.

"I'm going to go with him, Gi! He's taking me to meet some of his friends. You'll cover for me with the mistress, won't you?" Her eyelids batted, cheeks flushed pink.

"I don't think it's a good idea."

"Gi, please. This is important." She sounded almost childlike in her pleading.

Gyong-ho knew that she could not say no. She wanted to very badly, but the word would never come; not to Il-sun. Never to Il-sun, who was sunshine itself, who only ever played and never took anything very seriously.

"Okay," was all she said.

"Thanks, Gi!" Il-sun replied, almost squealing. She turned around with a bounce and ran back toward the young man. Halfway there she recomposed herself and was a woman again, full of restraint and grace. She glided to the young man, sat sideways behind him on the seat of the scooter and put her arms around his middle. She pressed her cheek into his shoulder, and the scooter sped away.

The brilliant light of the sun began to fade into shades of blue as shadows grew longer. Gyong-ho walked in the direction of the setting sun feeling the temperature rapidly drop, a reminder that summer had not yet arrived. She felt hollow inside, as if there had never been any substance to her at all.

In an attempt to fill the void that was usually filled with Il-sun's girly chatter, she thought about the turning of the planets around the sun. The cosmos was an enormous equation whose numbers were so large even her uncanny mind could not conceive them. But then she thought about "yes" and "no," positive and negative. She remembered playing a game where Il-sun was thinking of an object, and Gi had to guess what it was by asking only yes-or-no questions. For Il-sun it was just a way to pass the time, but for Gi the concept was profound. She thought of it numerically, so that yes was represented by the number one and no was represented by the number zero. In a flash she could see that all information could be represented using various combinations of yes and no, positive and negative, one and . . .

It was no use. She could not distract herself from her jealousy by getting lost in abstract ideas. She felt an uncomfortable churning in her stomach. Who was this young man to steal her friend away? How could Il-sun be so callous as to abandon her for this man she barely knew? She felt anger condensing out of her jealousy. She was betrayed and alone, and the cockroach was the one holding Il-sun. She began punching herself in the arm. At first she merely tapped, but then the strikes came harder and harder. The pain she was causing her flesh gave an outlet for the pain she was feeling in her heart. Tears welled up in her eyes, but they never rolled down her cheeks. She could not bring herself to sob. She did not want to release her anger and indignation yet. She wanted to hold on to it for a while.

She reached the orphanage and made the necessary prostrations to the photographs of the Great and Dear Leaders in the foyer. There was a light smudge on the glass just below Kim Jong-il's left eye. She went to the cabinet, took out the special cloth for cleaning the portraits, and polished the glass until it was again glistening. She then went in search of the mistress. The mistress's bedroom door was closed, and Gi knocked lightly.

"Who is it?" came the mistress's voice from inside.

"It's Gyong-ho. We're back from work, miss," she replied through the door.

"Why are you so early?"

"Our class was cancelled."

"Il-sun?"

"She went upstairs already, miss."

The lie nearly caught in her throat. She went up to bed alone.

21

The young man's body was firm, and Il-sun wished she could press herself fully into him. He fired up his scooter and they peeled away down the street. The spring air felt refreshingly cool on her face and bare throat as they zipped across the city. Il-sun felt important being on the scooter as they passed the throngs of people having to walk and ride bicycles. The young man used the horn to scatter the people who were walking in the middle of the road. It was a rare thrill to ride fast through the city on a scooter.

They sped through intersections and Il-sun smiled at the pretty girls in uniform who were standing in the middle, directing traffic. She marveled at their expressionless faces and rigid choreography as they conducted the scooter through the crossroads. In truth they seemed superfluous, considering the lack of traffic, but she liked seeing them all the same. As she made fleeting eye contact with them she squeezed the young man tighter as if to say, Look at the man I have; aren't you jealous? The girls were hired specifically for their beauty. And loyalty, of course. *Maybe one day I will get a job directing traffic,* Il-sun thought.

After a time they pulled up to an apartment building near the university. The young man stopped the motor and lit a cigarette. The sun was getting low in the sky, but he kept his dark glasses on. Il-sun liked the way he looked in them — powerful.

"So, who are these friends I'm going to meet?" Il-sun asked as she hopped off the back.

"Just some associates. Some guys I work with."

"If they're friends of yours, I'm sure I'll like them," she said, smiling at him.

He didn't respond, and Il-sun wondered if perhaps that comment was too intimate. She would have to remember to play it a little cooler.

The young man opened a compartment at the back of the scooter and withdrew two bottles of whiskey and a carton of cigarettes.

"I can't stand the acorn liquor they usu-

145

ally serve," he said. "It gives me a headache."

He led her to a set of stairs at the side of
the building and took her to a second-floor
apartment. She was surprised that no one
stopped them to check their papers on the
way in. Maybe the *inminbanjang* was out.
Voices could be heard through the door,
laughing and talking loudly, as well as faint
music. The young man knocked out a
rhythm on the door which Il-sun assumed
to be a secret knock. The deadbolt clicked
and the door opened a crack. Part of a face
appeared and looked from the young man
to Il-sun and then back again. The face disappeared and a voice boomed out, "Hey
everybody! The party has arrived!" The door
flew open and they were ushered inside.

The air in the apartment was thick with
cigarette smoke, and Il-sun had to control
herself to keep from coughing. The music
playing in the background was not like
anything she had ever heard, and she was
sure it must not be Party approved. She
could see that it was coming from a portable
music player of a kind she had never seen
before. It was a marvel of a contraption and
she would have liked to have inspected it
more closely, but she did not want to appear rude or unsophisticated. Eight people

were sitting on the floor of the apartment, all men except for one, and the young man introduced Il-sun around. Most of them went only by unusual nicknames, like Rooster, Pistol, Wart, and Pepper. The young man explained that they had all met in the army several years ago, and the names just stuck. Glasses were handed out and the whiskey bottles were opened. The young man distributed packs of cigarettes to everyone.

Il-sun had a hard time concealing her nervousness. Not only was she the obvious outsider in a group of close friends, but the whole scene felt conspicuously illicit. This was not a safe place to be if the police decided to come looking, or if the *inminbanjang* were to come to check people's papers. The young man noticed her hesitation and put his arm around her.

"Relax, Il-sun. These are all my close friends. Nothing will happen to you here."

"I'm just a little nervous, I guess. I mean, what if the police come, or one of the neighbors reports this?"

The young man chuckled patronizingly. "Let me tell you a little secret: Everyone has a weakness. If you can figure out a man's weakness, you can own him. Let's just say that I have a talent for knowing people's weaknesses. I happen to know that one of the head Party cadres has a weakness for foreign films of a certain variety. I also happen to have a source for those films and can deliver them to him. He is grateful for my service, and he keeps the dogs away. He knows if he doesn't keep the dogs away, then I talk, and my downfall leads to his downfall. You might say I deal in self-preservation. And he is but one of my clients. Really, I have the best job security of anyone in the city. So have a whiskey! It will help you relax." He filled a glass and handed it to her. It burned going down, but it also calmed her nerves.

She found herself sitting next to the other woman at the party, whom everyone simply called Cho. Il-sun did not ask about her first name. Cho had long, straight hair pulled back in a barrette. Her lips were painted bright red and her eyelashes were thick with mascara. Makeup was a luxury item that Il-sun may have enjoyed were she not an orphan, and it was a wonder that Cho could afford to use it so heavily. She was wearing a short skirt that defied conventional propriety, and her shirt was revealing of small breasts that were pushed up and inward in an attempt to make them seem larger. Her age could have been anywhere between twenty and thirty-five. She was casually ignoring the taboo against women smoking, cradling a cigarette with a raptor's hand, her fingernails impossibly long and painted to match her lips. She looked down her nose at Il-sun, her eyes swimming with whiskey.

"You know, he likes it when I call him Gianni," she said, slurring her words almost unintelligibly.

"What?" Il-sun asked, confused.

"Gianni. Your friend. He likes it when I call him that. He heard it in a movie once. Thinks it makes him sound tough."

"Oh," replied Il-sun, still confused.

"You're pretty. What do you do, teacup?"

"I'm a seamstress. At the White Butterfly."

"Seamstress?" She laughed a wheezy, alcohol-laden laugh. "I could help you make a lot of money, I bet, with your looks."

"Thank you," Il-sun said, uncertain if it had been a compliment. Then, to be polite she asked, "What do you do?"

Cho laughed again, but her eyes were hard and calculating. "I am what they call a flower-selling girl." Several of the men nearby who had been listening chuckled and winked at each other.

"But what do you do in the wintertime?" Il-sun imagined that it must be difficult to make a living selling flowers in the winter-time.

Cho slapped her thigh, her laughter becoming more of a cackle. "What do you do in the wintertime?" she mocked. "That's the best joke I've heard in a long time. Did you hear that, Gianni? I told her that I'm a flower-selling girl, and she asked me, what do I do in winter?" All eyes were on Cho as she cackled uncontrollably.

"You have had enough to drink, Cho," the young man said.

"To hell with you, Gianni, or whatever your name is."

Il-sun felt like she had just been the butt of some inappropriate joke, and she was embarrassed not to have understood it. She was also grateful to the young man, who seemed to be standing up for her. The only person laughing now was Cho.

The evening wore on and the last of the whiskey was poured into glasses. Conversation was getting more and more brash. One of the men in the group, a gaunt young man who went by the name Wart and was missing one of his front teeth, lifted his glass and said, "To the Dear Leader!" His tone was irreverent, to the point of being sarcastic.

"To the Dear Leader, and his dog!

Waaaaooooooo!" replied a drunken voice.

"You are the Dear Leader's dog," said another man, thinking he was being more clever than he really was.

"No, Cho is the Dear Leader's dog. She's his bitch," said another, and the room erupted in laughter. Cho and Il-sun were the only ones not laughing. Il-sun was uncomfortable with the blatant disrespect she was hearing. She had never before heard anything but praise and adulation for the Dear Leader. Though she herself had thought such things, and only the night before had spit on his image when no one was looking, she knew that to say such things in public could have dire consequences.

But the horrors were not over yet. As a coup de grace, the young man, her young man, stood up clumsily and grabbed the photo of the Dear Leader off the wall. He then unfastened his trousers, pulled them down below his buttocks, bent over, and rubbed the image of the Dear Leader against his bare backside. The room went silent. That went too far, even for the ill-mannered group. Coming out of a stupor, seemingly oblivious to the offending gesture, Cho remarked, "I haven't seen those fine haunches for quite a long time, Gianni."

She then slumped and passed from consciousness.

22

The orphanage mistress awoke with a start, hearing a motor come to a stop on the street outside. Vehicles at night usually meant an inspection by the secret police. Typically these were routine, conducted by bored officers who only wanted to put check marks on a list and proceed to the next residence. Sometimes, however, they were more serious, targeting specific people suspected of ill behavior. Regardless, everything had to be in top shape. Could someone have found out about her Bible? Could one of the children have turned her in for receiving foreign goods? She was out of bed and putting on her clothes in a flash.

She rapidly went over a list in her mind of the things the inspectors would want to see: proper maintenance and positioning of the portraits of the Great and Dear Leaders, proper identity cards for all the residents seventeen or older, birth certificates for the younger ones, public areas cleaned and well maintained, et cetera. She fought down a wave of panic as she realized that she had not been very diligent about her duties lately. There might be any number of infractions that she was unaware of. If they did a thorough inspection, they might find the gifts that the young man had given her, and she immediately regretted saving all the little foreign scraps in her Bible. She pushed those thoughts from her mind. This was probably just routine, and the girls were usually very good about keeping everything together.

She went to the foyer and flipped a light switch, and was glad to see that the power was working. Of course, they would want the power on during inspections to make their job easier. She scrutinized the portraits of the Great and Dear Leaders. With relief she found them to be glimmering and spotless, as was the surrounding foyer. She felt a welling of pride for her girls; they had taken up the slack where she had been neglectful.

The mistress went quickly from room to room, but everything was in order. She had been anticipating a loud knock at the door, but it was unusually slow in coming. She went back to the foyer and peered out a window overlooking the street. As her eyes adjusted, she was just able to make out the silhouettes of a motor scooter and two people. She had been expecting to see a military truck — her sleeping mind, always on guard for the approach of inspectors, must have magnified the whine of the scooter. Curiosity, more than her duty as *inminbanjang,* compelled her to light a lamp and walk out the door.

The people standing next to the scooter did not hear the door open and close, nor did they see the mistress as she approached them. The glow from her oil lamp lit the figures enough to see that they were locked in a passionate kiss. She recognized the clothing of the woman as being a uniform from the garment factory. As she got nearer, she recognized the pretty form of the impish Il-sun. She was not exactly surprised to see her, of all the orphans, breaking curfew and making out with a young man on the street at night.

"You have some explaining to do, Park Il-sun," said the mistress, her tone conveying both disappointment and understanding. Il-sun peeled her face away from the man's, at first terror-stricken but then defiant, her eyes glassy from alcohol. As Il-sun turned to look at the mistress, the light from the lamp lit the face of her lover. The mistress's heart missed a beat and she felt instantly short of breath. The young man, her young man, was holding the young and pretty orphan, had been kissing her hungrily, his hands digging shamelessly into her buttocks. His face was now expressionless.

"Get inside. Now!" she commanded. Il-sun very slowly removed herself from the young man, keeping eye contact with the mistress as she did so, her mouth a triumphant sneer. She walked past the mistress in slow, fluid strides rendered top-heavy from alcohol. She was making an insubordinate show, taking her time to reach the front door. The orphanage door slammed, leaving the mistress and the young man alone on the street.

They stood facing each other. He lit a cigarette, inhaled, almost said something, then exhaled. He took another thoughtful drag, looking at the mistress. Her eyes were unnavigable storms above a sea he had no intention of crossing. They were unreadable to him. He exhaled and then flicked the half-smoked cigarette into the street, wanting to say "What did you expect from me?" But he said nothing. He looked a little sad, as though he wanted to explain something to a child. It was a look that said "If you only understood, then you would see why there is no need for me to be sorry. If anything, that is what I'm sorry for: that you don't understand, and that I don't need to apologize."

He mounted his scooter and, without looking back, drove into the night.

23

For Gi, survival in the gulag had two faces. The first, her political mask, meant becoming the perfect *Chosun* girl. She became obedient and self-effacing. She worked hard without thought for her own well-being; everything was done for the glory of the Dear Leader and the benefit of the state. She learned to hold all her feelings deep inside where even she could not feel them. She became properly ebullient and effusive at the sight of the Dear Leader's image, but otherwise her face had taken on the grim, defeated look that was standard issue for all prisoners.

The other face of her survival was social. Aside from the strict regulations for behavior laid out by the Great Leader, there were subtle rules that applied only in the gulag and were enforced by the children themselves. There was an unofficial hierarchy among the inmates that dictated who got the best portions of food, who got to bunk in the choicest places, who got to keep the odd extra blanket. Learning the intricacies of this system took months. Whereas the political rules of behavior were clearly written out and rehearsed each day, the social rules had to be intuited or learned by trial and error. She quickly learned who the key players were, but learning how to keep them all satisfied was nearly impossible.

Food rations at the prison camp were meager — even the prison authorities did not make pretense to the contrary. It was understood that because Gyong-ho was one of the lowliest of citizens, she was undeserving of full rations. Most of the meals were nothing more than a thin maize gruel, often bulked up with sawdust. There was never any meat, or any promise of meat. She did, from time to time, benefit from the vegetables of the prison gardens, but the simple, unadorned fact was that all the prisoners were starving. It was understood that survival of the fittest was the ruling principle of the gulag. They were in a slow race between the failing point of their bodies and the unlikely event of their release.

Even in the worst of conditions, over the long run, people will fall into a routine and eke out a semblance of normalcy. This was true within the prison camp as well. Death and despair were Gyong-ho's constant companions, but daily events took place around her with surreal detachment. Friendships between inmates formed, gossip circulated, and people laughed — albeit with acidic sarcasm and infrequently. Even the prison guards, who meted out abuses of all kinds every day, did so with a business-as-usual air. When people come to feel that lives are cheap and survival is a moment-to-moment event, the grieving period becomes short. To meet someone is to be grieving for her already. Her actual passing becomes a formality.

24

Gyong-ho slapped at Il-sun's cheeks in an attempt to wake her. Her toxic smell reminded Gi of the factory foreman — almost flammable. Also, there was something faintly raw and masculine to her scent, but there was no time to think about that. Dawn was breaking and it was nearly time for them to go to work. Failing to rouse her, Gi solicited the aid of two other girls, who helped half drag, half carry her to the outdoor bathing room. Together they stripped Il-sun completely and sat her in a small enamel basin. The morning air was bone chilling and their breath came out in dragons of steam. Il-sun made a half-hearted attempt to resist, but lacked the ardor to have any effect against the determined girls. Gi poured buckets of cold water over her head and body, eliciting a series of protests and curses. Then Gi took a cloth, lathered it up with precious soap, and scrubbed her from head to toe. Il-sun broke away suddenly to vomit into the drain. Gi rinsed off the soap with more cold water, and then wrapped her in a towel, patting her friend dry. She wished there were time to do it with more care.

Il-sun was finally able to stand on her own. She smelled better, but her breath was still caustic. Gi dressed her in a fresh uniform and helped her walk into the kitchen. The mistress was sitting on a stool in a corner and looked over at them with red, bleary eyes. She looked as if she had not slept.

"Put some water on for tea," she said in a rough voice.

Gi obliged the mistress after sitting Il-sun down on a stool. Il-sun lay her head down on the counter, groaning. It seemed that she was trying not to look at the mistress. The mistress, on the other hand, seemed quite interested in Il-sun. It was hard to determine what was on the mistress's mind. She was appraising Il-sun and struggling on the inside. Clearly something had happened between them. Gi was afraid that the mistress knew that she had lied to her. She hated to disappoint the mistress.

The water on the stove came to a boil, and the mistress put several heaps of tea leaves into the pot. To Gi it looked like a whole week's worth of tea. There was silence while it steeped. The tea came out nearly black when the mistress poured it into three teacups. She handed a cup to Gi, and then set one down in front of Il-sun. Gi could not see the bottom of her cup — she had never tasted such strong tea. Il-sun looked up with an expression that said she would have liked to have thrown hers across the room; instead, she put her cold hands around the cup. She was still shivering from the bath.

The mistress inhaled as if about to speak, but then exhaled mutely. She inhaled again, and then held her breath for a moment before speaking, as if she were smoking her words. "You two will be leaving here soon," the mistress finally said, sighing. It came out without the pique Gi had expected. "I have filled out the necessary paperwork, giving you my high recommendations, and an apartment should become available within a month or two. You will be living together."

"Thank you, miss," said Gi.

"Gyong-ho, I know I don't need to tell you this, but I will say it for your sake, Il-sun, because I don't think you quite get it. It is a very dangerous world we live in. I'm not talking about the Americans or imperialists or enemies that we cannot see. It is dangerous right here, in this city. In this country. We are always being watched. Everything we do, everywhere we go, everyone we talk to is seen and recorded. Do you understand me?"

"No, I don't think I follow you," said Il-sun looking up at the mistress with a cold stare, her voice filled with sarcasm. Gi wondered where the animosity was coming from.

"Then let me make myself clear," said the mistress, emphasizing each word. "He is dangerous, Il-sun. He is not whatever he says he is. He is lying to you and using you and leading you down a path from which you may never recover. I think you know that he operates an illicit business. At the very least your *songbun* will be tarnished. At the worst, your association with him will brand you as an enemy of the state. People disappear for that to a hell you cannot possibly even imagine. Ask Gyong-ho. She knows."

Il-sun shot a surprised glance at Gi, whose eyes were starting to roll back in her head. She was entering one of her episodes. Il-sun brought her focus back to the mistress. "And how do you know that he operates an 'illicit' business? Could it be that you use his services? Who are you to threaten me?"

Something that the young man had said to her had stuck in Il-sun's mind, lodging there because of the simple truth in it: "If you can figure out a man's weakness, you can own him." She knew the mistress's weakness, and it was time to use it.

"I am not trying to threaten —"

"I know about the book," Il-sun said with sharp triumph.

The mistress dropped her cup.

Gi counted seventy-two shards skipping across the floor.

The mistress was lithified and bloodless. Slowly the feeling returned to her fingers and her heart resumed beating. Color came back to her cheeks and the shock on her face dissipated. She met Il-sun's fierce stare with a look of doleful resignation.

"You are trying to frighten me, but all I feel is sad. Very, very sad." The mistress stood up and walked out of the room.

Gyong-ho and Il-sun walked in silence. They were going to be late, which was causing Gi to twist at the fabric of her blouse in nervousness. The foreman would be molten.

The argument between the mistress and Il-sun was deeply disturbing. Gi and her friend were being pulled apart at the very fibers that connected them, and she felt as if a piece of herself were being removed. It was painful. She wanted to be a part of Il-sun's life, but Il-sun wasn't sharing herself anymore.

"Gi, I think I'm a woman now," Il-sun finally said, breaking the silence between them.

25

When Gyong-ho and Il-sun arrived at the factory, the other women were already at their stations in a frenzy of work. The foreman scowled at them as they entered.

"Song Gyong-ho! You're late! This is most unacceptable," he shouted loudly enough for all in the room to hear.

"I am very sorry, comrade foreman, sir. It is my fault and I am unworthy of leniency. I will work through all the breaks today to make up for my insolence."

"Indeed you will. Now get to your station!"

Nothing was said to Il-sun.

The girls made it to their stations, Gyong-ho hurrying, Il-sun shuffling her feet. Gyong-ho went immediately to task, working faster than she had ever worked before. She knew that Il-sun would be well below her quota today and she wanted to make up for it. Il-sun's behavior was insubordinate beyond reason, and Gi could not imagine that she could skate by this time without punishment. Hopefully it would be no more than severe public humiliation at the next self-criticism meeting. If she admitted her transgressions publicly before anyone else got a chance to bring them up, and if she showed an appropriate amount of remorse, it might be enough to keep her from worse punishment.

In her rush to catch up with the quota, Gi nearly ran her hand through the sewing machine. She had seen it happen before when the needle of a machine lodged itself in a worker's index finger. The needle stabbed right through the bone and stuck between the second and third knuckles. The force of the motor then lifted her whole hand into the carriage of the machine. The woman had gone pale and, in shock, could not release the power pedal. Her finger was crushed by the straining motor.

Il-sun made a halfhearted attempt to do her job, but she eventually laid her head down and fell asleep. Gi kicked her several times to try to wake her, but to no effect. Oddly, the foreman paced his usual rounds but said nothing to her, as if he had not even noticed. This filled Gyong-ho with dark foreboding. The breaks came and went and Gyong-ho sewed while Il-sun slept.

At the end of the day, the whistle blew and the women went through the ritual of stacking trousers neatly for the daily tally. Gyong-ho was well above the quota, though the quality of her work was marginal. Il-sun had few pairs of trousers at her station. Gyong-ho split her own pile, giving most to Il-sun. Now they were both well below the quota, but Il-sun had a better chance of redemption.

"Comrade Song, I am deeply, deeply disappointed in your performance today." The foreman's tone was patronizing. "You have offended the very idea that this great society is founded on. Just look at this pathetic pile of trousers! Are you aware that you are far below your quota for today?"

"Yes, comrade foreman, sir. There is no excuse for my behavior. I have failed the Dear Leader." Gyong-ho kept her head down while she spoke the deprecation.

"I would say you have. You have put a smirch on the great lineage of the *Chosun* people. I would be well justified in having you tried for treason."

Gyong-ho went cold. Her lips trembled and her voice quavered as she replied, "No punishment would be too great for my offense, comrade foreman, sir."

"The Dear Leader saw fit to give you a second chance. Because I try to model myself in his great likeness, even though I am a far lower being, I am going to follow his example. I will give you one chance to redeem yourself. Because of your insolence, my factory is not meeting its quota. You will stay tonight, all night if you have to, until you make up the shortfall. Is that understood?"

"Yes, sir, comrade foreman, sir. You are too generous. I will not fail the Dear Leader."

"No, you will not."

Il-sun was standing at her station with her head down. She looked nervous and uncertain.

"Are you waiting for something, Comrade Park Il-sun?" asked the foreman gruffly.

"Sir?" Il-sun looked up at him, confused.

"You have a meeting to attend, don't you, comrade? The Party Youth meeting that meets after work? You are going to be late."

"But, sir . . ."

"Did I ask you to stay? Get off my factory floor. Now!"

"Yes, sir." Il-sun looked sheepishly toward Gyong-ho, who was ghost white, then headed toward the door.

26

Il-sun felt terrible. She was walking alone to the building of the Party Youth for the weekly meeting, the absence of Gyong-ho following her like an unwanted companion. She had not imagined that Gi would be punished on her behalf. Gi had sacrificed her own well-being, giving her the trousers she had made. She did this every day, and yet Il-sun never really thanked her or gave her anything in return. Not even friendship, lately. *What is wrong with me?* she asked herself. *I have been so selfish.* She thought of the mistress and her heart sank even lower. She had been especially cruel to the mistress, who had done nothing but care for her for four years. *What was it she said this morning? "You are trying to frighten me, but all I feel is sad. Very, very sad."* She hated disappointing the mistress. She felt like walking directly to the orphanage to apologize, but it would have to wait until after the meeting. She had stirred up enough trouble for one day. She wanted to tell the mistress that she would never tell anyone about *John and Daisy.* In fact, she would return the book that evening. How could she make up for her behavior, to both the mistress and to Gi?

Her thoughts were interrupted by the approach of a scooter. She turned to see the young man, his newsboy cap missing, his sunglasses high on his nose. He looked unusually disheveled.

"Il-sun, get on. We have to talk. Quickly!" He sounded panic-stricken.

"I have to go to the Party Youth meeting. I can't be late."

"That's what I need to talk to you about. You can't go to the meeting. Get on and I will explain everything." He looked around nervously. Il-sun hesitated. "Hurry!"

She climbed on the back of the scooter. She knew she was going to have to verbally thrash herself and conjure real tears of remorse at the next self-criticism meeting if she was going to get out of this. She vowed that she would step back in line and change her behavior. For once, she longed to be the picture-perfect *Chosun* citizen.

The young man drove them to a run-down area of the city where the roads were still made of dirt and gravel and the houses were shacks cobbled together from odd scraps. They parked at one of the nondescript houses and he led her inside. No one else was in the one-room building.

"Where are we?" asked Il-sun.

"This is my cousin's house. We'll be safe here."

"Safe? What's going on?"

"We're in serious trouble, Il-sun. Very serious trouble." He was speaking rapidly and he seemed uncharacteristically frantic.

"Trouble? Why?" As soon as she asked, she thought of the events of the night before and knew the answer. He had gone too far with the image of the Dear Leader.

"I'm glad I found you before you got to the Party Youth meeting. They were going to accuse you there of high treason tonight. They want to make a public example out of you."

Il-sun felt faint. She had never imagined that she could be in so much trouble. "Are you sure? How do you know?" The strength was gone from her voice. She knew inside that it was true.

"That guy at the party last night, the one we call Rooster. It turns out that he is an informer. He told his superiors about what I did last night to the photograph. I thought for sure he was okay, but I was wrong. Now everyone at that party is suspect."

"But what about your contacts? Can't they step in for you?"

"Now all they can do is buy me a little time. That is the only reason I was able to find you." He swallowed hard, perspiration ringing the underarms of his shirt and rolling down his forehead.

"What can we do?" Il-sun felt tears in her eyes.

"We have to leave the country. Tonight."

"Leave the country? How? Where will we go?" The prospect of leaving the country, though she had romanticized the notion in the past, was terrifying in these circumstances.

"That's why I came to get you. We have to stay here until it gets dark. I've used my contacts to get a truck and some forged travel documents. I can't tell you all the details now in case we get caught."

Il-sun broke down sobbing. She collapsed into his arms and cried on his shoulder.

"Look, don't cry. We aren't going to be caught. It is just a precaution. I have crossed the border many times. In fact, I do it every week; it's simple. As long as you do exactly as I tell you, then everything is going to be alright. Okay?"

She tried to look brave, sucking in her tears.

"Okay."

27

Foreman Hwang was sitting at his desk, looking over a pile of papers. *It's amazing how much paperwork it takes to make a person disappear,* he thought. *That's the problem today: too much bureaucracy.* He put down his pen and sat back in his chair. He felt tense. He looked at the paper bag under his desk. *I could sure use a release . . . Not yet, there is work to be done.* He bent over his papers again.

His thoughts drifted to Gyong-ho, still on the factory floor, alone, completely focused even though she had been working nonstop for twelve hours. *She is such good Party material, yet the new guard will never let her in. Stupid pencil necks have no brains,* he thought. He looked again at the paper bag. *No, too early. Of course, she could improve her* songbun *with a good marriage, then they might let her in. After all, she was only a child when she was in the camp, and only because* of her parents. *But who would want to marry her?* He peeked at the paper bag again. *Maybe just a teaser?* He reached into the bag and his hand landed on a roll of magazines. He pulled back as if he had touched something hot. *No, the bottle first. Always the bottle first.* He put his hand back in the bag and found one of the bottles. He pulled it out and opened the cap.

Ah, whiskey. He poured himself half a glass. He could never quite give it up. When he was someone to know, in the army, he had gotten used to it. Whiskey was like currency in those days. *If anyone wants to get something done, just take old Hwang a bottle of whiskey, they used to say.* He preferred the black label, but the red would do. He raised the glass to his lips, intending to take a small sip to savor it, but drained the glass instead. He poured another, this time to the brim.

He hated his job. Stupid pencil necks placed him there after the accident. It never would have happened that way in the Great Leader's time. *Kim Il-sung, what a man! A leader like that only comes along every thousand years. The son had to go and mess the whole damned thing up! Everyone hungry, letting people get away with things, and then they pretend it's not happening.* He took a

177

long swallow. Then another. He refilled the glass.

I was on my way to being general! I had the songbun *for it; I had the credentials. I was the one everyone came to. I was the one everyone was talking about. Then that stupid dimwit had to pull the pin.*

It was a training day; one of the rare days when they were allowed to use live ammunition. The foreman, or colonel, as he was then called, was invited along to inspect a sergeant putting his troops through the paces. First it was rifle fire, then bayonets. The finale would be a demonstration on the use of grenades. *The boys looked fine. The boys looked really fine.* At some point there was a commotion, and a lot of shouting. Someone screamed, "Put the pin back! Put the pin back!" The foreman turned around — the boys were scattering in all directions, running. Right in front of him was a young boy, maybe sixteen or seventeen. He was a dim-witted half-breed boy from near the Chinese border. The Great Leader would never have allowed someone like him in his army. It was an abomination. The boy lifted his hand as if to offer something. He looked confused. It was a grenade. The pin was in his other hand. The foreman dove away, but a moment too late. The sound engulfed him, the percussion jarred him, shrapnel tore mercilessly through his body. He felt hot all over with pain. He was sure he was dying. There was the smell of smoke and burning flesh. There were fingers everywhere. The boy was lying not too far away, his arm torn off, half his face a smoldering crater.

The foreman lived through his injuries, but his career did not. He was told that a lame military commander gave the troops the wrong image. They placed him as the foreman of the factory instead. It was the best they could do, they said. Apparently he had hidden enemies. *Never would it have happened in the Great General's army!*

He drained another glass. He felt very tense. He needed a release. The whiskey was working: It was time. He reached into the bag with a timid hand and pulled out the bundle of magazines and unrolled them on his desk. *Yes! Yes! This is what I need,* he thought. On the cover was a shirtless man in army fatigue trousers. His body was well defined, muscles tensed like a cat ready to pounce. *So what if he is an Imperialist blondie?* His blood stirred. He opened the magazine hungrily. He perspired as he saw the photographs of young men, all in army fatigues, all undressing. As he turned the

179

pages the young men wore fewer and fewer clothes until finally their stiff male organs were revealed, oiled and in full view, like well-maintained rifles. His body responded to his excitement and he felt the familiar stiffening between his legs. He rubbed his organ through his trousers and opened the other magazines on the desk, spreading them out so that he could see all of them at one time. He was starving for it.

Then he snapped to his senses. It was too much. *I have to stop this behavior!* In a single movement he rolled the magazines up and stuffed them back into the bag, and poured another whiskey. *What a dirty habit!* He would never do it again, he promised himself. He would burn the magazines and never ask for more. He was a pervert. His father would have been so disappointed.

He forced himself to focus again on his paperwork. It would be easier now, after the whiskey. He shuffled the papers, added names, signed at the bottom, sealed them with a rubber stamp. Everything was almost in order.

He thought about Gyong-ho again. *What a waste of potential!* It was so unfair that such a good Party candidate should fall by the wayside while other spoiled and thankless weaklings were able to take the oath. *If*

180

only she could marry —

The solution exploded right in front of him. *I should marry her! I have good* song-bun; *maybe not what it used to be, but still fully respectable. She will attend classes, she will become a leader in the Party riding the tails of my* songbun. He would do it for the Great Leader, for the glory of *Chosun.* He would marry her, a woman, and expel his dirty fantasies, exorcise his dirty habits. Maybe they would even have children. *Why not? I am not yet too old, and she is certainly young enough.* But would she want to? *Of course she would want to do it! What better offer would she ever have, being a castaway orphan, and not a very pretty one? I must tell her my decision at once!*

The foreman stood up quickly and had to steady himself on the desk. He had had more whiskey than he realized. He made his way to his office door and opened it. The sound of a lone sewing machine chugged into the night. He stepped out of his office into the near blackness of the factory. Gyong-ho was sitting at her station, illuminated by a single lightbulb.

"Song Gyong-ho!" the foreman bellowed. It came out more loudly and sternly than he had intended.

Gyong-ho started, shocked out of some

181

dark reverie. She stood and lowered her head. "Yes, comrade foreman, sir."

"Comrade Song, please come into my office. I have something I would like to discuss with you."

"Yes, sir."

The foreman disappeared into his office. Gyong-ho reluctantly followed. When she entered his office, he was standing at a window behind his desk, looking out. He had the flammable smell, similar to Il-sun that morning. She noticed the glass of amber liquid on his desk.

"You might be surprised to know that I don't hate you," began the foreman, his speech slurred. *That did not come out quite right,* he thought. "I know you think I do, but I don't. I am hard on you, yes, but I don't hate you. The Great Leader is hard on all of us, asking that we make sacrifices, but he does it because he loves us. Do you understand?" He turned around and sat at his desk, appraising Gyong-ho. *She looks almost like a boy,* he thought. *Almost like a boy.* "I am hard on you because I see the light in you. You are the perfect citizen." *Yes, she will make a very fine wife. She will dress in army green and keep her hair short, just for me,* he thought. *She will love me.* "I have decided to marry you, Gyong-ho."

His words were a fist, a punch to her stomach. She collapsed forward, catching herself on the desk with both hands, her breath short. The way he stated it, stripping her of volition, stripping her of her humanity, she was a beast he had bought at auction, each day a day closer to slaughter. She felt fear, but something else stirred there too. It was anger. She was doubled up over rage, boiling but tightly capped in her stomach. There was nothing to do for it — every possible action was equally useless. Except suicide. She could end her life. In that way she could have control.

The foreman stood up, looking at the bent form of Gyong-ho, uncertain how to read her response. Suddenly he was in the early days of his career, still a sergeant. Those were really the best days. And nights. All the men bunked in close quarters, the smell of their overworked bodies permeating the nights, permeating his dreams.

He walked around Gyong-ho until he was directly behind her. She was still bent forward, hands on the desk, her backside sticking out. "Stand up, soldier!" he commanded her.

She did not, or could not, respond.

"Stand up, soldier, or it will be latrine duty for you!" He shouted even louder. He

183

was traversing time to a place when he felt truly powerful; maybe even happy. His body felt a stirring of excitement. "Stand up, or face the consequences, soldier!"

Gyong-ho had left her body. She was counting pencils, and pieces of paper, and dust motes. She was lost in the orbiting swirls of dust glinting in the electric light. She was lost in planetary forces and numbers too big to comprehend.

"I warned you, soldier!" The sergeant reached around Gyong-ho's waist and found the string holding her trousers up. He untied it and pulled her trousers down to her knees. He stood back and admired her backside. "Almost a boy," he said, not meaning to say it out loud. "Almost a boy."

Gyong-ho heard the faint sound of a zipper and the rustle of fabric behind her. She heard the labored breathing of the foreman as he stepped nearer. She could smell his smoke, his body odor, and his flammable breath. She heard him grunt in frustration. She felt something soft being tapped against her buttocks, lightly at first, and then with greater and greater urgency.

The sergeant was the foreman once again, standing in his pitiful office, pain shooting up his leg, his lifeless prick in his hand. He looked at the bare buttocks in front of him, distinctly feminine and repulsive.

"You would make a terrible wife!" he roared in anger, grabbing Gyong-ho by the shoulders and throwing her to the floor. When she looked up, the foreman had turned his back, pulling at his zipper.

"Pull your pants on. We're leaving."

28

Il-sun was steeped in regret. She was sitting on the floor in the dimly lit shack, her back to the wall, fear slithering in a ball inside her stomach. Since the sun had gone down, most of the people from the party the night before had arrived. The woman, Cho, had a look of nervous concentration etched into her face, ignoring a cigarette burning in her tight claw. She was far less crass when she had not been drinking. The men of the group seemed at ease, but men always had more to prove by wearing masks of bravery. The air was tense, and the inhabitants of the shack were mostly quiet and keeping to themselves. The young man had left, saying he had some arrangements to make. He assured her that he would be safe, but she still worried. Mostly she was sad that she would not get to say goodbye to Gi — Gi would be devastated. She worried that Gi would not have anyone to talk to. She was going to have to leave the orphanage soon, with no one to look after her. She wished she had been a better friend.

She thought of the orphanage mistress and winced. Now she would not have the chance to apologize to her. Maybe there would be a way to send a message, to her and to Gi, to let them know she was safe. That thought perked her up a little. The young man seemed capable of anything, so perhaps sending a message would not be too much to ask. Il-sun also worried about leaving the country. *Chosun* was the most powerful and prosperous nation in the world; how would they endure in the poor, oppressed, imperialist South? Cho had said they were going to *Hanguk,* but maybe she was only guessing. The young man certainly had not said anything. China would be the more logical choice.

She tried to cheer herself up with more positive thoughts. Maybe she and the young man would be married. *He knows how to drive, so he can get a job as a driver,* she thought. *There are not many jobs more prestigious than that. They will certainly need skilled people like him, wherever we are going.* As a driver he would have status and money. And she could work as a seamstress, until they had children, of course. *We will have each other, which is the important thing.*

After what seemed an interminable wait, she heard the young man's scooter pulling up outside. He came into the shack bearing a large bundle. Il-sun ran up to him and threw her arms around him, squeezing tightly. He stiffened under her touch, and she realized that maybe such a display was embarrassing for him in front of his friends. She would have to remember that in the future.

"Everyone, put these on. The truck will be here soon," said the young man, dumping the bundle onto the floor. It was an assortment of army fatigues. "We will be posing as an army workforce, dispatched to one of the border towns to the south. If anyone asks, we are a relief team helping to build a new factory for the glory of the Dear Leader. It is better to leave the talking to me.

"We will be stopping at one checkpoint on our way. That's the most dangerous part of the drive, and there's no way around it. I already have clearance through the checkpoint just outside the city, so we won't have to worry about that one. Since we are driving at night, just pretend to be asleep. All the guards know me, so there shouldn't be any problems. But keep your mouths shut anyway. That goes double for you, Cho."

Cho shot him a dirty look.

So Cho had been right; they were headed to the South. Il-sun felt a stab of disappointment — she had felt a twinge of hope that if they escaped to China, she could be reunited with her brother. But then, she could not hold on to the belief that he was still alive. *At least the language is the same, and we won't have to put up with the dirty Chinese,* Il-sun thought. *Maybe we can join a reunification movement in the South, and show the poor* Hanguk *the superiority of* Chosun *ways.*

They dug through the pile of clothes. They were ill-fitting and rough. Il-sun hoped that they would not have to get out of the truck at the checkpoint, because their bodies and these clothes were conspicuously mismatched. A vehicle rumbled to a stop outside, and the room went quiet.

"Relax, everyone. It's just our truck," the young man assured them.

A door slammed, and muffled shouting came through the walls, followed by a short shriek of pain. Even the young man tensed at the unexpected sound. Seconds later, the door to the shack flew open and a middle-aged man with a limp stumbled in, leading a skinny girl gruffly by the arm. He threw the girl into the center of the room, and Il-sun had to step back as a powerful wave of odor from the man assaulted her. It was the foreman and Gyong-ho.

"Gi!" Il-sun exclaimed, running to her friend. Gi's face was white, her eyes completely blank. Il-sun held her close.

The foreman handed a stack of papers to the young man. "You can have this cunt, too," he managed to say, barely able to stand, pointing to Gyong-ho.

"I don't have papers for her. She can't come," said the young man, leafing through the stack the foreman had given him.

"You'll take her. That's an order, soldier!"

"You're drunk, old man. I can't take her if I don't have papers. It's too risky."

The foreman drew a pistol from inside his shirt and pointed it waveringly in front of the young man. "Take her or I'll shoot you. I'll shoot *all* of you!" he threatened, raising his voice and wheeling around. "She was my wife once, when she was a boy. I can't stand the sight of her. Take her!"

"Put the gun down, Hwang. You're not making any sense," said the young man. He seemed unruffled. He looked thoughtful and calculating, and a smile tugged on the corners of his lips. "Okay, old man. I'll take her."

he doubted that was the only thing.
truck coughed and wheezed its way
he countryside. The engine sounded
sun like an old man complaining of
itis or gout. The pace varied greatly
he terrain: Going uphill the truck lost
and crawled, the engine whining at a
pitch. Going downhill it roared and
d up so much speed that Il-sun was
that they were going to lose control.
hat felt like hours they went onward,
passing a single vehicle. Several times
ung man turned onto different roads,
little more than dirt tracks slicing
gh otherwise undisturbed vegetation.
d said that they would go to great
s to avoid villages and outposts.
ually they always found themselves
n the deserted highway.
as a clear night and the stars were
ficent. Il-sun wished that Gi could
em, but she remained unresponsive.
particularly fond of the stars and, in
chnical way, she even liked to talk
them. Il-sun felt excited by the
ure in spite of her nervousness — she
ver been outside the city limits. Even
only uncertainty loomed before her,
s glad that she would never again
sit in the garment factory or listen

"What are you doing?" hissed the man called Wart through his missing tooth.

"This will work out in our favor," replied the young man, speaking mostly to himself.

29

It was past midnight when Il-sun, Gi, Cho, the young man, and four of the other implicated partygoers piled into the flatbed military truck. The young man was in the driver's seat, accompanied in the cab by two of the men. The others climbed onto the bed of the truck. The young man gave them blankets to protect against the night chill, but nothing to pad the hard wooden truck bed. It was going to be a rough ride. Also in the truck bed were two full military-style duffel bags containing their civilian clothes and six jerry cans of fuel. Conspicuously absent was the man called Rooster, who had turned them in. He had seemed somewhat quieter than the rest of them, Il-sun recalled. Everyone was dressed in army fatigues, except for Gyong-ho, who was still in her factory uniform.

Nerves were taut as the young man navigated the city streets to the edge of town —

even a military vehicle could [...] attention at night. The truc[k...] checkpoint at the outskirts [...] they were motioned throug[h...] tion. The young man tosse[d...] to the guard on duty, who [...] sleepy acknowledgment. Il-[...] ho, who shivered dispropo[...] chill of the air. Her eyes [...] and she still had not spoke[...]

"What's wrong with her[...] was said with a mixture [...] condescension.

"She gets like this som[e...] passes in a minute or t[wo...] frightened," answered Il-[...] for a moment back to wh[at...] said about the labor cam[p...] it was true. It would expl[...]

"I hope she doesn't bl[...] next checkpoint," said W[...] what he's thinking, bring[...]

Il-sun was happy that [...] a shock to see the forema[n...] the young man; but the [...] knew a lot of people. S[...] foreman was one of the [...] him through some kind [...] kind of weakness could [...] man have? He was cert[...]

but s[...]
Th[...]
into [...]
to Il-[...]
arthr[...]
with [...]
heart [...]
high [...]
picke[...]
afraid [...]
For w[...]
never [...]
the yo[...]
some [...]
throu[...]
He h[...]
lengt[...]
Event [...]
back [...]
It w[...]
magni[...]
see th[...]
Gi wa[...]
her te[...]
about [...]
advent [...]
had ne[...]
though[...]
she wa[...]
have t[...]

to the foreman lecture. She wondered if she would have to go to Party Youth meetings in *Hanguk,* or if those, too, were a thing of the past. One thing felt certain: that with the young man she was sure to be important. She imagined herself a beneficent bringer of culture and wisdom to the *Hanguk* people, who had for so long been deprived by their imperialist overlords.

Eventually the truck sputtered and came to a stop. The young man got out and emptied three of the jerry cans into the dry gas tank. He checked on the passengers in the back and offered them water from a plastic jug. Everyone, except for Gi, took turns going into the bushes to relieve themselves and indulged in the opportunity to stretch their legs. Il-sun was grateful for the reprieve, because the ride had been rather bouncy and uncomfortable. She hoped that the young man would offer them something to eat — her belly was grinding against itself. She knew that eventually the sensation of hunger would stop on its own and then she would not notice the lack of food for several more hours, but for the time being it was making her anxious. She knew better than to ask. She didn't want to appear weak in front of the young man.

Before too long they were back on the

road. The two passengers who had been riding in the cab exchanged places with the men who had been riding in the bed of the truck, with much grumbling and bickering on the part of the former. Il-sun felt exhausted but too excited to sleep. The rough ride would not have allowed for sleep anyway. The constant sound of the engine was starting to hurt her ears and she wished for a reprieve from it.

The truck slowed suddenly and Il-sun peered around the side of the cab. There was a building in the distance with an electric light blazing, fighting a losing battle against the looming darkness. *That must be the checkpoint,* Il-sun thought. Suddenly her heart was in her throat. She knew that this was the most sensitive part of the journey, and that if this went wrong, she could be lost forever in the prison camps. The other passengers seemed to tense as well. She could see soldiers preparing for their arrival. From this distance they looked like flies circling a lightbulb.

30

Gyong-ho's vision was distorted, and everything moved in slow motion. The foreman had grabbed her arm, and half dragged her out of his office, through the loading dock doors and into a truck. Sound and event separated in her mind, so that she seemed to hear everything several moments after it happened. There was no sensation in her body — she had become perfectly numb. They were driving through the city, everything stretching in her peripheral vision. Suddenly they were stopped and the foreman was pulling her out of the truck. She heard a shriek, and then realized it had come from her own mouth. She was thrown into a room, and Il-sun was there. Was it really her? Then they were in the truck again, only she was in the back this time. Numbers merged with forms and became distillations of ones and zeros. Yeses and nos. Then the humming of the engine broke it all down, and she dissolved into memory.

She had run from it for several years. She had put up a good fight, but now she was cornered and worn out. There was nothing left to do but give in. The relief of giving up overpowered her fear. The footsteps behind her echoed faster and closer. She turned and embraced him.

Days blended together, one being very much the same as the next. Gyong-ho became a fog of reeducation, confession, hunger, soreness, and fatigue. She had been in the camp for two years — she was ten years old — already forgotten to herself, a loyal daughter of the Dear Leader whom she had disappointed so completely, who was smiling on her even as he punished her. It was for her own good. The routine was constant, numbing, and severe. It was so constant and numbing that the day when her name was called during morning reeducation, she did not at first recognize it as her own. She no longer identified herself as an individual, and as it dawned on her that the tall, shadowy man in the doorway was in fact calling her, she was shocked back into herself. She stood and her feet obediently went to him, carrying the rest of her body reluctantly with them. Faces turned to her, already having done their grieving, passively curious about whether she would ever return.

The man, walking behind her, took her to a place she had not seen before. The building was more substantial than the rest, made of concrete block. It was long and narrow, with small windows high on the walls, and they entered through one side of it. The man brought with him his very own atmosphere of dominance, like the world itself was his alone to punish. He had no face. No soul. He told her to walk to the end of the corridor. His hard soles echoed loudly behind her, the sound of his long stride pushing her forward faster than her natural pace. He directed her into a small, dirty room.

The room was damp and cold. There was a wooden table and a chair, and nothing else. The door clicked shut behind her. She was told to sit on the chair with her hands on the table. He stood behind her, his shadow casting darkness over her. He asked her questions, she answered them. He disliked her answers, and asked them again more loudly. He issued some warning, but she could not hear what it was. He asked questions; she answered them, yes and no. Yes and no. He told her to stand. She stood, hands still on the table. He told her to remove her shoes. She kicked them off her feet. She was standing in a pool of water, her feet aching with cold. He ordered her to remove her clothing, which she did. She had never been naked like this before, in front of a man. She flushed with shame. He asked questions. Warm liquid ran down her leg. He laughed. He asked questions over and over. She responded yes and no, yes and no. He showed her a long metal rod with a rubber handle. He pressed it into her ribs and a painful shock passed through her body. She convulsed uncontrollably. He asked his questions again. She screamed her answers between sobs, yes and no, until she was no longer sure which was which. His questions came faster and louder, he shocked her when he was displeased. He grabbed the back of her neck with a gloved hand and forced her forward onto the table. He pushed the tip of the metal rod into her rectum, asking questions. She cried out, screaming yes and no at random, begging him to stop. He turned on the device and she convulsed.

The world slowed down — maybe someone had turned time itself off. A pleasant numbness settled in her bones. She looked at the window and could instantly see three hundred thirty-six water spots. The number was as clear as the spots. There was a line of seventy-eight ants on the windowsill, each an individual and yet still a part of the seventy-eight. She broke through a barrier in her mind and numbers poured in, permeating everything. Numbers interacted and danced inside her head, mingling and reproducing, dividing and multiplying effortlessly. Shapes in her vision broke down into simpler shapes, their angles and sides forming relationships that made them all numerically comprehensible. The wall slid across her vision and her shoulder hit the floor painfully. Her vision faded into black.

31

The young man engaged the engine cautiously, approaching the checkpoint slowly. His instructions to the passengers had been clear: Do not speak unless directly asked a question, respond as briefly as possible, and refer everything back to him. The passengers pretended to sleep. Il-sun tucked Gi's head into her arm and drew a blanket over her empty, staring eyes.

The truck came to a stop under the single bright streetlight outside the building. It seemed an isolated outpost, with no village apparent nearby. Of course, it would be difficult to see a nearby village at night if they were rationing power, as they most likely were. The building was a small, square, concrete block structure with a tin roof. There was a barricade across the road, with two soldiers standing at attention on either side of it, and a sign that told all motorists to have papers ready.

Il-sun could hear boots on the asphalt, approaching the driver's side door. She heard a greeting of familiarity from the soldier, and a friendly exchange with the young man. There was laughter. It sounded like they were indulging in some good-natured ribbing. Perhaps this would go easily after all. The engine revved and it seemed that they were about to move forward.

"Stop!" A voice shouted from somewhere near the concrete building. "What is this?" The engine died down again.

"Just routine, sir. A workforce brigade on their way to relieve some troops," shouted the officer standing by the truck.

"Have you seen their papers?"

"All is in good order, sir."

"Have you searched the vehicle?"

Il-sun tensed. If they were forced out of the truck it wouldn't take a very keen eye to discover their ruse. They did not look very soldierly.

"No, sir," came the reluctant reply.

"We have to keep sharp, soldier."

"Yes, sir." The soldier's voice hardened as he once again addressed the vehicle. "Alright, everybody. You heard the man. Everyone, out of the vehicle. Come on." He clapped his hands twice to stir them all to action. Il-sun turned cold, yet a film of perspiration appeared on her forehead. Gyong-ho showed no signs of being aware of her surroundings.

The young man jumped out of the truck and began shouting, as would befit a man of higher rank ordering his underlings. "That's right. You heard him. Out of the truck. Wake up! This is the Great General's army, let's look alive!" He looked in the bed of the truck and gave a hard, wide-eyed nod toward the lump of Gyong-ho. Il-sun understood the gesture to mean to keep her hidden.

The men in the cab jumped out of the truck and stood at attention. Il-sun remembered that they had all spent some time in the military, so this would come more naturally to them. She figured that the safest course would be to follow their lead. She peeled herself away from Gyong-ho and, trying to be inconspicuous, covered her under a pile of blankets. Maybe they would not look there.

Everyone was out of the truck and lined up at attention. The young man stood in front of them, his tight and confident posture making up for the poor fit of his clothes. He was playing the role perfectly by drawing attention to his professionalism and away from his appearance. Il-sun opted to do the same, and made her face into the image of soldierly efficiency.

The soldier shined a flashlight into the cab. He was very young, maybe twenty years old, with lopsided ears; and his easy-going nature ran contrary to the nosy job of vehicular searches. He scanned the surfaces of the cab very quickly, then turned his attention to the bed. Again, his search was quick and perfunctory. The commanding officer, a man in his mid-thirties, was standing in the doorway of the building with his arms folded.

"The truck is clean, sir," the young soldier declared.

"No, no! You aren't doing it right!" shouted the officer. "You need to look under and inside things. Feel the cushions for any suspicious lumps, things like that. If you are at all suspicious, then take your knife and open the upholstery." Then he added quickly, "But you better be certain before you do that to any official vehicles." This was clearly more of an educational exercise than a serious search, and for the moment anyway, his attention was on correcting the young soldier rather than on inspecting the ragtag group standing at attention.

"Yes, sir." The young soldier started over, looking again in the cab.

"We don't get many vehicles this way," said the officer to the young man, sounding apologetic. "I have to keep my men trained."

"Of course, sir," said the young man. "Are you new to this post? I haven't seen you before."

"Just transferred. I must have pissed somebody off."

"I'm sure it's not as bad as it looks, sir."

"Worse."

The young soldier pressed on the seats, opened the glove box and ran his hand along all the surfaces inside the truck. He peeked under the seat, and pulled out a carton of cigarettes. "I found something, sir," he said with a tone of pride.

"Very good. What is it?"

"A carton of foreign cigarettes, half empty."

"Bring them to me. And their travel papers."

"Yes, sir." The young soldier glanced for a moment at the young man, looking guilty, then handed the articles to his superior.

The officer first looked at the papers, sifting through them casually, then looked toward the group, counting heads to be sure he had the same number of papers as there were travelers. He was not bothering to read the documents, only concerning himself with having the correct number. He still had not observed the travelers very closely. He walked toward the group and addressed the young man.

"Did you know about these?" he asked, indicating the cigarettes.

"Yes, sir!" The young man put emphasis on the word *sir*.

"Are they your cigarettes?"

"Yes, sir!"

"At ease. You don't need to shout. I can hear you just fine. How did you manage to get a hold of a carton of fancy cigarettes?" His query sounded more friendly than threatening.

"They were a gift, sir. For driving a dignitary, sir." The young man did not waver in his act. Il-sun was impressed.

"I was just curious. I've never had a fancy foreign cigarette before. Do you mind if I try one?"

"Help yourself, sir," the young man said, nodding toward the carton.

"Do you have an open pack? I only want one." The young man reached into his pocket and drew out a pack. He knocked the butt of the pack to extract a cigarette, and handed it to the officer. The officer sniffed at it, inspecting the paper, the clean, square ends, and the filter. "Do you have a

207

match?" The young man withdrew a box of matches, and struck one for the officer. The officer took three thoughtful drags, looking vacantly toward the streetlight, consumed by the smoking experience. He then ripped the filter off and tried a drag without it. The subordinate soldier looked on, as if waiting for a trial verdict. Finally, the officer handed the partially smoked cigarette back to the young man, the vacant look on his face replaced by a look of certainty. "It's a bit like smoking air, isn't it?"

"Sir?" asked the young man, unable to hide his confusion.

"I mean, they're a bit weak, aren't they? People talk these up like they're so special, but to me it's a little too much like breathing. I prefer *real Chosun* cigarettes, even rolled in newspaper, to that crap. I want to feel 'em burn." He wasn't being condescending, just honest. His informal tone relaxed the young man.

"I guess everyone has different tastes," offered the young man.

"What a boring world this would be if everyone were just the same, eh?" The officer smiled and chucked the young man on the shoulder.

"I agree with you, there," said the young man, slipping seamlessly from subordinate to charming.

"Right," said the officer, coming out of his reverie and back to business. "How is that search coming, soldier?" Il-sun tensed again. She had thought that maybe that business had passed. "Anything unpatriotic or otherwise antirevolutionary back there?" He was bored and his tone was facetious. The search, for him, was over.

The soldier, missing the officer's nuanced dismissal, snapped to attention and went back to the truck.

"Not the sharpest kid, but at least he's enthusiastic," the officer said under his breath to the young man, rolling his eyes. He shrugged at the young man and then looked on in an avuncular way. The soldier flashed his light into the bed of the truck, lifting the blankets that were haphazardly strewn about. He was being thorough, wanting to impress his superior. Il-sun held her breath. The soldier poked at the shapeless bundle that was Gyong-ho. She did not make a sound, but the soldier recognized the density as being distinctly corporeal. He pulled at the blanket and uncovered the shivering Gyong-ho.

The officer perked up, his casual air gone. "What's this?" He looked at the paperwork that was still in his hand, and then counted heads once again. "What is the meaning of this?" he demanded of the young man. The young man swallowed hard, but kept his wits.

"Just a little recreation, sir." He was again the professional soldier.

"What do you mean, 'just a little recreation'?"

"A flower-selling girl we picked up in the city. We couldn't exactly get paperwork for her through official channels, if you know what I mean. The boys at the factory site need a little companionship." Then he added another hasty "sir."

The officer looked thoughtful, the corners of his mouth tight and downturned. "This is out of the ordinary," he said after a moment. The young man cursed to himself for finding the one man in all of North Korea who could not be bribed with foreign cigarettes. He had no choice but to try another tactic.

"She's not exclusively for them, you know, sir."

"What do you mean?"

"I mean, we could let you give her a try, right here and now, if you like. You would be doing us a favor, really. Let us know how she is?"

The officer rubbed his chin with his

fingers thoughtfully. It was a lonely outpost. "Bring her over here," he said finally. "I want to have a look at her." The soldier got into the bed of the truck and forced Gyong-ho to get up and step onto the pavement. He led her over to the officer. "Maybe you're right. Maybe I should have a talk with her in private. You can wait in your truck."

"You heard the man, everyone back in the truck!" the young man commanded.

"But —" Il-sun tried to protest.

"Get in the truck! Now!" The look on his face was truly frightening. Il-sun felt powerless to help her friend, but she wanted to do something. The men got immediately back in the truck, but Il-sun and Cho lingered.

Cho rolled her eyes and said, "I can't believe you men!" She turned in the other direction and walked toward the concrete building. The officer and the soldier were just stepping Gyong-ho inside and were about to close the door.

Il-sun could not hear what Cho was saying to them, but her hands were quite animated. Fortunately they were distracted enough by what she was saying not to notice her long, red fingernails — a sure giveaway that she was not truly a soldier. The men looked from Cho to Gyong-ho and then back again. Listening to what she was saying, their faces went from incredulous to concerned. Finally they released Gi, and Cho walked her back to the truck untouched.

"How did you manage that?" asked Il-sun.

"It was easy, teacup. I told them she has a social disease."

"A social disease?"

"Yeah. I told them that if they screw her, their peckers will turn black and fall off. They didn't believe me at first, but then, who would want to take that chance?"

Il-sun looked at Cho through new eyes. The women got in the truck, the young soldier lifted the barricade, and they drove off into the night.

32

Mother was the next to die. She had succumbed to some combination of sickness and
starvation. By that time, Gyong-ho was numb
and calloused by the hardships of the gulag,
and her mother was a stranger to her. She
had no tears to shed. If she felt anything at all
about her mother's passing, it was relief; but
even that was barely a sensation at all.

Days, weeks, months, and years passed
meaninglessly. As she grew, her body twisted
from lack of nourishment and overwork. She
retreated into the abstract world of numbers,
leaving little more than the shell of her body
to cope with the rigors of prison life.

Gyong-ho did not have any feelings about
God, but she did believe in angels. She
believed in them because she had met one,
no matter that she was flesh and bone. This
angel appeared in the gulag, young and clean
and beautiful, sometime after Gi's mother
died. She smelled fresh, like sunrise. She was

a new prison guard, unsullied by the filth of mind that infected everyone else. She did not yell, she did not beat, she did not threaten. She just was.

The angel was the new guard in charge of reeducation, and she was impressed by the quick and seamless way in which Gi could answer questions about even the most minute of details regarding the life and history of the great *Chosun* nation and its rulers. She began to reward Gi for her exceptional memory with little bits of extra food and lighter daily work. Gi learned to play into the angel's favor by being ever sharper and quicker. This naturally caused many of the other children to be jealous, but it did not matter — any extra calorie or comfort could be the difference between living and dying.

Gi became the angel's "special helper," which entailed little more than sweeping the classroom floor and tidying odds and ends. Most days this kept her out of the fields and factories. From time to time the angel would sneak food to her from her own home, which often included small portions of rice. Though by most standards it was a meager amount of food, in the gulag it was a feast that helped her maintain her strength. The angel could have been punished for this, Gi knew.

"I always wished I could have a daughter,"

the angel would sometimes say.

One day, as Gi was walking to the morning education class, the angel met her halfway there. This was highly unusual, though nobody questioned it. Nobody much cared what happened to the prisoners, including the prisoners themselves. The angel instructed Gi to follow her. She took her into the building where the dark man used his electric prod on her — Gi became short of breath. She assumed that finally the infection of cruelty must have spread to the angel too, and now she was going to be tortured by the most beautiful person she had ever known. The angel took her into a small room and told her to keep quiet, even though nobody else was around. Then she commanded her to strip down, and Gi obeyed. *Now the pain will start,* Gyong-ho thought, dispassionately. It was as if it were happening to someone else. But instead of pain, the angel handed her new clothes to wear. They were too big, but they were clean.

"If anyone asks, tell them you are my niece, okay?" said the angel. Gyong-ho nodded. "Listen to me, Gyong-ho," she continued. "I am getting you away from here, to a much better place. We will probably never see each other again."

"No!" shouted Gyong-ho. She could not imagine life without the angel.

215

"Shhh!" The angel put her finger on Gyong-ho's lips. "Listen. My sister runs an orphanage, and she has agreed to take you. It will be much better for you. Trust me. My boyfriend has agreed to help. His father is an important man, and he has a car and can arrange all the appropriate paperwork. My boyfriend will drive you to my sister, and she will take care of you."

"I don't want to leave you!" Gi watched herself say it, and saw wetness in her eyes from tears, but was unaware of feeling anything. The outburst had come from some distant part of her biology, where feeling must still be happening without her.

"You must. You will die if you stay here. I will miss you, Song Gyong-ho."

Gi nodded.

The angel led her outside the compound, where a shiny black automobile was parked. She opened the back door and helped Gyong-ho inside. She then walked to the driver's window and said a few brief words. Gyong-ho watched her recede as the car drove away.

33

It was a little past dawn when the truck came to a wrinkle in the landscape. The high fence and razor wire that marked the demilitarized zone, or DMZ, came into view. The DMZ was an ideological cleave splitting the Korean peninsula in half: communists in Pyongyang to the north, and capitalists in Seoul to the south. Flanked on either side by opposing and powerful militaries, the DMZ was a pair of parallel fences, approximately four kilometers apart, running along the thirty-eighth parallel from coast to coast. Between the electric fences was a terrifying gauntlet of land mines that made the prospect of crossing it in one piece a near impossibility, not to mention the guard towers with machine gun nests on both sides. The irony of this inflammable and politically charged barrier was that the complete lack of human activity between the fences created an amazing nature preserve where plants and birds thrived. The two Koreas had been facing off at the DMZ for roughly a half century: technically in a cease-fire with no peace agreement ever signed. The Korean war was still smoldering.

The young man guided the truck down a dirt track. He had hoped to make this approach under the cover of darkness, but there was nothing he could do about that now. His contacts in this region were high ranking and well lubricated with bribes, so anyone seeing him was likely to turn a blind eye; but one could never be too careful. It had been a close call at the last checkpoint. He aimed the truck down a steep gully and was glad for the truck's high clearance and stout, knobby tires as he straddled rocks and rolled over large exposed roots. He would have been happier if the truck had had better leaf springs to absorb impact, but he was in no position to complain: He was lucky to have a truck at all. He almost felt sorry for the people riding on the rigid wooden planks in the back, who were most certainly bruised and miserable.

The landscape was stark and dusty, dotted with scrub and clumps of dry grasses. The rising sun painted the surroundings in pinks, reds, and gold, and cast long, blue shadows. It was going to be a warm spring day. A lone jet cut a long vapor trail across the otherwise cloudless sky.

The truck came to a stop at a small natural rock amphitheater where the dirt track dead-ended. The men got out and began clearing piles of deadfall away from the rock wall. In a few moments they had uncovered a cleverly concealed cave with a mouth large enough to fit two trucks side by side. It looked to Il-sun like an empty eye socket in a parched human skull. The young man came back to the truck and emptied the two duffels into the bed, spilling their civilian clothes on the dirty wood.

Gyong-ho raised her head and looked around, confused. "Where are we?" she asked.

"Gi!" Il-sun threw her arms around her. "I was so afraid for you! We are at the DMZ!"

"The DMZ? How did we get to the DMZ? Why?"

"I have to leave the country, Gi. I'm in trouble."

"What happened? You can't leave the country! That's absurd!"

"I have to, Gi. I've been implicated in antirevolutionary activity. If I stay, I'll end up in a prison camp for sure."

"How did this happen? Why am *I* here?"

"I'm not sure. Foreman Hwang brought you when he delivered the truck. He was drunk and angry. I think you need to come too, Gi."

"She has no choice," interjected the young man. "This is a one-way trip."

Gyong-ho's brow furrowed deeply in an attempt to remember how she had gotten there. She remembered the foreman grabbing her arm — she was still sore there — but everything else was a muddle. She was too confused to feel scared. "But how will we get across the DMZ? Nobody can get across it. And besides, the Americans —"

"Everybody, listen up," the young man interrupted. "Change back into your old clothes now. This tunnel will take us past the fence into the DMZ. Once we are there, you have to do exactly as I say. Step exactly where I step. If you stray off my path, you will probably step on a land mine and blow your legs off. I won't stop to pick up the pieces. If we're seen by either side, we will be shot on sight; so be quiet and don't make any big, fast movements, is that clear?" He looked around and everyone nodded. "I have made this trip dozens of times and this route is secure. The natural features of the landscape will keep us mostly hidden. When we get close to the fence on the other side, there is another tunnel that will take us safely into South Korea. I have friends who will be waiting for us over there."

"What about papers when we get to the other side?" asked Cho.

"My friends have taken care of all of that."

"What about Gyong-ho? They aren't prepared for her," asked Il-sun.

"We will take care of that later. It won't be a problem. The *Hanguk* are not as bothered with identification as the *Chosun*."

They changed back into their clothes, except for Gyong-ho who was still in her factory uniform. The young man put the fatigues into the duffels and handed flashlights to the men of the group. He then passed the water jug around, and they all drank from it until it was empty. "Okay, follow me," he commanded, lighting a cigarette. They made a line and filed into the tunnel. Gi grabbed Il-sun by the arm and stopped her.

"I have a very bad feeling about this. I'm scared," Gi whispered.

"Our lives are going to be different. We just have to get used to that."

"I don't want to go. I didn't agree to this!" As the reality of the journey they were about to embark upon dawned on her, she began to feel panicked.

"What's holding you girls up, let's go!" shouted the young man.

"I'm glad you're here with me, Gi. It's going to be okay," said Il-sun.

"What are we going to do over there? The *Hanguk* are starving. We won't know anybody; how will we eat? Who will look after us?"

"He will look after us, Gi," Il-sun said, pointing at the young man. "Don't worry. His friends will take us in and we can get jobs. He will probably work as a driver, and maybe we can work in another garment factory. He said it's not as bad as we think over there. And besides, you heard him: There really isn't a choice at this point. If you stay, where will you go? You'll be stuck in the middle of nowhere without food or water. You have no travel papers. You will probably end up back at the prison camp."

Gi shuddered. The prison camp. She remembered it clearly now. She found that she could sift through the memory, like going through ashes from a recently extinguished fire. She didn't want to disturb the ashes too much, but for the first time she could look plainly into the memories. The demon was no longer pressing at her. She took a deep breath and clenched the hem of her blouse.

"Okay," she said finally, seeing no other choice.

They walked into the cave, the light from the mouth of the tunnel getting smaller behind them. The smell of dry brush was replaced by the smell of damp earth.

"Why is the tunnel so big around?" Il-sun asked the young man.

"The Great Leader Kim Il-sung started digging this tunnel many years ago," he replied. "He wanted tanks to be able to get through to the other side for when we reclaim the South. They got about a third of the way through the DMZ. I'm not sure why they stopped."

"How did you learn about it?" asked Cho.

"I found it when I was in the military, when I was stationed near here."

The four flashlights diluted the darkness. The ground was flat and smooth, having been made for vehicles, and easy to walk on. The tunnel was quite straight, though they could not see the end of it from the mouth. It was supported at regular intervals with large wooden beams; clearly great care had gone into the engineering and construction of it. Along the way there were inscriptions carved into the earthen walls commemorating workers who had died during construction, as well as proclamations of devotion to the Great Leader.

As they went deeper into the tunnel, the air became cooler and moister, and the darkness seemed to hang thicker around them. The air was stale and moldy, causing Gyong-ho to sneeze. Il-sun began to feel claustrophobic. About fifteen minutes into the journey they came across a red line painted around the circumference of the tunnel, and a sign that read Demilitarized Zone. "We're crossing the northern border of the DMZ now," the young man said. "We will be out of the tunnel soon." Several minutes later they could see a faint light in the distance. Il-sun was impressed by the undertaking of making such a long underground road, even if it was never fully completed. Surely the Americans and their puppet regime in Seoul could never construct anything so sophisticated. In another twenty minutes the grand tunnel tapered into a gradual earthen ramp heading toward a narrow opening into the light.

The young man halted the group before exiting the tunnel. "From this point forward, do exactly as I do and stay on my trail. There are land mines everywhere in the DMZ. Don't speak unless you absolutely need to, and be as quiet as possible. If we do run into trouble, then run to the south fence. Your chances of survival are greater over there. If anyone gets shot, don't stay behind with them. Just run."

The group tensed. It dawned on them that soon they were going to be fully exposed on some of the most dangerous ground on earth. They followed the young man into the sunlight.

The sun had climbed and it was now late morning. The sky was still clear and the air was warm. The tunnel ended in a secluded depression in the earth that was hidden from either side of the DMZ. The air was alive with bird sounds and thick with the smell of foliage. The men cleared away a pile of dead brush from the side of the tunnel to reveal several wheelbarrows. Without a word, each of the accompanying men took a wheelbarrow and filed in line behind the young man, who was beginning to walk along a discernable path.

"What are those for?" Cho asked rather loudly, pointing to the wheelbarrows.

"Shut up, woman, we are in the DMZ!" came the harsh reply of the young man, looking back with a stern face.

As promised, the path was concealed by the folds of the landscape. The southern fence was visible only for brief moments, and at those places the path was well hidden by trees. The narrow trail was well worn. Obviously it had been used often. This part of the journey seemed so easy and the day was so lovely that the walk was actually enjoyable. Sooner than Il-sun had expected, the young man stopped the group in front of another tunnel entrance. This tunnel was much narrower than the last, and so low that it looked as though they were all going to have to crouch to walk inside.

The young man spoke in a loud whisper, "We are at the second tunnel now. This one is fairly short. Since we are about to enter *Hanguk* territory, we need to take some precautions. I need you to hand over all of your identification and any *Chosun* currency that you are carrying. If you are caught with it, you will be tortured and executed by the imperialists."

He looked around expectantly. No one moved immediately: to be parted from one's identification was a huge offense in the North. It was almost like being asked to strip naked — a very personal thing to do.

"You can't go over there with it. It won't do you any good anyway. Like it or not, we can't go back to the North. So please, hand over your identification and your money. It is better for you if you do." The young man spoke authoritatively.

Il-sun reached into a pocket in her blouse and proffered her identification and a small stack of folded *won.* Gyong-ho followed suit; then, reluctantly, so did Cho. The young man put the materials in a shirt pocket and turned around, saying, "Follow me."

"But what about them?" asked Cho, pointing to the men of the group.

"We gave it to him earlier," responded one of the men.

"Alright, let's go. It's not safe to linger here," said the young man, disappearing into the tunnel.

Il-sun and Gi followed him inside. Cho delayed, her forehead furrowed in uncertainty. The man who was missing his front tooth, the one called Wart, stepped forward, bowed, and opened his hand in the direction of the tunnel as if to be a gentleman holding a door open for a lady. Cho went in reluctantly. The men followed, their wheelbarrows barely able to fit inside the tunnel.

The tunnel was distressingly low and narrow for Il-sun. Insects crawled along the close walls, and spiderwebs crisscrossed everywhere, sticking to her face and hands and getting caught in her hair. There did not seem to be enough air in the tunnel and she had to fight down waves of panic. In her imagination the integrity of the walls gave way and she was buried alive, suffocated and squeezed to death. The light of the flashlights strobed through the spaces between moving limbs, creating undulating shadows all around, making her feel dizzy and a little nauseous. To distract herself she made conversation with the young man.

"Is this another invasion tunnel?"

"No. Some of the laborers who were working on the other tunnel may have defected to the South by making this one. We had to widen it quite a bit after we found it. It was only big enough to crawl in before."

Il-sun shuddered at the thought of the tunnel being any smaller.

"But why would anyone defect to the South?"

Il-sun's question went unanswered.

Within a few minutes the tunnel dead-ended and a wooden barrier barred their way. The young man leaned hard against it and pushed. The barrier fell forward and landed with a heavy thud in a cloud of dust. Fresh air and blinding sunlight rushed into the seeming vacuum of the tunnel. Il-sun was relieved. One by one, the group emerged under the South Korean sky.

34

On reflection, crossing the DMZ was a rather anticlimactic affair to Gyong-ho. It was almost too simple, being more of a pleasure hike than a flight from certain imprisonment, and she wondered if all barriers were ultimately like that: more substantial in the mind. Even the looming threat of land mines took on an abstract impotence under the clear, blue sky and on the well-worn path. She had half expected to be met on the *Hanguk* side of the border by a squadron of ferocious American imperialists brandishing guns, standing at the ready to run her through with their gleaming bayonets; she was surprised to instead step out into a peaceful, beautiful day. She had imagined the soil of South Korea to be dry and barren, life burned out of it by the hostile ravages of war and impoverishment. But the landscape she stepped into was much like the landscape she had left at the northern border: low scrub and grasses with occasional trees in a setting of dusty hills.

The young man ordered everyone to take cover under a nearby tree as a precaution in case a helicopter or airplane were to patrol overhead. He then took a telephone out of his pocket and unfolded it. Gi had never seen a mobile phone before and marveled at it in disbelief. It looked altogether too small to house the necessary components. The young man hit some buttons, spoke into it, then folded it back up and returned it to his pocket. He turned around slowly, surveying the area.

"We are about forty meters south of the DMZ. Welcome to South Korea," he said with a smile.

Il-sun put her arm around Gyong-ho. She was pleased to have made it across the border safely. Gyong-ho, however, could feel no relief: She was terrified of whatever lay ahead. Cho lit a cigarette, her eyes shifting nervously from side to side.

Within a few minutes Gi heard the sound of an approaching vehicle and saw its dust as it navigated a circuitous road in their direction. The men of the group stiffened and made furtive glances toward the tunnel, assessing how quickly they could get back into it. The young man stood there calmly, wearing his sunglasses and smoking.

A vehicle unlike any Gi had ever seen before pulled up to where the young man was standing. It was long and sleek, with darkened windows. It had a pointed snout, as if its makers could not decide whether to make an automobile or an airplane, and it had a large, square door on the side. To Gi it looked like it might have come from outer space, but the young man referred to it as a minivan. It was two-tone blue and had a large dent near the rear. Two strangely dressed men, both Korean, got out of the van and greeted the young man. He returned their greeting, and it was clear by their informality that they had met before.

One of the men was quite tall, with shaggy hair, and wore wire-rimmed glasses, and his face sported several days of thin stubble. From his demeanor and the way he interacted with the other men, Gi could tell that he was the one in charge. The other man was average in height, though next to the tall one he appeared short. It was an illusion augmented by the fact that he was very overweight. Gi had never seen a fat person before, and she could not stop staring at his round profile. Both men dressed with what appeared a planned haphazardness. They were both wearing trousers of rough denim.

The tall man had on a T-shirt that was printed with the image of a screaming, long-haired man holding a guitar. The fat one was wearing a short-sleeved button-down shirt. It was hideous attire and she wondered why anyone in his right mind would leave his house looking like that. Then she remembered: These were the impoverished and backward *Hanguk.* Perhaps they could not afford more sensible clothing.

The three men were having an animated conversation; Gi could not make out the words. The young man pointed toward his group and the other two men looked over, their eyes lingering on the women, and nodded in acknowledgment. The fat man handed over a wad of bills. They looked like green imperialist dollars; Gi had seen pictures of them before but had never actually held any. The young man counted. He looked displeased, and pointed to the group again and said something. The other two men shook their heads decisively. Then their voices rose and Gi could just make out some of their conversation.

"I brought you three," the young man said.

"We never discussed a third one. That changes everything," replied the tall man.

The fat man was turned away from Gi, and his comment was lost in the wind.

"But I can't take anyone back with me. You know that." The young man was almost whining.

"I'll tell you what, because we have done such good business in the past, I'm willing to cave in a little bit here," said the tall one, sounding annoyed. "We'll give you one hundred for the skinny one, but that's it."

"She's worth a whole lot more, and you know it," said the young man, holding his ground.

"Supply and demand, Gianni. Supply and demand." The wind had died down and the fat one's voice could be heard. "The demand here is low but the supply is high, so the price comes down. But I guess they don't teach you capitalist economics up there, do they?"

"Do you see any other buyers?" said the tall one. "Either take the hundred or you can take the skinny bitch back with you."

The young man looked thoughtful, not yet ready to be defeated. "I had to stick my neck out to bring her here. One hundred is too low, but I'll tell you what: give me one hundred fifty's worth in whiskey and we can have a deal. I know you pay less than that for the whiskey, so one hundred fifty in whiskey really only costs you one hundred, or even less. You break even on the whiskey but you profit from the girl. And I'm happy because I have more whiskey than I would have had in dollars, and it goes farther in the North. You see? That way we both come out ahead."

The men looked at each other and then nodded. "You learn fast, Gianni," the tall man said with a smile.

Gyong-ho looked nervously toward the tunnel, wondering if she was fast enough to run back across the DMZ before the men caught her. She did not understand the conversation, but she knew that something was dreadfully wrong. It sounded as if they were negotiating a price for her; but that was absurd.

"So that's three hundred plus the usual cigarettes and whiskey for each of the two girls, plus an extra one hundred fifty, in whiskey, for the skinny one, right?" recapped the fat man.

"Right," replied the young man. He nodded toward the men from his own group, who stood and rolled the wheelbarrows to the van. They began unloading boxes from the back, supervised by the fat one. The young man and the tall one walked over to the women sheltered under the tree.

"Ladies, this is Mr. Choy. You are going with him and his friend now. You must do as he tells you."

"But aren't you coming with us?" Il-sun asked, her eyes wide and her skin draining of its color. She must have been hearing the conversation as well.

"No. I have a business to run back home. Mr. Choy will take care of you from now on." He would not look directly at her.

"I don't understand," Il-sun whined. "You can't go home! They'll put you in a prison camp for sure!"

"It seems that I was wrong. Rooster isn't an informer after all. I'm too important up there for anyone to want to arrest me anyway. Don't worry about me; I'll be fine." There was a note of sarcasm in his voice.

"Then I'll come with you! I can help you!" The pleading in her voice was painful to hear.

"Explain it to her, Cho; I'm sure you've figured it out. I have work to do." He turned and walked back toward the van.

"We've been sold, teacup. Gianni sold us out."

PART II

35

Gianni stood in the sunlight, his dark glasses giving his face an impassive look. He stood with his weight on one leg, hand on his hip, holding a cigarette and watching as the other men hefted boxes and cartons into wheelbarrows. Gyong-ho had a feeling that he would not be one of the ones rolling a heavy wheelbarrow back across the DMZ. He was a cockroach waiting for a giant shoe.

Il-sun sat looking stunned, disbelief rippling in waves across her face. "But I'll make a good wife," she said under her breath to no one in particular. "I'll make a very good wife."

Gyong-ho sat, shocked and afraid. Was it only yesterday that she was fantasizing about moving into a private apartment with Il-sun? How far away that seemed. For how long would that be postponed? Could it be forever? *My God, is this for forever?* Panic coiled inside her chest. A bargaining voice began chattering inside her desperate mind, trying to claw its way back across the DMZ. *I'll be a better citizen. I'll work harder. I will love the Dear Leader more!* What did it mean to be sold? What would be demanded of her, wherever she was going? She imagined being ground up in the wheels of the ravenous imperialist machine, toiling in a mine or breaking her back tilling the infertile South Korean soil. Wherever she was headed, the outlook was not good.

Mr. Choy stood in the shade near the women and watched the goods being unloaded from the van. Once the wheelbarrows were full, the men bowed to each other and closed the rear hatch. The ones with the wheelbarrows disappeared into the tunnel under Gianni's watchful eye. Gianni then stepped up to the mouth of the tunnel and turned, giving a perfunctory wave to Mr. Choy and the fat man. He glanced briefly at the women under the tree, but upon seeing them his head jerked reflexively the other way. His body stiffened and his face betrayed a moment of regret. But just as quickly his face hardened. He turned and scurried into the tunnel.

After securing the wooden cover and placing a pile of branches to hide the tunnel entrance, the fat man joined Mr. Choy under the tree. The men stood over the women, looking down on them.

"Welcome, bumpkins, to the Republic of Korea," began Mr. Choy. "I am Mr. Choy, and my associate here is Mr. Lee." His speech was accented and informal. Gyong-ho had never heard a *Hanguk* person speak, and she was surprised by how differently he spoke her language. Mr. Choy's voice was smooth, if a little high-pitched, for such a tall man. "I believe we can have an amicable arrangement between us, providing you do as you're told and don't make trouble. If you make things difficult for us, we will make things difficult for you, understood?" The women did not respond other than to stare terror-stricken at the man. "Let me outline the basics for you: First, you are here in the Republic of Korea illegally. You have no official papers, so if you go to the authorities they will hand you over to the Americans; and I think you know what they will do to you if that happens."

Gi shuddered. If it was anything like the labor camp, she knew all too well.

"We will protect you from that fate," Mr. Choy continued, "as long as you do what we say.

"Second, if you try to run away, there is no one who will help you. You will likely be

241

murdered or end up being turned over to the military, who will torture you for information about your Dear Leader."

Mr. Choy paused to allow it all to sink in. Understanding and denial pulled at Gyong-ho in a well-matched tug-of-war, and her face contorted under the strain. This could not be happening; and if it were, then surely it would all be over by tomorrow.

Tomorrow!

"We have to be at the factory tomorrow!" Gi burst out.

Mr. Choy looked at her, a malicious smile spreading across his face as he pinned her down with his eyes. He said nothing, but his silence communicated everything clearly. They would not be going back to the factory tomorrow.

"You saw that we paid Gianni a large sum for the pleasure of your company," Mr. Choy continued after the silence had a chance to sink in. "And you can probably guess that we didn't do that just to be friendly. So here's the deal: We will consider the amount that we paid for you to be a loan, to be paid back by you — with interest, of course. Also, we will give you a place to live, food, and clothing. You must pay for all of that as well."

242

if only from the consequence of not wearing one. She was afraid that if she took it off, she would be at risk of catching some grave, and possibly terminal, mental infection. Or at the very least, she would be sent back to the gulag.

"It's just a pin," Cho said. "It won't be of any use over here."

As much as that made sense, Gyong-ho could not make her hands move to take it off. What if Mr. Lee told Gianni, who then told the orphanage mistress, who would have to report it to the head of the Party Youth? If she took it off, everyone would know. Wouldn't they? Finally, her hand moved as if struggling against some great force, shaking as she fumbled with the clasp. Here was another barrier, another DMZ, where the mental hurdle was so much greater than the physical one. Even as the pin slid out of her blouse, she was already thinking of how she would explain this at the next self-criticism meeting.

36

The women were made to lie down in the back of the van, covered by a blanket. The ride was hot and bumpy, though no more uncomfortable than being in the bed of the truck the night before. After a time they came to an asphalt road and the ride smoothed out. The van had made several turns over the course of a half hour, and unable to see out the windows, Gi was beginning to feel nauseous.

Finally, Mr. Lee shouted to them that they could come out. They threw off the blanket and came timidly forward to a bench seat directly behind the two men. Mr. Choy was driving. Mr. Lee offered them water from a plastic bottle.

"It is thanks to our Dear Leader that we have enough clean water to drink," Gyong-ho said as she received the bottle.

The two men broke into uproarious laughter.

"I love you Northerners," said Mr. Choy, his face red from laughing. "You say such funny things."

The women shifted uncomfortably. The men's laughter was shockingly irreverent. Just hearing such insolence was practically a crime, and the only way to assuage their sense of guilt would be to report it; but to whom? They were in *Hanguk* now. There was no one to report it to.

Gyong-ho was in an alien world. The van was moving with great speed down a wide paved road, and there were lines of cars stretching in both directions for as far as her eyes could see. Thousands of cars and trucks were hurtling past one another at extreme speeds. It was terrifying. The *Cho-sun* roads, by contrast, were practically devoid of traffic; one vehicle coming along every few minutes, at most. In the North, most of the vehicles were old military trucks, all painted the same green color. In the city, an occasional luxury car was seen, but that was uncommon. On this *Hanguk* road there was an endless variety of cars and trucks of various sizes, shapes, and colors. She never knew that there could be so many different types of vehicles. She wondered how the people of the South, as impoverished as they were, could afford them all.

Mr. Lee turned in his seat to face the women.

"Are you ladies hungry?" he asked.

The women looked at each other in shock. No one had ever asked them that before. It seemed like a rude question, too obvious and personal, like talking about intimate bodily functions. In *Chosun* nobody ever asked, "Are you hungry?" Hunger was a given. It was a question a person asked only if there was an option to eat and one might actually opt not to. What kind of barbarians were these people in the South, to ask such indelicate questions?

Receiving no clear reply to his question, Mr. Lee continued, "Well, I'm starving."

Gi could not hide her horror. His statement was beyond rude, beyond scandalous. Mr. Lee, the only truly overfed person she had ever seen, saying out loud that he was starving. She was not sure if she should be angry or ashamed or sad, so she felt all three at once.

"Shall we give the bumpkins a treat?" asked Mr. Choy.

Mr. Lee nodded.

They were just entering the outskirts of a large city. Mr. Choy turned off the road and pulled up to a small, square building with a huge red-and-yellow sign in front. Most of the writing on and around the building was in strange foreign script. Mr. Choy commanded the women to remain silent, then pulled the van up to a rectangular board. There was writing all over it, though little of it made sense to the women. Mr. Choy rolled down his window, and a heavy smell wafted in. It was an awful, meaty, sickly sweet smell, but it reminded Gi of her hunger all the same. Her stomach gurgled. A voice emanated from a speaker in the rectangular board. Mr. Choy spoke back using so many foreign words that Gi could not understand him. The van then pulled forward to a window where a woman in a strange paper hat was visible behind the glass. She opened the window and handed Mr. Choy three white paper bags, which he in turn handed to Mr. Lee. After giving the woman a small handful of currency, Mr. Choy engaged the van, and, within only minutes of leaving it, they were back on the road with the bags of warm food. It seemed a small miracle. *Could food be so easy?*

Mr. Lee opened the bags and passed Gyong-ho a warm bundle wrapped in paper, which she unfolded carefully. Inside was a soggy bun surrounding a slab of grayish meat. There were odd sauces mixing inside the bun, white and pink. A single green leaf and a slice of tomato were also tucked inside. She felt conflicting waves of hunger and revulsion. She had not had meat in months. She had not eaten anything for over a day, but there was something decidedly weird about this food that gave her pause. She raised her eyes toward the men in the front of the van, not trusting them. Mr. Choy was watching her in the rearview mirror, as if he were enjoying her discomfort. It was a look of amused fascination mixed with condescension, and Gi quickly lowered her gaze. Finally hunger overpowered her uncertainty and she devoured the sandwich feverishly. Cho, with similar hesitation and suspicion, inspected the food. She sampled a long, fried, starchy string, holding it between her fingernails, being careful not to touch it with the pads of her fingers. Deciding that it was edible, she ate her whole portion in a matter of seconds. Il-sun looked despondently at hers without taking a bite. The shock was too much.

Gyong-ho gawked as the van came into the heart of the throbbing city. Traffic weaved dangerously around them; the air was thick with exhaust and exotic smells; tall buildings scratched the turning sky. The cacophony was unlike anything she had ever heard before: engines revving, tires rolling on asphalt, the muffled bass lines of music emanating from countless vehicles. Sidewalks thronged with a disordered tangle of well-dressed people — not the stained, ragged, and groveling masses she had been led to imagine populating *Hanguk*. It was an unintelligible soup of activity. Where, in *Chosun,* there would have been gigantic signs proclaiming the superiority of the workers' paradise and the magnificence of the Great Leader, there were billboards paying tribute to soap and perfume and cars. All in all, it was a dizzying swirl of information too vast and complex to understand, even for the unusually gifted Gyong-ho. Where were the long, grim faces and pleading, desperate eyes?

Mr. Choy navigated the van to a less frenetic part of town, seemingly on the outskirts. Here the buildings were less well maintained, and rubbish collected in untended piles along the street, as if placed there by the eddying force of the wind. Here and there small groups of rough-looking young men stood surveying the street, their watchful eyes attuned to some shifting urban tide. In contrast to the heart of the city, this street had a dense quiet about it that felt more like the sound inside the barrel of a loaded gun waiting to go off.

It was afternoon when the minivan parked alongside a four-story building that was a cake of cracked concrete and dirty glass. Some of the windows were cracked or covered with cardboard. Cigarette butts and bottle caps littered the sidewalk in front. The building loomed, seeming too heavy for the plot of ground on which it stood. Gyong-ho half expected to see it sink. The women were ordered to get out of the van, and Mr. Lee led them to a dark entrance-way. There was an electronic keypad affixed to the wall next to an iron gate and he pressed a series of buttons. There was a buzzing sound and Mr. Lee pushed the gate open. Gyong-ho had never seen such a device, one that could unlock a door just by entering a code. Part of her mind held a detached fascination in spite of her fear. They followed Mr. Lee into a dark corridor, with Mr. Choy bringing up the rear. The corridor was heavy with stillness, and their shoes echoed off the concrete floor. There were unmarked doors on both sides that looked to Gi like shady sentinels with their backs turned, looking over their shoulders, hiding something.

They were led to a set of stairs at the end of the corridor and climbed to the fourth floor, Mr. Lee red-faced and out of breath. There was another metal gate at the top of the stairs, this time secured with a chain and padlock. A young man, who looked to be no older than twenty, with spiky black hair and thick silver and gold chains around his neck, was sitting on a stool behind the gate. He acknowledged Mr. Lee with a nod.

"We own the whole building," said Mr. Lee to no one in particular. It was an odd comment that seemed almost housewifely coming from such a brusque man. "This is Razor," he said, indicating the young man. "He's here for your . . . *protection.* If you need anything ask him." The young man with spiky hair nodded apathetically and withdrew a key from his pocket, unlocked the gate, and ushered the party inside. They were in a long corridor, similar to the one on the first floor, with doors on both sides. The doors scowled at Gyong-ho as she crossed the threshold of the gate — she counted six on each side. They were led to the third door on the left. Mr. Choy shepherded the women inside.

37

Gyong-ho found herself in the entranceway of a small apartment. Just inside the door was a short hallway, opening into a large room in which beige paint was peeling in the corners. The place was lit by a solitary window on the far wall, under which there was a small, round table with two chairs. To the right was a kitchenette, not really separate from the room, outfitted with a two-burner electric stove, a heavy, cast iron cooking pan, a stainless steel sink, and, to Gi's astonishment, a refrigerator. To the right of the kitchen was another, smaller room furnished with a European-style double bed, two pillows, and a couple of blankets. The apartment was a bit musty, but it was clean.

"We were only expecting two of you, so you will just have to make do with three of you in here," said Mr. Choy. "Toilets and showers are down the hall, but the door only opens from the outside. If you need to go, knock and Razor will let you out, one at a time. I'll bring some supplies when I return." With that, Mr. Choy turned on his heel, walked out of the apartment, and closed the door with a loud *bang.*

Beyond the terror of finding herself a prisoner in a foreign land and facing an uncertain future, there was an even deeper discomfort brewing inside Gyong-ho. She felt exposed and anxious in a way that she had never felt before. It was a heavy sense of guilt at being complicit in a terrible crime, and her conscience was pressing her to confess it. She cast a penitent look at the blank wall where the portraits of the Great Leader and the Dear Leader were supposed to be; neither had there been portraits at the entrance of the building as they came in. She had never been anywhere that did not have the venerable leaders watching over her. Not to have the portraits was one of the greatest felonies possible, the punishment of which she knew only too well. The apartment felt vast and empty without them, and she was afraid that the local *inminbanjang* might come with the secret police and take her away in the night. Without the portraits to look over her, and stripped of her Kim Il-sung pin, she felt vulnerable to the evils that raged in the world outside the Dear Leader's protection.

"These guys must be important," said Cho, seemingly unaware of the danger. "Look at this refrigerator!" The refrigerator was a small white cube. She bent over and opened it, and a light blinked on inside. Owning a refrigerator, or a television or electric fan, was one of the ultimate status symbols in *Chosun*. Only the very wealthy could afford them. The refrigerator was empty, but Cho put her hand inside it anyway to feel the wonder of the chilled air.

"I want to go home," Il-sun said quietly, coming out of her daze.

"This is home, teacup. The sooner you get used to that the better it will be for you," Cho replied.

"What do you think they want from us?" asked Gi.

"Haven't you figured that out yet?" Cho asked with sharp amusement.

Gi looked down in shame of her own ignorance.

"I can't do it. I won't!" Il-sun burst, and then began to sob.

"Do you think you're too good for that, teacup?" Cho's voice was full of ridicule. "What, did you think Gianni was going to take you away and marry you? What a fool!

Let me tell you about your
He sold you, sold us all, for
whiskey. The only person he c
himself. He's gone now, teac
forget about him. You're in the n
try now." Cho turned away from
walked toward the window. Il-su.
wailing and fell to the floor. Gyong-.
confused, not understanding the con
about the meat industry. She knelt ne.
Il-sun and draped her arms around her.

Cho looked out the window for a mome
thoughtfully, then she softened. She turne
and put her arms around the two girls on
the floor. "I'm sorry. I didn't mean to be
unkind. Look, we're in this situation now
and there isn't a lot we can do about it. I
was tricked too, and I feel angry about it.
But you heard Mr. Choy. If we work hard
we can pay off our debts; then eventually
we can either get papers or try to go back
home. I've been selling flowers for two years
now. You get used to it."

Cho's comment upset Il-sun more than it
comforted her, and she cried harder.
Gyong-ho was perplexed by the connection
between selling flowers and the meat industry. She wished Cho would stop speaking in
riddles, but she was too ashamed to ask for
clarification.

38

Il-sun was numb. First she had had the biggest fright of her life, fearing that she was going to be arrested for treason and all that that implied. Then there was the horror of having to flee the country and nearly being arrested at the checkpoint. It was all going to be okay, though, as long as she was with Gianni. She had been feeling a kind of giddiness lately that she had never known before, something biological, and possibly even spiritual. Whenever she saw him, her heart would race and her palms would begin to sweat. When he said her name, which was not often, she would quiver from someplace deep down — she might have been the only woman, or certainly the most important woman, in the world. Whatever the feeling, she no longer felt like a girl. He had promised to lift her out of mediocrity. He had promised that he would take care of her. He had promised so much. All of that *had* to

mean something, didn't it? Because her feelings for him were so strong, didn't he also have to feel that way about her? Gianni was supposed to be her man: It felt like destiny.

Love, in *Chosun,* was meant to be a partnership to benefit the glory of the state. Even the popular films portrayed love as a happy sort of friendship where the couple comes together in some revolutionary cause. Personal satisfaction and glory are an insignificant secondary element of love. For romance, one had to read between the lines. Even still, the married seamstresses at the factory would giggle knowingly and make vague, lurid references to the marriage bed. She had not understood those comments much, until recently.

But now the shock was too much. Gianni had deserted her — no, had sold her, to strange men in a foreign country. It was unimaginable. She retraced every moment she had spent with him to try to find where she had gone wrong. What had she done to upset him? Surely there was some inner failing that she could have mended, had she been aware of it, and he would not have been so eager to abandon her across the border, away from him forever. Had he meant none of the sweet promises he had whispered in her ear, the ones that had a way of undoing buttons and untucking blouses? Could a man lie about such sacred things?

The ride in the van from the DMZ was a blur. Even what must have been a fascinating glimpse of the imperialist-occupied South went unnoticed. Wave after wave of terror, grief, denial, and even moments of utter resignation had rippled through her; and the balance of those feelings was to feel nothing. There was no fight at all inside her. It had been drained out of her the moment Gianni broke her heart.

Someone handed her some food in a paper wrapper, and Gyong-ho encouraged her to eat it, but she could not. Hungry as she had been since her mother died, she could not open her stomach to it. The thought occurred to her that if she never ate again, she would die; and that seemed fine — a sweet relief. Even being shepherded into the building and taken up the stairs to a small apartment, she did not take in the details. It was not until the lock clicked shut behind her that the gravity of their situation began to take hold.

Il-sun had only the vaguest of notions why two *Hanguk* men would want to buy women. She was still so close to her innocence that it was almost easy to retreat back into it, but Cho brought that effort up short with her snappy innuendoes. The world now was much too big a place.

39

It was dusk when Mr. Choy and Mr. Lee returned, bringing with them a sack of rice, a few vegetables, canned food items, towels, and a bar of soap.

"Once we know we can trust you, we'll fix your doorknob so you can open the door from inside your room. You'll be able to use the toilet and go to the showers freely," Mr. Choy explained. "There is always someone at the gate and you are not to leave this floor unless you are chaperoned. For the time being, you will be doing most of your work in this building. We will bring you food and supplies."

"But we have to pay for them, right?" asked Cho.

"We will keep a running tab, and do all the accounting for you. Once you pay off your debts, as I have already said, then we will work on getting papers for you; but not before."

"How long will that take?" asked Il-sun.

"That all depends on you: how hard you work, what kind of work you do for us, what kind of a tab you run up, that sort of thing,"

"What are our choices for work?" asked Il-sun.

"For the two of you," he pointed to Il-sun and Cho, "there are more options because you're pretty." He then looked at Gi. "I'm still not quite sure what to do with you," he said. "What's your name?"

Gi's mumbled reply was unintelligible.

"What was that?"

"Her name is Gyong-ho," said Il-sun, scowling.

"Gyong-ho? A boy's name?"

"My parents wanted a boy," whispered Gi.

"Well, you don't have quite the looks that these two do. But there are still options."

"What *are* the options?" asked Cho, frustrated by his elusiveness.

"Okay, I'll spell it out. Have you bumpkins heard of the Internet?" He said the word *Internet* in English. They had not, so they shook their heads.

"The Internet is an information system that reaches around the world that people access using computers. You do know what computers are, don't you?"

They nodded.

"When you connect to the Internet, anything you want to know, you simply type it in and the information just pops right up, complete with pictures, sounds, and video."

The women looked incredulous. If such a thing existed, surely *Chosun,* the most advanced, sophisticated society in the world, would have it.

Mr. Choy chuckled woodenly. "I have seen this before with you Northerners. You think your culture is so superior, with your Great Leader and all, that you don't believe in anything you haven't seen before. I'll show you tomorrow. Anyway, there is a lot of money just floating around the Internet — people buying things all over the world. If there's one thing that's certain, sex sells. Men all over the world will pay good money to watch a pretty young girl take her clothes off. It's called a strip show."

"So all we have to do is take our clothes off for this . . . Internet?" asked Cho. Gi and Il-sun looked terrified.

"That's one option," Mr. Choy replied. "Of course, that doesn't pay as well as other things you could do."

"Such as?" Cho's frustration was apparent.

"Well, men will pay more if you're willing to do things for them, like if they ask you to touch your tits, and you do it for them in real time, right there on the Internet. Then, of course, you get paid more."

"Real time?" Gi was unaware that there could be a distinction between real time and any other time. *Could there be artificial time?*

"It's an Internet saying. It means it's happening right now and streaming on the Internet live." Mr. Choy could see that the women were still confused. "You'll understand it when you see it. But the fastest way to pay us back," he paused to make sure they were listening, "is to see private clients."

"What does that mean?" asked Il-sun, her face losing its color.

"You know what it means," snapped Cho severely. She folded her arms across her chest. Il-sun looked stung, and hung her head. Gyong-ho was confused. "So how much time, if we see 'private clients'?" Cho asked.

"Could be as little as six months, if you work hard."

"And if all we do is take our clothes off?"

"*Quite* a lot longer," Mr. Choy said enigmatically.

Cho looked away thoughtfully. Then she turned back to the two men and asked, "Do you have a cigarette?"

Mr. Lee reached into his pocket, withdrew a half-empty pack and handed it to her, along with a book of matches. Cho tapped the pack to remove a cigarette and lit it. She took two deep drags. Everyone stood in silence as the women absorbed the information.

"And what happens if we refuse?" Cho's arms were still folded across her chest, her clawlike hand clutching her cigarette.

Mr. Choy took on a hard, stern look, the hint of a dangerous rage rippling across his eyes. It was a look that said his friendly, accommodating exterior was a thin crust over a far more volatile core. He smiled wryly and said, "If you refuse to work for me, I will have no choice but to hand you over to the American army, who will rape, torture, and kill you. Of course, the choice is yours."

As dusk gave way to night, the alleyway below came to life. Bright lights lit up the walls of the building next door and flooded the apartment with a red glow. The street outside, which had been relatively quiet during the day, teemed with vehicles. Loud music was emanating from somewhere nearby, a driving bass line and pounding drums causing the apartment to pulse and vibrate. For Gyong-ho, the sound was overwhelming and made her anxious.

The activity within the building increased after dark as well. The gate guarded by Razor opened regularly, hinges squeaking, and closed with a bang. Voices drifted up and down the hallway and doors slammed. Male laughter cut through the thin walls. In the apartment next door there was a rhythmic slamming of something hard against their adjoining wall. A woman groaned loudly over and over again, sighing and calling out. A man grunted wildly into the night.

Il-sun, Gyong-ho, and Cho were exhausted from lack of sleep. The women bedded down in the small European-style bed, Cho and Gi on the outsides with Il-sun in the middle. It was a tight fit, even for three small women, and they lay with their arms around one another for lack of anywhere else to put them. Gi enjoyed the closeness with Il-sun and was comforted to inhale her sweet scent. She had not showered — none of them had because they were afraid to ask to leave the apartment — and there was an earthy pungency to Il-sun's sweetness that Gi liked. She smelled real and alive, almost animal. In spite of her exhaustion, Gi could not sleep. *Chosun* nights were quiet and dark, even in the city, and the constant

267

intrusion of sounds was too much for her. The apartment felt vulnerable without portraits of the Great and Dear Leaders to protect them.

As Gyong-ho lay there with her eyes closed, she listened with wonder to the sound of traffic. She could hear layers of traffic, in an endless radius, like floating in a vast sea of motors and tires and horns. It was as spectacular as it was terrifying. Finally, about an hour before dawn, she fell into a fitful sleep.

40

Mr. Choy awoke at eleven, the whore still passed out in his bed. *At least she didn't puke on the satin sheets,* he thought to himself. His mouth was dry and tasted like gin, so he put on a silk robe. His apartment was long, and each footfall jarred his aching head as he padded his way to the kitchen at the other end. It was very modern, crisp, and clean — almost industrial — made of stainless steel and glass, exposed iron beams and concrete. The length of the apartment offered large picture windows with a spectacular view of downtown Seoul. Business was good. He poured himself a tall glass of orange juice from a carton, and drank it back in one lift of his arm. The fog on his brain lifted a little.

Training day. That's what he always called the day after a new shipment of girls arrived. It meant a lot of work, and probably some kicking and screaming. *You never can tell how a girl will take to the business,* he thought. *Some take to it like fish to water, others never get the hang of it.* Most of the girls Gianni delivered were inexperienced and naïve. A lot of the younger ones were still virgins, and he doubted whether some of them even knew what sex was. But what could he expect from Northerners? He much preferred dealing with career sluts, girls who came to the business on their own, but the profit margin was lower. They always demanded payment. It was worth putting up with a little kicking and screaming from the North Koreans.

He wished Gianni would stop getting them so young, but the price was right and he normally had good taste. With the exception of the twisted, scrawny one. What was the story with her? *It doesn't really matter,* he thought. *There is a niche market for girls like that.* "Never neglect your niche market, and be prepared to diversify," his business professor used to say.

A groaning sound came from his bedroom, and a moment later the naked, bedraggled whore came shuffling into the kitchen. Her black hair was a chaotic, lopsided nest and there was a pained look in her makeup-smeared eyes. He was confused for a moment — he thought he had come home with the tall one with the flower tattoo. Not that it mattered.

"Put some clothes on and get out of here," Mr. Choy said dismissively.

"I need some money," she replied through the agony of her hangover.

If I were a different sort of man, I would have hit her for that, he thought. *I shouldn't have to pay her — I'm her boss. But I never hit women, unless I have to. I respect them, as long as they know their place.* "I was too drunk to get it up," he said, wondering if it was true.

"I need money for the bus."

Mr. Choy rolled his eyes and went to a desk. He got a handful of *won* from a drawer and shoved it into her fist. "Don't spend this on drugs," he said, though he doubted she would follow his advice — he would not have. She turned and went back to the bedroom, presumably to retrieve her clothes.

He turned his thoughts back to the new *Chosun* girls. He was not looking forward to training day. It was sometimes such a struggle. It might be quicker if he just beat the girls into submission, but he preferred subtle manipulation to violent coercion to get his way. It took longer, but girls always performed better if they felt they had some control over their situation. Not that he was above violence, if it was necessary — that was what Mr. Lee was for. But he felt that if the girls reached the conclusion on their own that whoring was their best option, and they believed that they could work their way out of it if they did what was asked of them, then they ended up being better prostitutes; ergo: more profit over a longer term. It was a simple business strategy, and yet he was astounded at how few men in his position understood that, preferring to bludgeon their whores to exact the desired behavior. Then again, he had studied business at the university.

The Northerners were particularly easy in this regard. They were already so disoriented and fearful of "imperialists" and Americans that controlling them was a simple matter of telling them that they would be turned over to the American army for torture if they disobeyed. It was an extremely effective lie. Truthfully, if they were to escape they would be welcomed as defectors by the government; but there was not much danger of their finding that out, being under lock and key.

The door slammed as the whore left his apartment. *I hope she didn't steal anything,* he thought.

41

It was early afternoon when Mr. Choy and Mr. Lee arrived at the women's apartment. They entered without knocking — Mr. Choy liked to be firmly in control. He knew his chances of getting them to comply willingly were better if they were on edge. He brought with him some takeout from a local restaurant — showing a kind side would make them more eager to please him. He wanted them to associate his presence with the smell of food. *Just like training a dog,* he thought. He knew that the women would have slept poorly, and they would be bored and nervous from being locked up for so long. They would welcome his visit just to break the monotony. So it was important to enter with a smile, show interest in their well-being, and downplay their captivity.

"Good afternoon, girls!" he said cheerfully. He swooped into the apartment, Mr. Lee waddling in behind him, and placed the cardboard takeout cartons on the table. "I've brought food from one of my favorite restaurants. Dig in!"

The girls looked at him, uncertainty and fear in their eyes.

"Don't be shy. It's good, and I know you must be hungry."

"How much is this going to cost us?" asked the one with the long fingernails, looking skeptical.

"No, no! It's a gift from me and Mr. Lee. It won't go on your tab. Think of it as a welcoming gift," Mr. Choy replied, a syrupy smile dripping upward on his cheeks.

The women timidly approached the table and peered into the cartons. There were noodles with chicken and vegetables, pork stew, kimchee and rice. The food smelled wonderful and their mouths were watering. Mr. Lee went to a cupboard and found three plates and some chopsticks, and handed them to the women. They dove into the food hungrily, sitting on the floor while Mr. Choy and Mr. Lee watched.

"Were you comfortable last night?" Mr. Choy asked, wicking a note of concern into his voice, knowing full well that they were not. The women looked at him without saying anything. He knew that they would be afraid of voicing complaint, because doing so in the North would have landed them in trouble. "The bed was probably a little small for the three of you. Was it too small?"

There was a long, expectant pause. Finally his eyes met the eyes of the prettiest girl, and she nodded.

"Mr. Lee, they have insufficient bedding. Make a note: We need to bring them another bed and some more blankets." Mr. Lee drew a small notepad and a pen from his pocket and began to write. "Is there anything else you need?" There was another long pause as the women looked at each other. "Anything at all? A fan, perhaps? It's a little stuffy in here. Mr. Lee, put a fan on the list." A fan was considered a luxury item in the North, available only to the elite. They never would have thought to ask for it, so by suggesting it he was reinforcing his generosity. *How easy it must be,* he thought, *to be the Dear Leader.*

"We can't afford these things, if you're charging us for them," said the one with the fingernails, frowning.

"Don't worry about that. Soon you'll be making plenty of money. Really, you have no idea how easy it is here." The women looked at one another, a shiver of fear passing through them. Seeing their reluctance, he said, "You have nothing to worry about.

You'll have more than enough food, a safe place to live, and the work isn't very hard. I think you're going to like it here. Trust me: I have helped a lot of girls in your same situation. Before you know it, you'll be on your own and you can do what you like. In the meantime, enjoy yourselves! Have fun with it."

There was a long, quiet pause while he allowed what he said to sink in.

"We need a chamber pot," burst the one with the long fingernails, becoming bolder. "Since we can't leave the room on our own. I had to bang on the door for fifteen minutes before Razor finally let me out last night."

"Okay, we'll get you something."

"And we need another chair," she said.

"Alright, did you get that, Mr. Lee? Another chair. Anything else?"

The women remained silent.

"Alright. Mr. Lee, would you please go and collect the things on your list for these ladies?" Mr. Lee made a quick bow and left with his list in hand. "I have a treat for you," he said after Mr. Lee made his exit. "I've hired, at my own expense, a beautician to come and give you all makeovers."

"What's a makeover?" asked the pretty one.

"*Hanguk* women *love* them. The beautician will fix your hair, paint your nails, and do your makeup. Then she is going to dress you in some fancy clothes. You'll be beautiful *and* glamorous."

42

Gyong-ho had slept fitfully for a few hours. When she awoke she did not feel refreshed. She washed her face and hands with soap and water and then dared to look out the window for the first time. Below was a narrow alleyway strewn with rubbish. There appeared to be some sort of shop below, but from the sharp angle of her vantage point she could not see what it was. The narrow bit of sky that she could see was blue and cloudless. The morning progressed with the same tense boredom that had dominated the previous afternoon in captivity.

In the early afternoon, Mr. Choy and Mr. Lee arrived with food. Gi had never had food from a restaurant before, except for the unusual lunch from the previous day. It came in curious cardboard packaging, and there was enough to feed six people, even though only the three women were eating. It was still warm and flooded the musty apartment with comforting and delicious smells. The dishes were full of meat and alive with flavor. It was the best food she had ever eaten. So far, South Korea was full of contradictions.

Mr. Choy was being overly friendly, which was in contrast to his businesslike detachment of the day before. This made Gyong-ho suspicious. He seemed interested in their comfort, and promised to bring them furnishings. She would have preferred to have photos of the Great and Dear Leaders to hang on the wall, but she had been afraid to ask. She felt a pang of sadness about the bed, because it would mean that she would no longer have an excuse to hold Il-sun while she slept.

Later a young woman arrived carrying a plastic bin of supplies. She was short with long, black hair pulled back and secured with a stylish barrette. She wore tight blue jeans, a plain, light-blue blouse, and black, flat-soled slippers. She had a stony, expressionless face and spoke in monosyllables, and averted her eyes from theirs. She instructed the women to shower in preparation for their makeovers, and led them down the hall to the door just opposite the restroom. The room was tiled from floor to ceiling, and there was a drain in the floor. Four showerheads protruded from one of the walls, each with corresponding controls. The women stripped, leaving their clothes and towels on a bench provided for that purpose.

Having grown up in a girls' dormitory, Gi was not typically bashful about taking her clothes off in front of other women; but in this circumstance, because of the trauma of their ordeal and the sense of exposure she felt in their new surroundings, she felt the need to cover her chest with her arms. She was now seeing her body as a thing to be viewed and judged. She became aware that there might be a good and bad when it came to bodies, and she was fearful that hers would not measure up. What was it that Mr. Choy said? *"Well, you don't have quite the looks that these two do."* She watched as Cho and Il-sun stepped up to the showers, bodies tapering gracefully from shoulders to waists, hips elegantly flaring, buttocks rising in smooth mounds, long, sculptural legs ending at dainty, perfect feet.

She had appreciated the bodies of other girls, but never before as a comparison to her own. Her own legs were skinny and bony, her feet appearing too large. Her body twisted slightly to the left, and her left shoulder hung lower than her right. Her hips did not flare seductively, but came up straight from her sticklike legs. Her chest caved in, dented on the right side where a prison guard had slammed her with a rifle when she was nine. Her nipples had gotten larger in the last few years, but her breasts had not, remaining mere bumps protruding from her rib cage. With these observations came the thought that she may be somehow less desirable, less lovable, because of her body; and that made her profoundly sad.

"Gi, get in here. The water comes out warm!" exclaimed Il-sun. She was the girl Il-sun, not the woman, calling almost playfully to her friend. It brought Gi out of her maudlin thoughts.

Gyong-ho stepped into the shower. It was a thing of wonder. It was controlled by a knob at navel height, and as she turned it, water shot from the showerhead in fifty-two tiny streams. As she continued turning the knob, the water got progressively warmer. She had known about heated water for bathing, but she never believed that she would ever get to experience it like this. She turned the knob so that it was all the way to the hot side and stepped into the stream, allowing the heat and pressure of the water to loosen her muscles below her skin. Her body relaxed and the tension of captivity was momentarily forgotten. Il-sun passed her a bar of soap, which was super-bright white and lathered easily as she rubbed it with her hands. She reached up to work some of the soap into her dirty hair, but Cho stopped her.

"No, use this," Cho said, smiling and handing her a pink plastic bottle. "It's real shampoo!" For the first time, Cho was not a caricature — the thick makeup had washed off her face and she looked her age: nineteen. Gi put the bar of soap on a ledge and poured some shampoo into the palm of her hand. It came out as a thick, rose-colored ooze. It had a sweet, floral smell that made her think of summertime, and it foamed up deliciously as she worked it into her hair.

The women lingered in the shower, savoring the heat, carefully scrubbing every part of their bodies. When finally their hands and feet had become wrinkled from the water, they turned off the showers and toweled off. Not wanting to put their dirty clothes back on their clean bodies, they wrapped themselves in their towels and went back to their apartment.

In their absence, the young woman had set up a chair in the light of the window and arranged an array of bottles, jars, tubes, and brushes on the table. She instructed Il-sun to sit in the chair, and gave Cho and Gyong-ho a pile of magazines to read while they waited.

Cho and Gi sat on the floor and began looking through them. The magazine in Gi's hand was so glossy that it was sticky, and it was full of all kinds of unusual images and words. It was overwhelming to her senses: the tackiness of the paper, the bombardment of colors and shapes, the discordant smell of too many different types of perfume wafting up from the pages. There were words in Korean, but also occasional Chinese characters and foreign words that Gi could not read. Each page seemed to compete with every other page for her undivided attention. Advertisements were unheard of in *Chosun,* so it was difficult for Gyong-ho to grasp the concept of what they were. Cho said that the pictures were sexy, but Gi did not fully understand what she meant. They certainly caused her to feel strongly. Maybe that strong feeling was "sexy." She did notice that, without fail, every photograph showed people with regular features and lithe, strong bodies. Their faces were free of blemishes, their teeth perfect, and their eyes clear. Their clothes looked expensive and well matched, albeit, in many cases, oddly styled and immodest.

Want was a sensation that, for Gyong-ho, had been mostly relegated to the desire for food. But now, looking at the pictures, there was a new kind of want. She found herself wishing she could have a watch, and fancy shoes, and rounder eyes, and fuller lips. Want was like a fire catching inside her, getting out of control as she turned the pages. To want, she knew, could be dangerous: Wanting leads to asking for something you do not have, which is as good as telling the Dear Leader that he is not providing well enough for his beloved people. *Wanting is treason.*

She dropped the magazine.

Not once, on any of the pages, was there a reference to the Dear Leader. The articles did not begin with a preamble of gratitude for his beneficence and wisdom, nor were there any photographs of him. She became fearful that somehow the Dear Leader might know that she had perused the imperialist magazines, that she had wanted something beyond her reach, that she had enjoyed a hot water shower and not given him proper thanks. She was afraid that because of his disappointment in her, secret police would come in the night and steal her away. She was suddenly very much aware of her captivity and felt wrenched by homesickness. She missed the regularity of her days: the orphanage, walking to work with Il-sun, the fearsome foreman, the Party Youth meetings. She wanted to see Mr. Choy right away and beg him to take her back. But Mr. Choy would never do it. And now her life was hanging in unbearable uncertainty.

"They will never know, teacup," said Cho. She must have been struggling with the same thoughts. Gi was unsure which would be worse: Their knowing, or the idea that no one would ever know.

The beautician worked on Il-sun for over an hour, cutting and styling her hair, cleaning and painting her fingernails and toenails, and doing her makeup. When she was finished, Il-sun looked like a page out of one of the imperialist magazines. There was not a single blemish that could be seen. Her lips were a deep shade of red, painted in a pouty kiss, her cheekbones defined by a touch of shadow. Her hair had been cut to shoulder length, curled, and clipped up in the back. She looked ten years older: twenty-seven rather than seventeen. Gyong-ho wanted to place her on a pedestal in the window and sit for hours watching the sunlight pass over her beautiful face. The young woman offered Il-sun a hand mirror.

"Is that really me?" she asked. Il-sun shifted the angle of the mirror and inspected herself from all sides. She lingered for a long time, watching herself as she changed her expressions: smiling, scowling, flirting. She seemed captured by her own beauty, as if in looking at herself the whole rest of the world simply melted away. It was a clue into Il-sun's personality, Gi realized, an explanation of her embodied contradictions: self-admiration. When she flirted and teased and made the whole world want her, she was really only admiring herself through the eyes of other people.

Cho went next, though she was less patient for the process and pressed the beautician to be quick. Even so, at the end of it she looked more mature and sophisticated. The beautician's makeup style was less heavy-handed than Cho's, and she came out looking almost demure, rather than like a carica-tured flower-selling girl, her normal look. The beautician did not bother cutting Cho's hair because of her restlessness, but instead pulled the front of her hair back and plaited it down the back of her head, giving her an innocence that Gi never would have guessed was possible.

When it was Gi's turn, she sat in the chair nervously as the beautician applied various creams to her face. The beautician looked at her from different angles, puckering her lips and knitting her brow in concentration, and then wetted Gi's hair and began selectively snipping at it with sharp scissors. She then used a blow dryer — a contraption that was unheard of in *Chosun* — and styled her hair. She sprayed Gi's hair with something from a can and instructed her not to touch it. After the haircut, the beautician busied herself applying makeup to Gi's face. Gi had never worn makeup before, and she enjoyed the way it was applied, with light brushes, soft swabs, and pencils. The beautician held up several tubes of lipstick, comparing their colors with Gi's complexion. She settled on a frosty pink and daubed it on gently, and then told Gi to roll her lips together. The lipstick tasted a little like crushed flower stems, but in a pleasant way. The beautician cleaned and filed Gi's fingernails and toenails, digging into the nail beds to scrape away embedded grime. At times the sharp end of the tool jabbed painfully, but even that was pleasant. She then brushed on several layers of polish that matched the color of her lipstick. When the beautician was done, she handed Gi the mirror.

Gi could not believe that she was looking

at herself. Her pale skin glowed with warmth. The liner and shadow around her eyes made them stand out in a pleasing way. The blush on her cheeks altered the shape of her cheekbones so that she no longer had a drawn look. It was a miraculous illusion and she understood why Il-sun had been so captivated by herself. Looking in the mirror, Gi saw herself as almost pretty. She was certainly more feminine.

"Wow, Gi! Look at you!" Il-sun exclaimed. Gyong-ho couldn't help but smile.

43

Mr. Choy was sitting at a desk in his office, observing the live streaming of a dozen sex shows on a monitor. Frankly, he was bored. This was not where he had imagined himself being at the age of thirty-six — he had had such high aspirations. When he was eighteen he had been accepted to an American university. It was the most exciting time of his life. He left his home in Seoul a vigorous and promising teenager with the dream of graduating with honors, starting a corporation of his own, and having his picture on the cover of *Forbes* magazine by the time of his thirtieth birthday. But things had not gone according to plan.

He arrived at the University of Washington in Seattle looking very out of place in a business suit and tie. His hair was conservatively trimmed above his ears and he spoke textbook-perfect English. He had thought that these things would help him win friends and impress his teachers, but they only made him a target for ridicule from the shaggy, tightly muscled fraternity boys who prowled the campus. He had not been warned of the shock and loneliness of living in a foreign country without friends or family nearby. American movies had not prepared him for the reality of living among Americans, with their loud, brash manners and disrespectful airs, or their heavy, fatty, overly sweet foods. His first year in the States, his face was a greasy terrain of acne and his own odor offended him.

Timid and lonely, a stranger to everyone, Mr. Choy wandered the streets near the campus during his free time, looking for some form of solace. One day, he happened upon a dollar cinema not far from the university. He loved movies and he needed an escape, and the price of admission fit his student budget. He purchased a ticket to what he thought was a popular film; the title certainly had been similar to the one he had seen on posters around town. He realized his mistake soon after the film started — an understandable confusion with a play on words — and he almost rushed out of the theater in embarrassment. He had grown up a very proper young man. Once the action started, however, he could not take his eyes off the screen. He stayed, and in the dark anonymity of the theater he discovered something about himself: He loved pornography. In Korea, women had been chaste, untouchable creatures from fairy tales who giggled behind their hands and turned away from him. It always felt like they were laughing at him, and it made him feel small. He was shy and had never been on a date. He did not even really know what a woman looked like without her clothes on — he was a late bloomer.

He became a regular at the dollar cinema. It fascinated him. He enjoyed seeing all the parts of women that were normally shielded from view. He loved watching them be penetrated and pleasured in all the many different ways women can be penetrated and pleasured — it opened a whole new world to him. He even harbored a fantasy of becoming a director of pornographic films, though he did not take it very seriously; he still had a plan for success and intended to see it through.

Mr. Choy finished his degree, a business major with a minor in computer science — not with honors, as he had hoped, but well enough. He expected that the American business world would prove more disciplined and open to his talents than the university had been. He had a million bright ideas and boundless energy: Certainly one of the large corporations was bound to snap him up and make him a star. Rejection, however, was around every corner. The rich brats who failed the same courses in which he had earned As and Bs were getting high-paying jobs in companies owned by their fathers or their fathers' friends while doors were repeatedly slammed in his face. For an unknown, unconnected Korean kid the gates to success seemed closed.

At the time, an underground Internet porn community was beginning to develop in Seattle. The Internet was just taking off as a common household service, and more people than ever were using computers to explore the world. Terms like *downloading, uploading, cyberspace,* and *virtual reality* were becoming commonplace. With his background in computers and his penchant for porn, and because nothing else was working out for him, Mr. Choy was poised to enter the business at just the right time. Pornography, it seemed, had found its ideal medium in the Internet.

Having been the model business student, he put together a stellar business plan using sound statistical data to show the profit potential of a website he hoped to launch.

He needed only startup capital, and not even much of that. So, taking the textbook approach, he went to the bank. His project would have been given the green light for sure — the business plan was perfect — except for one sticking point: The banks were not keen on the idea of funding a pornographic endeavor. "It just isn't the right image for our bank," he heard over and over again as he was being shown the door.

Frustrated and defeated, he set up a meeting with Uncle Lyong. Lyong Chung-min, the leader of the Korean organized crime syndicate Blue Talon, had a reputation for rough dealing, violent extraction of moneys owed to him, and outright extortion. It was difficult to be Korean in Seattle and not have some dealing with Uncle Lyong, though most everyone tried to avoid it. The most disturbing part of meeting him was his amiability. He spoke to Mr. Choy in soothing, familiar tones as if he were a favorite son rather than a complete stranger he would be willing to cripple over an unpaid loan. Nervously, Mr. Choy pitched his idea with the same professionalism he had used at the banks. It was unnecessary. Uncle Lyong did not care what he was funding. His business was in extracting exorbitant interest under the threat of bodily injury — he knew he would get his money, one way or the other. Uncle Lyong reassured Mr. Choy that he was "in the family now." Mr. Choy did not find this reassuring.

Mr. Choy did the numbers, and even with the excessive interest on the loan, his website would clear a nice profit. Blue Talon proved to be a valuable resource for a pornographic upstart, with its connection to prostitution and the naked, desperate underworld that feeds on such industry. It was a nice symbiosis.

The problems started occurring after Mr. Choy made his final loan payment to Uncle Lyong. He had assumed that he was now clear of Blue Talon, and could build his business as he saw fit. He still had plans to branch out and develop his more legitimate corporation. But he was wrong. The debt was cleared, they agreed, but there were other fees for "services" that had to be paid out regularly. The main service turned out to be the *not* breaking of his legs with an iron pipe; which, when it came down to it, he was willing to pay for. Mr. Choy could hardly complain; he was still making money hand over fist, and Uncle Lyong was quick to point that out to him. Still, he craved autonomy.

When, finally, Mr. Choy had made enough money, he decided to move back to Korea and start over. As a "gift" to Uncle Lyong, he handed over his website and all its future profits. He believed he would not have been able to walk away, literally, if he had offered anything less in tribute. Korea was just enough behind in its Internet marketplace development, a trend that would not last for long, for Mr. Choy to once again find himself ahead of the curve, and he quickly established himself as the king of the Seoul Internet porn industry. It turned out that profitability was even higher, because his general overhead was much lower; not to mention that he no longer had to pay Blue Talon's fees.

With his first taste of success, Mr. Choy hungered for more. It was not enough just to make money. He needed to make more of it, no matter how much of it he made. And making money was easy. Mr. Choy realized that the difference between building a business and building an empire is that a business spends much of its time and energy managing its supply line, while an empire focuses on dominating the whole market by owning its supply line. When it came down to it, his commodity was girls; and to become a major player in his market he needed to own all aspects of the girl industry: Internet porn, porn videos, dirty magazines, brothels, and strip clubs. But to truly own his supply line, he also needed to own the girls.

That is how Mr. Choy started dealing in refugees. When he first started out in Korea, he worked mostly with known prostitutes and drug addicts, or other women who were just plain desperate for cash. They entered into the business quite willingly, but they always demanded payment. This cut painfully into his profits. His business professor had said, "Always look for ways to cut the overhead." And that is what he did.

One day, quite by chance, he happened upon two defectors from North Korea — a mother and teenage daughter. They had just arrived, telling an unlikely story of fleeing across the DMZ. They were filthy, frightened, and hungry and had no place to go. They had fled their home in a border village in the North because they were afraid that the daughter had been heard saying something disparaging about the regime. They said that their *songbun* was already bad, and they were scared of being sent to a forced labor camp. They were terrified of what would happen to them if they were caught, and they begged him for shelter. They would do anything, they said. Mr. Choy smelled opportunity.

He told the women that he would be willing to hide them and keep them safe from both Kim Jong-il and the American army, their two biggest fears, as long as they would work for him as prostitutes. Seeing no other option, they quickly complied. They never asked for money, not realizing how central money is in a capitalist society. In the communist North, except on the black market, money was a formality; the bulk of items were distributed with ration cards. The women were accustomed to austerity, so it was inexpensive to feed them, and they were content to live in a back corner of a warehouse, which cost him nothing. They were not the most attractive whores, but they worked hard and had plenty of customers. Once they were worn out, he was able to sell them off as wives to desperate farmers. From a business perspective, it was an exceptional return on his investment.

Mr. Choy's business mind recognized an untapped resource, and he used his associates in the black market to set up trade across the DMZ. It was a crazy idea, and that is why it worked. "Be willing to try the untested idea," his professor used to say.

"Challenge the assumption." It was assumed that the DMZ was a flawless barrier, and no one in his right mind would attempt to bridge it. Trading across the DMZ turned out to be surprisingly easy, once he found the right channels to go through. He had to bribe a colonel in the South Korean army, who was happy to divert patrols from specified locations for unlimited "companionship" in Mr. Choy's sex gallery. Because of the political situation between the two countries, North Korea was suffering heavy trade embargoes, severely limiting the availability of luxury items. The people in power did not like being deprived — it undermined their authority — so it was easy to find high-level North Korean officials who were willing to pave the way for the black market on that side of the DMZ. He was put in touch with a wormy young man who, for some reason, liked to be called Gianni. Gianni was already doing a brisk trade in liquor, cigarettes, and dirty magazines using abandoned invasion tunnels that had been built by the North. Gianni readily agreed to bring attractive young women across the border to Mr. Choy, and they came to a price that was agreeable to both of them. Mr. Choy's overall output and risk were low, but his profits were high. His professors at the university would have been proud.

A knock at the door startled Mr. Choy from his reminiscing. In walked the beautician, with the three Northerners in tow.

44

Cho had never expected to amount to much. She went to all the meetings, prostrated to photographs when it was appropriate, gave the rote adulations and self-criticisms, but she never really tried to advance herself. Why bother? Her *songbun* had been bad to begin with, and to even think about overcoming it she would need some exceptional, nearly superhuman skill *and* connections to someone important; she had neither. Her grandmother was Japanese, and though she had been considered loyal enough to avoid the purging of suspicious persons, her family continued to bear the mark of shame. As a girl, Cho had all the usual fantasies: She would marry an officer high in the ranks of the Dear Leader's army, have a baby, or maybe two, and do something great for the glory of *Chosun*. Early enough, however, it became clear that that life was not meant for her. Her parents discouraged such hopes, believing it was better for their daughter to know the truth — that she would marry a factory or farm laborer, that she would always be under greater scrutiny because of her ancestry, and she would always be passed up by opportunity.

Food had been scarce for almost as long as she could remember. She and her mother often foraged for hours in the hills; and almost as often came back empty-handed, having found only enough to sustain the effort of looking. In the worst of times they ate unimaginable things, and suffered bellyache as a result. The outcomes of their desperate experimentations were nearly more lethal than the hunger that eroded them day after day.

Cho learned, at the dawning of her teenage years, that she did have a single asset, and that asset could provide at least something to abate the hunger. She was blessed with regular features and flawless skin. Her teeth came in straight and white, and her eyes were well set and proportioned for her face. She was not the prettiest of the pretty girls, but she knew how to be cute; and cuteness, she learned, could be leveraged for food. A disarming smile well timed could yield a dumpling, or a bite of kimchee, or a piece of fruit. It was not enough to put extra flesh on her skinny frame, but at least it kept her from eating grubs.

Cuteness in a girl gives way to something else as her body matures, and there came a time when a smile was no longer enough for the dumpling man to give up one of his precious morsels. *A feel. Just a feel. You'll like it, too.* And then just a feel, too, became not enough. The day Cho lost her virginity to the dumpling man, he gave her three whole dumplings — one for each member of her family. In that moment she felt the remaining ember of the girlhood fantasy of the soldier, the baby, and the glory of *Cho-sun* smolder and go cold inside her. This path of survival, and that path of happiness, did not cross.

Cho was able to provide a little bit for her family this way. They never asked, and she never told. She brought home scraps of food and everyone lived — not happily, but with hearts that beat and lungs that drew in air. She did what she did gladly, because it meant beating death. But one day, a friend of her father's happened upon her in an alley when she was working for a small bag of flour. She begged him not to tell, but he went with the news to her father anyway. To save face, her father threw her out. She was only seventeen.

Cho hardened like steel around the deep ache of her excommunication. She had nowhere to go, but shamed and outcast, she could no longer stay in her parents' village. She risked going into the city without having the proper papers, and when a soldier threatened to arrest her for it, she bought her freedom with the only "currency" she had. The man was a dealer of identities, his position as a railway guard granting him access to the pockets of the hundreds of unclaimed corpses that collected in train stations, and he set her up with papers he had taken off a dead girl of the same age. Cho Soo-yun was an orphan who eventually succumbed to hunger on the street. Her family had all perished as well, so there would be no one who would know the difference. It felt wrong to use the girl's personal name, Soo-yun, Perfect Lotus Blossom, as if she might come back from the dead to reclaim it; and besides, she could not live up to such a name. She decided to go only by the family name instead.

Cho was able to slip seamlessly into the girl's "official" life, joining her Party Youth organization and taking over her ration cards. No one had seen the girl for several years, and the story she gave of having survived a prolonged sickness was plausible. There was never any plan for the future, only a plan to live until the end of the day. She worked in the alleys and slept wherever. She ate. Never much, but enough to stay alive.

She met Gianni through the usual channels. Spending time with his crowd always led to extra scraps and crumbs. He had an endless supply of cigarettes, and he sometimes brought her exotic makeup and clothing. He was good looking, more because of his confidence and abundance than because of his features. Sometimes she fantasized that one day she and he would —

But she always knew that that was what it was. Pure fantasy. Still, she had never expected this kind of betrayal from him. She thought she had become immune to this kind of hurt. The street had hardened her, but maybe not enough.

Living is to go forward. Shed the past as easily as you would shed a coat.

These were her mottos. She knew she could withstand anything.

45

Mr. Choy sat behind his desk appraising the new girls from the North. They had cleaned up very well, even the skinny, twisted one — she was almost pretty. Having them professionally made over was a tactic to distract them from their fears and misgivings about their new living and working arrangement. It gave them a sense of luxury and abundance that they most certainly never felt before, which would soften their resistance to their new life. It also enabled Mr. Choy to assess their maximum earning potential. He had to come up with a value for each woman, and that value was based mostly on how she looked.

The beautician had done well in choosing outfits for them. The pretty one with the heart-shaped face was stunning, with her hair clipped up in the back and several well-placed rogue strands framing the sides of her face. The makeup erased the childish softness that was still in evidence on her teenage face, giving her a maturity that was not really there. Her lips were painted in a seductive, dark red kiss. She was dressed in a black, ankle-length gown held delicately on her shoulders by thin satin straps. Her full bosom filled in the top of her dress, the inner slopes of her breasts rising out of the garment, as tempting as low-hanging fruit. The dress tapered at the waist, and then flared with the natural curves of her hips. It was slit up both sides all the way to the upper thigh, and exposed, in moments, the tantalizing shape of her legs as she walked. It was a view that promised much but revealed little. She was adorned with black high-heeled shoes made of straps that crisscrossed elegantly over her feet and around her ankles. She teetered a little as she walked, obviously needing more practice walking in them. Her toenails were painted a dark red to match her lips and gave Mr. Choy the sense that she might be edible from floor to ceiling. She would be a good earner.

The one with the long fingernails was wearing a royal blue velvet dress that came down just above her midthighs. It fit loosely, but suggested the shape of her body well when she moved. The beautician had outfitted her with a padded bra to augment her shape, to great effect. As she moved about the dress lifted up, revealing the tops of her black thigh-high stockings, clipped to an unseen garter belt above. It was the perfect touch of provocateur to an otherwise classy look. Her shoes were closed at the toe and squared off, with tall, blocky heels and square buckles attached to straps in the front. Her face was clean and pretty, the sides of her hair pulled back and braided.

The smaller girl with the crooked body was the most transformed of the three. Her hair was styled with flourish, countering the length of her face, which was too long. The makeup did wonders for her color and brought attention to her eyes, which sparkled. One would not call her pretty, but she had an interesting face that grew in appeal the more he looked at it. *She might do well on the Internet, from selective angles,* he thought. *She will probably look better in two dimensions.* The beautician had cleverly concealed the girl's stick-like proportions by outfitting her in a peach colored, floor-length Chinese dress with a high collar and half-length sleeves, and a subtle pattern woven into it with silver threads that glinted in the light. The dress was slit up one side to the knee, showing just enough skin to make a person curious. It did a pretty good job of hiding the girl's asymmetries. On her feet she was wearing simple flat-soled black slippers. *On second thought, she might do better entertaining drunk sailors and college kids at the club,* he thought. *Where it's dark.*

The women looked nervous.

"You ladies look wonderful!" he exclaimed, spreading his arms. Now was the time to be charming. "Turn around so I can get a better look at you."

The women looked at each other timidly.

"Come, now. I won't hurt you."

The pretty one stepped forward awkwardly in her shoes, pale with terror, and turned around.

"Very nice!" Mr. Choy complimented. "You look just like a movie star! Now you," he nodded at the sassy one with long fingernails.

She did not move, but cut him a fierce look. His face darkened suddenly.

"I'm not asking, I'm telling. Turn your ass around," he said through gritted teeth. He swallowed to keep from becoming irate. His temper tended to flare.

The sassy one stepped forward, more confidently than the pretty one had, but no better in her heels. She spun around quickly. Then the crooked girl did the same. Mr.

Choy composed himself again, putting on a mask of absolute civility.

"I want to show you something," he said to the women. He dismissed the beautician with an impatient hand gesture. The girls watched with uneasy expressions as she left them. "I promised that I would show you the Internet today. Get behind me and watch." He sat down again at his desk and turned on a computer. The girls crowded in behind him, more from fearful obedience than curiosity. "Just about anything you can think of is on the Internet, and you can access it instantly. You see this blinking line? All we have to do is type something there and hit the Enter key, and bang! Ten thousand related articles will come up. What do you want to look up?" he asked, already knowing the answer.

"The Great Leader, Kim Il-sung," responded the crooked girl as if by reflex. It was the same response all the girls from the North gave. Mr. Choy had the sense that it was the "correct" answer.

"Alright. Watch me type it in. See? Now hit that button," he said to the crooked girl. She reached forward hesitantly, as if the keyboard might bite her, and pressed the Enter key. "Now look, see how fast that was? Each of those headings links to a web page.

And see here? That is the total number of pages that contain some reference to Kim Il-sung. Well over one million." The girls were impressed, but not convinced. "So we use the mouse — that's what this thing is called — and choose the heading that seems most likely to give us the information we want. You see, there is quite a variety. Let's just go to this one, *'Kim Il-sung: A legacy of failed Stalinism?'* " He clicked on the link.

The page changed, and had both Korean and English words. Mr. Choy was sure that the girls could not read English. The web page read, in Korean:

In the half century since the birth of North Korea, what has become of the Worker's Paradise? A country riddled with famine, oppression, concentration camps and corruption, it is little wonder that there are signs that the world's only remaining Stalinist state is beginning to collapse. North Korea, home to the world's fourth largest military, is controlled by a single dictator, Kim Jong-il, the son of the country's founder, Kim Il-sung. Kim Jong-il maintains absolute control of his people through fear, propaganda and persuasion in what is perhaps the world's most bizarre and dangerous personality cult . . .

"Imperialist rubbish!" shouted the pretty one.

"Well, I always say, 'don't believe everything you read on the Internet,' " replied Mr. Choy. He always enjoyed how the Northerners responded to that article. "Anyway, that's just one example." He typed rapidly on the keyboard and another page came up. "This is our website." This one had a light pink background and pictures of women in risqué outfits striking suggestive poses. Music began to play in the background as soon as the site loaded, and the girls looked around, mystified by the source of the sound. Mr. Choy pressed a button that led to a special area of the website that he had designed specifically for training day. He did not want the girls to see anything explicitly sexual at first. The page showed thumbnail images of the faces of beautiful women, and Mr. Choy explained that the thumbnails were a gallery of videos that a customer at the website could pay to download. He showed that by clicking on the thumbnail image, a video of the girl shown would begin to play. The videos were of young women strutting and making eyes at the camera. All the women remained fully clothed, though they ran their hands up and down their bodies in a sensual manner.

"This is the kind of thing that I want you girls to do. No problem, right?" The girls did not respond, their faces like stones. He showed them the entire gallery of ten videos. "So let's try it. You can start working off your debt right now!" Mr. Choy brought excitement into his voice, hoping that it would help them feel more enthusiastic. "How about you?" he asked, looking at Il-sun.

"My name is Park Il-sun," she said, looking offended.

"Very well, Il-sun, how about stepping in front of the camera? You saw how easy it was."

It looked as if she might refuse, but then she cast a look toward the girl with the fingernails, remembering how Mr. Choy responded when she was slow to do what she was told. After a moment she nodded.

Mr. Choy led the women into the next room. It was long and narrow, with light blue walls. At one end was a camera on a tripod, a video monitor on the wall, and a computer on a small table. Mr. Choy stood at the camera and told Il-sun to stand at the other end of the room.

"Alright, Il-sun, look at the camera for me. You should be able to see your face on the monitor."

"Gi! I'm on the television! Look at that!" exclaimed Il-sun, pointing at the monitor. Seeing herself, she momentarily lost her apprehension. To Mr. Choy it was a good sign that she would be one of the compliant ones.

"Okay, so when you have a client on the Internet, you will see yourself in the monitor, and he will write instructions, which you will be able to read at the bottom of the monitor, like this . . ." Mr. Choy typed on the computer, and the word *smile* appeared on the screen. "All you have to do is follow the instructions. It's that easy. So give me a big smile."

Il-sun forced a smile.

Mr. Choy zoomed the camera out so that all of Il-sun was in the frame. He then typed "Turn around." Il-sun spun around awkwardly.

"No, no, no. Not like that," Mr. Choy corrected. "Turn around like it's the best feeling in the whole world, like turning around is your very favorite thing to do. Do it slowly. Remember, you're not turning around for you, you are turning around for the camera; and the camera wants to look at you. The camera thinks you're beautiful. Now try it again."

Il-sun turned around again, this time more slowly.

"That's right, now use your hips. That's much better. Look directly into the camera now and blow a kiss. Great! You're a natural! Now watch." Mr. Choy punched a few keys on the computer and the video of Il-sun turning around replayed on the monitor. She was fascinated watching herself. Mr. Choy recognized the look of a girl with vanity, and he knew how to work with that. "Okay, let's try again. Remember the videos I showed you? Do you remember the attitude that those girls had? That's what I want you to do. Can you do that for me?"

Il-sun nodded.

"Great. Alright, now turn around again, but use your hands on your body. Pretend that your hands are really a man's hands touching you. Just like the other videos, okay?"

"Am I paying off my debt right now?" she asked.

"Sure. Now turn around."

"Okay," she responded. Il-sun looked at the monitor and a change came over her. She was a temptress, looking coyly at the camera. She smoothed her hands up and down her body as she slowly turned around, exaggerating the swing of her hips. She kept her face to the camera as she turned, flirting with her eyes. She even seemed, for a moment, to be enjoying herself.

"Great!" Mr. Choy hit a few buttons and replayed if for her. She watched it intently. "Okay, let's let the other girls try it. You," he pointed to Cho.

"We call her Cho," said Il-sun.

"Right. Okay, Cho, show us what you've got."

Cho stepped nervously in front of the camera. Even though she was no stranger to the sex trade, she had never worked in front of a camera before. She giggled to hide her embarrassment, even though her face showed a deep strain of fear.

"Don't be shy. Look at the monitor. See? You're beautiful!" Mr. Choy had focused on her face. He typed "Dance for me" on the screen, and then zoomed out to show her whole body.

"The only dance I know was the dance my Party Youth group performed at the Dear Leader's birthday festival," she said to him.

"Whatever dance you've got," he replied.

Cho started humming what sounded like a military march, then stepped around in a circle, kicking high. She moved her head and arms in rigid opposition, a stiff smile plastered to her face. Kicking her legs caused her to teeter perilously on her shoes and she nearly fell over.

"Cho," Mr. Choy interrupted her, laughing openly at her. "That's not what I had in mind. Remember what Il-sun did just a minute ago? That's what I want you to do. I'll put some music on to help you get in the mood." He typed again into his computer, and music played from hidden speakers. "Remember to watch the monitor and follow the instructions there."

Cho tried to emulate what Il-sun had done, but she was nervous and her movements were stiff. It did not help that she was finding it difficult to balance on her shoes — standard-issue *Chosun* heels never came quite so high. Mr. Choy typed something into his computer. Cho stopped dancing, squinted at the monitor so that she could read what he had written, and then she put her hands over her breasts.

Mr. Choy exploded. "No! Don't stop dancing to read the fucking instructions! I thought you would be better at it than this." His patience had suddenly evaporated and his smiling veneer cracked. It was as if someone had flipped a switch and changed him into another person entirely. "Also, when a client tells you to touch your fucking tits, you don't just put your hands on them. You stroke them, like a goddamn man would. Make it sexy, for crying out loud!" He was on the verge of a dangerous meltdown, and he knew he needed to keep himself in control if he was going to get these girls to comply. He took several deep breaths, recomposing himself. He put his charm back on as if it had been a hat that had simply fallen off his head. He smiled, and said sweetly, "Can you do that for me?"

Cho stood, paralyzed, fearful of further inflaming Mr. Choy's anger.

Mr. Choy looked from Cho to Il-sun and then to Gyong-ho. His face was glowing red. He forced two deep breaths, then said, "I have a better idea." He drew his mobile phone from his pocket and punched a button. "Send Jasmine over here," he commanded. He closed his phone with a snap and returned it to his pocket.

A couple of minutes later the door opened, and a statuesque woman in her midtwenties with intelligent eyes walked into the video room. She was wearing a lacy blue halter top that exposed her midriff, denim shorts that barely concealed her panty line, and red platform shoes that had spikes for heels.

"Teach these girls how to be sexy. I'm going to step out for some air," he said to the

woman. Mr. Choy left the room, his office
door closing with a loud bang.

46

The woman stood for a long moment, looking from Gi to Il-sun to Cho and back again. It seemed to Gi that she was appraising them, but in a completely different way than Mr. Choy had. *"Chosun?"* she finally asked. They nodded at her. The woman's face was unreadable, though some deep thought seemed to ripple there. "Let's bring some chairs in here. This might take a while," she sighed. It was difficult to tell if she was feeling put out or just sad. They followed her into the office, where they found some folding chairs and took them into the video room. They set them up in a loose circle and sat down.

"My name is Jasmine," she said after a long pause.

"Jasmine?" asked Il-sun. It was unusual name.

"Most of the girls here go by English names. It's to make it easier for our international customers." She paused again, and then continued, "I have seen quite a few *Chosun* girls come through here. Do you know why you're here?" she asked. The women did not respond. "I mean, do you know what Mr. Choy wants you to do?"

"Well, he wanted me to dance in front of the camera," Cho replied.

"Do you know why he wants you to do that?" No one spoke, so she answered her own question. "It's because he makes a lot of *won* every time you do. Did he show you the website?"

The women nodded.

"Did he show you the whole website, or just the page with the girls dancing with their clothes on?"

"Just that page," said Cho.

"I thought so. You didn't volunteer for this, did you? You are here illegally, and now you don't have any choice but to do this, right?"

The women looked at each other, then Il-sun nodded.

Jasmine gazed at the floor, a significant look crossing over her face, but its meaning was indiscernable. "Look, you're not going to be wiggling your ass in front of the camera with your clothes on. You need to know that right up front. Mr. Choy may

320

post those cute little videos as teasers on his website, but there isn't any money in it. He may tell you that you have the option to do whatever work you want to do, but ultimately he will make you do what he wants you to. The only reason you are here is to make money for Mr. Choy: otherwise he wouldn't have bothered with you. It's better that you know that now, rather than finding out when he makes you do something that you don't want to do. My advice to you: Do whatever he tells you to. He's dangerous when he gets angry. Trust me, whatever it is he asks of you will be a whole lot better than the consequences if you don't. I've seen girls beaten. Badly. If you do what he asks, you may not like it, but at least you won't get hurt. Do you understand?"

The women looked pale. Cho nodded.

"With that said, once you get used to this business, it really isn't as bad as you might think. Getting used to it is the hard part. You're going to feel dirty; and to be honest, that feeling never quite goes away. But you will get used to it."

"Are you in debt to him too?" asked Il-sun.

"Not technically," Jasmine sighed. "Not in the same way you are. But I'm stuck, too."

There was something about Jasmine that

Gi liked. She was intelligent and honest. What was unreadable about her before, Gi could see, was really a deep layer of compassion. She knew instinctively that she could trust her.

"How are you stuck?" asked Il-sun.

"Well, I wanted to go to university to study computers, but I didn't have any money. I was eighteen. I met a girl who worked at one of Mr. Choy's clubs; she was a stripper. She told me how easy it was to make money by working for Mr. Choy. She was paying her way through university at the time. Anyway, I went to the club and checked it out, and Mr. Choy hired me on the spot. The girl was right — the money was good — and I was well on my way to getting my computer degree. I nearly finished it, but then my father died unexpectedly. He had a lot of debt, and without any income, my mother was about to lose her house. She had always been a housewife and didn't know how to make a living, so I had to help her. I had to stop school and take on more shifts at the club, but it still wasn't enough. I knew that some of the other girls would see private clients in the back rooms for extra money, and I just sort of fell into it. I was terrified, but I didn't really have a choice. Five years later, I'm still doing it.

Now I don't have my degree, and nothing I could do would pay enough money. On top of that, I'm a good earner for Mr. Choy, and I'm afraid that if I quit he might do something bad to me or my mother."

Her story lingered in the air for a while before she took a deep breath, then continued. "Anyway, there are three — no, four aspects to this business that Mr. Choy might have you do. The first is live Internet chat and strip shows, where you chat with a guy and he tells you what he wants you to do. Normally you just strip and blow kisses into the camera. Usually they want you to touch your pussy, or pull on your nipples, or something like that. Then there are live strip shows at the club, which include pole dancing and lap dances. There are porn movies and magazines. If you don't know what those are, I can show you. And then, of course, seeing private clients — whoring."

Gyong-ho did not understand much of what Jasmine was saying, but she knew she did not like it.

"In this business, we have to pretend to be what men want women to be, not what we really are," said Jasmine. "Just look at the way I'm dressed. These shoes aren't any good for walking, and this shirt certainly doesn't keep me warm. But I wear them

323

because when I do, men get turned on and can't think straight. They open their wallets and we suck the money right out of them. For me, I would just as soon wear a rice sack — it would be warmer — but then I wouldn't have enough money to pay for my mother's living expenses.

"Really, it's all about what's between your legs. Men want to get at that more than anything. The trick is, you keep it barely out of their reach so they keep wanting it more. The longer you keep them wanting it, the more money they spend trying to get it."

Gi understood, at least, the concept of what she was talking about. She had learned about the vacuum of wanting when she looked through the fashion magazines earlier that day. It was the lethal danger of capitalism that the Great Leader had warned about.

"I'll be frank with you. Everything in this business is about pleasing men. Period. It doesn't matter what you want or what will make you feel good. On the one hand, that's bad for us. But on the other, it's good because it makes it easy. Once you understand men, then you can be in control of the situation. Mr. Choy will still be the boss, of course. There isn't anything you can do about that. But what I mean is, men are not really all that complicated. They like tits, they like ass, they like pussy, and they like a pretty face." Jasmine paused and looked at the women to make sure they were following her.

"I read an article one time," Jasmine continued, "where scientists did an experiment with male turkeys. They discovered that male turkeys will try to mate with a stuffed, dead female turkey just as readily as they would a live one. They fight over it and do everything a turkey does to try to impress a female turkey, even though it isn't real. When the scientists replace the stuffed turkey with a piece of wood that is roughly the same shape as a female turkey, they try to mate with that too, and fight over it. In the experiment, scientists kept reducing the wooden turkey, taking away parts of it, and still the male turkeys tried to mate with it. Finally, the fake turkey was reduced to nothing more than a piece of wood vaguely the same shape as a female turkey head, suspended on a string. The male turkeys even tried to mate with that! Men are just like turkeys — it doesn't matter how artificial we are, they will still behave the same way.

"That's why the Internet is so successful for us. Men will get excited and pay good money, even though they aren't getting anything tangible for it. When you think about it, it's pretty stupid, but they do it anyway." She paused and looked at the *Chosun* women, giving them time to absorb what they had heard.

"So, what does it mean to be sexy?" Jasmine asked, rhetorically. "The problem is, everyone has different tastes when it comes to sex. For some men it's big breasts, for others it's long hair, for others it's short skirts. But all these things are secondary turn-ons. I have been in this business for five years, and in that time I have been with hundreds of men. The one thing that I have found that most men find to be the biggest turn-on is when they think they're turning *you* on. This isn't because they actually care about what you're feeling. It's because it makes them feel more powerful, and better about themselves. It's about their egos and not the women they are with. Here's a secret that will help you get the hang of this business: Men are insecure. Most men come to see a girl, even on the Internet, to help them feel better about themselves. It really isn't about getting off, like most people think. They want to think that they are making you wet between the legs, making you moan with pleasure and lose control of yourself — all because of them. They think that it proves their manhood. For some reason, men always want to know that they have been the biggest and the best, even with a prostitute.

"Now let me ask you a question: What turns *you* on?"

Gi was uncomfortable. Not only was she sure that it was a very personal question, she also did not fully understand what it meant.

"Do you know what turns you on?" Jasmine asked. The women remained silent. "I'll tell you what turns me on. I like a man's eyes. You can tell a lot about the way a man is going to treat you by looking into his eyes. I also like a smooth, low voice. When a man whispers in my ear, it sends chills down my spine. I really like it when a man reads to me; not that it has happened very often. I think intelligent, confident men are sexy. I like to think that a man can carry on a conversation with me."

Gi was starting to understand the question better. She thought of how Il-sun walked as if the sun existed for the sole purpose of shining on her. She thought about how Il-sun's lighthearted nature caused her to feel more at ease. She realized that these were her own turn-ons. She thought back to the night at the orphanage when being so near Il-sun caused her body to respond and she wanted to press herself into her, to merge with her. *That must be "sexy,"* she thought.

"Men have a hard time understanding that what turns a woman on usually has more to do with who her partner is and how he treats her than how big his cock is or what kind of a car he drives," continued Jasmine. "That's because men get turned on by superficial things. A man will judge a woman by the size of her breasts, so he naturally assumes that women are going to judge him by the size of his penis. He is so concerned about that, that he becomes insecure. And that's where we profit."

"I never thought of it that way," said Cho. "I was a flower-selling girl back home, but I never analyzed it like that."

"Most people don't, but Mr. Choy is a smart businessman. He asked me one time, 'What business are you in?' I thought it was a trick question; I mean, wasn't it obvious? I fuck men for a living, and that's what I told him. 'No,' he said. 'Anyone can sell pussy. Pussy is everywhere. You're selling self-esteem.' 'What do you mean?' I asked him. He said, 'When you're with a guy, make him think he is the only guy in the whole world. Make him think he has the ability to please you unlike any man you have ever been with. It will mean so much more coming from you, having been with so many men. When he's done, beg him to come back again so you can get more of his kind of loving. That's how you bring the customer back. If the guy just wanted to get off, he could have jerked himself in front of the TV. A man comes to a prostitute to feel good about himself. That's what business you're in.' "

They all sat in silence for a little while, absorbing everything that was said. "Well, Mr. Choy doesn't like his assets to sit idly," Jasmine said. "So I assume he's going to put you to work tonight. It's already almost nine and business starts to pick up at around ten, so I should get into some details with you. I have to ask because you look so young, and it has been an issue with the girls from the North before: Are you virgins?"

Il-sun looked at the floor, looking embarrassed, but said nothing.

"Like I said, I have been a flower-selling girl for two years now. What do you think?" said Cho a little venomously.

Jasmine looked at Gyong-ho who, being put on the spot, could not pretend to know what was going on. "What is a virgin?" she asked weakly.

"Do you know about sex?" Jasmine asked, trying to be delicate.

Gi shook her head and looked down, embarrassment glowing red under her makeup.

"Do you know how babies are made?" Jasmine asked.

"Yes," mumbled Il-sun with a dry throat, but Gi said nothing, shaking her head again.

Jasmine's eyes glistened with tears, but she held them in. She didn't speak for several moments, it appeared, to keep herself from crying.

"I didn't know, teacup," said Cho to Gi, consolingly. "I would have said something."

Finally, Jasmine composed herself. "Have you menstruated?"

Gi nodded. It had happened for the first time a year earlier, when she was sixteen. She woke up one morning and there was a small dot of blood in her underwear. Il-sun had already been having her period for several years — the orphanage mistress referred to it as "the visiting friend," so she knew to expect it. Gi's period had come only once since then, and again there was no more than the one dot of blood in the morning. She knew that Il-sun's period came monthly, and that there was significantly more blood over several days. Gi suspected that there might be something wrong with her own cycle, but she was too afraid to ask anyone for help.

"Do you know what a man looks like naked?"

"Of course," said Il-sun, a little defensively.

Gi shook her head again, and wondered if the shame would never stop.

Jasmine patiently explained the mechanics of sexual intercourse, as well as conception and birth. She also went over basic sexual anatomy, and explained sexual pleasure. For Gi it clarified a lot of things, including the book *John and Daisy*, Il-sun's compulsion to see Gianni, as well as her own impulses toward Il-sun. She looked over at Il-sun, whose face was expressionless, and Gi could not tell how much of this was new information for her. Cho looked bored.

"Anyway, that's what we do here, and what Mr. Choy is going to expect you to do. Do you understand?"

Gi nodded. She found the idea of having a man inside her revolting, and she began to tremble with fear. Would Mr. Choy really make her do that?

"Look, this isn't how you should be learn-

331

ing about sex. You should learn about it with a nice young man your own age who loves you. Unfortunately that just isn't an option. It might help you to understand how sex works if I show you a video." Jasmine walked over to the computer and began typing. "Mr. Choy produces porn movies. Bear in mind that real sex is different from porn sex, but this will be better than trying to figure it out on your own with your first client. Also, a lot of men come to us wanting things they have seen in porn movies, so it doesn't hurt to know what it is they are expecting."

On the video monitor a film began to play. Cho sat with a smug expression, unimpressed. Il-sun and Gi watched, shocked and horrified.

47

Cho followed Jasmine to the first floor of the building. They walked down a short corridor to a locked door, for which Jasmine had a key. On the other side was a long, narrow room that ran the length of the building along the alleyway, three stories directly below the women's apartment. To Cho it felt like being in a long aquarium, because the whole wall facing the alley had been replaced by picture windows. About a dozen women were standing or sitting behind the glass, looking out into the alley, like mannequins on display. There was one door opening into the alley, likewise made mostly of clear glass, which was manned by an imposing fellow with a deep scar on one cheek.

Mr. Choy and Mr. Lee had arrived not long after Jasmine had shown the *Chosun* women the film. Gyong-ho went with Mr. Lee and Il-sun went with Mr. Choy; where,

Cho did not know. All she had been told was that she was going to the alley shop with Jasmine to do her "night work." Living on the streets had taught her to be fierce, but even so, she could not help but feel concern for the other two.

"We call him Runner, though I don't know why," said Jasmine, indicating the man at the door. "I don't think he could run to the end of the block. He handles all the money and brings your clients to you. He is also here to protect you, in case anyone gets unruly. I have seen him break heads before."

"How does this work?" asked Cho.

"We call this the meat shop. Basically, you just sit in the shop window like a slab of meat. Guys come along and look in at the girls through the windows. When they see something they like, they pay Runner, who brings them to you. Each girl sits in front of a door, which leads to a little bedroom. Literally just a room with a bed."

"So, all you do is sit there and wait for clients?"

"Well, not exactly. You're supposed to flirt with the guys as they walk by. Try to make them pick you. Mr. Choy wants you to flirt with everybody, but between you and me, you should be a little choosy. If you see someone you really don't like, you can try to make yourself unappealing. It doesn't always work, but it's worth a try. But don't let Runner see you do that."

"Who comes here? I mean, what kind of clients?"

"We get all kinds. Mr. Choy likes to think that he is running a quality establishment, so he charges more than your average street-walker. That keeps the lowlifes to a minimum. Basically, we take anyone who can pay. We get a lot of American servicemen."

"Americans?" asked Cho, concerned. It was known that Americans were inhuman brutes.

"Yeah, they smell funny, but they pay well. You get used to it. If you have any problems, have Runner come and get me. I'm working here tonight, too."

Jasmine introduced Cho to Runner, who showed her to her window space. He was a man who tended to speak in grunts and head nods. Cho peeked inside her little room and was pleased to see that at least it was clean. She then sat on a stool in the window and waited for her first client.

So far, she reflected, things did not seem all that bad in the South. She had eaten well since arriving, had had a hot shower, had been given nice clothes to wear and an apartment with running water *and* a refrigerator. Considering everything, her life seemed to have improved, in spite of having been double-crossed by Gianni. The fact that she was not free to come and go as she pleased did not bother her too badly, as long as she had a warm place to sleep and plenty of food. It was only temporary anyway, since eventually Mr. Choy would help her get papers. With a private bed and someone else to organize the business, even the flower-selling business had an air of luxury to it. In the North, her business had been mostly back alley quickies for food or ration cards. Here, once her debt was paid, she would be making her own cash.

A group of young men strolled by the window, looking in. She stood up and passed them a steamy look, hiking her dress just over the top of one of her stockings, like Jasmine had shown her how to do. The men paused and kissed at her through the glass. She walked up to the window, put her hands on the glass and stood with one knee crossing demurely in front of the other. It was a calculated look of coyness while also showing off one of her legs. One of the young men mouthed, *"Saranghae,"* "I love you," through the glass, causing his friends to erupt in laughter. They continued on their way, doubled over and pounding each other on the back.

The gesture stabbed unexpectedly at Cho's heart. Tears rushed forward and she had to strain to keep them from flowing. She thought of the dead dream that would never be, of the soldier and the baby and the glory of *Chosun.* Would loving her, a prostitute, always be a joke? She was a woman whom men used for pleasure, then discarded. She was too dirty, touched as she had been by so many men. Could she ever be innocent again? But then she hardened her heart with the cold thought of survival. *What is love if you cannot eat?* Love was a luxury item unavailable to women with her low *songbun.*

As the night progressed, the alley became a flurry of activity. Her first client was a married man in his sixties whose only desire was to watch her undress and to touch her naked breasts with his hands. Her second client was a serious-looking businessman in a fancy suit who thrust inside her exactly three times before climaxing. He never even took off his tie. The next man was drunk and slammed numbly into her for a long time before he finally passed out. She had to get Runner to escort him back out to the alley. She had seen a total of fifteen clients before the night was over — she had never seen so many in a day before. She was glad, however, because she knew she must be well on her way to paying off her debt to Mr. Choy. She was that much closer to freedom.

A little before dawn, Jasmine came to fetch her. They walked back into the building and Jasmine escorted Cho to the fourth floor. Thoughts of love were left behind to crust over and dry out on crumpled sheets. Razor unlocked the gate and let Cho in.

48

Gyong-ho was led out of the building by Mr. Lee and shoved into the backseat of a small green car. There was another young woman in the backseat with her, but Mr. Lee forbade them to speak. She was about Gi's own age, maybe younger, and was dressed similarly, in a fancy gown and makeup. Gi counted exactly fifty-six sequins around the collar of her neck. The girl had a blank look on her face and did not acknowledge Gi when she got in the car. Mr. Lee climbed into the driver's seat and drove off down the street.

After Jasmine had shown her the video, Gi felt sick to her stomach. Under the best of circumstances, she felt no desire to have sexual intercourse with a man. The mystery of their bodies held no allure for her — especially after seeing the raw, unfeeling way the man in the video probed the young woman on the screen. Was that woman like her — at the mercy of Mr. Choy, sold unwillingly and now only going through the motions to survive? How could anyone derive pleasure from watching such a thing? Would she, too, have to go through those same motions?

Mr. Lee drove to the end of the block and turned right. The world swirled again with numbers. Gi counted sixteen cars parked on the right side of the street, three of them blue; and eight cars parked on the left side, two of them white. They drove another block, seven cars passing them in the other direction, two of them red. They made another right turn and drove four blocks. By the time they double-parked in front of a dark building with heavy music pouring out its doors, red cars, blue cars and white cars had been passed and calculated, their sums and products and squares demystified and known. The colors of the *Chosun* flag, in numbers represented by cars on *Hanguk* soil, could not be distilled into any of the magic numbers that seemed to govern the laws of existence, like the square root of two or the ratio of a circle's radius to its circumference.

Mr. Lee got out of the car and told the women to follow him inside. A large, muscular man stood at the blacked-out doorway with his arms folded across his chest. He nodded at Mr. Lee as they went into the building. The room was dimly lit and thundering with music. The sound hurt Gi's ears. They went to the back of the building, past a lit-up bar with a harried bartender serving a thirsty crowd and a series of stages with poles at their centers. Women were dancing around the poles, taking their clothes off, and Gi wondered if that was why she was there — only to dance. She knew she would not be very good at it. Finally they went through a set of swinging double doors and the music was muffled. There was a row of booths on both sides of a long hallway, partitioned off by heavy black curtains.

Mr. Lee stopped and turned to the women. "The boss said that you two are going to be my hand-job and blow-job girls tonight. If any of your customers gives you extra money, you hand it right over to me, you got that? I'm going to search you at the end of the night, and if I find so much as a single *won* on you, I'm going to beat you until you're bloody. Got it? You get the two stalls at the end. Sit in your stall and I'll bring your customers to you. Get 'em off quick, because I don't want there to be a line. Now off you go!" He turned on his heel and walked out.

"I don't know what to do," Gi said, panicking. "What does he want us to do?"

The young woman snorted and turned away without answering the question, and disappeared behind the curtain of her booth.

Gi peered into her own booth. It was small, maybe about two meters square, and very dimly lit with a red light. There was a small bench inside, a wastebasket, and a stack of paper towels. She sat on the bench and waited.

A few minutes later, she heard Mr. Lee leading a person into the hall. They went to the booth across from Gi's, and Mr. Lee said tersely, "Blowjob." He walked briskly out. Gi could hear the voice of the young woman, then some response from the man. She decided to risk taking a look.

She stole across the hallway quickly, and then pulled the curtain back just enough to look in with one eye. The young woman was on her knees, head bobbing up and down, her hands on the man's bare buttocks. His trousers were bunched up around his ankles, and his right hand was clutching the back of the young woman's head. The girl gagged and choked occasionally but did not stop. Eventually, the man let out a loud grunt, and the thrusting stopped. The woman pulled back and spit and coughed into a paper towel. She looked over and caught Gi's eye, giving her a caustic look. Gi dropped the curtain and scurried back to her booth, mortified.

She felt a knot in her stomach as she realized that it was only a matter of time before Mr. Lee brought a man into her booth. Should she count the seconds? She wondered, if she focused hard enough, could she make time itself come to a stop? Could she escape somehow, maybe slipping unnoticed past the muscular man at the door? Where would she go if she could? The thought of being caught and turned over to the Americans for torture crossed her mind. Would their torture be better or worse than what she was expected to do in that booth?

She heard the swinging double doors open, and her stomach tightened. She heard two sets of footsteps coming down the hall. The curtain of her booth was pulled back and a man staggered in. Mr. Lee stood outside the booth and grunted, "Hand job," and turned on his heel.

She steeled her courage and stepped out of the booth, and asked to his back, "Mr. Lee, I don't know what hand job means."

He turned around with a look of contempt, brought his hand to the front of his lap and made a back-and-forth gesture with his fist. He then stormed out the door.

Gi reentered the booth. The man standing there appeared to be in his midtwenties and reeked of alcohol. His eyes were glassy, and just standing there he was swaying as if off balance. He smiled at her, and even appeared a little embarrassed. "My name is Cha'an. This is my first time here," he said, nervously.

Gi nodded, not knowing what else to do.

"What's your name?" he asked.

The question caught her off guard. She had not expected anyone to want to know her name. The thought of giving it to this man was vile, as if doing so would be a terrible violation worse than the sexual act she was expected to perform. Giving him her name would be like handing him a chunk of her soul which she would never be able to retrieve. If she told him her name, he would leave with it, and keep it with him forever, tying her to him in his memory. Even as she thought it, she realized that this man *would* be a part of her forever. This man would leave a stain on her that would never wash off. Suddenly it was not fear that she was feeling, or even nervousness. It was grief. It was not just this man, but an endless line of men over an undetermined period of time who would all be leaving their stains on her. All those men would always be a part of her, slowly pushing her out of herself, crowding the finite space of her soul until there was no room left for her. She was grieving the loss of herself.

The man stood there expectantly, but receiving no reply, he just shrugged his shoulders and unfastened his trousers. His pants fell to the floor, and automatically Gi's eyes followed the movement.

"I'll bet you've seen a lot of those," the man said. It was the kind of stupid thing a person says out of nervousness, and he seemed to realize it. Gi just stood there, wondering what the consequence would be if she simply refused to touch him. His penis was ugly and wrinkled, and appeared to be shrinking. Aside from the video Jasmine had shown, this was the first time she had seen one. She was too frightened and appalled to be fascinated by the difference from her own anatomy.

"Aren't you going to touch me? I already paid," he said, whining.

Gi realized that her time was up. The seconds leading up to this moment had all drained away, and from this moment forward this is who she would be. Her fingers made contact with him, and he jumped back.

"Your hands are cold!" he shouted, and then giggled nervously. "Maybe you should warm them up first."

Gi heard footsteps in the hallway, and Mr. Lee passed another customer to the young woman across the hall. He then shouted into Gi's booth, "Are you almost done in there? There's another one waiting." His heavy footfalls disappeared once more out the door.

Gi rubbed her hands together, then placed them for a moment under her armpits. Then she reached for the man again. She grabbed his organ with the tips of her fingers, the way a person would grab a dead mouse by the tail — as if to hold it without actually touching it. It was soft and warm under her fingers. From watching the porn video and from the gesture that Mr. Lee made, she had the impression that the man would want her to pull on it rhythmically; so she gripped him gently between her fingertips and pulled. As she touched him, his body responded and she felt him get larger underneath her fingers. She tugged and pulled on it, much like how she would imagine one would milk a cow. The man closed his eyes.

"Put your whole hand around it," he said.

Reluctantly, she gripped him in the palm of her hand and pulled.

"Not so hard," he said.

She lightened her grip and began sliding her hand back and forth. The man responded by moving his hips to meet her hand movements. He then put his hand over hers, and began stimulating himself, through her hand. Gi understood what Jasmine had meant about men being turkeys. He didn't really seem to care whether or not she was there. His eyes were closed, and he was making all of the movements himself. She was just a passive participant in his fantasy. It felt dirtier that way, somehow.

His breathing was getting faster and he stroked harder. Then he stopped, panting, and said, "I'll pay the extra money. Give me a blow job."

Gi looked up at his face.

"I want you to suck my cock," he said. "Now!" He put his hands on her shoulders and pushed her to her knees. A shock of pain went through her legs as she hit the floor. His stiff penis was directly in front of her, looming large from such a close angle. She had not expected the pungency of the man's sexual smell. She had not thought of its having any particular odor, though now it overwhelmed her — a strong, sour, earthy odor — and it turned her stomach. She knew what was expected of her, but she could not bring herself to put her mouth on it. "Come on, I'm almost there!" he begged. "Suck it!" He grabbed the back of her head and forced it toward him. His penis mashed against her nose and lips, and he began to grind it into her face. "Open your mouth. I want you to suck my cock!" She parted her lips and he thrust himself inside her. The taste was powerful and the tip of his penis made contact with the back of her throat. He started thrusting himself in and out of her mouth, but sickness overcame her and she retched, vomiting all over him and his trousers and onto the floor.

"What the fuck?! You bitch!" he shouted loudly, pulling back. The swinging doors opened and Gi could hear footsteps running down the hallway. Mr. Lee pulled the curtain open, mouth agape.

"What happened here?" he demanded.

"I told her I would pay the extra money for a blow job, then the fucking bitch puked on me," whined the man.

Mr. Lee whistled loudly and a man dressed all in black came running through the double doors. "Take this gentleman upstairs to a private room where he can get himself cleaned off, then send a girl in to service him properly," Mr. Lee ordered. He then turned to the man in the booth, "I am awfully sorry about this. She's new. We're going to take you upstairs where you can get cleaned up, and then send you a full-service whore to take care of anything you need — on the house. Afterwards, come on down and have a free drink at the bar."

The man stepped out of his spoiled trousers and followed the man in black out the double doors. Mr. Lee then turned to Gyong-ho, who was choking and crying on the floor. He reached in and grabbed her by the hair, lifting her up to standing. She made a swallowed scream. "Clean this shit up," he said to her in a loud, angry whisper. He was still holding her hair, pulling her head back. "If you ever do that again, I'm going to take you in the back and teach you a lesson you will never forget. We have customers waiting, so get cleaned up." He turned on his heel and marched out the door.

49

"Would you care for a glass of champagne?"
Mr. Choy asked Il-sun as soon as her
friends had been taken away. They were in
his office, and his charm had been restored.

"What's champagne?" she asked.

"I can't believe a beautiful woman like you
has never tried champagne," he said, pro-
ducing a bottle from a small refrigerator
behind his desk. "Don't the men up North
know how to treat a lady?" He untwisted
the wire restraint and removed the cork
from the bottle with a loud *pop.* "All the
most sophisticated ladies drink champagne,"
he said, pouring golden, bubbly liquid into
two tall-stemmed glasses.

"Thank you," she said, receiving a glass.
She was wary of Mr. Choy, but also curious. She lifted the glass to her lips and
sipped. The liquid was sweet as it passed
over her tongue and tickled in her throat as
it went down. After she swallowed, it left

her mouth feeling tingly and dry. It was wonderful.

"With your looks, you can go far in this business. I have a feeling about you, Il-sun," said Mr. Choy

"You do?" She took another sip of champagne.

"Don't let what you've seen here frighten you. I'm going to take care of you. Ease you into it. You only have to do what you're comfortable with, and that's all."

Il-sun nodded, in spite of her apprehension. She pushed Jasmine's earlier warning out of her mind.

"You're a natural at this. I can tell," Mr. Choy continued. "A lot of girls have the right body for it, but they don't know how to carry themselves. But you — you have that special something. I know it can take some adjustment for a girl like you to get used to this business. But I can take you a long way. I could even make you famous."

"Famous?" Even in North Korea there were famous people, movie stars and music idols, who were the pinnacle of glamour and prestige.

"You start here and get the hang of Internet dancing. Maybe we'll have you try it once or twice at the club. If you learn fast, I can probably get you into the movies within a month or two. If you work hard and have enthusiasm, I'd say your success is assured."

Il-sun smiled in spite of herself. She looked away to try to hide it — she did not want him to know that his flattery was having an effect. "But I don't want to take my clothes off in front of anybody," she replied.

"Why not?" he asked with exaggerated shock on his face. "You're so beautiful, and everyone should get the chance to admire your perfect body. It would be a shame to keep it hidden. You're a piece of beautiful art, like a sculpture, and you deserve to be appreciated. Have some more champagne." He refilled her glass — the first one had gone down easily — and removed a hard-cover book from a shelf above the desk. He handed it to her. It was a book of black-and-white art photography nudes. "Look at these pictures. They're a celebration of the human body! A woman's body is the most beautiful thing in the world," he said, outlining her figure in the air with his hands. "And it should be admired. That's what our business is: the appreciation of the female body. We celebrate it."

Il-sun looked away again, hoping to suppress another smile that was tugging at the corners of her lips. It only made her feel coy, which was compounded by the champagne — it was very different from whiskey. She then focused on the book in her hands. It was mostly photos of women in waterfalls, or sprawled on rocks, and she had to concede that they were beautiful.

"Where are Gyong-ho and Cho?" she asked, attempting to conceal her being both embarrassed and flattered, and to remind herself that, even though Mr. Choy was being nice, she was still his captive.

"Look, everyone has a different area of this business where they can excel. You have something special that we need to cultivate, and we can do that best here, at the studio. I'm grooming you for the movies. If you're successful here, then you will be able to take care of them. Those girls don't have the same star quality that you do, but there are other things they can do. Don't worry about them. They will be well looked after, I promise. When I'm done with you, after you clear your debts to me, you will have money and prestige. You will have all the rich food you could ever want to eat, a car, a nice house, people to do your cooking and cleaning. They can live with you in your big, fancy house, if you want." He then brought a chaste, avuncular tone into his voice, and said, "Now let's get you in the studio so you can show us what you've got!"

Il-sun followed Mr. Choy across the hall to a door with a sign that read, "Studio 1." Just inside the door was an L-shaped desk where three busy men wearing headphones sat behind computers. They gave Mr. Choy a brief nod. Wires snaked from the desk to a long row of partitioned stalls, each with a camera, monitor, and lights facing into it.

"These are the dancing studios," Mr. Choy explained. "Customers come to our website, select a girl they want to watch dance, and then the girl dances for them live. It's that easy. They pay by the minute, so your job is to keep them interested for as long as possible. Do you think you can do that?"

"I'm not sure."

"Think of it as going one step closer to getting your papers."

They went to the stall closest to the control desk, and Il-sun walked in. Mr. Choy turned on the lights, and Il-sun winced until her eyes adjusted to them.

"Now, you remember how you danced for me earlier?" Mr. Choy asked.

"Yes."

"Just do that. We have a set routine here that maximizes how long the chump will stay online watching you. The trick is to draw it out as long as possible; so the rule is, you dance for two minutes without taking anything off. You can make like you're going to, but your job is just to tease them. Remember, they're paying by the minute. There are bells that chime every sixty seconds, to keep time for you. After two minutes, then you can start taking your clothes off, slowly. At five minutes you're down to your bra and panties, at seven the bra comes off, and then at nine, the panties. After that, you start touching yourself. It becomes a masturbation show."

"What's a masturbation show?"

"We'll worry about that when we get to it. For now, let's just work on the first part. Remember, this is a celebration of your beauty, like in the book I showed you. Just so you can get used to it without any pressure, we'll do a practice run. Ready?"

Il-sun nodded. She was feeling self-conscious and walked around the pole timidly. She had still not mastered walking in high heels, and the champagne made her feel top-heavy.

"Okay, here we go. This is just for practice. Going live in five . . . four . . . three . . . two . . . one . . ."

50

Mr. Choy flaked a couple of small crystals into a glass pipe. *Just a maintenance dose,* he thought. *Just enough to get me through.* He had almost lost his temper with the Northern girls; and losing his temper, he knew, would work against him. He struck his lighter and held the flame to the bottom of the glass. A moment later, the *hiroppong* began to bubble and smoke. He put his lips to the pipe — *just a small kiss,* he thought — and drew the smoke deeply into his lungs. Oh, how it hurt! Oh, how wonderful the hurt! He exhaled and considered reloading the pipe, but thought better of it. It was time to put the new Northerners to work.

Mr. Choy found Mr. Lee in Studio 2 on the second floor, and together they went up to his office. Jasmine was just finishing with the Northerners. The sassy girl was accustomed to whoring and did not really need training, so he sent her to the alley shop with Jasmine. The skinny girl he sent to the club with Mr. Lee, for lack of anything better to do with her. If she did not earn her keep, he would send her out of town with Mr. Lee, and he would —

No, it would not come to that. If he failed to turn a profit with his product, that was his own failing. The pretty one stayed. He knew just the right tactic to take with her, and he was eager to bend her to his will. This was the part he enjoyed — the seduction. He did this for every one of those giggly girls who wouldn't give him the time of day when he was younger. Every time he brought a girl into the business, he felt vindicated.

He sweet-talked the pretty Northerner and plied her with champagne. He could see the fear in her eyes, but also the vanity. She longed to hear words extolling her beauty and, above all, her specialness. He doled them out, with just enough restraint to be believable. He then ushered her across the hall to the Internet studios, where he coaxed her to strike a pose on the pole. "Going live in five . . . four . . . three . . ."

Il-sun put her hand on the pole and arched her back stiffly. She knitted her brow in concentration and began to dance. It took a minute for her to start dancing away the nervousness, but it melted quickly enough. She was almost completely lost in the dance, but then she stumbled on one of her shoes.

"Take the shoes off, for now," Mr. Choy instructed. "You can practice dancing in them tomorrow."

She kicked the shoes off, which helped her balance, but then the minute timer rang. She shook with a start, hesitated, and then stopped altogether.

"What's wrong?" asked Mr. Choy. He felt a surge of anger rise sharply from somewhere in his bowels . . . No. Anger could come later.

"I'm sorry. I've never really been naked in front of a man before. I'm scared."

"Is that really true?" he asked, his voice suddenly thick with sarcasm. He doubted that she had *never* been naked in front of a man — Gianni tended to sample his own merchandise — and he wanted to get past this hurdle as quickly as possible. He forced a smile, and said, "You're doing fine."

Il-sun looked at the floor, her face turning bright red, but she did not respond.

Mr. Choy took a deep breath. "Okay, let's watch what you did so far. I was recording you so that you can see what you look like." He nodded at one of the technicians at the desk, and Il-sun watched herself on the screen.

"Well, what do you think?" Mr. Choy asked her.

"I was a little bit stiff. I can see how nervous I was. I also had a funny look on my face. Can I try it again?"

Mr. Choy gloated inside. He was right to play to her vanity. "As many times as you like. We have all night."

Il-sun began again; this time she was more self-possessed. Her nervousness evaporated quickly and she seemed to lose herself in the dance. She even threw in some flirtatious glances at the camera. When the bell rang, she stopped.

"Can I watch it again? I want to see if it was better that time."

Mr. Choy felt his anger rising again — it was so much harder to stave it off when he was high. He hated it when people did not do what he wanted them to. He clenched his fists at his sides and bent his lips into a smile. "Of course," he said.

She watched the monitor with her head cocked to the side, evaluating her performance.

"Are you satisfied?" asked Mr. Choy.

"I can do better," she responded.

"Alright. Let's go all the way through this

time, okay?"

Il-sun did her dance again, and Mr. Choy had to admire how quickly she was improving. The bell rang again, and then she looked into the camera, bringing her hand to the strap of her dress. Her timing was perfect. She moved the strap off her shoulder in a sultry way, but then stopped again.

"I'm sorry, I —"

"Just take off your goddamned clothes!" Mr. Choy shouted, his violent frustration breaking through. "This isn't a fucking ballet, it's porn!" He then grabbed the rack of lights and, with a growl, threw them to the floor. Lightbulbs exploded, sending a shower of glass into the studio. Mr. Choy began to huff away, but then turned around and pointed a finger at Il-sun. "You have to pay for that!" Then he turned and walked out.

All activity in the studio ceased, and Il-sun stood there, shocked. The click of typing on keys, which had been constant white noise in the background, stopped, the men at the desk distracted by the outburst. A woman peeked around the corner from the stall next to Il-sun's. As soon as the shock wore off, Il-sun began to weep.

One of the technicians eventually appeared with a broom and a dustpan and cleaned up the glass. He then righted the rack of lights and replaced all the bulbs. Nobody looked at or spoke to Il-sun. After fifteen minutes Mr. Choy reappeared. There was no trace of his outburst left on his face, and he was smiling. He spoke in a quiet, measured voice.

"Shall we try that again? We're going live this time, so I want you to go all the way through it."

Il-sun was afraid of setting him off again, so she took up her position at the pole, tears still streaming down her cheeks. The voice of a technician came over a speaker, saying, "Going live in five . . . four . . . three . . . two . . . one."

She danced without much heart, but she did not stop. When the bell rang, she slipped a strap off one shoulder, and then the other. She reached behind and pulled the zipper of the dress down her back. She peeled the front of the dress slowly off her breasts, exposing a lacy white bra underneath. It was a perfect contrast of innocence and sophistication, the white bra under the black dress. She danced around the pole, and eventually slid the dress off her hips and down her legs. The beautician had chosen her underwear well, Mr. Choy noticed. They were the perfect cut to show off Il-sun's seductive form. She continued to cry, but she did not stop the dance. Mr. Choy felt himself getting hard. He liked it when a girl cried. He would enjoy watching this again and again.

The bell rang again, and Il-sun glanced up at Mr. Choy. Fear flashed in her eyes before she looked away and undid the clasp of her bra. She placed her arms in front of her chest, holding her bra in place, and turned her back to the camera. Her bare back was a flawless landscape to Mr. Choy. She let go with her arms and the bra fell to the floor. Looking down, she turned slowly toward the camera, her arms folded just under her breasts, her nipples pointing at a slight angle upward. Mr. Choy was transfixed as he watched the light shift across her breasts and glint off her tears as she turned. She stood, full frontal, and lifted her eyes to the camera without lifting her chin. Tears fell from her cheeks onto her breasts, mascara running in two rivulets down the sides of her face.

The bell rang. Il-sun put her thumbs into the waistline of her panties, and she slid them down her long legs. Mr. Choy was salivating and nearly drooled. He had not seen anything this erotic for a long time. She stepped out of her panties and stood there, motionless for a whole minute, holding her legs together. Her pubic hair was scant but dark. Her belly was flat. Her breasts were firm handfuls. She was innocence and temptation all wrapped up into one, and Mr. Choy knew that he had struck gold.

A buzzer went off, breaking the spell. The customer had gone offline.

Mr. Choy and Il-sun stood facing each other for a long moment. The look in her eyes was both fear and hatred. He had not expected to see the defiance that was pushing through her humiliation. He liked that. He clapped slowly.

"Very good. Now, that wasn't so hard, was it?" he said in a syrupy sweet voice. "Now clean up your face. Another customer is waiting."

51

Il-sun awoke to a loud banging on the door, then the squeaking of hinges. She could tell by the daylight filtering in through the single, spotty window in their small apartment that it was late morning. A man came into the apartment and shouted, "It's time to get up. The boss wants you to clean the studios." Il-sun arose groggily, returning from her dreams only to find herself still a captive in South Korea. The orphanage mistress had been helping her fold the laundry. She had been dreaming of home.

"He never said anything about cleaning," Cho said saucily, sitting up and rubbing sleep from her eyes. Cho had slept on the futon that had been delivered in their absence the night before and now dominated their living room. Il-sun and Gi shared the small European-style bed.

"He did just now, so get up!"

"We need to eat something," Cho said,

cutting him an icy look. The man was in his midthirties, with a thick neck and a crew cut. He looked like the kind of man who was just smart enough to follow orders. He reminded Il-sun of a dog who had been kicked often — he looked both afraid and mean.

"I'll give you fifteen minutes to get ready," he barked, and stepped out of the apartment.

Gi got out of bed and went to the sink to spit. Il-sun had noticed her getting up throughout the night to do that, but was afraid to inquire about it. Her own night had been bad enough, and she could not bear to hear what Gi had gone through. She had a feeling that whatever it was, it must have been even worse than having to strip off her clothes. Now, in the dirty light of their only window, she could see the faraway look in Gi's eyes. There would be no talking to Gi about anything for several hours.

The women got dressed in their old clothes, and then Cho served up the remainder of the restaurant food. Il-sun and Cho sat in silence while picking at cold noodles. Gi did not touch the food, and stood at the sink, her back to the others, unmoving except to occasionally clear her throat and cough. Cho seemed foul tempered, but

365

more from lack of sleep than anything else. She had a look on her face that forbade conversation. Il-sun wanted to talk about her embarrassment and fear from the night before — she needed comfort and re-assurance — but her companions were in no shape to commiserate. That would have to come later.

The man came back and ordered the women to come with him. Reluctantly, Il-sun and Cho stood up and began to follow, but Gi made no movement. Il-sun walked over to her and touched her hand to her shoulder.

"Gi . . ."

"I'll be okay," Gi whispered.

Il-sun was surprised that Gi was able to respond at all. Gi turned, and Il-sun put her arms around her. Gi softened under the touch. Il-sun held her close, as much to receive comfort as to give it.

"We don't have all day!" the man shouted back to them, breaking the embrace.

The thick-necked bouncer led the women downstairs to the alley shop, where a young woman was wiping down one of the picture windows.

"The alley looks worse in the daylight," Cho remarked.

"You've been here?" asked Il-sun.

"I worked here last night."

"I have more cleaners for you," the man said to the woman who was cleaning the glass. Without another word, he left them.

The woman looked up from the window, and then turned back expressionlessly to finish the pane. She was dressed in a stained T-shirt and a knee-length skirt, and had her hair pulled back in a ponytail. She looked as tired as Il-sun felt. When she was finished with the window, she approached them.

"There is a bucket with rags and window cleaner over there," she said, pointing. "People like to paw at the glass, so we have to clean both sides every day. They will let one of us out under supervision to clean the outside." Her voice was droopy, like her eyes. She threw a cautious glance at the bouncer by the door. It looked like a habitual movement. "After we finish with that, then we clean the rooms. We have to strip the sheets and make sure everything is stocked and dusted."

"Are you *Chosun?*" Il-sun asked. The accent was unmistakable.

The woman gave a blank look, then nodded. "They treat us differently, you know. They think we're stupid because we come from the North."

"How long have you been here?" asked Cho.

"I don't know. Maybe six months. I came from Kaesong. I was promised . . ." she glanced over her shoulder and swallowed. "I live across the hall from you."

"What's your name?" Il-sun asked.

"It doesn't matter," she replied, looking down at her feet. "It just doesn't matter anymore."

Il-sun felt her heart sink even lower. She could see her own future in the woman's exhausted eyes.

"They only make the *Chosun* girls do the cleaning," continued the young woman. "Because they don't have to pay us."

"After six months, you must at least be close to paying off your debt to Mr. Choy, though. Right? Then you probably won't have to clean anymore," said Cho hopefully.

The woman did not say anything, a sour look darkening her face.

"How many *Chosun* live here?" asked Cho.

"Maybe ten, or twelve. It changes all the time. We all live upstairs."

"Where are the rest of them now?"

"I don't know. Maybe they have been taken to clean the nightclubs." She looked outside for a moment, gauging the time by the quality of daylight, then threw another quick glance toward the bouncer. "Look, there really isn't time to talk. We need to finish up here so we can clean the Internet studios. I like to be done in time to take a nap before night work starts. You girls start with the rooms while I work on the glass. Be thorough. If Mr. Choy sees anything out of place he goes crazy." With that she went back to the window.

The women went to work, busily detailing the rooms. All the soiled sheets were taken to a laundry facility in the basement. Il-sun was in awe of the laundry machines, which required no more work than loading the sheets, adding detergent, and hitting the Start button. How was it that the South could have such things, where in the North a woman's hands were chapped and roughened by wringing clothes in cold water and caustic soap? After the alley shop had been thoroughly cleaned, the women went methodically through the rest of the building, sweeping, mopping, and dusting. The first floor housed the alley shop on one side and a small video production studio on the other. The second and third stories were wholly dedicated to Internet studios, where they had to clean around all the activity that was continually going on. It was a twenty-four-hour business.

They had finally finished cleaning the building by dusk, and the nameless young woman told them that they would probably have an hour or so until they were summoned for their night work. She then left them without a word.

In their absence, someone had brought a pile of clothing and left it in a heap on Cho's futon. The beautician had explained the day before that the company had a wardrobe department, of sorts, that was stocked with all styles and sizes of women's clothing appropriate for the pleasure industry. Mr. Choy wanted his women to look nice and clean. Along with the clothes were some basic makeup and hair supplies.

Jasmine came to their apartment not long after dark. She helped them prepare for the night by assisting with their hair and makeup. She also wanted to see how the *Chosun* women were holding up. Jasmine's eyes were ringed by sadness, for herself, Il-sun could tell, but also for their plight. It felt good, at least, that someone cared, even if there was nothing Jasmine could do to help them. Jasmine talked more about the business, about how to steer clear of Mr. Choy's wrath and how to be safe. She also talked about herself. Il-sun had the impression that she did not have many friends to confide in. She was resigned to her life, her dream of studying computers long abandoned.

Jasmine's mobile phone rang, and she answered it. It was Mr. Choy telling her to bring the women down for work. They went downstairs, nervous and glum.

52

Il-sun arrived at the Internet studio expecting to see Mr. Choy, but he was not there. There was no glass of champagne or sweet talk about the celebration of the female form. Instead, she was roughly met by one of the technicians, who looked up and pointed. "I need you in the third stall. Now!" was all he said.

She went directly to the third stall, and before she even had time to think about it, the technician's voice came over the speaker and said, "Going live in five . . ."

She danced, fearful of what would happen to her if she did not do as she was told. She was tired and sore from the night before, but she forced herself to keep moving. One dance after another, the night wore on. She was barely able to catch her breath between performances, and her prickly tongue stuck to the roof of her mouth for lack of moisture. Nobody offered refreshment. Finally, after many hours, another woman arrived to take her place — Il-sun did not even bother to look at her face. She could barely lift her feet to climb the short flight of stairs to their apartment. She fell onto the bed and into a deep, deep sleep.

Day after night after day after night, the routine of cleaning and dancing was repeated until Il-sun lost track of how many days and nights she had been in *Hanguk*. Each day blended into the next, and she was too tired and aching to care. Disoriented and deprived of sleep, her home at the orphanage felt like it belonged to an aeon in the past, distorted by time and coming from a vague dream. Had there ever been a garment factory, a *Chosun*, a Gianni? When she thought of Gianni her heart lurched and the acid taste of bile crept hand over hand up the back of her tongue. At times she longed for him, or the idea of him, telling herself that he had made a mistake, that he had not meant to sell her to Mr. Choy. At other times she danced to spite him, flaunting her naked flesh to an unseen stranger on the Internet — a stranger who wanted her, who would pay to look at her.

Look at me now, Gianni. You could have had this.

53

According to Gi's count, she had been in *Hanguk* for exactly twenty-one days, had given three hundred seven blow jobs and two hundred eighty-six hand jobs. Mr. Lee had slapped her four times and called her a whore sixteen times. Now she knew what that meant. She'd dared to put her hand on Il-sun's shoulder exactly eight times as she watched her sleep. Those were qualitatively the best eight moments of the last three weeks. She still had not seen a photograph of the Dear Leader.

She hoisted his image into her mind and tried to hold it there. She could not recall enough details, she was sure of it. She should know every pore and hair. When they repatriated her back to the North, if they tested her worth by asking her to draw his face, she knew she would fail. She was not good enough. So she traced his image with her fingertips, rendering his hairline, his square glasses, his tall forehead, his pouting mouth, the disappointment in his eyes, on walls and windows.

Gi found a newspaper in the club, on a dirty table. It was early and the club was still mostly empty. She would not have picked it up, out of fear that she might be punished, except that on the cover was a photograph of the Dear Leader. *At last!* Even for that she might not have taken the risk, but the newspaper was folded so that the crease ran across the Dear Leader's chin. It was an outrage and an abomination! A *Chosun* newspaper never would have dared to place his photograph over the crease. Seeing the desecration of the image sent her into simultaneous paroxysms of fear and rage. She was deeply afraid that someone might report the abused image in the North, and that she might somehow be implicated. She was enraged that a person would so carelessly or, even worse, so maliciously damage his image. She had not seen a photo of him in weeks, and had barely even heard mention of his name, even from her companions. It was wrong that this was how he should come to her, disrespected and cast aside, like rubbish. So much like her.

She was also afraid of what might happen

to her if she did not take steps to rectify, as best she could, the damage to the photograph. This might all be an elaborate test, she realized, set up by her Party Youth organization to assess her worth as a *Chosun* citizen. Maybe all of it — the trip across the DMZ, Mr. Choy, the curtain booth with the red light — was part of an elaborate trial of her devotion to the Dear Leader. She resolved to do the right thing, to prove herself once and for all.

She cast her eyes furtively around. Nobody was watching. She reached down quickly and opened the paper, smoothing out the front, careful not to read any of the words printed there — they might say poisonous things unapproved by the Party. She ripped around the bar napkin–size photograph and then tucked it inside her bra, over her heart. She was afraid of what Mr. Lee would do to her if he found it, but she was even more afraid of what might happen to her if she did not take care of the image of the Dear Leader.

After her work was done for the evening, she reported to Mr. Lee for the nightly search. Some nights the inspections for hidden cash were only cursory, and she hoped that tonight Mr. Lee would have other things on his mind. Other nights he performed more demeaning searches.

He started by looking inside her shoes. Then he made her remove her top, which he turned inside-out and shook. Gi swallowed hard. It looked as though tonight he was being thorough. Next he ordered her to remove her skirt, and then her panties. She held her breath that he would not ask her to remove the bra. He sometimes let it go, but it was unlikely. She was not lucky this time, and he asked that she hand it to him. The search was humiliating, being naked in front of the overfed, bullying Mr. Lee, and he seemed to enjoy her shame. She removed her bra, trying to fold it over the photograph hidden in the left cup, but the movement was not lost to Mr. Lee. His brow furrowed and his muscles flexed.

"Give me that!" he demanded, reaching for the bra.

Gi had no choice but to hand it over. She lowered her head, tensed, and waited for the blows to come.

Mr. Lee unfolded the bra and the photograph of Kim Jong-il fell out of it, swirling on the air as it floated to the floor. Mr. Lee picked it up, frowning. Gi closed her eyes. Soon he would strike her.

Instead, however, he laughed. She was standing alone with him, naked, and he was laughing at her. Her saliva began congealing in her throat and she wanted badly to spit, but she held it in. She felt that she might suffocate on it.

"Of all the things you could try to hide from me," he said through his laughter, "you try to hide this?" When he spoke it sounded as if he had a mouthful of pebbles. "I don't know what you Northerners see in this little rat. Don't worry, it's not worth beating you over this. You can keep the photograph." He dropped it and the bra to the floor and left the room, his cackle receding with him down the hall.

Gi would have preferred being beaten. Of all the responses she could have imagined a person having to the Dear Leader, that was not one of them. She could understand a person feeling fear of him, awe of him, respect for him. She could even understand a person feeling hate for him: It was an appropriately strong emotion for someone so grand. But Mr. Lee laughed, as if the tendrils of the Dear Leader's power did not reach him. He laughed off the Dear Leader as if he were no more than a minor irritant, easily neutralized and completely inconsequential. It was a disturbing response and it shook Gyong-ho to the core. Until she crossed the DMZ, she had never met a person for whom the Dear Leader was not absolutely central. The Dear Leader was credited with everything good. Could it be that there was a limit to his power?

She took the photograph home and more carefully trimmed the edges. She then used a flour and water paste to stick it prominently on one of the bare apartment walls. It was inappropriately small for the size of the wall, and it was hard to make out the details from across the room; but it served to assuage Gyong-ho's feelings of fear and emptiness that were caused by not having any photos of him at all.

She studied his face in detail, memorizing every curve and hair. She would pass the test.

54

Every night for weeks Il-sun did nothing but work in the dancing studio. She eventually developed a routine that she could do even when she was half asleep. As long as she focused on her future prospects once her debt to Mr. Choy was paid, the work was almost bearable. She ached to go home, but the longer she was absent, the more dangerous it would be to return. Anything unaccounted for in *Chosun* was suspicious, especially time.

Once she got past the initial humiliation of being naked in front of Mr. Choy, the technicians, and the anonymous clients on the Internet, she started finding a comfort in her body. In many ways it was less tense than working under Foreman Hwang at the garment factory, with his heavy smell and impossible quotas. Secretly, she even had to admit to herself that she enjoyed being looked at and admired. She liked the thought that the technicians and her clients were excited by her body. She felt powerful, being able to manipulate men by the way she looked and moved.

Mr. Choy was waiting outside the studio when Il-sun arrived. It was a rare event, since he could watch everything from a monitor in his office and relay instructions with his mobile phone. She tensed instinctively at the sight of him, and her heart began to race. When he saw Il-sun, however, he was all smiles and charm.

"Good evening, Il-sun!" he said, his voice lilting and smooth. When he used her name she felt special. He almost never used it, and never when he was displeased. "You have been doing a great job here. I mean it. You are one of the best dancers we have ever had."

In spite of herself, Il-sun felt elevated by the praise. "Thank you," she replied.

"I think you might be ready to try something new. We're going to put you in Studio Two tonight."

Studio Two was referred to by the other women as the "masturbation studio." Il-sun suddenly went cold. That was different from just taking her clothes off and flirting at anonymous clients. It was a much more vulnerable thing to do, to touch herself so intimately in front of the camera. She wanted to refuse, but she swallowed her fear, knowing that if Mr. Choy wanted it, it was going to happen whether or not she was willing.

Mr. Choy sensed her hesitation. "It's not much different, really, than what you have already been doing. But the best part of it is, you get paid more for it. If all you ever do is dance, then it will take a really long time to pay off your debt. Years, probably. But if you do this, then you will pay it off faster. Trust me, I think you'll find it easier than dancing anyway. It's less active. A lot of the girls prefer it, once they've done it."

Il-sun knew that to be a lie, but it was better to keep Mr. Choy in a good mood. She nodded consent.

"Good girl! Come with me," he said, putting his arm around her shoulder. He walked her down to Studio Two. His arm was hard and heavy. It felt toxic, like it was radiating something that would make her sick if he held the contact for too long. She was glad that the walk was short.

The layout of Studio Two was identical to that of Studio One, on the floor above, but instead of there being a pole in the middle of each partition, there was a sofa or a bed.

"Okay," Mr. Choy began. "This isn't so

difficult. Like dancing, everything is timed, and a bell rings for every minute the client stays with you. Watch the monitor, because sometimes they like to give you instructions. You can read, can't you?"

Il-sun nodded.

"For the first three minutes, you just tease the guy. Touch yourself through your underwear, offer glimpses, but nothing more. Then take your top off, just like in the pole studio. Draw it out for two minutes. Then the same with your panties. Make a show out of it and exaggerate your pleasure. Pinch your nipples, move your hips, make groaning sounds. There's a live microphone hanging from the ceiling, so the client can hear you. Touch yourself with your hands, but don't put your fingers inside until the ninth minute —"

"I have to put my fingers inside?" Il-sun was appalled. Nobody had told her to expect that.

"That's what they're paying for," he replied, raising his voice. His eyes hardened for just a moment, and then quickly softened. "There is a dildo on the table next to the sofa. Don't put that inside until at least the twelfth minute, okay?"

She swallowed dryly and nodded. She walked into the studio and looked around.

383

She was glad that the bright lights blotted out the lens of the camera. She picked up the dildo on the table. It was made out of rubber molded to look like a penis. It was, however, extremely large, and the thought of putting it inside her caused her to panic. She did not think it would ever go in; at least not without considerable pain.

"It's too big," Il-sun finally said, turning her head to Mr. Choy. "I can't use this."

"Nonsense!" shouted Mr. Choy. He did not sound angry, exactly, but there was a rising note of displeasure in his voice. "You're one of Gianni's girls, so I know you're not a virgin." That comment stung Il-sun deeply. It made her feel cheap and dirty. "Guys want to watch you be stretched open. If it were any smaller it wouldn't look right on video."

"There is a bottle of lubricant in the table drawer," said one of the technicians over the loudspeaker, trying to help, but it only compounded her embarrassment.

Il-sun doubted that lubricant would make it much easier, but it would be better than nothing. She opened the drawer and spread lubricant on the dildo. She realized that her nervousness was not going to help matters, but she could not control that.

"Going live in thirty seconds," said the

technician.

Il-sun knew that there was no point in obsessing over her dread. She took a position on the sofa and waited.

"Going live in five . . . four . . . three . . . two . . . one."

Il-sun began to strip. She flirted with the camera in the way she knew was expected of her, following the timing bells. She could see Mr. Choy standing with his arms folded, observing her. She could not see his expression because of the lights, and his glasses reflected them like two glowing monster eyes. A bell rang and she began rubbing herself through her undergarments. Another bell rang and she removed her bra, and then after another bell, her panties. She felt herself flush with embarrassment as she spread her legs, opening herself to the camera, but she did not stop for fear of Mr. Choy's fury. She continued to rub herself. She was too scared to feel pleasure in it, but she pretended all the same. A bell toned and she reached for the dildo on the table. The bell rang again, and she knew there would be no stopping. With one hand she spread her labia, and with the other she pressed the tip of the dildo into the entrance of her vagina. She took a deep breath, and on the exhalation she pushed it into herself.

Her vagina started to give way, and for a moment she thought the dildo was going to slide in easily; but it quickly became too thick and she felt a tearing pain. She stopped and withdrew it, taking a couple of deep breaths. She tried again, pushing, but again she could not open enough to comfortably accept it. She tried one more time, determined, weighing the fear of pain against the fear of Mr. Choy. She pushed hard and she felt as if she was being ripped apart as the tip went in.

The pain awakened anger inside of her. She was no longer afraid. She hated Mr. Choy. She hated Gianni. She hated Foreman Hwang. She hated the Dear Leader. She withdrew the dildo, screaming, "Fuck you!" She then threw the dildo at Mr. Choy. Taken by surprise, his reflex to duck came late and it hit him square in the face, knocking his glasses askew.

Mr. Choy exploded. To be defied was bad enough, but to be outwardly attacked was too much. He picked the dildo up off the floor and ran at Il-sun, who lifted her legs and crossed her arms over her face in self-defense. Mr. Choy lifted the dildo high over his head, and began beating her with it mercilessly. Soft though it was, he hit with such force that it stung badly. She kicked and punched at him, but he was so much larger than she that it was useless. His eyes were wide and his lips set in a rabid snarl. He reached with his left hand and wrapped it around her throat, pinning her to the sofa. He then took the dildo in his right hand and forced it between her legs. She fought hard, and it was difficult for him to overcome her, but eventually she succumbed. He positioned the dildo over her vagina, and then thrust it with all his might. She felt a searing, ripping pain as the dildo entered her. He kept pushing and pushing until it was as far as it could go. Il-sun nearly vomited as she could feel the intrusive object all the way in her belly. She thought she might die, choked to death by the wild Mr. Choy. She hoped she would. The pain was unbearable, and she felt herself slipping from consciousness.

Mr. Choy released the death grip on her throat and her vision began to fade back in. She coughed. Mr. Choy stepped back from her and she rolled onto her side, tears streaming down her cheeks. She reached between her legs and removed the dildo, causing almost as much pain as when it went in.

"I want you ready in twenty minutes; and I want you to do what you're told!" Mr.

Choy screamed at her. He turned and stormed out of the studio.

Il-sun rolled her face into the cushion of the sofa, wrapping her arms around herself, and sobbed.

Several minutes later she got up, holding her lower abdomen, and started making her way toward the restroom, without even bothering to put her clothes on. It hurt to walk, but not as much as it hurt her pride to walk past the technicians who had all witnessed her being violated. She kept her head down.

She could hear the clack of high-heeled shoes running to catch up with her. She did not turn to see who it was. A moment later, an arm wrapped around her shoulder and she was accompanied to the restroom. Once inside, Il-sun looked up at her companion. It was a *Hanguk* girl she had met briefly a couple of times in passing. Like many of the women in Mr. Choy's empire, she had chosen to go by an English name, Susie.

Il-sun stood at a sink, holding herself up with her hands, and broke down sobbing. Susie, without saying a word, rubbed her back and stood with her until the tears subsided. Il-sun turned the faucet on and washed her face, then she made eye contact with Susie in the mirror.

"He is such an asshole!" Susie said. "I can't believe he did that to you."

"What can I do?" pleaded Il-sun. "He scares me so much. I don't have anywhere to go."

"I know. I know," replied Susie in a consoling way.

"When will this ever end? Can you tell me that? When?"

"We don't always have a choice about what we do. I hate this business."

"Then why don't you leave? You're one of the free ones. Not like me."

"I may seem free, but I'm not. Not really."

"Then how did you end up here?" Il-sun asked, wiping the remainder of her tears away with the back of her hand.

"When I was sixteen I had a boyfriend who was going to the university. I would have done anything for him. He wanted to have sex with me, so I let him, thinking he would love me if I did. He didn't want to use a condom, and I was stupid and said okay. We did it once, and that was it. I was pregnant.

"I came from a good family; my dad is an executive in a big company. When he found out that I was pregnant, he went through the roof. He kicked me out of the house, saying I had shamed him. I didn't have anywhere to go, so I lived on the streets. I begged for help, but I didn't have enough to eat. I miscarried. I went back to my dad and begged him to take me back, but he wouldn't have me. Said I no longer existed to him. I was crushed.

"Eventually, a man offered me money if I would suck him off. I was desperate, so I did it. I tried to find a good job, but I was only sixteen and no one wanted me. Whoring was the easiest way — in fact, the only way — I could find to make enough money to eat and afford a place to live. Then I fell in with Mr. Choy. He did not pay me as much per job as I was making on my own, but he could get me more clients, so I started working for him. And now there's this Internet thing. So, now I'm stuck too."

"How do you deal with this?"

"I'll tell you. Actually, I'll show you," replied Susie, reaching into her purse. She withdrew a small glass object and a plastic bag filled with a white substance.

"What's that?" asked Il-sun.

"This is *hiroppong*. It'll make you feel great. Even after that shitty episode back there."

"How?"

"We're going to smoke some of it right now. Trust me, it's what you need to get through this." Susie took a small chunk of the *hiroppong* out of the bag and loaded it into the glass device she was holding — it was a kind of pipe. Susie then brought the pipe up to her lips. She took a plastic lighter out of her purse and then held the flame to the bottom of the pipe. In a few seconds, the *hiroppong* turned from solid to liquid, then began to bubble and smoke. Susie inhaled.

An odd smell, vaguely like burning plastic and ammonia, filled the restroom as Susie exhaled a long stream of smoke. "You take it in, and then hold your breath for a moment so that it gets into your bloodstream. You start to feel really good almost immediately," Susie instructed.

"I'm not sure . . ."

"Trust me. It will take away the pain. You will feel like the most powerful woman in the world, and you'll be able to get the job done. You heard Mr. Choy. He wants you back in there."

Il-sun took the pipe and Susie loaded it with more *hiroppong.* "You won't regret this, I promise you. Now hold it in your mouth. I'll tell you when to inhale. Since it's your first time, just take a little bit and see how you feel." She held the flame of the lighter under the pipe. "Okay, now inhale."

Il-sun inhaled and tried to hold her breath, but the smoke hurt her lungs. She felt like her chest was on fire and she went into a fit of coughing. Susie laughed. "I did that the first time, too," she said.

The coughing subsided and Il-sun began to notice a peculiar feeling taking over her body. At first she just felt dizzy, but that was quickly replaced by a feeling like electricity shooting through her bones and out of her fingertips and toes. The pain in her body was replaced by a light, transparent feeling. She felt like she might even be hovering off the floor. It was the most wonderful feeling in the world. Colors became sharper, sounds became clearer. She felt like if she wanted to, she could jump and touch the ceiling. She was powerful. Infinitely powerful. She could do anything; in fact, she just might do . . . *everything.* Everything! She would do everything!

She looked down at herself and realized she was still naked. She was beautiful! Having a body was the most wonderful thing ever. It felt so good to be alive. She looked at Susie and realized that she was beautiful too. They were the most beautiful people in the whole world, standing side by side in the restroom. And they both could do everything.

Il-sun and Susie floated out of the rest-room and back into the studio. They walked past the technicians, who looked up and then averted their eyes. They apparently felt bad about what they had seen Mr. Choy do.

"It's okay!" exclaimed Il-sun to them. "I'm okay!"

Il-sun glided into her stall. She could do it, and it would be beautiful.

"Are you okay?" asked the technician over the loudspeaker.

"I'm great," she responded.

"Are you ready to try again?" He sounded uncertain.

"I'm ready," she said.

"Going live in one minute."

Il-sun put her clothes back on and struck a pose on the sofa.

"Going live in five . . ."

Il-sun needed to move fast. She knew it would be better that way. The minute bell seemed to take an eternity to ring. She stripped forever, and the whole world was watching her. The whole world loved her. She was the most beautiful thing on earth.

The buzzer rang. The customer went off-line. She had not even taken off her top.

"What was that?" asked the technician. "What's wrong with you? Just do it like normal."

"Wasn't that wonderful?"

"No, it was awful. The customer thought so too. Do it right, or Mr. Choy will come back. You don't want that."

"Okay. Sorry. I'm really sorry. Sorry. I'm ready to do it again. Sorry. It's hot in here. I'm ready. I said I'm ready! Why is everyone so fucking slow today?"

"Calm down, please. Just relax and do it like normal, okay? Going live in thirty seconds."

"Okay. I can do it.

"I can do it."

"Five . . . four . . . three . . . two . . . one."

Il-sun would never need to sleep again. She told the technicians that she could stay for another whole shift; but they would not allow her to. She went back to the apartment and paced until the others came home. They were exhausted. She watched them sleep, impatiently. The sun came up, and then the woman across the hall knocked on their door to tell them it was time to clean. Il-sun felt like she could clean all day.

But the *hiroppong* gave out soon after she reached the alley shop. She came crashing down from her high all at once, and all the darkness of her life closed in around her.

She felt like weeping, but she was too tired for even that. She was no longer immortal or beautiful. She hated her loathsome, ugly self.

Somehow she made it through the cleaning shift, but then fell into a deep sleep. Her friends could not wake her for night work. Fortunately Mr. Choy was not on site that evening, and the technicians took pity on her by allowing her to rest. When Il-sun came to, their neighbor was knocking on the door for cleaning duty the next day. She got out of bed with a terrible headache and overwhelming thirst. She hurt all over. She remembered being violated by Mr. Choy and she seethed with anger and embarrassment. Her skin still stung where he had struck her. Her throat was sore where he had throttled her. Her vagina ached. She felt dirty inside and out.

Cho and Gyong-ho stared at her wide-eyed. She was bruised in the places where she had been hit, and there was a red and black ring around her neck. They asked her what happened, but she did not feel like talking about it. She was hungry, but all she really wanted was more of Susie's *hiroppong*. She needed to feel that way again.

55

Gyong-ho was lying on her side, facing Il-sun's back, watching her shoulder rise and fall with her breath, counting. Could she dare touch her again? This time the urge to do so was not entirely selfish: Il-sun looked in terrible shape, and Gi longed to offer comfort. Il-sun was beaten and bruised, and even though her body was filling in quickly from three weeks — twenty-four days, by her count — of better nutrition, she appeared to be deflating. Something of her essence was draining out of her, leaving her hollow. Gi once again felt a stirring fury, like when Foreman Hwang had told her he was going to marry her, and was once again disappointed that such a strong emotion — like her love — could be so useless. There was nothing she could do about it. Her greatest fear was not of the damage that this life could inflict on her, but for what it could do to Il-sun. If Il-sun lost the power to attract sunlight, then there would be no light left for Gi — the sun did not shine for her.

Gi waited until she was almost choking before getting up to spit. It seemed that the substance of her blood was slowly being replaced by something thicker, each day she worked behind the curtain. If she spit enough, maybe her veins would not solidify with it. And spitting was the only outlet for her anger. She spit, not only to clear her blood, but also to spit *on* something. She wished it could be Mr. Lee or Mr. Choy, but she would never dare. Between breath six hundred eighty-one and breath six hundred eighty-two she fell asleep.

The next morning, they performed their cleaning routine as normal, and then went back to the apartment to get ready for night work. Jasmine was still in the habit of coming to help them get ready, even though they did not really need the assistance anymore. She enjoyed their company. When Jasmine saw what Mr. Choy had done, and once she had drawn the story out of Il-sun, she fumed.

"He seems to be getting worse all the time," she said. "When I first started working for him, he never lost his temper. He was always a cool manipulator, not an outright bully. Mr. Lee, on the other hand, isn't above hitting a woman, but Mr. Choy would never do that. Now he flies into a rage at the littlest thing. It's like he can't control himself, and he's always high." She paused thoughtfully, looking out the window, and then added, "There has to be a way out."

"What can we do? I don't think I can carry on," said Il-sun. "I don't want to do it anymore. I just want to go home."

Jasmine sighed, then hoisted a stiff smile to her lips. "Let's see what we can do about those bruises," she said to Il-sun, reaching for the makeup.

56

The next night, Jasmine burst into the apartment and closed the door behind her. Gi was accustomed to seeing her in the evenings, but tonight she could tell that something was different. Jasmine called them into the living room, and they gathered on Cho's futon.

"I'm getting us out of here," Jasmine said, in a whisper.

"*What?* How?" asked Il-sun.

"I've been chatting online with a man from Kwangju, one of my regular Internet clients. He has offered to marry me."

"But what does that have to do with us?" asked Cho.

"I agreed to marry him if my mother and sisters could live with us. You're my sisters!"

"What about Mr. Choy?" asked Il-sun. "How can we leave? We're guarded all the time."

"I have a plan, but before I tell you, I need

to know that you're willing to take a risk. Will you leave with me?"

"I'm not sure," said Cho. "We have been here for almost a month and I have been working really hard. I must be getting close to paying off Mr. Choy, and then he'll help me get papers and start paying me real money. Who's to say if Kwangju will be better?"

"Look, I didn't want to tell you before because I didn't want you to get discouraged, but Mr. Choy is never going to help you get papers. He isn't keeping track of any tab because he has no intention of ever letting you go. I have seen a lot of *Chosun* girls come and go, and none of them have ever been allowed to go free. Honestly, I think he sells off the ones who don't earn well." Jasmine lowered her head, and then said, in a barely audible whisper, "I have seen this happen too many times without doing anything about it. I can't live with it anymore."

"But he said —" Cho began, defensively, but stopped herself. "I was wondering about that," she continued in a low, defeated voice. She sighed heavily. "Okay. Whatever it is, I'll do it."

"Me, too," said Il-sun. "I can't keep doing this."

"Gi?" asked Jasmine. All eyes turned to Gyong-ho, who did not speak right away. Her life in Mr. Choy's empire was unbearable, but facing even more uncertainty might push her past the breaking point. At least she knew, more or less, what to expect where she was. This was not the kind of decision that growing up in *Chosun* prepared her for. Where was the wisdom of the Dear Leader to guide her?

"Gi, we can't leave without you," said Il-sun. Then she added, "I don't want to lose you."

That was the one thing that Gi needed to hear, and it propped her against her fear. "Okay," she said. "I'll go."

"So what's the plan?" asked Cho.

"As soon as you come back from cleaning tomorrow, one of you will go into the restroom and wait there for me. I will come up right after you're done with the cleaning — that's when there's the least activity in the building. Razor will be at the gate, and I've seen how he looks at me. He sits there bored all day, and I know he wouldn't mind getting laid. I'll come to the gate and seduce him. He'll let me in, and I will take him to the restroom and let him have his way. When we get into the restroom, whoever is in there will leave and let the others out of the apartment. Then all of you will go out the gate and down to the street level."

"What if Razor locks the gate after you come in?" Il-sun asked.

"I won't give him the chance. As soon as he opens the door, I'll be on him, kissing him and squeezing his ass. He won't be able to think straight. It should work just fine; but if it doesn't, then . . ." Jasmine swallowed, then cleared her throat. She did not want to say the next part, but she had to. "Whatever the outcome, I have to be on that bus to Kwangju. My mom is already on her way." She looked down with a guilty look, but she did not linger on it. "You need a code to get out the front door. The code is thirty-seven thirteen. That's three, seven, one, three. Then you hit the Pound button. That's the one that looks like this," she said, drawing a pound sign on the window with her fingertip. "The door will make a buzzing sound when it unlocks. As soon as you're out the door, turn left and run to the next block. From there, turn left. Walk two-and-a-half blocks, and you will see an alley across the street on the right. Go down the alley to the little noodle shop. Wait there for me. Any questions?"

"Where will we go from the noodle shop?" asked Cho.

"From there we will walk together to the bus station — about fifteen blocks. Our bus for Kwangju leaves at nine, which should give us plenty of time. Agreed?"

"What will happen to us if we get caught?" asked Gi.

"Let's not think about it," said Jasmine.

57

Cho did her night work with a knot in her stomach, but with proud resolve knowing that she was taking an active step to escape her captivity. It was much easier to put up with the work knowing that it was her last night on the job. She slept fitfully when she got home, trying not to think of all the things that could go wrong with the plan. It seemed far-fetched and cobbled together. There was no way to know for sure what would happen, in the end.

The morning came all too slowly. Their neighbor arrived at the usual time and the women went off to clean the building. Cho felt a twinge of guilt knowing that they were escaping, leaving the young woman behind with Mr. Choy. She would have to fend for herself. The day would not go quickly enough, even though she dreaded the danger of escaping. She wanted to get it over with.

When the women finally climbed the stairs at the end of the day, they were met with a shock — it was not Razor at the gate, but one of the other bouncers. He was older and, by appearances, less gullible. He was one of Mr. Lee's bullying friends, and all the women feared him. Already it was not going according to plan. The women looked at each other with uncertainty as they were let in. Did this mean that the plan was off? Cho decided to play her part through and went directly to the restroom to wait for Jasmine.

She sat in one of the stalls for what felt like an endless quarter hour. The door swung open and someone walked inside, but it was only one of the other women who lived on the floor. She came and went. Cho continued to wait. After another quarter hour, the door opened again, but it was only the bouncer, without Jasmine.

"What's taking you so long?" he said in a gruff voice.

"Some things just can't be rushed," Cho replied, trying to sound sweet. Her heart was beating in her throat. He closed the door and his footsteps receded down the hall.

Cho was becoming quite anxious and, after several more minutes, decided to peek into the hallway. She opened the restroom door a crack and peered to the end of the hall. Jasmine was standing at the top of the stairs. She was dressed to seduce — in a miniskirt, a low-cut blouse, and strappy stiletto heels. Cho saw the shock register on her face as she realized that the man behind the gate was not Razor.

"Oh, hi. Where's Razor? He's usually minding this floor," said Jasmine with a slight quake in her voice.

"Day off," replied the bouncer.

"Well, I can't say that I'm upset by it. You're awfully handsome," she said, recovering herself quickly. "You know, I've had my eye on you for some time."

Cho was relieved — Jasmine was still going forward with the plan.

The bouncer either grunted in response, or mumbled something that Cho could not hear.

"I'll bet all the girls try to go home with you," Jasmine said, batting her eyelashes flirtatiously.

"I'm married," he responded. It sounded more like a command. A command to leave him alone. Cho felt her heart sink. It wasn't working. But Jasmine was not so easily deterred.

"Well, she sure is a lucky woman. I'll bet

you please her all night long," she said, reaching between the bars of the gate to run her finger down his chest. "I wish someone would please me all night long." Her voice was syrup. Cho could not see what effect it was having on him.

"I told you, I'm married," he said again. It sounded like he was beginning to weaken, but perhaps Cho was only imagining it.

Jasmine pulled her hand back quickly with a hurt look in her eyes. "I didn't mean to offend you." Her voice was suddenly cold and injured. Cho admired Jasmine's subtlety. Now the bouncer felt like he had to apologize for something, even though he did not know why. He was flustered, losing his edge of gruffness.

"I'm sorry, I didn't mean —"

"It's just that, a girl like me doesn't get many chances to have a strong, handsome man like you. You're a great lover. A girl can tell these things, you know, just by looking at a man. I haven't been pleased by a real man for such a long time . . ." Jasmine let the thought trail as she offered a steamy look through the bars. "Maybe you could let me in and we could . . ." She allowed that thought to trail also.

The bouncer unlocked the gate. It was working! They were going to escape! Jasmine charged inside, causing the bouncer to step back. She put her arms around him and kissed him hungrily on the lips. He kissed back. She pressed herself into him, grinding with her hips, pushing him away from the gate. "I'm so hot for you," she said. "I want you so badly." She put one of her hands on his buttocks and squeezed. "Take me right now," she commanded. The bouncer started unfastening his belt. "No, not here," she said. "Someone might see."

"Where?"

"The bathroom," she said, exaggerating the breathiness of her voice. She grabbed his hand and started pulling him along the hallway. He had forgotten to lock the door! It was going to work!

Cho stepped back in the bathroom, listening to their footsteps in the hallway as they approached. They stopped halfway to the restroom. Cho peeked out again.

"Wait, I have to lock the gate," he said. Cho's stomach clenched.

"No, I have to have you now," she replied, pulling on his hand.

"It will just take a second." He peeled his hand from hers and turned around before she could protest further.

"Shit!" Cho said aloud, without meaning to. Jasmine heard and looked over. The bouncer assumed it had been Jasmine.

"Be patient, honey. Good loving like mine is worth waiting for," he said.

Cho ducked back into the bathroom.

Jasmine came in first, with the bouncer right behind. She had a wide, frightened look in her eyes. She made eye contact with Cho and shook her head.

"Finally finished?" sneered the bouncer when he saw Cho. "I hope you flushed."

Cho walked out the door and stood there as it closed behind her. What were they going to do now? Jasmine would still leave, but Cho, Il-sun, and Gi were stuck. The thought was too much for Cho to bear. She had settled in her mind that she was leaving tonight, and she was determined to make it happen; but how?

Suddenly an idea struck her and her feet responded by taking her down the hall. She opened the door to their apartment and stepped inside, leaving the door wide open.

"What happened? Is it time?" asked Il-sun frantically. They were all tightly wound.

Cho did not answer because she did not want to lose the momentum of what she was about to do. She was desperate. She went to the stovetop and grabbed the cast iron skillet. It was still full of leftover vegetables, so she dumped the food onto the floor and walked out of the apartment.

"What are you doing?" asked Il-sun.

"Be ready to leave when I say so," was all she said as she disappeared down the hall.

Cho marched with purpose to the restroom door. She opened it and stepped through quickly. The bouncer was standing, facing Jasmine against the wall, thrusting himself hard and fast into her. His trousers were around his ankles and Jasmine's skirt was hiked up around her waist. Jasmine looked up with terror in her eyes as she saw Cho with the frying pan lifted high above her head. The bouncer sensed something and turned his head.

"What the fu—" he began to say as Cho brought the heavy pan down on the crown of his head. He slumped instantly as the sickening crunch of his skull and the reverberations of the frying pan echoed off the tile walls. He fell to the floor, twitching, the slope of his head permanently changed. Jasmine shrieked.

"Let's find his keys!" Cho said, pushing the horror of what she had just done out of her mind.

Jasmine could not move. She stood there wide-eyed, with her hand over her mouth. Cho bent down and searched the bouncer's pockets. She found the keys and leveled a look at Jasmine.

"Are you coming?" she asked, with a calm, steady voice.

Cho's voice brought Jasmine out of her shock, and the women left the restroom without looking back.

Gyong-ho and Il-sun were already standing in the hallway.

"The gate is locked!" exclaimed Il-sun.

Cho showed her the keys. She walked to the gate and unlocked it. The women stepped through it and onto the stairs. The stairs were interminable as they jogged down to the ground floor. Freedom was so close, but the danger was still so high.

They made it to the ground floor without seeing anyone. Jasmine stepped up to the keypad at the front door. She could not press buttons fast enough, and in her hurry she pressed the wrong key. The door refused to open.

"Come on!" shouted Cho in frustration. They were almost out.

"I'm doing the best I can!" replied Jasmine. She finally pressed the correct combination and the door buzzed. They could see the fading light of dusk on the other side of it. Jasmine pushed and the door gave way. The women crowded through it, turned left, and ran right into Mr. Lee.

58

"What's going on here?" shouted Mr. Lee as the women collided with his bulky frame.

A moment of shocked uncertainty passed between Mr. Lee and the women.

"Run!" yelled Cho, breaking into a sprint.

Mr. Lee moved surprisingly quickly for such an overweight man, and managed to grab hold of Cho's arm in an iron grip just before she was able to bolt out of reach. She wriggled, trying to break free, but he twisted her arm painfully and she screamed.

Jasmine turned and ran in the opposite direction, but a man jumped out of a parked car and tackled her on the sidewalk. He half dragged her back to the front door.

"Any of you try to run like that and I'll break her fucking arm off. Get inside!" Mr. Lee commanded. They stepped back into the building and the door closed behind them with a fateful *click*. Holding Cho with one hand, he reached into his pocket with the other and produced a mobile phone. Using his thumb he dialed a sequence of numbers.

"It's Lee. We have a problem," he said into the device. "The Northerners tried to bolt . . . Yeah, the new ones . . . What do you want me to do? . . . Okay. We'll be waiting." He closed his phone with a snap, and said, "Come with me. You first. Up the stairs."

With their hearts pounding they trudged up to the third floor, followed by Mr. Lee, who was still holding on to Cho, with the man who had tackled Jasmine bringing up the rear. Mr. Lee took them into Mr. Choy's office and closed the door behind him.

"Sit against the wall in those chairs," Mr. Lee barked. "And no talking!" He made another call on his mobile phone, but there was apparently no answer.

"Where is Kang?" he asked the women.

They did not reply.

Mr. Lee turned to the other man. "Go up to the fourth floor and check on Kang. He's not answering his phone." The man left immediately.

The silence while they waited was excruciating. Mr. Lee sat at Mr. Choy's desk facing the women, staring menacingly at them. The women mostly kept their heads down and eyes averted. Gi cleared her throat several times, wanting to spit but had nowhere to do so. Several long minutes passed as the women steeped in their anxiety. Mr. Lee's phone rang, causing everyone to jump.

"Lee here," he said, answering the call. "He's what? . . . Is he alive? . . . Get someone to help you. Who's in the studio? . . . Call him and take Kang to the emergency room — I don't care if his head was fucking cut off, I don't want an ambulance here. We don't need that kind of attention . . . Just take him and dump him off. They'll know what to do . . . You call his wife; I have more important things to do." Mr. Lee snapped his phone shut.

My God, I just killed a man, thought Cho as the brunt of her actions hit her full force. She looked at her clawlike hands in disbelief. *The hands of a murderer,* she thought. Cho felt self-disgust for the violence she had committed. Even if the man did not die, she was guilty of murder in her mind. There had been such anger in her heart seeing the bouncer slam himself so unfeelingly into Jasmine, using her for his own gratification as if she were not there at all. The intent to kill rose straight from her liver to the frying pan without pausing in any of her more sensible organs. She brought the pan down

414

and hit him, hoping he would die. Now she realized that the man had a name — Kang — and he was dying and leaving behind a pretty, young wife who would never fully heal from the grief of losing him. She felt that her guilt might consume her. She wished that she had the power to turn the clock back and make a different choice. Who was she to have wanted a better life?

Mr. Choy came bursting through the door.

"What's going on?" he demanded.

Mr. Lee stood up. He seemed afraid of Mr. Choy's wrath as well.

"They hit Kang over the head and stole his keys. I caught them as they were running out the front door."

"Where is Kang now?"

"On his way to the emergency room. He's still alive, but they say it looks bad. His head is bashed in."

Mr. Choy looked at the women, who were sitting in folding chairs in a line against the wall. His eyes landed on Jasmine. "You did this, Jasmine?"

Jasmine kept her eyes on the floor, tears rolling off her cheeks.

"I'm hurt that you would do this to me, after all we've been through. You're one of my best." Mr. Choy could not keep still. His body twitched randomly and he shuffled on his feet, moving from side to side.

"What should we do with them, boss?" asked Mr. Lee.

"Let me think, goddamn it, Lee!" shouted Mr. Choy, causing Mr. Lee to flinch. "Shut up when I'm thinking!"

Mr. Choy had a wild look in his eyes. His pupils were wide like coins. He kept scratching and picking at his face. An open sore on his cheek wept. "I can't exactly keep them now, can I? Can I, Mr. Lee? Not after they've tried to kill one of my men. They could be dangerous. *Dangerous,* Mr. Lee!"

"Clearly," responded Mr. Lee.

"Well, if I can't keep them, and I can't give them away . . . You're supposed to laugh when I make a joke, Lee."

"Joke, sir?" There had been no apparent joke.

"I can't give them away. That's funny. I can't keep them, and I can't give them away. Get it? Get it?" He grabbed Mr. Lee by the shoulders and shook him. "Get it?"

"I think so," said Mr. Lee, his face showing more fear than understanding.

"Well, what do you do if you can't keep something and you can't give it away?"

"I really don't know," said Mr. Lee with a pained look on his face.

"That's because you didn't go to university. You sell it, Lee! You sell it! We're going to sell these bitches to the highest bidder. Find me a buyer!" he ordered, and stormed out the door.

59

The thin strip of sky visible from the apartment window showed a cloudless, early-summer day. Gyong-ho wondered if she would ever again get to go out to enjoy the sunlight. It had been three days since they had tried to escape, and they were only allowed out of their apartment once a day to empty their chamber pot. The apartment stank even with the window wide open and the fan on.

Gi contemplated jumping out the window. Suicide seemed a dignified response, she thought. She was certain that if she dove headfirst she would die from the fall. That thought alone — that she had a quick way of dispatching herself — gave her enough courage to live through another day, tedious and uncertain as it was.

There was not much to say. They had nearly escaped, but failed. There was nothing to apologize for, no blame to cast. Jasmine could not have arrived any earlier. They could not have made their way down the stairs any faster; and even if Jasmine had gotten the gate code correct on the first try, it would not have made much difference. Mr. Lee would still have been right outside the door. The only regret in the room was felt by Cho, for hitting the bouncer. She regretted every murderous thought she had ever had. There was no real vindication in striking back. There was nothing left to do now but wait.

Gi found herself once again contemplating what it meant to be sold. Mr. Choy had said that he was going to sell them to the highest bidder. Who would buy them, and for what purpose? How much money was a human life worth, and how does one arrive at that sum? She held on to a glimmer of hope that her new owner would be more kind. Her biggest fear was that she would be separated from Il-sun.

The women were running out of food. They had at first been too scared, and then too proud to ask for more provisions. There was plenty of water to drink, and they knew that they could hold out for a few weeks, albeit miserably, if they had to. They still had a bag of rice and a shallow, lightweight aluminum pot to cook it in. Everything that was heavy or sharp had been removed from the room. Gi could not blame Mr. Choy for taking precautions, but she thought it wholly unnecessary. She did not think even Cho had the heart to inflict more violence.

At around midday, Mr. Choy and Mr. Lee arrived with two bouncers. Mr. Choy looked rough, with dark circles under his dull eyes. His skin was a grayish color, and he walked as if the percussion of his feet on the floor hurt his head.

"I finally found a buyer for you," he said with a ragged voice. He scratched at his face and then looked under his fingernails as if expecting to find something there. There was nothing. "An old business colleague of mine. I got a pretty good price, too. All in all a good return on my investment. Now you are going to go on a little journey, and you'll be out of my hair forever. Just in time, too. I need to make room for Gianni's next shipment. He has two new cuties for me, and they need your apartment."

"Where are we going?" asked Jasmine.

"You'll know when you get there."

"How is Kang?" Cho burst out suddenly, like a cork giving way under pressure. She had been trying to hold the question in, but she no longer had the strength. She looked as if she might cry.

"Oh, you care about him now, do you? You should have thought about that before you reshaped his skull," Mr. Choy said venomously. "Kang is alive. Barely. They say he is going to have permanent motor damage, though it's too early to know how bad. He's in and out of consciousness. Are you satisfied?"

Cho hung her head, holding back a wave of tears. She did not want to give Mr. Choy the satisfaction of her regret. She wished it had been him. She wondered if she would feel bad if she had smashed his head instead.

As they walked out of the apartment, Gyong-ho reached for her portrait of the Dear Leader — she did not want to be without him. But then she thought of the new *Chosun* girls who would be arriving. She thought about how confused and frightened and alone they would be, so far from home. They needed him more than she did, she decided, and left the portrait where it was. Maybe it would offer some comfort.

Mr. Choy made the women walk in single file down to the street, flanked by the bouncers. At the curb was the dented minivan in which they had arrived in South Korea from the DMZ.

"This is where we say good-bye," said Mr. Choy with melodrama. "I know how much you'll miss me. I'll completely forget you in a couple of weeks, but you'll remember me forever."

That statement made Gyong-ho seethe. She knew it was true, that he would always be a scar on her soul that she would feel and remember every day. She also knew that he would forget them, like a man forgets a thousand other little business decisions made in the construction of the big picture. That he knew it too, yet still inflicted his abuses, put the final punctuation on his evil. He was a man festering with hate, and his very cells lacked the organelles of compassion that, collectively, gave a person conscience. Gyong-ho had suffered torture, humiliation, subservience, and sexual abuse, and yet had never, until now, felt hatred. She could see that all of her previous abusers had, in some way, been victims themselves, acting through the pain that the world had dealt them, and she could forgive them. But Mr. Choy was not a victim and she could not forgive him.

Hate burned like acid, corroding her innocence even more than the sexual acts he had forced her to commit. Hate demanded vengeance and retribution, the million acts of which cascaded through her imagination in images of violence and pain. With every drop of hate that condensed inside her, something else, pure and wholesome, was squeezed out. It was an infection that she had caught from him, making her blister inside — she would never again be free of it.

She locked her eyes on his, and he was momentarily transfixed. Coming from such a meek and broken girl the power of her gaze took him by surprise. Maybe, if he had not been coming down from amphetamines, he would have been immune to it; but he was weak and depressed and exhausted. He was blindsided by her stark, wordless honesty and became lost in her eyes. They were terrible, beautiful eyes. She released the essence of her soul with full force into her eyes and showed him the hate he had bequeathed her. For one crystal clear moment he could feel the horror of what he was spreading in the world. He stepped back, as if punched. She had infected him with something too.

60

Mr. Lee sliced his way through the city in the minivan, the four captive women subdued and sullen, crammed together on the bench seat in the back. After an hour of driving through traffic, well into the outskirts of the city, they came to an area dominated by warehouses and industry. Smoke belched from factories, and the view was overwhelmed by large, blocky buildings with iron beams and no windows. The van pulled into one of the many indistinguishable tin-clad structures.

Inside the warehouse was a semi truck with a twenty-foot steel shipping container strapped to its bed. There was a long ramp leading from the ground to the bed of the truck, and men were scurrying about, stacking boxes at its side.

"Get out," Mr. Lee ordered, and the women piled out of the van. A short, thin man with a permanent stoop scurried up to

Mr. Lee.

"Everything's ready, sir. Just like you asked." The man's voice was high and nasal. He oozed sycophantically, carrying himself in a way that reminded Gyong-ho of a dog humping the leg of his master.

"Is there enough food and water? One of them died last time," said Mr. Lee.

"Yes, sir. I remember," the man said, lowering his head and raising his left hand. His little finger had been amputated at the second knuckle. "I'll never make that mistake again."

"Good. Let's have a look," said Mr. Lee, walking to the ramp in the back of the truck. He and the man disappeared into the shipping container. A minute later they reemerged. "I think that should be fine," said Mr. Lee. The man looked relieved, unconsciously rubbing the knuckles of his left hand.

"Okay, girls, listen up," Mr. Lee said. "You're going inside that container, and you will be in there for a couple of weeks. There should be enough food and water, but use them conservatively or you will die. Do you understand?"

The women nodded.

"Alright. Put them inside," Mr. Lee commanded.

PART III

61

Il-sun vomited into the bucket. She had been doing that on and off for days, and Gyong-ho assumed that it was due to the constant pitching and rolling of the shipping container. They were at sea. Gauging by the alternating light and dark that filtered in through the small vent holes at the top of the container, the ship had sailed for two days before docking again; and Gi had hoped, in spite of what Mr. Lee had said about how much time to expect inside, that they would be released soon. For a little more than a week, by Gi's count, the ship sat at dock. By day she could hear the rumble of heavy machinery, and by night a ghostly quiet. Then, once again, they took to the sea.

Each day, under the sun, they baked inside the hot steel box, and each night they froze. They were shut into a special compartment at the end of the container, their quarters cramped and unyielding. The air in the small room became thick with the odor from their unwashed bodies, and from the waste barrel that was lashed to the back of the container. The waste barrel's vent to the outside seemed to do little to eliminate the smell. They made a great effort to conserve their water, drinking only when the thirst became unbearable, and only enough to moisten the insides of their mouths. Even so, their water barrel was emptying at an alarming rate. The constant and unpredictable movement caused by the churning of the sea brought on bouts of nausea in all the women, especially when the seesawing became particularly intense. It was constantly dark, the only light coming from the vent holes and a single flashlight with failing batteries. The vent holes served to keep them from suffocating but did little to circulate the stale air. Darkness and uncertainty and the unceasing bombardment of foul smells made time come to a near standstill. There was nothing to do to absorb the impact of time, and it thrummed endlessly onward. Their food was a salty assortment of nuts, crackers, dried fruits, and packaged goods — all things to compound their thirst — and the women cursed whomever had provided for them. After the first week their bowels had become solidified, painful rocks in their bellies.

Shortly after they set sail, Cho got her period. Nothing was furnished for this inevitability, another ignorant oversight of the men who provided for their journey. It was decided that they would relegate one of their precious blankets to the job of absorbing the expelled blood, adding to the already pungent atmosphere. A few days later, Jasmine had to sit with the blanket bunched between her legs.

"I suppose you'll be next," Cho said to Il-sun, trying to bring levity to the situation, as well as to alleviate her own embarrassment.

If they could have seen Il-sun's face, the other women would have watched her turn white. The silence that followed spoke volumes.

"You will be getting your period, won't you?" asked Jasmine.

Again, Il-sun responded with silence.

"You're not pregnant?" asked Cho, shocked.

Il-sun broke down, sobbing. Jasmine put her arm around her and squeezed, and no one spoke for several minutes. Finally, the crying subsided enough for Il-sun to squeak out a few words.

"I haven't had my period, and I'm usually very regular. My breasts keep getting bigger, even though I haven't eaten much. I get sick every day," she said through her tears.

"But how? I thought you said they weren't making you pull tricks," Jasmine asked.

Silence.

"Mr. Choy?" asked Jasmine.

"No," replied Il-sun, almost inaudibly.

"Gianni?" asked Cho, incredulity, and perhaps jealousy, in her voice.

Il-sun nodded, even though the other women could not see her, and sobbed with renewed vigor.

Gi felt as if someone had hit her over the head. Gianni had made love to the beautiful Il-sun; and Il-sun had allowed it, even welcomed it. She thought back to the night at the orphanage when she had wrapped herself around Il-sun, not even fully aware of what she was doing, and she cringed. Maybe if she had read *John and Daisy* she would have known better what to do, and Il-sun would have acquiesced. She had lain with a man, when lying with a man was an optional, innocent thing to do. She was ahead in the race for experience, and in some small, competitive way, Gi felt jealous of that too. On top of it all, she felt jealous that Il-sun was now going to be a mother. Her child would be supreme in her affections, and there would be yet another layer between herself and Il-sun.

And then she hated herself for these feelings. Il-sun was in pain, facing the onerous task of raising a child in the uncertainty of her situation. They had no idea where they were going, though they knew it was far, far away. Would she be able to care for herself, let alone a small child? Would she be bringing the child into a world of happiness, or a world fraught with pain and hardship? There must be a million uncomfortable questions boiling inside Il-sun's mind, and she needed support. *Perhaps,* Gyong-ho thought, *I can be a second parent, like a father, to the child. Maybe this is how I can be close with Il-sun.*

Il-sun's pregnancy gave the women an excuse to feel happiness, which they clung to after so many days — about two weeks since they left Seoul, by Gi's best guess — in the dark privation of the container. It helped them take their minds off their thirst and hunger. They enjoyed doting on Il-sun, and insisted on increasing her comfort, even at their own expense. Gi vowed to drink less water so that Il-sun could take extra. Il-sun was given a blanket to cushion the rough wood floor, and they insisted that, for hygienic reasons, she sleep farthest away from the waste barrel. Il-sun tried at first to protest the added luxuries, but Jasmine reminded her that it was for her baby, the uncounted fifth person in the room, and she gave in.

The journey continued, seemingly without end, and the monotony of it chipped away at their sanity. Each of them went through phases of babbling, giggling, crying, and testiness. The constant darkness caused them to have vivid hallucinations, and at times it became difficult for them to distinguish between dreaming and waking. For a whole day Gyong-ho insisted that Foreman Hwang had come into the container demanding that they mend his torn trousers. For hours she would not believe that it did not happen. Finally she realized the absurdity of what she was saying and fell into a sullen quiet.

Even Gyong-ho had lost count of time, though she knew it had been weeks, and they were scraping the bottom of the second water barrel. The women felt weak and had no energy left for talking. Their tongues were as good as cemented to the roofs of their mouths for lack of saliva, their heads ached from dehydration, and their lips were cracked. They remained lying down, in spite of the painful sores that had developed where their bones rubbed away their skin against the floor. Gi would have been happy to let herself slip from life, but the thought of Il-sun and her unborn baby kept her from giving over to death completely. Of the women, she was the only one who maintained enough will to live to continue going to the water barrel. So she brought water to the others, keeping them just barely alive. She gave Il-sun twice the amount of water — it could have been counted in drops — and made sure she ate at least a little. The others had stopped eating completely. She knew that in a matter of days they would all be dead.

Just when Gi was about to give up, the last warm spoonful of water sloshing in the barrel, the sea calmed and their boat stopped. She assumed that she was hallucinating when the sounds of machinery pierced the quiet of their container. Then the room spun about in a dizzying way and landed on solid ground. Gi slipped in and out of consciousness, events unfolding in a dreamlike way. There was the sound of a truck, and of her mother singing to her, and then she was under the sky in the DMZ. She could hear the boxes being removed from the other chamber of their container, and muffled voices. She heard a padlock click, and cool, fresh air filled the space around her. There was more light than she had ever seen before, and the sound of retching as their foul air was breathed in by the person who opened the door. Then the foreman and Gianni stood in the doorway, kissing; but that was impossible and she blinked it away. It was a man with an electric prod and she screamed, but only dust came out of her cracked mouth. She blinked and it was a man, but his hands were empty.

Il-sun was being helped to her feet and led out the door. Gi forced herself up for fear that they would take Il-sun away and she would never see her again. When she stood, however, the ocean moved through her and she could not keep her balance. She did not have the strength to stand on her own. Jasmine and Cho were led away, and then a man came and helped her walk out of the squalid room.

Voices shot through the air in a torrent of unintelligible language, and the light was painfully bright. They were again inside a metal warehouse. The women were made to lean against a corrugated tin wall, while a man with shears cut their putrid clothes from their bodies. In places the cloth had to be painfully ripped from the flesh. The man choked from time to time as he did his job, the stench of their fouled bodies nearly overpowering him. Once the women were naked he appeared with a hose and doused them with a pressurized stream of water. The water stung like needles, but they ignored that, trying to capture the liquid in their hands so they could drink it. Realizing that his efforts to clean the women were going to be thwarted by their efforts to drink, the man reduced the pressure and let them drink their fill from the hose. Once their thirst was quenched, he shot them again with the water, this time to less resistance.

Once they were thoroughly soaked, another man handed them a bar of soap, but they were too weak to effectively scrub themselves. Someone barked orders, and there was some arguing; then two men appeared with rags and roughly scrubbed the women. Gi was deeply embarrassed by having her naked body so thoroughly handled by a strange man, but she lacked the strength to protest. Besides, she was relieved to be rid of the filth. They were once again hosed off and stood shivering, dripping dry against the wall.

A well-dressed Korean man walked in and

stood in front of the women, looking at them with a hard, cold stare. He seemed displeased. He was in his sixties, with mixed silver and black hair. His face, when he was younger, would have been square and strong but was now well padded, with a slight sag in his skin. His eyes were hard slits and his mouth was set in a grim expression. His lower lip protruded slightly, with a fullness and femininity that was at odds with his otherwise wholly masculine appearance. He carried himself with power, and everyone shrank in deference to him. His stare bore into Gyong-ho, making her squirm. After a moment he turned on his heel and walked away.

62

Gyong-ho awoke in a strange room with her head pounding. She tried to sit up, but collapsed back on the bed, too dizzy to get up. She had to blink several times to clear her vision. Gray light was pouring in from a window, diffused through gauzy white curtains. It was an overcast day.

After the well-dressed man had walked away from them in the warehouse, Gi's legs buckled and she collapsed to the floor. It was the last thing she remembered. She had been unconscious since then and had no idea where she was or how she had gotten there.

She felt an agonizing thirst and tried to call out to get someone's attention, but it came out as a mute wheeze. Even so, she heard footsteps coming toward her, and a young woman appeared. The woman put her arm under Gi's head to lift it off the pillow and then raised a glass of water to her lips. The water had lemon in it, and she gulped greedily.

"Thank you," she tried to say, but it sounded like babble, even to her own ears. The woman pressed her finger to her lips.

The lemon water worked quickly to bring some vitality back to her, and she was able take in more of her surroundings.

She was lying in a narrow European-style bed in a small bedroom. The walls were covered in old, peeling wallpaper with a red floral pattern, and the hardwood floor was dented and scratched, and looked like it might have been there for a century or more. The ceiling was white plaster that was cracked in a crazed pattern radiating from an old light fixture. There was a table next to the bed with a cheap, modern-style lamp that looked out of place in the otherwise antiquated room. The air was cool and humid.

The woman who had helped her drink the water was short and slight, with a round face. She appeared to be about Gi's age, or maybe a couple of years older, with heavily painted eyes and hair dyed an impossible auburn color. She had a kind face that bore a look of genuine concern. She helped Gi up to a sitting position, and then piled pillows against the headboard so that Gi could be supported by them while she sat. The woman then took a bowl from the bedside table and fed Gi a spoonful of its contents. It was a thin rice gruel mixed with meat broth. Although she was ravenous, Gi could only eat a few spoonfuls before she felt full and slightly nauseous.

A groaning sound came from an adjoining room, and the young woman set the bowl back on the table and hurried out the door. Gi could not tell whose voice it was, but she hoped it was from one of her companions. She tried to get up to see, but as soon as she moved she was overcome by dizziness and had to sink back onto the pillows. She pulled the covers off her body and was surprised by her nakedness. She had lost precious weight — her ribs protruded and the bones of her hips were well defined by lack of flesh. Her arms and legs were fragile stems. She noticed that the sores on her body had been thoughtfully dressed with gauze and tape, and she felt grateful that somebody cared.

A while later the young woman returned and fed her a few more bites of gruel. Slowly her strength began returning. After the second feeding, the young woman helped Gi out of bed and to the toilet. She gave her a pair of panties and an oversized tee-shirt to wear. The effort of making the thirty-pace round-trip between the bed and the toilet was exhausting, and afterward she fell into a deep sleep.

After that, the young woman awakened her every couple of hours to eat gruel and drink water. By the next afternoon, Gi was able to stand and walk to the toilet on her own. The young woman, it turned out, could not speak Korean, so Gi was not able to question her about their location. Once she could walk, she insisted, using hand gestures, on going to see her friends.

Gi discovered that she was in a suite of four small bedrooms with an adjoining bathroom. At one time the suite was probably a two-bedroom apartment, complete with kitchen and bathroom, but the kitchen had been taken out and the living room and kitchen divided into two small bedrooms. Each of the women was in her own bedroom.

Cho, like Gi, was able to walk, if shakily, on her own. Il-sun was not yet walking, but she had some color in her cheeks, and smiled when Gi walked in. She looked relieved to see her. Nobody had information about where they were.

Jasmine was the worst off of all. She appeared to have a fever, and slipped in and out of consciousness. Her lips were badly cracked and bleeding, and she was in a state of delirium. She was drinking and eating, however, when the glass and spoon were lifted to her mouth. Gi saw it as a promising sign. All the women were very thin and pale, but alive.

On her way back to bed, Gi paused to look out her bedroom window. It was her first look into the new world she had entered. She counted the time from their flight across the DMZ — they had spent a month in South Korea, and about three weeks in the shipping container — and she figured that it must already be early summer. It did not look it, though. The sky was overcast and a light drizzle darkened the charcoal gray asphalt of the road below, and the air held a humid chill. She could see that she was on the second floor of an old redbrick building, but could not tell how wide or tall the building was. To the right was an intersection that had a lot of cross traffic, but the street below was relatively quiet. She could hear the steady stream of cars through the intersection, and overall it sounded just like Seoul. She was certain, however, given the amount of time they'd been at sea, that she was no longer in Korea. Directly across the street was another brick building, with cracks in the walls and a sagging roofline. At street level there were shops of various kinds, though she could not tell what they were selling: All the writing was in western-style lettering. Various cars were parked along the street. Two people were walking along the sidewalk directly below her, but they were shielded from view by a large black umbrella.

By the next day Il-sun was getting up on her own. In spite of the trauma of their ordeal, she had not lost the baby. "She's going to be a survivor just like us," Gi said to her.

Il-sun smiled and replied, "What makes you think she will be a girl?"

Gi did not have an answer. It just had to be a girl.

There was no improvement for Jasmine yet. The young woman fed her every couple of hours with thin gruel. The other women were starting to eat solid food, in larger portions and less often. Strength was coming back to them rapidly.

It was not until the fourth day of her recovery that Gi had built up enough strength to try opening the main door out of the suite. She had been afraid to touch the doorknob because she knew the mystery of their situation would be solved on the other side of it, and she did not want to uncover any grim truths. She stood in front of the door for several minutes before reaching out to it. Finally, after taking a deep breath and holding it in, her fingers wrapped around the knob and she turned it. The knob was fixed in place — they were locked inside. Confirming for herself that she was once again held in captivity drained the precious strength out of her body. She went to bed, closed her eyes, and escaped into numbers until she fell asleep.

By the fifth day Jasmine still had not improved and their caregiver brought a man into their suite to have a look at her. He was a tall Asian man in his midthirties, but he did not speak much Korean. He brought with him a bag of medical supplies, and Gi assumed him to be a doctor. He thoroughly examined Jasmine, looking into her eyes, her nose, her ears, and inspected the sores that still festered on her body. He took her blood pressure and temperature. He brought some pills out of his bag and handed them to the young caregiver and gave her instructions in his unintelligible language. Then he brought a bag of fluid and some plastic tubes out of his kit. He inserted a needle into Jasmine's arm, attached the tubes to the needle and then the bag of fluid to the tubes. He used a push pin to secure the bag in a high position against the wall.

"What is that?" asked Gi.

The doctor scrunched up his face at the question, his eyes rolling upwards as if trying to find the right words. Finally he said, "Food water." It was not correct Korean, but she understood the meaning.

"Will she be okay?"

He looked confused at first, not understanding the words, but he seemed to understand the concerned look in Gi's eyes.

"She fine week next," he said. "No worry."

The doctor then did a cursory inspection of the other three women, and indicated that they would be fine as long as they continued to eat and drink plenty of fluids. He then packed up his case and walked out the door.

Within a day Jasmine was much improved. Her fever abated, and with it left the delirium. As soon as Jasmine was able to stand on her own, their caregiver came less frequently, and only to deliver food and clean clothing. They were still not allowed out of the suite, and nor had anyone come to explain their circumstances to them.

A full week after arriving at their new location, the women were looking significantly more healthy and full in the face. The lock on their door jiggled, and in walked a stately woman, elegantly dressed in a fancy embroidered gown, followed by two large, muscular men.

"Come!" The woman shouted in Korean, standing in the doorway. Her voice rattled like an old truck, its huskiness caused by a lifetime of heavy smoking. The women came out of their rooms and stood before her.

She was short, but her posture was so erect and her poise so perfect that she seemed to tower over them. They would have described her as a tall woman, even though she was almost the shortest person in the room. She could have been anywhere from her midfifties to her midseventies, depending on how well or poorly she had aged, with her hair dyed black and pulled back in a tight bun. She had high, well-defined cheekbones, which were painted with a smear of rouge, and her eyebrows were penciled in over her eyes in a sinister arch. The outer corners of her eyes slanted upward, and her lips were pinched and plump and painted a deep shade of red. The skin of her neck was loose over hard, rope-like tendons. She wore a string of pearls and matching pearl pendant earrings that showed off the length of her neck. Her face

447

was slightly wrinkled, and she was beautiful and frightening. When she was younger her beauty must have stopped hearts and caused collisions. Now she did it with her hard, penetrating stare.

"So you're the new whores Choy sent from Seoul. Mr. Lyong is not happy." She stood in three-quarter profile, looking down her nose at them, her hands held together in front of her waist. She might have started singing an aria, standing like that. "I am Mrs. Cha, and I'm in charge here. You will do what I say." There was a pause. "When I stop speaking, you say, 'Yes, ma'am.' We do things a certain way around here."

"Yes, ma'am," the women said in unison.

"That's better. You girls are here to work, and I want you in shape. I am most disappointed that you arrived so ill. It cost Mr. Lyong dearly, and he let me hear all about it."

"Yes, ma'am."

"Here are the rules. One: You do what I say, and no arguing. Two: You are not to leave. Ever. Unless I say so. If I catch you trying to escape, my boys here will rough you up. They are not above taking out an eye or cutting off your toes. Three: This is a business and you are to treat the customers with respect. You give them what they want.

If you don't perform my boys will beat you black and blue." There was silence as the women absorbed this. Mrs. Cha stepped forward and slapped Il-sun hard across the face. The sound resounded through the suite and Il-sun cried out in surprise and pain. "I didn't hear 'Yes, ma'am'!" said Mrs. Cha with her voice raised.

"Yes, ma'am."

"Good. If you follow those simple rules you will have three square meals and a roof over your head. Make a habit of disobeying me and my boys will dump your body in the Puget Sound. Got it?"

"Yes, ma'am," the women chimed, though not knowing what the Puget Sound was. The message, however, was clear.

"I'll put you to work in three days. You better be ready by then," said Mrs. Cha. She turned to walk out, but Gi stepped forward.

"Ma'am?"

Mrs. Cha's head turned, viperlike, ready to strike. Gi could almost hear her hiss and see her split tongue taste her pulse in the air. "What do you want?"

"I'm sorry to bother you ma'am, but Il-sun is pregnant. She can't see men in that condition." It had taken all of Gi's courage to speak up. For anyone other than Il-sun, she would not have done it.

Mrs. Cha's eyes went wide and her nostrils flared. Gi stepped back for fear that her fire breath would reduce her to cinders. "No, she most certainly cannot!" she said, and stormed out of the room.

63

"You old bitch," Mrs. Cha said in English to herself into the mirror. She was sitting at an antique dressing table in her bedroom, removing eye makeup with a cotton ball. Where had all the lines around her eyes and mouth come from? A cigarette burned in an ashtray on the corner of the table. She pulled pins out of her hair and it fell in a black sheet down her back. The years of dye had made it course and brittle, where it used to be silky and soft. *The price of getting old,* she thought to herself. She found a silver-handled hairbrush in a drawer and ran it through her hair in long, meditative strokes. This ritual always felt particularly French to her, and she began to sing "La Vie en Rose" in a fair imitation of Edith Piaf.

Quand il me prend dans ses bras
Il me parle tout bas . . .

Chung-min had promised to take her to Paris, many years ago. That was one of many unkept promises that had kept her hanging on to him for so many years, hoping to extract a drop of intimacy from a man who was lithified by easy, dangerous money. *Old age is the sum of all the small bad decisions made in the ignorance of youth,* she thought.

She had been a fool to trust him. He always had other women — she knew that. He never even tried to hide it; but he always came back to her. She was the crown jewel in his collection of women, or so she believed. Like a fool, when she was twenty, that made her feel special.

When Mrs. Cha arrived in Seattle she was only eighteen, but she looked older. She had been sent there by her unusually progressive father, who encouraged independence and worldliness in his daughters. If Asian women had been in fashion then, and if she had been taller, she would have been a top model. Her features were perfect, her skin smooth and her hair radiant. She held herself with poise and grace, walking with confidence and even with an air of snobbery. She knew how to make the most of it too, with a flirtatious glance here, a toss of the hair there. It was fun being a beautiful girl with no attachments in a time and place when "free love" was becoming a catch phrase.

Her father had been an important and affluent man in Seoul, having made his money rebuilding the city after the North Koreans destroyed it in the 1950s. Mrs. Cha grew up speaking Korean, Chinese, and English with her father's business associates. She discovered that she had a knack for languages and a love for literature. In high school she had taken up French, Italian, and Spanish. She moved to the States to study language and literature at the university, picking up Russian and even a bit of Swahili. She read Hugo, Lu Xun, Tolstoy, Camus, Hemingway, Faulkner, Molière, Dostoyevski, and Nabakov, plus a run of trashy romance novels, all in their native languages, and loved them all. Her weakness was for Russian literature. She had dreams of one day becoming a renowned literary critic, and maybe even a novelist. At the very least she imagined herself working as a translator and editor for a large international publishing house, but none of that was to be. She had written a novel, a masterpiece, which was sitting in a box on the top shelf of a closet, that nobody had ever read. It had all the drama of Tolstoy and the psychology of Camus and the grit of Hemingway. But the success of that work belonged to an entirely different person — to an elite ex-model living in her fancy New York apartment, or the chief editor of an important literary magazine, not to the madam of a brothel owned by the Korean mafia. She had chosen her life, and the two worlds were not compatible.

The truth was, she had had a difficult time taking her own dreams seriously. She was easily the brightest student of literature that the university had seen for over a decade, but progressive as her father was, he still expected her to find a husband and become a subservient wife. She had been taught to be deferential and soft spoken to men, and as a result she found herself undermining her own ambitions. Then she met Chung-min.

Lyong Chung-min was a dapper, flashy, dangerous bad boy whose smile had the effect of sliding her panties off her legs. He was then a lieutenant for Uncle Jang, running heroine and speed through the port of Seattle and distributing it along the Pacific coast. He was confident and powerful, and being seduced by him made her feel special. He drew her slowly into the dirty underworld of Blue Talon.

At first she thought it was just an erotic

game, an odd fetish of his powerful sexual appetite that caused him to ask it of her. She would have done anything for him. It did not help matters that his fingers were inside her when he asked, and she was near climaxing. It was quite a turn-on.

"I want you to fuck another man for money," he said.

"What?!" she asked, incredulous, panting.

"I want you to fuck another man for money," he repeated.

"If that's what you want me to do," she replied.

"I do."

"Will you watch?"

"Maybe."

"What if I like it?"

"You won't."

"What if I like it more than I like fucking you?" she groaned. She enjoyed dirty talk.

"You won't."

"I might."

"No, you won't," he said, thrusting his fingers inside her roughly. It hurt. It was a gesture of threat, and for some reason it pushed her over the edge into climax. Looking back on it, it was not some kinky enjoyment of his threatening demeanor, or the pain caused by his fingers, but the fact that he was expressing a desire for her loyalty that made her orgasm. He wanted her to enjoy sex only with him. It was as if he was asking for some kind of commitment from her. It was the most intimate thing he had ever expressed to her in their relationship: It was an indication that he cared, and she fell for it.

"Stupid old bitch," she said to herself in the mirror.

What had started as an erotic game — his taking money from a man who then had sex with her — eventually became a job. By the time she realized that it was no longer a turn-on, that he in fact was her pimp and she was just a prostitute, it was too late to change the course of fate. She was now, irreversibly, a whore, full of shame masked by defiance. Then she aged. Then she became a madam. *Too late in life to switch career paths,* she thought. Another song by Edith Piaf flashed through her mind.

Non, rien de rien
Non, je ne regrette rien . . .

Her thoughts were interrupted by the sound of the front door.

"Grandma, I'm home." It was the strong, young voice of her teenage grandson. He already sounded like a man, and she was proud of him.

"I'm in here. Come and give me a kiss."

He entered the room and kissed her on the cheek. He was tall and handsome.

"Do you have much homework?" she asked him in English. He was going to go to university and become an engineer, or doctor, or anything that would keep him out of organized crime. She would see to that, and she was prepared to defy Chungmin if he came recruiting. He would leave her grandson alone; he owed her that much.

"I have an exam in physics tomorrow," he replied in Russian. It had been a game to them to alternate languages. He had inherited her talent.

"Then don't let this old woman keep you from studying!" she said in Italian.

"Ciao!" he said, smiling into the mirror, and then turned to leave.

"Don't forget to eat!" she said to his back in English. He went to his room and closed the door.

She went back to brushing her hair. Her thoughts turned to the new girls, and her heart broke a little. They were so young and naïve. She could tell from their accents that they were from North Korea — doubtless victims of the burgeoning sex trafficking business from that region. She wondered if they had mothers or grandmothers back home who worried about them — then she stopped herself. It would do no good if she allowed herself to sympathize with them. She had a job to do, and so did they. Their roles were clearly defined, which made things simple. Their lives were not going to be a pleasure cruise: This business killed off the weak and made the survivors strong. She felt bad for slapping the girl, but it was always better to assert dominance right at the very beginning. It would keep the girls in line. *Small kindnesses can come later,* she thought. *But for now it is better for them to see the rough edge of the business. How else am I to care for them?*

Her eyes fell on a small statue of the Buddha sitting on a wardrobe and the word *compassion* went instantly through her mind in half a dozen languages.

"You old bitch," she said to herself in the mirror.

64

At sea, Il-sun had thought she was going to die for sure. At times, in the misery of the shipping container, she wished she would. Would she see her mother and brother on the other side? Would she finally get to meet her father? These were not questions that had answers, but she longed to know.

She first suspected that she was pregnant two weeks after arriving in South Korea. Her period did not come — but that could have been the stress. Then the nausea began and her breasts were just a little plumper than normal. The nausea had not been too bad at first, and she tried to blame it on the *Hanguk* food — maybe the Americans were poisoning it. Maybe the plumpness in her breasts was just normal growth; after all, she was only seventeen, and admittedly she had been eating well. Once she was in the shipping container the sickness reached its peak, with the foul odors and the pitching of the sea. Even so, she knew.

What did it mean for her to be pregnant? She did not know how to be a mother; and how could she love a child that every day would remind her of Gianni and his treachery? In moments, some scraping part of her mind even thought that if she could get a message to him, he would bring her back and care for her and the baby; but she knew better than to put stock in that hope. Throughout her childhood she had fantasized about motherhood, and it was never supposed to be this way. But her body wanted this baby — the biology was so much more powerful than her will. Then when Gi, Jasmine, and Cho found out, and they doted on her so much, and it gave them so much hope, she could not help but feel a sense of pride and a desire to see it through. This baby made her special. And maybe she could use it as leverage in their new home. Whoever was to be her new master would surely take pity on a young mother-to-be. Would that be the dreadful Mrs. Cha? She was a woman too, so she must have sympathy.

When she awoke in her new room, she wondered if she was dead. Did the dead have beds with blankets? Did the dead suffer such deep, unbearable thirst? Then the young woman came in and fed her, and she knew she was still among the living — the girl was just so . . . plain, in spite of her brilliant auburn hair; and why would the dead need to eat? In a way, she was disappointed. Death would have made things easier. She put her hand on her belly, and instinctively she knew she had not lost the baby. It must have been fate. She still had a reason to feel special.

Gyong-ho was trying too hard to be helpful, and it was a little annoying. Il-sun loved Gi, but she hovered too close. She kept coming into her room to offer water and to fluff her pillows, holding an overly bright smile. Gi's eyes were always on her — she had such a loud way of being quiet — and sometimes Il-sun just needed some room to breathe. The look in Gi's eyes made her wonder if perhaps Gi craved her in the same way she had craved Gianni. Was it possible for a woman to want another woman in such a way? The book *John and Daisy* had certainly alluded to it. It seemed better to avoid Gi than to confront her.

Uncertainty gnawed at Il-sun from the inside. Would Mrs. Cha insist that she become a prostitute, even with a baby? At the very least she would have to wait until the baby was born to put her to work, and then perhaps Il-sun could find a way out of it. This baby would buy her time to adjust and come up with a plan.

Il-sun rubbed her belly and sang a lullaby. *I will be a good mother,* she vowed to herself as she fell asleep.

65

The door to the suite opened and Gi peeked out of her room to see who was there. She dreaded that it might be the frightening Mrs. Cha coming to spit curses at them. Instead, it was the same two men who had accompanied Mrs. Cha earlier that day, her bodyguards, but with another man who was carrying a small backpack and a toolbox. They came inside and closed the door.

"Mrs. Cha says it's time for your tattoos," said one of the men in accented Korean. Though he looked Korean, he was obviously not from there.

"Tattoos?" asked Cho.

"Everybody gets one," he replied, pulling his shirtsleeve back to reveal a small tattoo on the light skin of his lower arm.

"Why do we need tattoos?" asked Jasmine.

"Because you belong to Blue Talon now. If you try to escape, anyone from the organization can recognize you by the tattoo. You will have to cut your leg off if you want to be rid of it."

Gi blanched. She did not want to have anything permanently marking her body, let alone a brand that would connect her with an organization. Having a tattoo of a foreign organization would surely land her in the prison camp back home, and she still had hopes of returning one day. She wondered how it was going to be, living without one of her legs. How would she go about cutting it off?

"Please don't try to resist. We'll have to beat you if you do." His tone of voice indicated that he would not gain any pleasure from doing it, but he would do it all the same, if he had to. The women had little choice but to submit.

Cho stepped forward to be the first, putting on a brave face for the benefit of her friends. The tattoo artist asked her to lie down on her left side, exposing the outside of her right ankle. He swabbed an area of skin with alcohol, then took a device that looked like a pen out of the toolbox. He then opened a package and took out a small plastic tip with needles on its end, attaching it to the pen. He set up a vial of ink on a bedside table, and then went to work. The tattoo pen made a buzzing sound, and as soon as he touched it to Cho's skin she kicked involuntarily, stifling a scream. The two bodyguards grabbed Cho and held her down.

"I'm sorry!" she said. "I wasn't expecting it to hurt like that. You can let me go. I won't kick."

The two men looked at each other, and reluctantly let go. The tattoo artist brought the needle to her skin again; this time she gritted her teeth and endured the pain. The artist worked for about twenty minutes, and Cho's face was shock white and wet with perspiration. She was relieved when he pronounced the tattoo complete.

Gi looked down at Cho's ankle, which was oozing ink and blood, and gasped. It was not the gruesomeness of the reddish purple mixture pumping out of the tattoo that startled her but the image itself. Gi knew without a doubt that she would someday have to cut her own leg off. The tattoo was roughly two inches in diameter, situated just above the condyle of Cho's ankle. In the background were the symbols of the imperialist South Korean flag, with the *taegeuk,* or yin-yang, symbol rendered in blood red and dark blue, surrounded by four trigrams from the Chinese book *I Ching.* In front of the symbol, cutting across it at an angle, was a raptor's talon, sharp and poised as if about to grasp its prey. Oddly, the talon looked appropriate on Cho's body, her hands looking very much like the talon on the tattooed image. Otherwise, it was a horrific perversion of her flesh.

Seeing her friends' discomfort, Cho quipped to the artist, "You did alright, but could you move it just a little bit to the left?"

The attempt at levity worked, and the women laughed.

That evening, as Gi was lying down for the night, trying to keep the covers from rubbing against the dressings on her fresh tattoo, the door to their suite opened.

"Il-sun?" It was a man's voice.

Gi got out of bed to see who it was. Jasmine and Cho had done the same. It was the doctor.

"Il-sun?" he asked again, looking timid.

Il-sun poked her head out of her room. "That's me," she said.

"You have baby?" he asked.

Gi was relieved that her plea for Il-sun's condition had not gone unnoticed.

"Yes, I'm pregnant."

The doctor reached into his kit and took out a cardboard package. He opened it and handed Il-sun a small wand.

"Could you please?" he asked.

Il-sun took it and gave him an uncertain look.

Jasmine, sensing Il-sun's uncertainty, said, "It's a test to be sure that you are pregnant. You're supposed to pee on the end."

Il-sun shrugged and disappeared into the bathroom. She came out a moment later and handed it back to the doctor. They waited while the doctor kept an eye on his watch, and after a few minutes he looked at the tester and nodded.

"Yes. Baby," he said, and reached again into his kit. He opened a bottle and took out a pill. He then went into the bathroom and filled a cup with water, and handed both the pill and the water to Il-sun. "For baby," he said, looking at the floor.

Something about the doctor's mannerisms did not seem right to Gi. He appeared uncomfortable, but maybe he was just embarrassed to be in a room full of women in their nightshirts. Il-sun put the pill in her mouth and lifted the glass of water.

"Il-sun, no!" Gi shouted suddenly — an inner alarm was ringing. Il-sun gave her a funny look and swallowed the pill.

"Thank you," she said to the doctor. "You are kind to look after me and my baby."

The doctor did not reply. He simply

turned around, his eyes on the floor, and walked out the door.

"What was that, Gi?" Il-sun asked, scowling.

"I don't know. I just have a bad feeling."

"He was only giving me vitamins. For the baby," she said, and went back to bed.

66

The next morning their door opened and a woman wearing a miniskirt and a skintight tank top came into the suite. Gyong-ho recognized the outfit as the exaggerated sexualized styling of a prostitute, and she felt a sudden need to spit. There had been no need to ask what work they were expected to perform because Mrs. Cha had already referred to them as the new whores; but seeing their visitor that morning brought it back to reality.

"Mrs. Cha wants me to show you girls around the place," said the woman. Her accent was South Korean. She had an air about her of perpetual boredom, and she spoke through a large pink wad of chewing gum. "She says it's time you start pulling your own weight."

"Do I have to come?" asked Il-sun. "I'm not feeling very good this morning." Then she added, with a touch of pride, "Morning sickness."

"Mrs. Cha said one of you wasn't feeling so good," said the woman. "Naw, you don't have to come." She spoke as if she was either too lazy or too bored to give her words proper enunciation or her verbs proper conjugation. Gi noticed the Blue Talon tattoo on her ankle and shuddered, her own tattoo stinging anew. They were now sisters, of a sort. "Follow me," she said, and walked out the door.

Gi, Cho, and Jasmine stepped for the first time beyond the confines of their suite and into a long, narrow hallway. The corridor was inefficiently lit by a single, dim light that left both ends of the hall in darkness. The walls were cracked and peeling, and there was a vague, moldy smell coming from the frayed and faded carpet. There were other doors on both sides of the hallway, presumably leading to other suites. The women went down the hall to a set of stairs. The stairs were likewise poorly lit, and made of bare wood, but smelled better than the hallway. They creaked as the women descended.

The stairs opened into a large room with several small, round tables, a raised stage at one end, and a long bar running the length of the room. It was clean and nicely furnished. Behind the bar was a Korean man with a round face and a thin mustache, standing with his arms folded, scowling at nothing in particular. Sitting at the bar were two women, heavily made up and dressed for business in skimpy outfits, chatting idly with each other. At the end of the bar closest to the stairs was a stout door with a mean-looking, muscular man sitting on a stool next to it. He was reading a newspaper and looked up briefly when he heard the women enter the room.

"This is the bar," said the woman. "Where we meet clients. It's pretty much always open, but we normally aren't busy in the morning. That guy at the door is as much there to keep us in as he is to keep the customers in line. I seen him break a girl's arm before, when she tried to walk out. Broke her nose, too. He's called *Asshole*." She said *asshole* in English, then told them what it meant in Korean. "Uncle Lyong started calling him that, and now everyone does. He seems to like it, and anyway, the name fits."

"Does that door open to the street?" asked Jasmine.

"Not exactly. I'll show you," replied the woman. They walked over to the door, and the woman said something to Asshole in

English. Asshole nodded and then held the door open. The women stood in the doorway, looking out.

On the other side was a narrow room with dirty windows that looked out onto the street. The room was dingy and uninviting, a stark contrast to the room they were just in. There was a bar in this room as well, with a wary-looking bartender and several rough-looking men sitting on stools. They looked toward the women with hard eyes.

"This bar is a front for the real business in the back. If a guy wants a girl, or some blow or crank or pot, he tells the bartender a password and he lets him into the back room where all the action is. It helps keep the cops away. There's no back exit, so everyone has to come and go through here. Those guys sitting there all work for Blue Talon. They carry guns and keep the place secure. If you have thoughts of trying to escape, even if you get past Asshole, you will still have to get by them."

The woman led them again into the back room, where they turned and went through a door under the stairs. It opened into what appeared to be a disused restaurant, embellished with some out-of-place homey touches. There was an industrial kitchen in the back, a few tables, a television in the corner, and a window with a piece of plywood bolted securely where the glass should have been. They were the only people in the room.

"We call this the lounge," she said. "We cook and eat here. Whenever you're not working you can hang out in here, watch television or whatever. There's books and games on that shelf in the corner. We take turns cooking and cleaning up. We eat pretty good. Just don't piss off Mrs. Cha."

"She seems mean," said Cho.

"She can be a real bitch, but she's not quite as bad as she seems at first. Just do what she says and stay out of her way." She paused for a second to let it sink in. "Anyway, it's our turn to cook, so let's get to work before everyone starts grumbling."

They went into in the kitchen and began making rice, preparing vegetables, and sautéing meat. Gi had eaten well, if simply, since she had arrived, which puzzled her: It was known that outside of *Chosun* the world was a bleak, uncivilized wasteland. In reality, the opposite seemed to be true. Gi had never eaten so well or so consistently as she had after leaving her own country, even being a prisoner.

"What's your name?" Cho asked the woman.

"Everyone calls me Britney," she replied. "You know, after the singer?"

They did not know, but they nodded anyway.

"I'm Cho. Nice to meet you."

"Everyone goes by fake names," said Britney rudely. She clearly felt superior, or was trying to establish a pecking order with her at the top, or both. Cho felt hurt, but she masked it as irritation and turned coldly away from her. Britney blew a large bubble with her chewing gum, and it popped loudly. The *Chosun* women had never seen a person do that before, and they were impressed in spite of themselves.

"Britney, maybe you can tell us. Where are we?" asked Jasmine, trying to smooth over the turbulence that had appeared between Britney and Cho.

"What do you mean?"

"I mean, what city, what country. Where on the fucking planet are we?"

"You mean you don't know?"

"That is what I mean," said Jasmine, enunciating especially clearly. Relative to Britney's lazy speech, it made Britney sound all the more unsophisticated, deflating her air of superiority.

"Honestly, since I've been here, I haven't been outside much. Just a couple a times to do tricks here and there, but I was always with a chaperone. But I do know that we're in a city called *Seattle,* in the United States."

Gi dropped the pot of water she had been carrying from the sink to the stove. It landed with a loud clang on the floor, and water drenched her feet and lower legs. "What?" she said, panic rising from her abdomen into her throat.

"We're where?" asked Cho, her jaw dropping.

"Seattle, in the United States."

"But that's not possible!" exclaimed Gyong-ho.

"Well, you're here. You can believe it, or not," said Britney, some of the superiority creeping back into her voice.

"I figured we were probably in San Francisco, but I wasn't sure," said Jasmine. "I had a feeling we were in the States, but I didn't want to say anything until I was sure." She pinched her lower lip with her thumb and index finger. Her brow knitted as if she were trying to solve a difficult problem in her mind.

"Wow," said Cho, otherwise speechless.

The *Chosun* women had, from their earliest memories, been told that America was the world's most evil empire and its citizens the most blood-thirsty, oafish, inhumane people on the planet. Americans ate their own children and routinely shot their elderly in the back of the head. America was a land of chaos and confusion, ruled by an inferior species of proto-humans. The fact of their brutishness was even reflected in *Chosun* vernacular, referring to Americans, as a matter of semantic routine, as *Mee-guk nom,* or American bastards, rather than as *Mee-guk saram,* or American people. To think that all around them was a vast colony of these violent, maniacal, shifty psychopaths was harrowing. How could they live through it?

Gi, Cho, and Jasmine had finished making the morning meal and met several of the women who lived and worked in the brothel. They had come from all over the world, though mainly from Asia. Most were Korean, but there was one from Laos, two from Thailand, a couple from the Philippines, and one from somewhere in Africa — Gi had not heard of her country before and Jasmine said that she spoke French. Many of the women had the English language in common, and the ones who did not got by using hand gestures. Jasmine knew a little English, but the *Chosun* women did not.

After breakfast, Gi took some food up to Il-sun.

"I've brought you a bowl of soup," she said, smiling, as she entered her room.

"Thanks, Gi, but I'm not hungry." Il-sun managed a weak smile. She looked a little pale.

"But you need to eat. For the baby."

"My stomach hurts."

"Are you alright? Should I get the doctor?"

"No, I'll be fine. It's only a bit of morning sickness. Leave the soup. I'll eat it in a little bit."

"Would you like me to sit with you?"

"No, I think I'll try to sleep."

"Are you sure?"

"Really, Gi, I just want to be alone." Il-sun's tone had become exasperated, and the sting showed on Gi's face. "I'm sorry. I'm just not feeling good. We'll talk later, okay?"

"I understand," said Gi, trying to sound upbeat. "I'll check on you later." With that Gi turned and left. Reluctantly she went back downstairs.

Inside the lounge several women were sitting around a television set, watching with numb disinterest. Gi pulled up a chair and joined them, though no one greeted or even acknowledged her. She had never watched television before — her *songbun* had not allowed for it. Everything on the television was in English, and therefore incomprehensible. The images, however, were fascinating. The programs seemed to be depicting characters going through various dramas and shenanigans, some humorous and some serious. Absent from the shows were the poverty, depression, inhuman aggression, and deceitfulness that she knew to be rampant in America. Doubtless these were propaganda shows, depicting life in the United States in a far better light to try to fool their citizens and their enemies.

After a while, Gi closed her eyes and focused solely on the language. English was fast, loud, and punchy. It seemed a rather insensitive language without much nuance. All the same, she let herself be bombarded by it, allowing her mind to try to make sense of the sounds. At first it was meaningless and random, but eventually she started to discern repeating rhythms and consonant/ vowel relationships. Silently she mouthed what she was hearing. It felt funny, like putting shoes on the wrong feet. It was not a musical language, but she listened to it as if it were, guessing at the meaning by the pitch, intensity, and tone.

Different women came and went from the lounge all day, but Gyong-ho stayed, fascinated by the content the television offered.

Even Jasmine and Cho eventually went their own ways, to do what, Gi did not know. After a full day in front of the television, Gi had acquired a few English words, such as *go,* meaning to start something; *hi Al,* a greeting; and *turbo-chopper,* meaning something that cuts vegetables. Absorbed in the process of learning, she had been able to escape her imprisonment for an entire day. That night, she went to bed clinging desperately to a feeling of mental satisfaction.

67

The next morning the doctor came back to check on Il-sun. He took her temperature, felt her pulse, and looked into her throat. Gi noticed the Blue Talon tattoo on his lower arm; apparently he was property, too. The doctor gave Il-sun another pill, saying, "For baby." He left without making eye contact, and Gyong-ho's feeling of uneasiness returned. This time, however, she said nothing because Il-sun was so happy for the attention. It helped Il-sun feel that everything was going to be alright, and Gi did not want to ruin that for her.

A few hours after the doctor had left, a loud groan from Il-sun's room called the other women to her bedside. Il-sun was doubled over in pain, her face pale and dotted with beads of sweat.

"What's wrong?" asked Jasmine.

"Cramps. Horrible cramps," Il-sun replied through gritted teeth.

"Find someone who can get the doctor," Jasmine said to Cho, her face grave. Cho disappeared without a word. Gi held Il-sun's hand. The pain seemed to come in waves.

"It's probably just part of morning sickness," said Il-sun in a moment when the pain abated. The other women did not say anything, giving each other furtive, doubtful looks.

Cho had been gone for an interminable quarter hour, and then returned with Mrs. Cha. The room turned icy cold in her presence, her eyes fierce coals that looked capable of emitting rays of death. She stood at the foot of the bed, an improbable midwife. Il-sun gave a loud shriek of pain, and a pool of deep-crimson blood appeared between her legs. She looked up, terror-stricken and pale. Gi squeezed her hand, tears streaming down her face.

"The bleeding will stop soon," said Mrs. Cha flatly. "There is no need for the doctor." Then she turned and glided out of the room.

As the truth of what happened dawned on her, Il-sun began to sob. The baby had lifted her above her situation. It had given her a ray of hope and something to live for, and now it was taken away from her. The stark reality of her life clicked into place, like a sticky tumbler in a lock finally releasing, opening her awareness to the undeniable truth: She was a prisoner in a foreign country, being forced into prostitution, with no way of escaping. She wished she could die. Maybe she would bleed to death.

Another wave of painful contractions came over her and she expelled more thick clots of blood and tissue. The baby had come out. It was little more than a couple of centimeters long, with discernable arms and legs. She could not bear to look at it. Her tears stopped and her face became hard and stoic.

"Take it away," she said.

"Il-sun —" said Jasmine tenderly.

"Just take it away!" she shouted.

Gi reached down and scooped the fetus into her hands. It was small and nameless — qualities she could relate with. It was not fully formed, like her, and she envied it that it would never know the suffering that this world could provide. She took it into the bathroom, cradling it in her palm. Here, in her hand, was an ending that never had a beginning. There was a complicated mix of feelings, and Gi took a minute, looking at the fetus, to unknot them. She was sad, for Il-sun's pain more than for the baby. She

482

had enjoyed the bonding that Il-sun's pregnancy fostered between the women, and she knew that she would miss that. The baby had been an avenue that Gi could have taken into Il-sun's heart, but now that would never be. And in there, too, was an uncomfortable sense of relief: She would no longer have to compete with this child for Il-sun's affection. She hated herself for feeling that way, but it was an undeniable truth.

Gi had lived through a time, in the gulag, when life was especially cheap. She had watched impassively as girls perished, or were maimed or . . . forced into intercourse — now she knew what that was. She tried to feel something deeper for the small body that was in her hand, but it was not there. She knew that she was supposed to be torn with grief. Why would it not come? It was just another life, only this one would not be lived. It was probably better this way. "We all loved you very much," she said, wishing that she could feel those words — she really wanted to. It seemed that there needed to be ceremony. Then she lowered the body into the toilet, and flushed. Il-sun wailed loudly in the other room.

68

The next morning Britney came to their suite looking put out.

"Mrs. Cha wants me to get you girls ready for work," she said.

"Today?" asked Gi. Il-sun's miscarriage had been such a trauma that she had thought the whole world would need to rest from it. Apparently not the flesh industry.

"Yes, today," Britney replied.

"I don't feel good," said Il-sun.

"What, do you think you're better than the rest of us, princess?" said Britney rudely.

"No, it's just that —"

"Mrs. Cha said *all* of you were going to work today, and I'm not gonna argue with her. Neither are you, so get ready."

The women took showers and spent time doing their hair. Britney brought them clothes, makeup, and hair products. The shoes that they had brought with them from South Korea had disappeared when they were released from the container, probably thrown out with the rest of the fouled items that were found inside. They had been barefoot since their arrival, and it looked like that was not going to change. The clothes that they were given were ill-matched and fit poorly; but then, they would not be in them long enough for it to matter. It was a far cry from Mr. Choy's standard. Once they were ready, Britney led them down the stairs and into the bar. Mrs. Cha met them at the bottom of the stairs appearing regal and fierce.

"Alright, let me have a look at you," she said, glaring down her nose. She inspected each woman up and down and front to back. Her brow was pinched, as if she were assessing the work potential of oxen. She had a habit of clicking her tongue when she was in thought, which sounded to Gi like mild disapproval. She looked cursorily at Gyong-ho, and said dismissively, "Well, we'll see how you do." Gi had a feeling she was not really speaking to her, so remained quiet. Mrs. Cha paused at Il-sun.

"What have we here? Aren't you a pretty one." She circled around Il-sun as if zeroing in on a kill, examining her with an appraising eye. "I think you'll do well, even if you turn out to be a lousy lay." Mrs. Cha reached out with one hand and grabbed hold of Il-sun's face by the chin. She turned Il-sun's head from side to side. "But you won't be a lousy lay, will you? What is your name, dear?"

Il-sun's hatred showed on her face. She knew that the miscarriage had been ordered by Mrs. Cha — Gi had been right to be suspicious. Now she was being forced to prostitute herself only a day afterward. She was still having light cramping and spotting, but it did not matter to Mrs. Cha.

"I asked you your name," Mrs. Cha said, raising her voice.

There was a pause, and Il-sun stared back into Mrs. Cha's eyes. "Daisy. My name is Daisy."

"My name is Daisy, *ma'am*," Mrs. Cha corrected.

"Ma'am," Il-sun repeated.

"Better. Okay, this is how it works: You girls mingle with customers at the bar. I know you don't speak English, but it doesn't matter because those men aren't here to talk. Just be pretty, smile a lot, and do whatever they want you to. When a man wants to go with you, he pays me or the bartender. You take him up to your room and fuck him. It's that simple.

"Sometimes men will leave cash tips for

you. You're not allowed to have cash, and you will hand it over at the end of your shift. If I catch you hiding money, I will have your fingers cut off. I've done it before. I may be a bitch, but I'm not a crook. Those tips are yours and I'll keep an accurate log of how much you've made. Just ask the other girls here, and they'll tell you that I deal fairly that way. You can use your money to pay for things like cigarettes, or clothes, or whatever. We keep a shopping list and I have my boys go out a couple of times a week to buy things."

"Why can't we keep our own money, if it's ours?" asked Jasmine.

"Girls started thinking they could buy things like bus fare and plane tickets. We can't have that." She began to pace. "You're allowed two drinks while you're working to help calm your nerves. I don't want you getting sloppy drunk and making asses of yourselves. It's unprofessional. If you keep the customers happy and behave yourselves, I think you'll find it's not such a bad life in here. If you don't behave, I will make your life a living hell. Understood?"

"Yes, ma'am," they said in unison.

"Now, get to work," said Mrs. Cha.

Suddenly the room felt very large and Gi felt terribly small. Smoke was rising in thick plumes from cigars and cigarettes, and it lingered on the air as a dense haze. There was a collection of young Caucasian American men at the bar and another group sitting around one of the tables playing a game of cards, and Gi shuddered. Jasmine had tried to allay her concerns about Americans, telling her that men were men, no matter where they came from; but she could not overcome a lifetime of belief that Americans were evil monsters, that they were imbued with an inhuman propensity to violence and dishonesty. She knew that Cho had had to service Americans in Mr. Choy's sex shop, but Gi had been spared — they did not frequent the club where she worked.

"Cho and I have done this before," Jasmine said with a resigned sigh. "Just follow our lead. You'll get the hang of it soon enough." She stepped toward the bar with more confidence than Gi knew she was feeling, and the others followed. As they approached, the other women at the bar gave them cold looks and condescending stares that seemed to say "This customer is mine, so hands off!" It was apparently a territorial business. They sat at the far end of the bar, Gi on the farthest stool.

Jasmine turned and leaned her back against the bar with a practiced look of boredom on her face. Soon a man with too many chins staggered over and stood next to her. His eyes were bloodshot and he reeked of alcohol. He said something to her in English, more loudly than he needed to in order to be heard over the soft music that was playing in the background. She batted her eyes and looked him up and down. She leaned in close to him and whispered something into his ear, and he chuckled. The bartender drifted over, sensing a deal about to be made.

"Vodka and tonic, please. Heavy on the vodka," Jasmine said to him in Korean. The bartender nodded and busied himself making the drink. Jasmine's client was feeling talkative, and she nodded and smiled at him as if he were the most interesting man in the world. Truthfully, she probably only understood a small fraction of what he was saying, but he did not seem to notice, or even care. Jasmine downed her drink in two large gulps, shuddered, and then said something to the man in English, nodding toward the stairs. He nodded back to her, paid the bartender, and followed her up the stairs.

Gi felt a knot in the pit of her stomach, and she sat hunched at the bar trying to be invisible. Il-sun sat next to her, watching the women in action, fascinated and frightened. Cho went upstairs with a client soon after Jasmine, leaving Il-sun and Gi alone at the bar.

"Something to drink?" asked the bartender.

"Champagne," replied Il-sun.

"Fancy girl, are you?" he said sarcastically. "Girls don't get champagne, unless you pay for it."

"Okay. Whiskey."

"Neat, or on the rocks?"

"I don't know, just whiskey."

"Neat, then." He poured a glass and handed it to her.

Gi watched two more men enter the room. Asshole frisked them both, and they made their way to the bar. One of them noticed Il-sun and came directly over to her. He was in his late twenties, tall, thin, and wearing a dirty T-shirt and baseball cap. He smelled sour and unwashed. Il-sun stared into her drink looking like she hoped he would disappear, but he did not. He said something to her that she did not understand. She looked over her shoulder and saw Mrs. Cha glaring at her — she had no choice but to be polite. She conjured a plastic smile and looked back into her drink. She took a sip, and then another. The man ordered a drink and leaned against the bar, staring at Il-sun's breasts, which were still overplump from her pregnancy.

Mrs. Cha came and stood between them. She greeted the man as if he were familiar, and then turned to Il-sun.

"This is your first client, Daisy. Don't disappoint me." She said the words with a smile plastered on her face and a pleasant lilt in her voice, but her eyes were hard and threatening. Il-sun turned to the man and gave another forced smile. Mrs. Cha spoke to him again, saying something in English that caused them both to laugh. He handed her a small stack of green bills, which she counted with sharp movements. The bills sounded like a knife on a sharpening stone as they slid across each other in her hands. She nodded at the man and walked away.

The man threw back his drink and wiped his mouth with the back of his hand, looking expectantly at Il-sun. Il-sun glanced over her shoulder at Mrs. Cha, and then smiled at the man again. She took a long sip of her whiskey, held back a cough as it burned its way down her throat, then stood up. He followed her across the room and they disappeared up the stairs.

Gi had not felt this alone for a long time. She hoped that nobody would notice her sitting there and that Mrs. Cha would forget about her. The room filled up around her, and the sounds of talking, laughing, and drinking got louder and louder. Cigarette smoke burned her nostrils and the air was heavy with the smell of men. Jasmine returned, and then left again soon afterward with another client. Cho came and went similarly. Gi was not sure which was worse, being alone in anticipation of her first client or enduring the dizzying cacophony in the now crowded bar. She wondered if eventually the sounds would make sense to her the same way the sounds of the garment factory had become a kind of music. She listened for patterns in the chaos: the wavelike rise and lull in chatter, the random clinking of glassware, the nonsense music coming from across the room drowned out and absorbed into the thrum.

Mrs. Cha sat at the stool next to her. The expected chill that normally accompanied her was absent.

"What's your name, dear?" Mrs. Cha asked. Gi was surprised by the lack of malice in her tone.

"Gi-Gi-Gyong-ho, ma'am."

"Gyong-ho?"

"Yes, ma'am."

"Were your parents from the dark ages? Did they think by giving you a boy's name that they would turn their daughter into a son? I would say it almost worked, by looking at you."

"I don't know, ma'am." Gi was nervous talking with Mrs. Cha. She counted bottles behind the bar, then divided them by the number of steps up to her room.

"I'm not really here by choice either, you know. You'll get used to it. You will either get used to it or it will kill you. It's that simple. Most girls choose to get used to it. Have a drink." She turned to the bartender and shouted, "Gin and tonic!"

The drink arrived, clear and bubbling. Gi counted the ice cubes, and then the bubbles, and then multiplied them by the previous number that was in her head. She took a small sip, and it lit up the back of her throat. She coughed. The drink was bitter. She took another sip.

"It will give you strength. I'll be right back." Mrs. Cha got up from the stool, not quite able to mask the pain she felt in an arthritic hip, and left Gi with her drink. She returned a moment later with a bleary-eyed young man in tow. She said something to him in English, which he acknowledged with a nod. He was having difficulty standing.

"Gyong-ho, this is Justin," said Mrs. Cha.

"He just paid for your services, so take good care of him." Then she leaned into Gyong-ho and whispered in a frozen breath, "I told him your name was Toby. I gave you a boy's name, too. I always wanted a son." She then evaporated into the crowd.

Gyong-ho was frozen to the spot. She knew what was expected of her, but she could not will her legs to move. Her breathing became shallow and the room started to close in around her. She calculated the square root of the number of barstools. Mrs. Cha was watching her from across the room. She looked back at her client and multiplied the square root of barstools by the number of eyelashes on his upper lids. The lids of his eyes were sagging over dull red orbs. She felt something thick collecting at the back of her throat, and she wanted to spit. She looked again to Mrs. Cha, who was talking with Asshole and pointing over to her. Asshole walked over and grabbed Gi's arm. He said something to her client in English and laughed. He pulled her by the arm across the room and to the stairs while the client followed. At the base of the stairs, Asshole made a sweeping gesture with his arm, as if to cordially invite Gi and her client to climb them. As he did so, he squeezed her arm very tightly. The pain of his grip brought her back into her body, and she found the strength to go through with the task. She put one foot in front of the other and ascended the stairs.

Gi passed Il-sun on the stairway, neither acknowledging the other. Il-sun was grimacing as if she had just tasted something foul. The sun was not with her: Gone were the woman and springtime. For Gyong-ho, this alone was the worst part of losing her virginity, seeing Il-sun in such a state. It was more horrible than being stripped by the drunken imperialist. More loathsome than feeling his weight pressing her into the mattress. More vile than inhaling his toxic breath as he thrust his tongue inside her mouth. Worse, even, than feeling her insides rip as he forced his way inside her. All that could be beautiful was now tarnished because Il-sun, herself, was tainted. Beauty itself had given up on beauty — what chance did she have of recovery?

She raised herself from the mattress, her client passed out in a sodden heap. "Il-sun, I think I'm a woman now," she said to herself, half aloud. She had a kind of understanding now of when Il-sun had said those words to her. She put her clothes on and walked down to the bar.

69

The humiliation of Il-sun's life was now complete. She had given her virginity to Gianni, but she had not lost her innocence until she led the smelly American up the creaky stairs of the Blue Talon brothel. This was not the life promised to her by her mother: the one of a beautiful young woman with excellent *songbun,* courted by a good-looking man high in the Party. Something fundamental was now irreparably altered. It was suddenly clear to her that there would be no turning back, no reclaiming the life she believed was her birthright. All of that had changed. She snapped inside, all at once, and everything that used to be Il-sun drained out of her.

She would never forgive Mrs. Cha, who had sent the doctor with his killing pills to undo her one shred of happiness. She was sure she had done it out of spite. Mrs. Cha had it in for Il-sun from the moment she laid eyes on her — that much was clear by the way she slapped her, and by the condescending way she spoke. *She's jealous of me,* she thought. *Of the way men look at me!* Mrs. Cha had been pretty once, and maybe even beautiful. The hard fall from beauty had been unkind to her. Il-sun was determined to exact revenge.

There was routine at the brothel: All roles were neatly defined, and the rules were simple and spelled out clearly. Each day there were chores and a precise schedule of when she was to be entertaining customers at the bar. It reminded Il-sun, in a way, of the orphanage and the orphanage mistress, and how, in spite of railing against the routine and responsibilities, they had given her a sense of order. Without that regularity there was nothing to guard against the press of chaos from the outside world, which threatened to swallow her whole. What she would give to be back at the orphanage . . . But that thought would only bring her down. She was Daisy now, and there was no going back. To Daisy, there never had been an orphanage, a factory job, a Gianni. As Daisy she could take control.

It did not take long to make sense of the brothel hierarchy. Mrs. Cha was at the top, followed by Asshole, then the bartender, then the various Blue Talon thugs whose job it was to keep the place secure. It was clear where the prostitutes ranked — at the bottom, a commodity, like cattle or chickens. But the brothel was owned by Blue Talon, and Mrs. Cha was only its manager; she had to answer to someone: Uncle Lyong.

Uncle Lyong, it was rumored, would sometimes come to the brothel to let off steam. He had not been there in the month since Il-sun had arrived, but Britney told her that he doted lavishly on his favorite girls with fine gifts. Il-sun thought back to Gianni and the thing he said: If you know a man's weakness, you can own him. Mrs. Cha's weakness was that she was not the boss, and Uncle Lyong's weakness was being a man.

If Daisy could not choose where she lived, or when she worked, or what kind of work she performed, then she had to make the most of her situation. If she had to be a whore, then she was going to be the top whore; and if she could not gain Mrs. Cha's favor, then she would secure the affections and loyalties of the bartenders and bouncers — how did the Great Leader do it? — by promising bottomless love if only they

could prove their worth. She would seduce
Uncle Lyong and rise above Mrs. Cha.

70

Cho reached a breaking point. She kept looking down at her hands and thinking, *The hands of a killer.* She could still feel the sensation of Kang's skull giving way to the heft of the frying pan. She could still see his glazed eyes rolling backward. She could see the pool of crimson blood growing, like a halo, around his head. She had seen much gore and death in the streets back home — a prostitute's view hardens one to such things — but she had never before been its cause. She was blindsided by guilt and shame and regret, and those feelings would not stop.

The torturous weeks spent in the filth, darkness, and discomfort of the shipping container had eroded her strength to the point where she barely knew herself anymore. She kept wondering, *Why won't I die?* She had been a woman with strong knees and an iron spine, but now they could barely hold her upright. For a brief time, right after arriving in Seattle, she thought her strength was returning, that she would once again be the old Cho. She volunteered to be the first to get the tattoo, and she held her chin high her first day working for Mrs. Cha; but then her knees buckled for good, and she found herself on a long, dark spiral inward. There was no way out, no hope, nothing to strive for. She had held so much grief at bay for years, surviving on the street, just making it through each day, but now there was no holding it back. Grief poured from every cell of her body.

In North Korea she had been kept alive by asking, "Will I live another day?" Somehow that question, the fact that in it was a pinch of doubt, buoyed her, caused her to fight for her life. Now, in the brothel, living through the day was nearly assured: There was plenty of food and guaranteed shelter. She did not have to strain at all for her physical survival, nor did she have to stake a claim on life or defend it, yet it wore her down. In fact, all that seemed to matter to anyone was that her heart was beating and her flesh was warm. There was no conceivable end to this captivity. Under Mr. Choy there had been a pretense that she was working toward the goal of her freedom;

but here there was no such promise. She had no hope of this life opening to something better.

Without being able to go forward, she started slipping backward, into her past. She saw over and over again the angry, broken face of her father as he cast her out of his home. His shame, she knew, was not that she had sold her body for food — he had eaten the morsels gladly, without question — but rather that he was bowing to social pressure in throwing her out. His anger was not at her, but at his own weakness at not defending his daughter, at feigning pride so as to save face in his community. He had failed to protect her from the ravages of the world, yet gained strength from the product of her labor. On some level he had known, all along, where she spent her days. Cho loved her father, and she went without a fuss. She helped him save face by leaving and never looking back.

"Where do we go from here?" she asked herself when she stood outside her father's door. She felt less lonely, speaking to herself in the plural.

"Where do we go from here?" she said out loud in the Seattle brothel.

71

Gi looked out onto the street. Summer was making way for fall, and the few trees in the slice of view from her bedroom window were showing hints of yellow. She dressed herself in one of her three outfits, a light green summer dress that had been left behind by one of the many girls spirited away in the constant shuffling of girls, and went to perform her morning chores. She vacuumed the hallway and swept the stairs. Then she helped the kitchen crew clean up from breakfast. Afterward, she sat on a stool with her back to the bar, stone-faced, and waited. This had been her routine for the last three months.

Mrs. Cha was sitting across the room at one of the tables, going over a pile of papers. Apparently there was bureaucracy even here. Mrs. Cha looked up and gave an acidic smile.

"Good morning, Toby," she said in English.

Mrs. Cha's voice traveled down Gi's spine, causing her to shiver, and she lowered her head in a subordinate bow. She had understood Mrs. Cha — she spent all her leisure time in front of the television, decoding the English language. She knew that she was a *bargain price,* that Mrs. Cha was a *mean old bitch,* and that "Daisy" was a *top dollar whore.* In fact, she could understand most of what was said around her, even though she often wished she could not. She never dared to speak the new language — was learning English, the language of imperialists, a punishable antirevolutionary offense? Did that even matter anymore?

Two customers were sitting at the bar. They had looked up briefly when Gi walked in, but then turned back to their conversation. She was not the kind of girl that they were after; at least, not until they had had a few drinks. Men came and went through the brothel at all hours, and it seemed now that all of them were just one man, a carbon copy, coming and going. It did not matter who he was, anymore, Korean, American, African, they were all the same. Various members of Blue Talon also frequented the bar. They were a razor-sharp bunch, well dressed and professional; Uncle Lyong insisted on it. Sometimes they were there to deliver drugs or new women, and at other times they were there solely for pleasure. Gi was spared having to service them. They always went for the pretty girls like Jasmine, Cho, and "Daisy."

Mrs. Cha stood up, wincing from the pain in her hip, and walked toward Gi. Gi felt herself shrinking as she approached, creating a dizzying parallax as Mrs. Cha grew larger in her field of vision. It was all she could do to keep from falling off her barstool.

"I have a gift for you, Toby," said Mrs. Cha, holding out her hand. "We need something to shine you up."

Gi opened her palm, and Mrs. Cha dropped a pair of sparkling clip-on earrings into it.

"I bought them with your tip money. You do get tips, you know? They're adding up."

The other women at the brothel lived for their tips, so that they could buy personal items — it was the only thing that gave them a sense of control over their lives. Jasmine spent hers on soaps, shampoos, lotions, and scents, Cho's went almost entirely to cigarettes, and Il-sun — Daisy — who by far collected the most, spent hers on clothing. Gi wanted nothing to do with money. It made little sense to her, valuing things in dollars; and that which she most longed for could not be purchased.

"See how good I am to you, Toby? Put them on," Mrs. Cha said in English.

Gi obliged, and the clips pinched her ear-lobes uncomfortably.

"Thank you, ma'am," she mumbled in Korean.

It was almost noon when Gi had her first client for the day. She never made an effort to attract men. Normally Mrs. Cha was severe with girls who did not flirt and try to earn their keep, but for Gi she let it slide. Most of the men who went with her were lured by the price. She led the faceless man up to her room and closed the door behind her. She went through the motions, undressing and lying naked on the bed. These violations were painful and sickening, but over the months she had lost sensation in her body, as if it were no longer her own. She found that she could lie passively, allowing *it* to be done to her, while her mind escaped into ever deeper concepts, shapes, and numbers. Anyway, resistance only made it worse. She sensed that the men who came to her all wanted something more than they were receiving, some intangible connection that they tried harder and harder and faster and faster to make until they were spent and yet still unsatisfied. Whatever it was, she knew they were looking in the wrong place, that she did not have it to give to them.

Gi handed Mrs. Cha three meaningless imperialist dollars, her tip, and returned to her stool at the bar. Mrs. Cha folded the money with a quick, practiced movement and slid it into a bulging bag at her waist. She then turned back to her ledgers.

Daisy made her first appearance in the late afternoon, once the bar had gotten considerably more crowded. Gi watched her materialize at the bottom of the stairs, all hips and attitude. She was dressed as a *schoolgirl* — Gi had learned that word in English — in a short red-and-black plaid skirt, knee-length white stockings, black Mary Jane shoes, and a low-cut white blouse. Her hair was pulled into pigtails on the sides of her head in an attempt to make her look barely pubescent. Mrs. Cha had one time ordered her to dress that way, to humiliate her for an insolent comment she had made; but Daisy turned it around — it was her most successful act, and now she enjoyed flaunting it in front of Mrs. Cha. Daisy stood for half a minute, framed by the entryway, without drawing the attention she wanted; she preferred when heads turned immediately. Gi could see a moment of frustration in her eyes.

"Anyone knowing how to pleasing lady?" she shouted across the room in English. It was a phrase that Britney had taught her to say, and was one of several collections of syllables Daisy had memorized to work the crowd. It meant nothing to her. Gi would have loved to have taught her how to say the phrase correctly, but Il-sun hardly spoke to her anymore; and when she did, her words usually packed the sting of condescension.

She had adapted to the work quickly. Daisy — a brash exaggeration of Il-sun's pride, superiority, and self-centeredness — replaced Il-sun from the first day, as if she'd been planted there in the seed of the man who first lay with her. It seemed that she had erased the past, and with it the common experiences that bonded her to Gi, Cho, and Jasmine.

All eyes in the room turned toward Daisy, and she glowed in the attention. She reached down to the hem of her skirt and slowly drew it up her thighs. Then in a quick movement, she flipped the front of her skirt up to her waist, and held it just long enough to reveal that she was not wearing underwear.

The men in the crowd cheered. Then she strutted through the bar, brushing past men, pinching them, and whispering into their ears.

Daisy's behavior was a shock to many of the women, whose captivity was a mark of shame and ever heavier sadness. Mrs. Cha demanded that all her girls smile and act happy, under threat of serious beatings; but it would not have taken a very keen eye to see beneath the act. The stress and strain of the situation, the loss of self and family, was hardened into the folds of the women's faces. It was a wonder that the men who frequented the place could not see it, or that they could ignore it for the sake of their own satisfaction. But Daisy's performance was unwavering.

Mrs. Cha sat in the corner, coiled up, viperlike and seething. She could not deny that Daisy's act and attitude were profitable, but she did not like losing control. Gi sensed a dangerous match brewing between the two, and she had no doubt who would get the better of whom, in the end. She had tried to warn Il-sun about it, but was snubbed. A self-satisfied smile erupted on Mrs. Cha's face, and she stood, clearing her throat.

"Gentlemen, can I have your attention,

please?" she shouted in English. Mrs. Cha
had a commanding presence, and the room
went instantly quiet. "I think you have all
had the chance to behold our lovely young
Daisy."

Men cheered and clapped.

"Daisy, please step up to the stage," Mrs.
Cha said in Korean.

Daisy's face darkened, and she did not
move.

"Does Asshole need to show you where
the stage is?" Mrs. Cha was all smiles —
most of the men in the room could not
speak Korean — but the threat was plain to
everyone else.

Daisy cleared her sour expression and
made her way to the low stage at the end of
the room.

"Gentlemen, we're going to try something
new today," Mrs. Cha once again addressed
the men in English. "We're going to auction
off a whole evening of Daisy's company. The
highest bidder takes her upstairs. We'll start
the bidding at two hundred dollars."

Gi could see Daisy straining to maintain
her composure. She could not understand
English, but she understood that Mrs. Cha
was getting the better of her. She caught
Gi's eye, and for the briefest of moments,

Gi thought she saw Il-sun, fractured, just below the surface.

72

Mrs. Cha summoned Jasmine before break-fast. Jasmine had been working all night, and the command to go down to the bar was unwelcome. What could she possibly want? Jasmine dressed and went downstairs.

Jasmine blamed herself for the fate of her three *Chosun* friends. Her plan to leave Seoul had been desperate, and not thought through — but she had needed to act fast. There was the offer of marriage on the table, and her mother had already left to live with her fiancé. She had to tell her mother some of the awful truth to get her to agree to go — that she was in trouble and needed to flee a dangerous gangster. Now what would become of her mother? She hoped that her fiancé would continue to take care of her, but she doubted he would feel much obligation to do so after Jasmine failed to arrive when promised. Deep down, she even wondered if the offer of marriage had been some kind of scam, but she would have dealt with that once she got to Kwangju.

She could not have lived with herself if she had not done something to try to help Gi, Cho, and Il-sun. She had seen too many enslaved girls cycle through Mr. Choy's sex galleries, aware of their fate without doing anything about it. But finally, working so closely with her three friends, she could not deny the truth: that being a witness, she was involved, and being involved, she had a responsibility to act. She hated feeling helpless. Were her friends worse off here than in South Korea? It was difficult to tell. In either place they would have spiraled into madness, eventually, and the strain was starting to show.

Cho was now continually hunched over, clutching a cigarette and muttering to herself. It was as if the bottom had dropped out of her mind and she had fallen into the abyss of herself. She had seemed so strong, but the loss of hope had crushed her. She kept saying, over and over under her breath, "Where do we go from here? Where do we go from here?" She was not eating much anymore, and she was getting frighteningly thin. Jasmine worried that if Cho did not pull herself together, at least a little bit, she would be unable to work. There was no telling what Mrs. Cha would do to a woman who could not earn her keep.

Il-sun had become a completely different person. Jasmine knew that the drugs could do that. Daisy had discovered soon after their arrival how to barter herself for *hiroppong* from the bartender, but the transformation began even before the drugs appeared. Jasmine had seen this kind of personality shift before, working for Mr. Choy. Sometimes the only way for a woman to endure the pressures of the flesh trade was to seal away some small kernel of herself where it could not be corrupted, and protect it with a tough external shell. Il-sun had done just that, by changing her name so that all the abuses happened to Daisy, a brash, confident, completely self-serving woman, instead of to herself. That way she protected her innocence with the hope that, someday, she would be able to return to it. Sadly, Jasmine knew that she could not.

Jasmine did her best to try to steer Il-sun away from *hiroppong,* but there was little she could do. Il-sun avoided her, and when confronted, she became defensive — communicating with her was impossible. Jasmine had seen many girls hit a rapid decline on the drug, corroding both inside and out

within a matter of months. It was a substance that sapped youth and tarnished
souls; and Il-sun was already exhibiting
signs of its abuse. She was tetchy and
sometimes paranoid. Her color was perhaps
a little ashen and her eyes were getting
colder and harder. The drug had not yet
claimed her beauty, but it was beginning to
close in on it. Jasmine's heart broke for the
inevitable track Il-sun's life had taken.

Gi had won a special place in Jasmine's
heart. She had been through so much in
the months that Jasmine had known her,
and clearly much more before they met, and
yet she still possessed a small, unquench-
able fire. The stresses of captivity and forced
prostitution were visible on her as well, but
she seemed to be holding up better than the
other two. She had a way of disassociating
that served well to protect her, though if
she ever escaped this life, she would have to
overcome that, too. For now, however, her
ability to retreat into her mind was saving
her life.

From her best guess, four months had
passed in Seattle, and time loomed endlessly. Nobody ever talked about leaving,
and after her previous failure, Jasmine was
wary to plan another escape. They were too
well guarded. Women came and went with-

out explanation, many of them in their teens, stolen or tricked from their homes, smuggled or lured thousands of miles away from their families, where they had no contacts and could not run back. Jasmine listened to their stories of kidnapping or betrayal in the early morning hours after work was done, when exhaustion lowered defenses and the bouncers were more likely to overlook hushed conversations. Women often disappeared from the brothel without warning, and nobody knew what happened to them. They had probably been moved to another brothel, maybe in another city or country where Blue Talon had a presence. Jasmine had met several women who had been relocated more than once — it was a large organization that had tendrils everywhere, it seemed.

Mrs. Cha was waiting for Jasmine at the bottom of the stairs.

"You're one of the clever ones," said Mrs. Cha with her sandpaper voice when Jasmine reached the bottom step. "It's better for a girl like you to keep moving."

"Better for whom?" Jasmine asked. She had a sinking feeling.

Mrs. Cha smiled her cold-blooded smile. "You're one of the clever ones," she repeated, and walked away.

"You're coming with me," said a muscular young man. He was one of the sharp-dressed Blue Talon thugs. There were two other women in the room, both wide-eyed and frightened. With tears in her eyes, Jasmine followed them out the door.

73

Daisy descended the stairs, crossing one leg sensuously in front of the other, pointing her toes enticingly as she stepped. It was all in the attitude, and even though no one could see her until she reached the bottom step, it was important for her to already be in character when she got there. She felt nervous, but she knew it could not show. Today was a special day.

Most days when she made her entrance it was the same old thing. She would linger at the bottom step and strike a pose — if she had learned one thing from Mr. Choy, it was how to strike a pose. If the crowd did not turn their attention soon enough, she would shout one of the English phrases she had learned. Some days, if Mrs. Cha was feeling particularly vindictive, she would say something sharp in response, knocking Il-sun off her pedestal with a slight in perfect English, and everyone in the room would laugh at her. Normally, however, Mrs. Cha said nothing and collected the money.

Daisy's heart was racing. Maybe it was her nerves, or just the *hiroppong.* She had hit the pipe, just a little, in her room only minutes before. If any day she needed it, it was today. She needed to feel *that* way if she was going to pull off the seduction of Uncle Lyong.

Mrs. Cha strictly forbade her girls to use *hiroppong* or any of the other substances that the bartender guarded and dispensed behind the bar. She said it made them edgy. But Mrs. Cha was not always around — even serpents need to sleep — and when she was not there, things relaxed. Il-sun had been plying the bartender with sweet promises and occasional favors, and now he gave her a steady supply.

Uncle Lyong had been to the brothel only once in the five months Daisy had been there; this was but one of Blue Talon's pleasure houses. He had come specifically to see a girl from Vietnam who had caught his attention, and he came through so briefly that Il-sun did not have an opportunity to impress him. But now that girl was gone, like Jasmine and so many other girls were suddenly gone, and Uncle Lyong would be looking for a new consort. It was rumored that the girl had so captured his heart that she convinced him to let her go home. Daisy found that difficult to believe, but it never hurt to hope that it could happen. For the vague promise of release, and for the expensive gifts Uncle Lyong was known to dole out to his favorite girls, there was a tense, competitive atmosphere among many of the women. Mrs. Cha had announced in the morning that Uncle Lyong would be coming in.

Daisy knew that she was considered the prettiest girl in the brothel, but would she suit his tastes? Men could be so particular. Jasmine had a special knack for peering into the motivations of men, and Daisy did her best to recall what she had learned from her. It was not only for the extra gifts that Daisy wanted to seduce Uncle Lyong. She wanted to reach above Mrs. Cha, to poison his mind against her. She wanted to hold Uncle Lyong's arm and watch Mrs. Cha squirm in obligatory politeness. And who knew? Maybe Uncle Lyong would be so taken by her that he would lift her, too, out of the brothel and give her a life of her own.

Daisy had planned carefully for this night for many weeks — she knew the opportunity would come, eventually. She had sized up Uncle Lyong in the two minutes he had spent there, and she believed she knew what kind of man he was. Her plan would be either a smashing success or an abject failure. While all the other girls were daubing on heavy makeup and squeezing into their skimpiest outfits to try to lure him with wild, dirty sex, Daisy was applying a simple skiff of white powder and donning a *Chosun-ot,* a traditional Korean outfit consisting of a loose-fitting, long-sleeved blouse and a floor-length, high-waisted skirt. She had saved her tip money and then requested the *Chosun-ot* when one of the bouncers did the shopping. There had been confusion at first, because in South Korea the same thing is called a *hanbok* — another perversion of the language no doubt orchestrated by the imperialist puppet government, but she no longer cared about those differences. She had originally asked that he take her with him so she could choose her own, but that was out of the question — she had not set foot outside the brothel since her arrival. So then she described the colors she wanted, and hoped he would get it right. In the end, the bouncer had done well enough. He said that shopping for a *hanbok* outside Korea was not an easy task, and that he did the best he could. Daisy was sure he had not put much effort into it, but she had to work with what she had. The *Chosun-ot* that the bouncer brought had a white blouse with black trim, and a royal blue skirt. It was simpler than she would have liked, but it would do.

After bathing, dressing, and applying powder to her face, Daisy spent a good long time fashioning her hair into a perfect bun on the back of her head. There was not a strand out of place — there could not be. Then she waited. She had to time her entrance perfectly. When Uncle Lyong arrived, there was a frenzy of activity downstairs. The women, the ones who were interested, anyway, were scrambling to be the first in the bar, but Daisy sat in her room and lit the *hiroppong*. Ten minutes later, after Uncle Lyong had had a chance to get an eyeful of all the women in the brothel, she descended the stairs.

She struck a pose in the frame of the stairway and stood stock still. As a course of habit, the women in the brothel turned to look at her on the stair, and as she had hoped, their collective gaze drew Uncle Lyong's attention. The women would expect her to shout one of her loud English phrases; but instead she was silent. She kept a neutral expression on her face, purposefully keeping her eyes averted from Uncle

Lyong. After a moment, she glided into the room, her *Chosun-ot* swishing on the air behind her, and sat at one of the empty tables across the room from him. Her head was bowed, and her gaze lowered. Daisy had made herself the image of conservative Korean innocence, perfectly virginal; and against the backdrop of raw flesh and base sexual provocation she was easily the most compelling woman in the room. That she sat aloof only served to set the hooks more deeply into him. Her plan was working. Uncle Lyong peeled himself away from the shell of women around him, walked over, and sat down next to her.

74

Gi watched Mrs. Cha watching the brothel. Mrs. Cha had keen eyes and a sixth sense and seemed to know everything that was going on, even the things that went on behind her back. She was patient, and acted in quick, decisive strokes. She was an ambush predator, a master of concealment and the surprise attack; and she seemed to enjoy manipulating her pretty playthings, occasionally savoring the act of ripping into the flesh of one of them with her sharp, hidden teeth.

As Daisy became bolder and louder, Mrs. Cha became quieter and more observant. Daisy mistook this as her own victory, and flaunted her disregard for the rules with greater and greater gall. She shirked her cleaning and kitchen duties, showed up for work in the bar as much as an hour late and manipulated the bartender for more than the allowed number of drinks. Watching from the sidelines, Gi could see that Mrs. Cha was not retreating or giving in, as Daisy assumed, but coiling even tighter, sharpening her senses, readying her aim — the more audacious she allowed Daisy to become, the more dramatic her downfall would be. This was a game to Mrs. Cha that she played, perhaps, to make her own life interesting; after all, if she wanted to, she could simply send Il-sun away as she had done with Jasmine, as she often did with girls she did not like or to make room for new ones.

The mood shifted, however, the night that Daisy descended the stairs wearing her *Chosun-ot.* Uncle Lyong drifted right over to her, forgetting for a moment to be manly, being pulled toward her as if by the softness of his own feminine lips. This struck a nerve with Mrs. Cha, and she visibly stiffened. Daisy had, either accidently or by design, tread across a boundary that Mrs. Cha would not abide. It was one of the few times Gi ever saw real emotion on Mrs. Cha's face. Anger. Revenge. As soon as Uncle Lyong whisked Daisy away from the brothel to take her to his private nest, Mrs. Cha descended upon the bartender, who shrank as she approached.

"I want you to give her more *hiroppong,*" she said to him in English.

"What?" he said, looking shocked. He had believed she did not know about his arrangement with Il-sun.

"Don't play dumb with me or I'll have your balls on a platter. I know you give it to her. I want you to give her more. A lot more."

"Yes, ma'am," he replied, shaking.

75

As winter came on, the rain never seemed to stop. The old building was a poor barrier against the damp and Gyong-ho was always cold. Sometimes she welcomed the extra body heat provided by her clients as they satisfied themselves on her. For a few days there was even snow, and traffic all but stopped in the brothel. It was a welcome reprieve.

Then the sun gradually returned, and for some time in the afternoons it would shine through Gi's window, where she would soak up its rays. The days got incrementally longer, the rain stopped, and the winter slowly turned back into summer. The air was once again rich with the smell of life. She lingered by open windows to inhale the change of seasons — she had been in the brothel for an entire year.

Cho smoked and mumbled to herself almost constantly. For no apparent reason she would blurt "Where do we go from here?" and "I'm not that stupid." It was distressing, and Gi wished she could talk to Jasmine about it. Jasmine would have had something insightful to say, she was sure — she had been a beacon of strength, and without her, since Daisy had claimed the better part of Il-sun, Gi was awash with loneliness. Gi found herself at a crossroads: Would she be pushed under and destroyed by the crush of captivity, or would she find her inner strength and continue to push against it? She could go either way. She looked inside and asked herself the question, Do I want to live? And, to her own surprise, the answer came back a resounding, Yes! She would do whatever it took to get through this.

Gyong-ho rarely spoke to Daisy. There were almost no recognizable traces left of Il-sun, though Gi was sure she still lingered there, under the surface, below the *hiroppong* and posturing. Il-sun had aged so rapidly that she could have passed for a rough forty, even though she had barely turned nineteen. Her eyes bulged and maintained a wide, hard stare. Her skin had lost its youthful color and sheen and hung loosely around her eyes. She picked at her face and arms constantly, and open sores wept on her sunken cheeks and her dry lips. Her teeth were a dark yellow shade, and some were even starting to turn black near the gums. Even with makeup, now, few men chose to lie with her. Mrs. Cha looked at her with smug satisfaction as Daisy sat, unaccompanied, at the bar.

For two months Daisy had been Uncle Lyong's pet. He had come often to take her away for the evening; and as she was walking out the door on his arm, she would pass Mrs. Cha a sweet and condescending smile. Daisy's air of superiority hit its peak at that time, and she outright refused to perform chores or work in the bar. She began ordering everyone around, like a princess; and though Mrs. Cha was immune to her commands, she did nothing to put her in her place. Then, without warning, Uncle Lyong stopped coming to the brothel. Daisy waited to be summoned by him, but the summons never came. When he finally did come back, he selected a newly arrived girl from Thailand to entertain him. Uncle Lyong was not going to save her from this life, and with that realization Daisy began to implode. She hit the pipe without restraint, and the bartender's supply of *hiroppong* for her was limitless. In her drugged ranting, she often made references to her superior beauty and excellent *songbun.*

Gi ached to soothe the deep wound that had caused Il-sun to be this way. She no longer desired Il-sun, as she once had, but she still cared for her deeply. Il-sun had nursed her back from a wretched state, and Gi wished she could do the same for her; but her friend was unapproachable and incoherent.

One evening in early August, Daisy was sitting at the bar, weaving back and forth on the stool, her eyes dull and droopy. Uncle Lyong walked in with several of his men. They had come for an evening of enjoyment after some tense business dealing. Uncle Lyong might have owned the whole world, by the look of his arrogant stride. His face was an unpleasable mask, cut in two by a sour grimace. When he came in, he ignored Daisy completely, as he had for months. If he even recognized her, it did not show. He found his favorite new consort and then went to sit for a game of cards at one of the tables. Something snapped in Daisy then, and she got up with a wild look in her eyes.

"You're my man, Gianni," she screamed, pointing at Uncle Lyong. The whole bar fell silent — no one ever dared to speak in a raised tone to Uncle Lyong, and it was especially inappropriate to point at him. She walked up to him, shaking her finger in his face. "You owe me, Gianni!"

Uncle Lyong stood, and everyone instinctively backed away from him. He turned to her, his eyes burning with fury, and the back of his hand made a sharp, loud sound on her face. He was a strong man, and he had cocked his arm wide, releasing it with tremendous force. Daisy spun from the impact and hit the floor. Her gums had been made soft by the *hiroppong,* and she spit two teeth into the palm of her hand. Il-sun gaped silently and then began to sob.

Uncle Lyong disappeared with his consort. Mrs. Cha stood over Il-sun, cold and triumphant. "You got what you deserve, cunt." Il-sun looked up at her with fear and hatred. "I have no more use for you. Get out," Mrs. Cha said with quiet command in her voice, pointing at the door. "Get out now, or I'll have Asshole throw you out. And never come back!"

"No!" shouted Gyong-ho.

Il-sun picked herself up off the floor. The room was silent. Even the customers, who did not fully understand what was going on, knew enough to keep quiet. Il-sun walked to the door with her head down. Before pushing it open she looked into the palm of her hand at her teeth. She then turned her hand sideways and allowed her teeth to fall to the floor. The clatter they made split the dead quiet like thunder. Such small teeth, such a loud sound. She pushed the door and walked out of the brothel.

The door swung shut behind her and chatter erupted. Business went back to normal. Gi ran to follow Il-sun, but was brought up short by Mrs. Cha's loud, raspy voice.

"Not you, Toby," she said in English. "I like having you around."

76

Gyong-ho worried constantly about Il-sun, who was now on her own and fending for herself on the streets of an unfamiliar, foreign city. How long could she live out there? Even though they had drifted far apart during the last year, Gi felt stripped of something crucial. One thing that had been getting Gi through the numbing nights and days had been the hope that Il-sun would shed the persona of Daisy, and they would be close once again. Hope had been a distraction from the raw endlessness of this life of subservience. Dispossessed of that hope, Gi found herself on the precipice of despair — the future was a bleak promise of only more of the same. But she thought of her life, of everything she had been through, and as difficult as it was, she could not give in now. She stepped back from the brink, not with the question "Why?" but with "How?" How would she escape this life? How would she foil her captors, find Il-sun, and resuscitate her? These thoughts gave her a singular focus, a reason to live yet another day. She knew that the DMZ had been just a mental barrier, and so was her captivity: a problem to be solved, fear to be acknowledged and defused.

Cho was broken. She slouched, mumbled to herself, and smoked constantly. She saw clients — she was now a *bargain price* like Gi. She ate sparsely and looked dangerously thin, even for someone from North Korea. But still she lived. Some part of her, too, was fighting to get through it, and Gi felt proud of her for that.

Faces came and went. Girls were moved from place to place to keep them unsettled and too disoriented to escape. Gi could not explain why Mrs. Cha would not part with her or Cho; they had been at the brothel longer than any of the other girls. Maybe she needed someone familiar to care for. Her grandson had left for college, and perhaps, like everyone, she craved stability. Or maybe no one else wanted two skinny whores from North Korea.

As autumn approached, tension began to build in the brothel. The bouncers paced nervously, and Mrs. Cha was more serious and grim than usual. Unsmiling men held meetings in a private room, after which they would leave without satisfying themselves on the girls. More bouncers fortified the brothel, and all the customers who entered were subjected to thorough body searches. Bit by bit Gi was able to piece together what was going on from scraps of conversations that she overheard. Apparently the Japanese counterpart to Blue Talon was trying to muscle in on their territory. Old agreements had been breached and now the more powerful Japanese were attempting to take over. Blue Talon expected to be attacked, but they did not know when or how. Uncle Lyong was in hiding, being an obvious target for assassination. Already two of his generals had been gunned down.

Gi caught herself thinking fearfully, *They are going to attack us!* It reminded her of the days back in *Chosun,* when there was constant fear that the Americans were going to launch an offensive. But then she had to consider whether or not she was even a part of "us." Who was she and where did she belong? She used to be *Chosun,* living her life for the glory of the Dear Leader's republic. Now the Dear Leader was a faint shadow in her life, powerless over her since she had crossed the DMZ. *Chosun* was no longer the mightiest of nations but an imaginary fortress across a wide, bumpy sea. But she was also not a member of Blue Talon — she was a possession. She was not any part of "us." What did it matter if the Japanese attacked and took over ownership of her? Either way she was only a possession. To her, us was Cho, Il-sun, and Jasmine. Us was the orphanage mistress and her sister, the angel who saved her from the gulag. Us was her grandmother, mother, and father. Us was all the seamstresses, orphans, prisoners, and whores.

"And we want our lives back!" she said aloud.

"What was that?" asked Cho.

"I said, we want our lives back, Cho. This isn't who we are."

Tires screeched on the street below; then came a sound like a heavy rock falling hard onto a wooden floor. Then another rock. Then a whole load of them falling in succession. Glass shattered, men shouted, and a scream pierced the afternoon. Gi had just finished dressing and her client was still lying on the bed. There was a dreamlike quiet that followed. She descended the stairs. Everyone in the bar was cowering under tables and in corners. Mrs. Cha made a frantic waving gesture at her from across the room. The door to the front room was propped open by the body of Asshole, who lay unmoving in the doorway in a red pool growing on the floor around him. Tires screeched again outside and a car sped away. Gi stepped over the body in the doorway and into the forbidden front room. The windows were shattered and men were sprawled every which way. Everywhere there were holes and shards of glass. She stood in the front room for a moment, comprehension coming to her in waves. She looked back into the brothel, and then out to the street. She knew that within a minute Mrs. Cha would recompose herself and that an opportunity would be lost. She thought of Il-sun, then she thought of Cho.

"I'll come back for you, Cho," she said under her breath. She stepped over the broken glass and onto the street.

PART IV

77

Gyong-ho had not worn shoes for over a year, and her feet were cold on the wet sidewalk. She ran blindly from the brothel, not bothering to look back. She did not know where she was going, and she did not care, as long is it was far away. She found a quiet boulevard and followed it in a straight line. After eleven blocks, she slowed to a brisk walk.

At first glance Seattle was the same as Seoul, full of cars and random noise. She had never been on her own in a foreign city, and the adrenaline of leaving the brothel gave way to fear. People stared at her when she walked by, and she realized that she must look as strange to them as they looked to her. She was not dressed for the autumn chill in the air, wearing only a thigh-length skirt and thin, short-sleeved top, and it must have seemed odd that she was walking down the street barefoot. She was afraid that her

Blue Talon tattoo was too conspicuous, and she did her best to conceal it against the buildings she passed. She wanted to find some way to cover it as soon as possible, but her first priority was to get as far as she could from Mrs. Cha and Blue Talon.

After a while the skyline of the core of the city came into view, a jagged crop of tall buildings huddled in the distance. The city seemed to funnel in that direction, and she needed a goal to keep her walking, so she headed toward downtown. Her feet began to hurt from the impact on the sidewalk and from the cold, but she did not dare slow down. She crossed a bridge and then found herself walking around a lake; and in spite of her desperate situation she had to admire Seattle for its beauty. Downtown was nestled between several low hills that were covered with houses and trees. The lake seemed to give the city a still center around which all its activity spun. The late-afternoon sun all but disappeared and the air became crisp, and she worried that she would not be able to find shelter. If not, she did not think she could live through the night.

Finally she found herself among the high-rises, and she could no longer believe that America was a desolate place. Exhausted, she stopped on a busy corner and watched the throbbing of the city. Such an assortment of people wearing a variety of styles, going in every direction and at different speeds. It was a wonderful kind of chaos. She had nowhere to go and no plan for what to do next. She thought about her decision to bolt, and wondered if she had made the right choice — at least at the brothel there was food and shelter. Would they punish her if she went back? But then she thought about that life and her impulse to leave it, and she realized that she would rather die taking control of her own life than suffer endless, anesthetic indignity at the hands of others. She stood on the corner, shivering, counting the people walking by. *I might die here,* she thought to herself. *Maybe that will be okay.*

A man shuffled along, pushing a wire mesh cart that was overflowing with random items. He almost walked past her, but then stopped and took a closer look. He was wearing a filthy yellow jacket and fingerless gloves.

"Your lips are blue," he said to her in a rough voice. He had a white beard and greasy hair. His eyes held the compassion of one who has suffered greatly over a long period of time. He looked down and saw that her feet were bare. "You don't have any shoes on." He said it as if he were filling in an equation: blue lips plus no shoes equals . . . He began rummaging in his cart and withdrew an old pair of sneakers and handed them to her. It was a generous offering, and she was thankful. The shoes were fetid, and many sizes too large, but none of that mattered. At that moment they were better than anything she could have wanted from the imperialist magazines she had looked through so long ago.

"Thank you," she tried to say in English. It was the first thing she had ever said aloud in the foreign language. It came out sounding more like "sank oo." The man understood anyway, and nodded.

"Follow me," he said.

Gyong-ho put the sneakers on her feet and walked behind him. She was grateful for the cushioned soles of the shoes, and the warmth they provided. As she walked, she noticed that the well dressed never looked at the wretched. It was like two parallel worlds coinciding but never intersecting. She followed the man for several blocks to an area of town that looked considerably older, with redbrick buildings and narrower streets. There was a line of people down one of the alleys, and the man joined the queue. "This is the food line," he said. "They serve a cup of soup to the homeless every night. They also have a women's shelter. They don't let men stay here. It's downright sexist, if you ask me, but I guess they don't want no fornicatin', it bein' a church and all. Anyway, I'll introduce you. They know me here." The line moved quickly and soon they were at the door of the building. A man with a clipboard was writing names down as people entered. "They'll want to talk at you while we eat; nonsense about God and stuff like that. Nothin' comes for free, I guess," he said in a whisper as they approached. "Hey, Rick!" he called to the man at the door.

"God be with you, Sam."

"Hey, Rick, this is my good frien', uh . . . what's your name?"

"Daisy." It was the first name that came to mind, and Gi immediately regretted saying it.

"Daisy what?" asked the man with the clipboard.

"Daisy Smith, if it's all the same to you," said Sam hotly. "Nosy prat," he added under his breath.

"Right," said the man, writing the name on his clipboard.

"She'll be need'n a place to stay tonight, too, I imagine."

"She will have to speak to Donna after the sermon, then. Let's keep the line moving."

Sam and Gi received foam cups full of soup and a dry roll each, and sat down at a long table. A man was droning on in the background about a man named Jesus Christ. The food was not very flavorful, but the room was warm. Gi scanned about, hoping to see Il-sun, but she knew it was unlikely she'd find her so soon — it had been about two months since Il-sun had been cast out, and there was no telling how far she had gone in that time. After the lecture was finished, Sam brought her to a tired-looking woman with droopy eyes.

"Donna, this is my good frien' Daisy Smith. She needs a place to stay."

"We're pretty full up, Sam."

"She doesn't have a place to go. I'm sure you can find some room for her."

"Well, where did she stay last night? Maybe she can go back there?"

"She can't go back there! Boyfrien' on drugs, waving his gun around! Termites eating her bones! No, she can't go back there."

"Has she tried Central?"

"No, she hasn't tried frickin' Central. That's fifteen blocks from here. She's here now, and she doesn't have no clothes. She has shoes cuz I give 'em to her. Where's your Jesus fucking Christ spirit?"

"Calm down, Sam, or I'll throw you out. It's routine. I have to ask. We don't have a lot of room, but I'll see what I can do." She disappeared behind a door for several minutes, then poked her head out. "Okay, Daisy, follow me. I'll show you to a bed."

"Sank oo, Sam," said Gyong-ho, and she bowed.

"Yer welcome. See ya around, Daisy."

Gi followed Donna through the door and into a small waiting room. Donna handed her a clipboard and a pen.

"Fill out this form the best you can. You can read, can't you?" asked Donna.

Gi nodded.

"You're not allowed to bring any possessions inside with you. If you have anything, we will keep it for you in the safe. We've had a problem with people spreading vermin, so you'll have to hand over your clothes for washing, and we'll give you something to wear until morning. You're allowed five minutes in the shower. You won't want more than that because it ain't exactly hot. We'll give you a pillow and a blanket, and feminine products if you need 'em. Wake-up is at seven, and you're expected to be out of here by eight. We'll give you a warm biscuit to eat on the way out. Once you're inside, you're not allowed to leave until morning. All the doors have alarms. Got it?"

Got it must mean "do you understand," Gi thought. She nodded. She began filling in the form, using Daisy Smith as her name. She had to think hard about what letter combination made the *th* sound, but then remembered the blue elephant on television singing a song about the friendship between the letters *T* and *H.* After handing the form back to Donna, she was led behind a locked metal door. As soon as she heard it click shut behind her, she heard every door that had ever clicked shut behind her and she regretted her decision to stay. She was paralyzed by fear. What if this had been an elaborate trick to get her into the imperialist gulag? She was now locked in and being asked to strip. The walls were sterile and lit by anemic fluorescent lights. There were no windows, and now that she was inside, she would not be allowed to leave. The *Chosun* gulag was bad enough — the American gulag must be even worse. What horrible labor would they force her into? She could not take another step forward.

"Don't take all night, now. I have things to do," said Donna. "Don't be afraid, I

548

won't bite ya. Give us those clothes of yours. Shoes too. They look like they need a good washing. Here, you can wrap yourself in a towel and head to the shower, just inside that door. I'll give you some pj's when you get out."

Reluctantly Gi removed her clothes and wrapped herself in the thin towel Donna had handed her. Donna stuffed the clothes into a mesh bag with a number printed on the side, then handed Gi a small plastic chip with the same number on it.

"You'll get these back in the morning," said Donna, indicating the clothes. "Show your chip at the counter tomorrow, and you'll get these back, fresh and clean. Now you have five minutes in the shower, then it's lights out."

Gi stepped into the shower room and stood under the water. The best she could say for it was that it was not cold, exactly. It was still better than any bathing experience she ever had in North Korea, using icy water and a small bucket. The soap smelled strong and antiseptic, and it burned her skin a little. Once she'd finished in the shower, Donna gave her a set of maroon pajamas and a pair of cardboard slippers. The cloth of the pajamas was surprisingly rough for being so thin. If this was the American gulag, at least it was clean.

Donna led her into a large room full of single beds. It reminded Gi of the orphanage, the way the women slept side by side in rows, and she scanned the room hopefully for Il-sun. The lights were dimmed but never fully extinguished for the night; and although the women were not allowed to talk after nine o'clock, there was constant noise. Women belched and farted, tossed and turned on noisy spring mattresses, one woman hummed to herself incessantly, and at least two could not keep themselves from bursting out with meaningless babble. Even with all this, and with her fear that she had just landed herself in a gulag, Gi fell into a fitful sleep.

78

"Alright ladies, rise and shine! Up and at 'em; it's seven o'clock," a woman shouted into the dormitory. "Turn in your blankets and your pj's and pick up your clothes." Women groaned, and chatter picked up where it had left off the night before. Gyong-ho opened her eyes and blinked a couple of times to clear them. The woman in the bed next to her was staring at the foot of Gi's bed. Gi looked down and saw that her foot and ankle were sticking out from under her blanket, her Blue Talon tattoo in plain view.

"I'd keep that hidden if I was you," she said. She was a blonde woman in her midthirties with dark bruises for eyes.

Gi said nothing and pulled her foot back beneath the blanket.

"Don't worry. I won't say nothin'," said the woman.

Gyong-ho watched the routine of the

shelter unfold, and then joined the line of women waiting to receive their laundered clothes. Gi gave her numbered plastic chip to a woman behind a counter, and the woman handed over the mesh bag with her clothes in it. Gi noticed a strong disinfectant smell coming from the bag; they apparently did not use the same fragrant detergent that was used at the brothel. Noticing that Gi's bag was particularly light, the woman said, "We have a free box, you know."

"A what?" asked Gi. She was glad that those words were easy to say. She was still timid to use the language.

"A free box. We have a box full of clothes from Goodwill. You might find some warmer clothes to wear. It's in that corner, over there," the woman said, pointing.

Gi went to the box and was happy to find an assortment of trousers, shirts, and sweaters. She found some things that looked like they would fit, including a pair of socks that would cover her tattoo. None of the shoes in the box were better than the ones Sam had given to her, but she was grateful to have shoes at all. The socks, anyway, would help her feet fit better in them. Without a second thought, she dumped her brothel clothes into the free box, and then went to the restroom to change out of her pajamas.

Once she was dressed, the tide of women at the shelter pulled her toward the exit. Just before leaving she was given a plain biscuit that was still warm from the oven. She bowed in gratitude, and walked out into the sunlight. It was a relief to find that she had not been tricked into the gulag.

During the day she wandered the city within a short radius of the shelter. She observed how people dressed and behaved, and made notes to herself on how best to blend in. She managed to go the whole day without so much as making eye contact with another person. The city was a wonder of abundance, and there were endless streams of well-dressed, well-fed people, carrying all manner of fascinating gadgetry. Could what she was told about America have been a lie? These people, though loud and lacking subtle manners, did not seem the monsters she had seen depicted on posters or heard about in the popular stories told back home.

She stayed at the shelter for four nights in a row, and during the days she familiarized herself with the city. Her distance from the shelter grew each day as she became more comfortable exploring her surroundings and as she realized that it was unlikely that anyone from Blue Talon would recognize her in the anonymity of the city. She did not know how she was going to find Il-sun out of the millions of people around her, but she had not lost heart. On her fifth night she arrived late at the shelter; she had been spellbound by a group of Peruvian men playing pan pipes outside a shopping complex and could not tear herself away from the sound. The music was fascinating, the way each musician played only a small range of notes, but worked with the others to seamlessly create broad and beautiful melodies. It was music that fulfilled the *Chosun* ideal because each person perfected his own small part, but to a greater, communal end. *The Dear Leader should love this music,* she thought, but doubted that he would — it had not originated in *Chosun,* and was therefore, by nature, inferior. Or, perhaps, a story would be told of how Kim Il-sung himself had created this music, and given it as a gift to the Peruvians to teach them the superiority of *Chosun* socialism. Only now was Gi beginning to realize that she had never really believed such stories of his magnificence, but convinced herself of their veracity only out of self-preservation. Not believing could be fatal. By the time she arrived at the shelter, it was already full and they turned her away. Fortunately, Sam had shown up for dinner and told her she could stay with him under the freeway.

Gi followed Sam to a culvert under two massive roads that were stacked on top of each other on skinny concrete pillars. It was a spectacular feat of engineering that it could withstand the forces of nature and gravity, and she felt a kind of fearful thrill as she stepped with Sam underneath it. She could almost sense all that heft pressing through the pylons and into the ground around her. The traffic overhead made a constant, fluctuating hum that, once her ears adjusted to the volume, was almost beautiful. Sam dug a spare woolen blanket out of his shopping cart and handed it to Gi. He then situated his cart between them and bedded down several meters away. Gi had assumed that, in exchange for helping her, he would want to use her in the way she had come to expect all men to want to use women; and she would have allowed it for his help. But to her surprise and relief, he turned away from her and almost immediately began snoring. He did not even try to touch her. This gesture of unconditional kindness made her cry the first of many healing tears.

79

The next day, Sam explained to Gi the
layout of the city using a tattered and faded
map from his shopping cart. Once he understood that she was looking for a lost friend,
he helped devise a method for finding her.
He had had tactical training in something
he kept referring to as Nam — he could be
very linear for a man whose imagination
regularly bled into his sense of reality —
and he came up with a sensible plan. He
explained to her that racial lines were rarely
crossed, even in the homeless community,
so her best bet would be to first scour the
city's areas that were dominated by Asians.
He circled the International District, as well
as various streets and blocks throughout the
city on the map.

"Now you gotta be careful when yer
lookin' fer yer frien'," he warned. "A lone
prostitute workin' the city is almost unheard
of. Normally they get picked up by a pimp

— always workin' fer the man. Anyway, if a pimp picked her up, which is likely, and he sees you come nosin' around, he's likely to pick you up too; and then you'll be right back where ya was. Pimps is mean sons-a-bitches.

"The area you think you was livin' before, that's the University Distric'. If she was kicked out, she probably went to another part of the city, just to get away. But she mighta left a trail, so you could start there. That was a couple a months ago, you say? Well, she didn't go to Wallingford or Fremont. Maybe Ballard or up north. She mighta gone up to Capitol hill, but she wouldna stayed there long. It's gettin' kinda yuppie. From there she coulda ended up in the Central Distric', if she was picked up by a pimp, but I wouldn't go there firs', if you can help it. You don't need to bother with Firs' Hill or Queen Anne. Let's see . . . If she's workin' the streets she might go downtown sometimes. It would be worth askin' around at the market. The missions in Pioneer Square is a good place to find people on the run. Yer best bet is to ask around the International Distric', see if any Korean girl matching her description came around lookin' for help. It may seem like a big city, but people remember things like that. We'll find yer frien'."

It took a few days, but Gi finally summoned enough courage to do as Sam suggested, and started her search in the University District to retrace Il-sun's steps. She found the street where the brothel was, tucked on a forgotten block between two more upscale streets. Sam had lent her an oversize rain slicker with a hood to better conceal herself. Even so, she did not dare get too close for fear of being discovered. From a distance she could see that the windows had been boarded up, and it was difficult to tell if the business was still operating. She did not linger long enough to see whether or not customers came and went. She thought of Cho with a stab of guilt. Was she still in there, enduring endlessness, talking to herself?

She tried to imagine where Il-sun would have gone from there. When Gi walked out of the brothel, she had turned left. Was that a logical choice, or was it random? Gi had chosen left because that was the direction to the quieter intersection. She felt more comfortable where it was less busy. Il-sun, on the other hand, preferred crowds and activity. She would have been drawn to the bustling intersection, Gi decided, so that is where she went.

Gyong-ho stood at the corner trying to look inconspicuous. She was alert to the danger of running into one of the bouncers, who might recognize her, but she did not see anyone she knew. In fact, nobody seemed to pay her any attention.

What would Il-sun have done at the intersection? Maybe she stood at the corner in just the same way, wondering what to do. Once she collected herself, where would she decide to go? Gi looked up and down the street. Everything was confusing and foreign. Then her eyes landed on a colorful sign halfway down the block, around the corner and across the street from the brothel. The sign had English, Chinese, and Korean letters advertising itself as a pharmacy and convenience store. Il-sun would have been drawn there because of the Korean writing, Gi thought. She would have gravitated toward the familiar. Gi walked to the pharmacy. As she got near, however, she noticed the Blue Talon emblem painted in the corner of the window, and felt a prickling sensation on her tattoo. Il-sun would have noticed it too. What would she have done? She would have kept walking. It was the natural thing to do: Keep walking and hope not to be noticed. Gi walked past the pharmacy and to the end of the block. Now what? She would have been too agitated to stand still for very long, and, not speaking English, she likely would not have dared to talk to anyone to ask for help. Il-sun would have walked, but to where? There was nothing at the intersection that stood out. She had already spent the effort walking in this direction, so she would not have backtracked toward the brothel. Gi decided to keep walking in the same direction down the street.

Gi allowed the exercise to clear her thoughts, hoping to see some clue about Il-sun's next move. She started counting her steps, out of habit, but then stopped herself: Il-sun would not have counted steps. She wanted to see the street from Il-sun's frame of mind. She walked for several blocks without seeing anything and began to feel discouraged. Perhaps it was hopeless to thread together a trail that was already months old. She was walking toward downtown — it seemed the natural direction to go — but had not yet made it as far as the lake when she came upon a shop window advertising a tae kwon do studio. The South Korean flag hung in the window, and there were posters on the wall written in Korean. If Il-sun had seen that, would she have gone inside? There were no Blue Talon emblems to be seen, but she still may have been wary of the *Hanguk* flag.

A class was in session, so Gi waited on a bench outside until it was over. After the last of the students filed out of the studio, she took a deep breath, for courage, and entered. She was surprised to see that the instructor was a Caucasian man, and she nearly turned and left without saying anything. Il-sun may not have been comfortable approaching an American, but this was Gi's only lead. She had to find out.

"Anyang haseyo," she said to him, and bowed. She hoped that, being a tae kwon do instructor, he could speak Korean.

He looked friendly but perplexed and gave an awkward bow. Westerners always looked funny when they bowed. He could not speak Korean.

"Hello," she then said in English. She was becoming more comfortable with how the language twisted and formed in her mouth. "My name is Gi-Gyong-ho."

"Nice to meet you. I'm Erik," he replied extending his hand. Gyong-ho grabbed his hand and shook it timidly. She realized she probably seemed just as awkward shaking hands as he did bowing. "How can I help you?" Erik had medium brown hair cropped short, a compact, well-defined body, and the grace of someone who had practiced martial arts for a long time. Gi hesitated for a moment, weighing the possible risks of talking with this man. Erik had a face that bore no malice, so she decided to trust him.

"I looking my friend. She name Il-sun, or maybe she Daisy. She Korean like me. Maybe she stop here, two months yesterday?" In her nervousness she had spoken incorrectly, but he seemed to understand.

"A girl did come by here several weeks ago." Gi's heart skipped a beat. "She didn't speak English, but she seemed to be asking for help. I couldn't understand her, so I took her to my teacher, Mr. Kim. Mr. Kim took her in for a few nights, but he had some problems with her. I don't know what happened to her after that."

Gi's heart sank. Il-sun could be trouble. The drugs had made her even more unpredictable than she was by nature. "You take me him?"

Erik scrunched his face for a moment, then he understood and frowned. "Mr. Kim's already upset that I passed your friend on to him. I don't think he'll be very happy if I bring him another homeless girl."

Panic rose from her belly to her throat. This was the only link she had to Il-sun, and if she lost it now she would not know what to do. She swallowed her panic and forced her thoughts to be clear. She remembered a television show in which a desperate woman was urgently trying to convey the importance of her struggle. What did she say?

"It's a matter of life and death!" Gi blurted, using the same inflection and strength in her voice as the woman on the television.

Erik seemed engaged in a turbulent inner struggle as he weighed Gi's desperation against Mr. Kim's anger. Finally he sighed and said, "Alright, I'll call him and see what he says. Wait here." He went to a phone behind a counter and dialed a number. After a moment he spoke into it, but Gi could not hear what he was saying. Then he looked up. "Mr. Kim would like to speak to you."

Gi took the receiver from him. "Hello?" She had never used a telephone before. There had never been anyone to call, and telephones were not so common in *Chosun,* especially for an orphan.

"Hello. You are looking for Park Il-sun?" Mr. Kim's voice was curt. He spoke Korean with a Seoul accent. Gi had expected puffs of air to come through the phone, like when someone whispers in your ear. She found it disorienting to talk with someone who was not in the room. But Mr. Kim had met Il-sun, and she used her real name!

Gi swallowed. "Yes."

"Who are you?"

"My name is Gi-Gi-Gyong-ho."

"I see. You sound *Chosun*."

"I am."

"And do you have a Blue Talon tattoo on your leg as well?"

"I do." Gi's voice was shaking and she was near tears.

"I can't help you. Your friend was trouble enough. Don't bring your problems to me."

"I'm truly sorry to bother you, sir. I don't mean to be difficult, but I really need to find my friend. She needs my help. If you could just tell me where she went —"

"I don't know where she went. I got her a job at my cousin's restaurant washing dishes, and he let her sleep in the storeroom. She was there less than a week. She was a lousy worker and she stole money from him. He had to kick her out."

"Could you tell me which restaurant?"

"No! I told you, I can't help you."

"I'm sorry to have bothered you," Gi said and hung up the phone.

"Is there anything else I can do for you?" asked Erik.

"No, thank you for your helping." Gi bowed and turned to the door.

80

Gyong-ho learned quickly how to thrive on
the streets. In many ways it was simpler than
survival in North Korea. Food was easy —
cast off but still edible from garbage cans
and dumpsters. There were no strict rules
of behavior that had to be adhered to, no
pins that had to be worn or meetings that
had to be attended. Hygiene was a more
difficult issue to resolve, but as long as she
went regularly to the women's shelter she
maintained a comfortable level of cleanli-
ness. Whenever she could not sleep at a
shelter, she stayed with Sam under the freeway.

Days passed, and then weeks, and then
months. Instead of being worn down by the
passing of time, Gi felt as if she were being
built back up by it. It was empowering to
be on her own and making a life, even a
meager one, in the city. She felt herself
becoming stronger every day. She still

searched for Il-sun at the various intersections and nodal points of the city. She inquired about her with all the homeless people and prostitutes she encountered, hoping for some clue. Nobody had seen her. Searching for Il-sun gave her purpose, even if she was starting to doubt that she would ever find her.

Seattle was full of interesting shapes and colors. Some buildings were little more than boring block towers made of concrete and glass. Others were designed to pull the eye skyward and lift the soul. Some looked as though they had been made to intimidate the other buildings around them, with imposing height and darkened glass, their windows topped by sinister brows of stone. For Gyong-ho there was much time, and on nice days she enjoyed walking and looking at the sights.

There was one marvel in the city that, for Gi, topped all other marvels, and she first happened upon it two months after her escape from the brothel. She often stared at it in wonder. It was, of all the buildings she had ever seen, a miracle of design. It was an intersection of mathematics and the human soul, and whenever she came near it, she was compelled to walk all around it to study it from every angle.

It was not the tallest building, nestled as it was between skyscrapers, and somehow that made it all the more grand. It was made of triangles of glass and steel, and within its rigid physical confines it seemed to undulate and ripple. It reflected light off its many angled panes, like a polished and faceted gem. It was oddly geomorphic, being both a natural megalith and a microscopic crystal. It was the thousands of chemical bonds of a complex molecule contorted by nuclear masses and the sharing of electrons. It was a building that had struck a deal with gravity, neither boastful of its vertical conquest nor cowed by Earth's constant tug. The sign on the door read Seattle Public Library.

Could she dare go inside? Would they even allow it? It took weeks for her to gather the courage to try. Gi stood at the door for over an hour wondering if her *songbun* was good enough. Finally she opened the door and walked in. A bored man in a blue-and-white uniform stood at the entranceway. He took no particular notice of her, so, with her head down, she walked past him.

The building was no less magnificent from within, and she quickly lost her apprehension. It was quiet and cathedral-like, in spite of a certain amount of bustle and conversation. It was clearly a building designed to catch and hold the light. *Maybe this is what it is like to be inside a grain of salt,* she thought. There was no regularity to the space that could be described in terms of blocks or symmetry, but it did have order and pattern. She let her feet take her of their own accord. She rode escalators and traversed floors. She walked between rows of desks and along balconies. She observed all the angles, and was awed by the interior distances. It was a monument to collective human knowledge — the structure itself gave the definition for the word *library,* and Gi did not have to wonder what it was. It was a dream come true.

Central to its function was a slow helix of books rising from the floor to the ceiling. It was a spiral of information on a gradual incline around a center. Gi walked the spiral, touching the books, smelling the volumes, buffed by the light coming through the triangular panes. So much information in such a small space! She could almost feel it in her lungs when she breathed.

The library became the center point from which all of Gi's activities sprung. It was her favorite place, and she would spend long hours, whenever she was not actively searching for Il-sun, perusing books under the slanted glass roof of the reading room. She discovered the mathematics and physics sections and pulled books off the shelves at random to read them. She learned the common methods of notating concepts that she had already intuited but did not know how to write. She learned whole new ideas that she had not considered before but that made perfect sense. She even uncovered a few things that she could not readily understand or that she outright disagreed with. The language of mathematics, she discovered, was learned in much the same way as the English language. There were rules of syntax, vocabularies, whole concepts distilled down to symbols, and even punctuation. Mathematics, at a point, transcends mere numbers and enters a conceptual realm. Whenever Gyong-ho opened herself into that realm, she entered a kind of euphoria, a deep state of bliss, and she wondered if that was the state of mind Il-sun was trying to achieve when she smoked the sugary *hiroppong* from her glass pipe.

Gi found a yellow notepad, and she filled its pages with the things she learned from books and the ideas they inspired in her. So far away were the Dear Leader and the many rules to please him.

81

Springtime on the streets of Seattle was truly spectacular. Trees seemed to be in bloom everywhere, showering the sidewalks in pink and white petals, and it reminded Gi of home. Gi had lived through the winter — the time of greatest trial for the homeless, when the weakest died in semifrozen lumps, according to Sam, in alleys and forgotten gullies.

"If you can make it through your firs' winter, you're gonna be okay," he had told her.

Gi arrived at the shelter late and they almost did not let her in. Donna had taken a liking to her, however, and sometimes bent the rules for her. Gi went to one of the small beds and closed her eyes to sleep. It was the usual chorus of creaking springs and random babble, and she had gotten quite used to it.

"I didn't mean to do it," she heard a voice

say in Korean as she was drifting off to sleep. She opened her eyes. Had she started dreaming already?

Then the voice came again, several minutes later. "Where do we go from here?"

Could it be? Gi got out of bed and padded her way in the direction of the voice. The lights were dimmed but not blacked out, and she could see clearly. She scanned the room.

"I hit him on the head."

Gi zeroed in on the source of the sound and crept closer.

"I hit him but I hope he didn't die. I didn't want him to die."

"Cho!" Gi exclaimed loudly. It was definitely her, lying wide awake on her bed and talking to herself.

"Shhhhhh!" someone hissed.

Cho pulled the blanket up to her eyes and remained quiet. She looked frightened.

"Cho, it's me! Gi — Gyong-ho!"

"Shut up!" someone shouted.

"Gi?"

Gyong-ho threw her arms around her friend and sobbed with relief, and with guilt for having left her behind. But Cho was alive. Cho held her tightly.

"I was so worried about you," said Cho.

The next morning Gi helped Cho find a pair of faded blue jeans and a green cable-knit sweater in the free box. The only passable shoes for her were a pair of cloth-bottomed Chinese slippers. They would not last long, especially if it rained, but they were better than the high-heeled sandals she had escaped in. Improvisation was critical to living on the street — it was the one thing Gi's life in North Korea had prepared her for — and Gi was confident that, with keen eyes, they would find better footwear for Cho within a day or two.

Gi had learned that it was important to manage her look. She was likewise dressed in blue jeans, seemingly the American uniform, but with a heavy gray cardigan over several layers of undershirts. She had found a pair of almost new sneakers in a dumpster, and they fit perfectly, but she had to intentionally scuff them up: If she arrived at the shelter with new clothes, they might not let her in. But if she allowed her appearance to get too shabby, there was the danger of being hassled by the police or attacked for sport by aggressive people who preyed on the meek. Her aim was to blend into the background, to find the look that could pass for legitimately homeless and rebellious youth alike. With that line blurred, people left her alone.

Gi led Cho to a bench at a public garden where they could talk and eat the rolls provided to them by the shelter. Cho looked the same as when Gi had left her: too thin and high strung, but at least not any worse.

"Things got really bad after you left, Gi," Cho began. "Several of the bouncers were dead. Word got out that the brothel had been shot up and customers stopped coming. Mrs. Cha was meaner than ever."

"What happened?"

"The police came, but they have some arrangement with Blue Talon. They didn't close us down, but business was bad and Uncle Lyong moved the whole operation across town. Then they started running me on the street. I had to stand on the corner and service men in the alley."

"How did you get away?"

"One night some drunk kid approached me. I took him into the alley, but he passed out before we got into it. My bouncer wasn't watching, so I left the kid and ran the other way. If they had caught me I'm sure they would have killed me. I just had to get away. I kept running and running. I didn't have any plan. I slept in some bushes. That was four nights ago. I walked toward the tall buildings. Then I met a *Hanguk* lady, and she helped me get to the mission. And now here I am, talking to you. I wish I had a cigarette."

"I'm sorry I left you."

"You did the right thing, Gi. You did what you had to, and I probably would have done the same thing. Have you heard anything about Il-sun?"

"Nothing. You?"

"No."

"Jasmine?"

"Not her, either."

They sat quietly for a time. Cho fidgeted constantly.

"What do we do now?" asked Cho. Gi was unsure if she was truly asking or if it was part of her babble, but she decided to answer anyway.

"We live. We eat, we find shelter, and we persevere. I have done pretty well, so far."

"You look . . . better than ever, actually."

"For the first time in my life I am making my own decisions. I do what I want to. We're free, Cho!"

"Free? What does that mean? I'm scared out of my skin. We don't belong here."

"We don't belong anywhere. Not here, not

in *Hanguk,* and not in *Chosun.* Not any-more. I don't even want to go back. We'll take care of each other. We'll make ourselves belong."

82

Gyong-ho oriented Cho to surviving on the street. With the warmer weather, they spent most of their nights sleeping outside in the parks, or under the freeway with Sam. Most days they spent at the library, Gi scribbling notes and Cho looking through magazines. It was becoming clear to Gi, however, that if they were going to rise up out of the street, they needed to find a way to start making money. Though she had learned how to stay alive by scrounging food out of the rubbish, it was a life fraught with dangers and discomforts, and it was obvious that most people in Seattle did not have to resort to that. Also, the organizations that ran the women's shelters frowned on long-term reliance on the shelters, and pressured the regulars to seek employment and independence. Gi's goal was to find some kind of living arrangement before the onset of winter.

One of Gi's regular stops was in the alley behind a Chinese restaurant in the International District where, on occasion, one of the cooks would offer her a small bowl of congee. She never begged for it, but would linger in the alley until he came out for a cigarette break. He normally offered. One day, the owner of the restaurant came into the alley looking for the cook while Gi and Cho were sitting on boxes and eating from the restaurant's ceramic bowls. She was an ancient and stony Chinese woman with a deeply creviced face. She saw Gi and Cho, then lit into the cook with rapid-fire scolding in Chinese. The man shrank from her, and Gi thought he might be reduced to tears. Finally, she turned her attention to Gi and Cho, and began screeching at them as well. The cook timidly interrupted her to tell her something, presumably that they could not speak Chinese, then she turned back and glared at Gi.

"Nobody eats for free!" she shouted in Korean.

Gi stood and lowered her head, and offered her bowl back to the woman, in the polite way, using both hands.

"We are very sorry to have caused you trouble. We have no money, but we will very gladly work for the food we have taken."

The woman paused, then gave Gi a sideways look. "What kind of work can you do?"

"We'll do anything."

"Can you clean?"

"Yes, ma'am."

"My cleaner is worthless. If you come back after closing, and if you can clean my restaurant better than she does, then I'll give you a full meal at the end of the night. But if you're stupid and lazy, then I better never see you around here again. Deal?"

Gi and Cho cleaned the restaurant with the highest attention to detail. They dug hidden grime out of corners and scrubbed every surface. The effort was not lost on the woman, and at the end of the night she gave them a generous meal, including precious morsels of roast duck, and a bag of leftover dumplings to take with them. Gi and Cho bowed deeply in gratitude.

"Come back tomorrow," the woman said curtly as she scooted them out the alley door.

Gi and Cho showed up faithfully every night and cleaned the restaurant. After a week the woman, Mrs. Ling, began to soften toward them, if only by being fractionally more polite. It turned out that the cook was actually her husband, and her way of displaying affection for him was to criticize his every action. She complained constantly that his generosity, or his wastefulness, or his lack of common sense was going to drive them to bankruptcy. He made a show of cowering from her, but they had found an equilibrium that would have been impossible to upset.

As the weeks went by, the Lings showed greater and greater kindness. As hard as Gi and Cho tried to keep themselves clean, the grime on the street found its way onto their clothes. Because they were working at night, they could no longer go to the shelter to shower or have their clothes laundered; so Mr. Ling took them home with him one night to let them bathe and put their clothes through the washing machine. And, since it was late, he gave them a mat and blankets and let them sleep in the garage. Gi learned later that it had been Mrs. Ling's idea to let them stay.

When the first cold night of the autumn hit, Mrs. Ling offered to let them stay every night in the garage, in exchange for housekeeping and as long as they were gone during the day. Also, they were allowed occasional use of the shower and laundry. To the homeless girls, this was the greatest generosity imaginable. Though the garage was not heated, it was shelter from the wind and rain, and they were able to gather enough blankets to insulate themselves from the cold. For the consistency and privacy, it was an improvement over the shelters.

All the while, Gi worked actively on her English and continued her studies at the library. She absorbed books on algebra, trigonometry, and geometry. She explored calculus and chaos and the mathematical principles behind the concepts of physics. She loved how numbers could be used to describe and predict the concrete world, and in that she found a bridge that helped her explain and validate her own existence to herself. She was real, numerically consequential, a vehicle with mass and velocity and substance.

Strength slowly returned to Cho. She fidgeted less and nearly stopped mumbling to herself. Without money she could not buy cigarettes, and eventually she stopped craving them. Gi hoped to see more of the old Cho come back, with her snappy comments and fearless attitude; but she seemed now permanently subdued, as if she were happy to be invisible. Regardless, Gi was grateful for her companionship.

83

Gi had been away from the brothel for
nearly a year and a half, and her quest to
find Il-sun had been almost entirely replaced
by the quest to improve her own life. The
odds of finding Il-sun now seemed improbable, though she still kept her eyes sharp.
She had done many double-takes, thinking
she had seen Il-sun out of the corner of her
eye, but it was never her.

One evening Gi and Cho were walking
through the International District, on their
way to clean the restaurant, when they
passed two women speaking Korean. They
were dressed like prostitutes, in short skirts
and stiletto heels, but it was not always easy
to tell: Sometimes women just dressed like
that in America. As they went by, Gi thought
she could detect the unmistakable *Chosun*
accent when one of them spoke.

"Excuse me, are you *Chosun?*" Gi asked,
incredulous. She had not met anyone from

North Korea since arriving in Seattle, and she did not expect that she ever would.

The women stopped and gave a wary stare. Then one of them shrugged and nodded.

"So are we," said Gi. There was another guarded pause as the women sized each other up.

"How did you get here?" asked the woman, finally.

"That's a long story," replied Gyong-ho.

The woman chuckled, and then nodded. How could it be anything but a long story?

"We've been looking for a friend of ours. She's *Chosun.* Her name is Il-sun, but she also goes by Daisy. Do you know her?"

"We know a Daisy," said the other woman. She spoke with a *Hanguk* accent. She was apparently glad to be part of a mystery solved; but then her face fell. Something had made her uncomfortable. The *Chosun* woman elbowed her: It would be in her nature to want to hide information — anyone could be an informer for the secret police. Gi and Cho understood her reticence all too well.

"You do?" Gi had only asked out of habit, and expected the usual negative response. She could not believe what she had heard.

The other women looked at each other,

but remained silent.

"She is my friend from childhood. We lost track of her, and I have been worried sick. If you know anything about her, or where I can find her, please, please tell me." Gi could not keep the note of pleading out of her voice.

"We know where they took her," the *Chosun* woman said, finally.

"Who is 'they'? Where?"

"Pill hill," the *Hanguk* woman said in English.

"Pill hill?" repeated Cho.

"She means First Hill, where the hospitals are," said Gi. "What's wrong with her? Is she alright?"

"It doesn't look good."

"Where can we find her? Which hospital?"

The women shrugged and walked away without another word.

84

Gyong-ho and Cho spent most of a day trying to locate Il-sun. They walked all over First Hill, going to the hospitals and speaking with unhelpful receptionists and harried nurses. Finally Gi realized that there was confusion with Il-sun's name: Korean names are typically given with the family name first, followed by the personal name. The person who admitted Il-sun made the mistake of thinking Park was her first name and Il-sun was her family name, and noted it that way on her chart.

Once they established which hospital Il-sun was in, they had to convince an ill-tempered nurse to allow them in to see her. She insisted that only next of kin were permitted on the terminal ward. Eventually she went off duty, and her replacement proved to be less of a stickler for the rules.

Gyong-ho and Cho were not prepared for the sight of her. There was no question that she was dying. She was emaciated and her hair had thinned to the point where her scalp was visible. She had sores and bruises festering here and there on her papery, pallid skin. Her breathing was rough and shallow, and she went into coughing fits that seemed powerful enough to break her frail-looking bones. She had tubes going up her nose and poking into her arms. She was completely wasting away. Even so, when they walked into her room she lightened considerably, even managing to smile.

Il-sun did not have energy to speak, so the women sat together holding hands and looking into one another's eyes. It was amazing how much could be said with only the eyes. There were looks that said "I'm sorry," looks that said "I'm scared," looks that said "I love you. I will miss you when you're gone." Gi stroked Il-sun's head and held her hand, and told stories, memories of being children together — and they laughed. The offenses that at one time seemed so big in their friendship fell away. Even their history, where they had come from and where they had been, seemed insignificant compared to being there together in that moment. The only moment there will ever be is right now — Gi had heard that somewhere, and now it made sense.

Nurses and doctors came and went. They were so busy that they rarely spoke to the women — they were impatient for Il-sun to die. They needed the bed. Gyong-ho was glad that Il-sun was at least not dying alone. She was there for her. After dark the head nurse came in and told them visiting hours were over. She looked for a moment like she might enforce it, but then she turned and left the room. A few minutes later she returned with extra blankets and a box of crackers.

"Sleep in bed next to me, like in the old days," Il-sun rasped to Gi. The effort of saying it was nearly too much for her. Gi climbed into the bed and put her arm around her. Il-sun felt hollow under her arm. Gi could not sleep. She counted Il-sun's breaths until dawn. Cho slept restlessly in a chair.

The next day Il-sun floated in and out of consciousness. Gi and Cho sat with her, leaving reluctantly only to use the bathroom. A young intern took pity on them and brought food from the cafeteria. They had no appetite, however. Tears came in bursts at unexpected intervals. Gi again held Il-sun through the night.

The following day Il-sun awoke with bright, alert eyes. Some energy returned to her and she even sat up in bed for a short while. Her voice was soft, and she seemed possessed of a deep calm. She told them, especially Gyong-ho, how much she loved them. The rise of energy was short-lived, however, and by noon she was unconscious again. To Gi she seemed like a piece of clockwork winding down. Her breaths came in shorter gasps, and more slowly. Her heart was a faint throb. The head nurse came in and said, "It won't be long now."

There were no more tears. The clockwork stopped — there was a little cough and then her body deflated. In one moment there was life, and in the next it was gone. It was that simple — the sweet release of death. Gi was lying in the bed next to her. She felt her final heartbeat. The last one pulsed strong. She died with her eyelids half open. Gi closed them with her fingertips.

85

After Il-sun passed away, something in Gyong-ho was liberated. The quest to find Il-sun had taken the focus off her own suffering, and enabled her to persevere. Through it she built her inner strength. Now that Il-sun was dead, the story of Gi's childhood had ended. The last remaining tether to who she had been was severed. She was ready to start over. If the child Gyong-ho was communist *Chosun,* and the adult Gyong-ho would be imperialist American, then she would have to resolve the conflict between the two within herself. The enemy, she decided, was not the communist or the imperialist, but the lack of understanding between them. If one has to be right, then one has to be wrong, in a polarized world. Yes and no. But between yes and no there is an infinite range of possibilities, a full spectrum of maybe. If you are stuck in either/or, then you are missing the infinite.

She went to the library almost every day after Il-sun died. She read books and filled notebooks with observations, thoughts, and equations. She would sit alone in quiet, blissful concentration.

"Is that the Olowati paradox you're working on?" a voice said over her shoulder, startling her.

She turned to see a tall, dark-skinned man with a wide smile and a pot belly standing over her. He was in his middle fifties and wore large, square glasses and a sweater with broad horizontal stripes that made him look wider than he actually was. She felt guilty, as if she had been caught doing something bad. "Yes," she said sheepishly.

"That's ambitious. Can I see?"

Gi handed the man her notebook, only because she thought it would have been rude not to. She would have preferred to keep her work to herself.

The man sat on a chair across the table and studied her work intently. His eyes darted around the pages as he chewed on his lower lip.

"My God, have you solved this?" he said after several minutes. "Jesus God, I think you might have solved it! Is this all your work?" He looked up at her in disbelief.

590

Gi nodded.

"Are you . . ." The man found himself speechless. "Jesus God." He looked back over her notes. "Are you Carlson's student?"

She shook her head.

"Well, you're not my student. You don't look old enough to be doing doctoral work, anyway. I'll be damned. What's your name?"

"Gyong-ho."

"You did this?"

His shock and disbelief were getting irritating. "Can I have my notebook back now, please?"

"Of course. Sorry. My name is Henry. Professor Henry Calvin. What school are you with?"

"School?"

"You're not at UW. I know all the upper-level mathematicians there. When will you be publishing?"

"Publishing?"

"Surely you are going to be publishing this soon. I don't mean to be forward, but I wouldn't mind being on your peer review board. I would love to go over this thoroughly."

"I don't know what you are talking about."

"This is your work? You didn't just find this notebook?"

"I need to go," said Gi, standing up.

591

"No, wait." Professor Calvin stood up and handed her a card. "Take this. It has my number on it. I'm having a gathering of all my post-grad students. If you wouldn't mind, I would love for you to come and present your proof to us. I know a couple of them have tried their hand at Olowati's paradox."

Gi took the card and looked at it. "People will be there just to discuss mathematics?"

Professor Calvin laughed. "Of course. That's what we do." He took the card back and wrote on the back of it. "That's the address. Six o'clock next Thursday. I'll supply the beer. You bring your notebook."

86

Professor Calvin's house loomed over the street, and Gi was afraid to knock on the door. He had seemed nice enough, but she was still not sure whom she could trust. As far as she could tell, meeting freely was something that Americans took for granted, but old fears die hard and she could not shake the dread that secret police might arrest the hapless partygoers. Still, the thought of meeting people who wanted to discuss the very things she thought about all the time was too exciting to pass up. She swallowed her fear and knocked on the door.

"Can I help you?" A young man answered, his lip curling slightly when he saw her. Although she was clean, Gi realized that she still looked like she came from the street. Her clothes were mismatched and all the wrong size and frayed around the edges. Her hair was unkempt.

"Mr. Professor Calvin invite me party

here," said Gi nervously. Her English always reverted when she was nervous, and her accent became exaggerated. She wished she had not come.

The man looked her up and down. "This is a private party —"

"Adam, who's there?" a voice boomed from behind the door.

"Nobody, Prof. C. Just a girl from the street."

"Maybe it's that Gung-ho girl I told you about. Let her in."

The young man stood aside, looking down his nose as Gi entered the house. The only home she had been in since arriving in Seattle was the Lings', and though theirs was large by *Chosun* standards, it seemed like a hovel compared to Professor Calvin's. Professor Calvin's home was full of colorful wall hangings and personal photographs. There were knickknacks on all the surfaces, shelves full of books, rugs, and nice sofas. The house had many rooms, and a back patio that overlooked Lake Washington. She had long ago discovered that the relative comfort of Americans was much higher than that of North Koreans, but she had not witnessed it quite so intimately until now.

"Welcome! Welcome!" Professor Calvin

extended his hand to her, his face full of warmth. She grabbed his hand awkwardly, and simultaneously shook and bowed. "Come and meet everybody," he said. He took her into a room with plush carpeting, a television set in the corner, and chairs arranged in a loose circle. A white dry-erase board was set up on an easel near the television. "Everyone, this is Gung-ho, the one I was telling you about."

There were ten people in the room besides Professor Calvin and Gi. They all looked up at her, many of them smiling — they were not all going to be rude like the man at the door had been. She shook hands and bowed. Someone offered her food from a tray, crackers with a pink spread. She was hungry but ate reservedly anyway.

"Where are you from, Gung-ho?" asked a pale woman with long, red hair. Gi got stuck on the woman's shocking green eyes and was nearly too stunned to answer.

"Korea," she finally said. She had learned that nobody in America knew the word *Chosun,* and that it was better not to be specific about which Korea. Americans always assumed she meant South Korea, if they even had a notion that Korea was a divided nation.

"And how did you come to the States?"

"On a boat," she replied. She was uncomfortable with the line of questioning. Everyone in the room chuckled. Apparently they had thought she was making a joke.

"I mean, are you studying here? Are you with a school?"

"No school."

"But you are working on Olowati's paradox?"

"I found it in a book. I thought it was interesting." Again people laughed, but she did not understand the joke.

"Where's your notebook? I was hoping you could give us a glimpse of your proof," said Professor Calvin.

"I left it with my friend. I can show you on paper, if you like." As she was getting more relaxed, her English improved.

"Without her notes? This should be good," said the man who had answered the door. His voice was dripping with sarcasm.

"Can you show us on the board up there?" prompted Professor Calvin.

Gi nodded and went to the board. "Olowati's paradox is written like this . . ." she began. She started writing a series of numbers and symbols. As she wrote she became absorbed in the problem and her nervousness melted away completely. The room fell captive as she went methodically through the problem. "Olowati's first misunder-standing of the problem was . . ." and she had to erase the board to write more equations and symbols. It flowed from her seamlessly. She filled and erased the board a dozen times, and after an hour and a half she had finished, "So Olowati's paradox isn't really a paradox at all." The room was densely quiet.

"My God . . ." said Adam, the rude young man from the door, as the silence began to wear off.

"I didn't catch all of that, but I have no doubt that she's right," said a woman in the back of the room.

"Did you follow that, Prof. C?" asked a man who was sitting sideways on a sofa.

"Without your notes?" said Professor Calvin in disbelief.

EPILOGUE

It was a beautiful spring day. Gyong-ho sat on a bench in front of the music building, as she did at this time every Monday, Wednesday, and Friday, and waited. Sometimes as early as three thirty-three, and once as late as three forty-nine, the object of Gyong-ho's fascination emerged from the music building. When she did, time would slow down and the rare Seattle sun would come out and shine just for her. She was beauty: all woman and springtime, natural curves gliding through space. She was unplucked innocence waiting to know herself.

The first time Gi saw her, her heart went cold. If Gi had not held Il-sun as she passed away, had she not stayed with her body until it was cold, she would have sworn it was her. The likeness was uncanny. More than her features, it was her rhythm, her cadence, the carefree swing of her hips. And it made Gi's heart burst. As she did every Monday,

Wednesday, and Friday between three thirty-three and three forty-nine in the afternoon, she cried.

The young woman passed, unnoticing as always, and walked to the north. Gi sat, feeling her grief, becoming lighter for it. Through her tears she saw Cho step out of the throng of students, still wearing her cleaning uniform, the small diamond on her engagement ring seeming to light up the rest of her.

"They must think I'm crazy," Gi said to her, forcing a smile.

"Geniuses are supposed to be crazy," Cho replied, sitting down and putting her arm around her. Her English had steadily been improving.

"It just hurts so much."

"Yes, it does."

"But it's getting better. Slowly."

"Yes. Yes, it is, teacup."

ACKNOWLEDGMENTS

I would first and foremost like to thank my wife, Michi Holley-Jones, for her unfailing support in every way, and her belief in me while I was writing this novel, even when things got tough. You are a constant inspiration to me and teach me daily about patience, kindness and empathy. This work would not have been possible without you.

Also, I would like to thank Greg Kahn for coddling the seed, for providing much needed encouragement, for hours spent combing through and discussing the first draft, and for giving me permission for all the chapter fifteens.

I would like to thank Lailani Kahn for talking me down when I really needed it. Also, thank you, Landhiji, for being an exquisite witness to the birth of a writer, sharing with me the excitement that goes with it, and bruising my arm when required.

Special thanks to Alice Walker for reading

the work, believing in it, and fanning the ember until it caught.

Thanks to my agent, Wendy Weil, for taking this on and working hard to find this novel a home.

A huge thank-you to my editor, Andra Miller, whose equal parts enthusiasm and insight helped this work find its potential. Also, deep thanks to all the folks at Algonquin, who propel their books with passion.

Thank you, Pierce Scranton, for believing in this work and being its champion.

Thanks to the anonymous LiNK intern (www.linkglobal.org) who offered verification of some of the details in this book.

I would like to thank everyone who read and offered feedback on the various drafts along the way. Special thanks to Cymber Lily Quinn, Lisa Fitzhugh, Jennifer Barr, Greg Kahn (because I cannot thank you enough), Margot Kenly, Brad Pearson, and Brad Smith.

And a huge mahalo to the Hale 'ohana, on whose ancestral land I was able to find the peace, inspiration, and time to conceive of myself as a writer, and to bring this novel into the world.

The employees of Thorndike Press hope you have enjoyed this Large Print book. All our Thorndike, Wheeler, and Kennebec Large Print titles are designed for easy reading, and all our books are made to last. Other Thorndike Press Large Print books are available at your library, through selected bookstores, or directly from us.

For information about titles, please call:
  (800) 223-1244

or visit our Web site at:
  http://gale.cengage.com/thorndike

To share your comments, please write:
Publisher
Thorndike Press
10 Water St., Suite 310
Waterville, ME 04901